Other books by Fred Patten

Best in Show: Fifteen Years of Outstanding Furry Fiction (2003)
Reprinted as:
Furry! The World's Best Anthropomorphic Fiction! (2006)

Watching Anime, Reading Manga:
25 Years of Essays and Reviews (2004)

Already Among Us; An Anthropomorphic Anthology (2012)

The Ursa Major Awards Anthology:
A Tenth Anniversary Celebration (2012)

What Happens Next: An Anthology of Sequels (2013)

Five Fortunes (2014)

Funny Animals and More: From Anime to Zoomorphics (2014)

Anthropomorphic Aliens: An Interstellar Anthology (2014)

The Furry Future : 19 Possible Prognostications (2015)

An Anthropomorphic Century

Stories from 1909 to 2008

Edited by Fred Patten

An Anthropomorphic Century
Stories from 1909 to 2008

Production copyright FurPlanet Productions © 2015
Cover artwork copyright © 2015 by Mark Brill

Published by FurPlanet Productions
Dallas, Texas
www.FurPlanet.com

ISBN 978-1-61450-244-9

Printed in the United States of America
First Edition Trade Paperback July 2015

To my sister, again.

SHERRY

One dedication is not enough!

Table of Contents

INTRODUCTION

Introduction

by Fred Patten

When did anthropomorphic animals begin? What does "anthropomorphic animals" really mean, anyway? Just thinking and talking like humans? The first fantasy talking animals, in Aesop's ca. 500 B.C. fables such as *The Town Mouse and the Country Mouse,* may have talked; but were never otherwise imagined as being anthropomorphized. It was not until late 19th-century and 20th-century children's picture books that they were depicted as walking upright and wearing clothes.

The medieval/renaissance Reynard the fox folk tale, set around the Animal Kingdom of King Nobel (sometimes King Leo) the lion, had a mixed illustrative history. Sometimes the animals were clothed and walked on two legs; sometimes not. The Oriental Monkey King characters usually wore clothes, but technically Monkey, Pigsy and the others were minor gods or demons, not mere animals. Most pre-19th-century talking animals, such as those in *The Life and Perambulations of a Mouse* by Dorothy Kilner (1783), were unanthropomorphized except for their ability to converse with each other and with humans.

Clothes-wearing, two-legged, human-like animals were "invented" in Lewis Carroll's *Alice's Adventures in Wonderland* (1865) and *Through the Looking-Glass* (1871). The White Rabbit who wore a waistcoat and watch; the bewigged frog footmen; Bill the lizard with his ladder; the Caterpillar with the hookah (well, it wasn't two-legged or clothes-wearing, but it had a very human personality)—they set off the vogue for animals that mimicked humans as closely as possible. Cassius Coolidge's mega-popular 1900s paintings of "dogs playing poker" helped. During the 20th century, animated cartoons, newspaper comic strips, and children's funny-animal comic books cemented their popularity.

In adult popular literature, they were slower to catch on. "Tobermory" (1909), the earliest story here, is just a cat who learns to talk. Dr. Lu-mie, the giant termite disguised as a human (1934), is also a solitary character. But more widespread anthro animals rapidly followed, in several stories by L. Sprague de Camp in the late 1930s and 1940s, and *Animal Farm* by George Orwell (1945). Numerous "space aliens" that were thinly-disguised funny animals appeared in 1950s science fiction. Robert Crumb and other underground comix artists popularized outright funny animals for adults in the 1970s. By the time furry fandom appeared during the 1980s and 1990s, anthropomorphic animals for adults were nothing unusual.

Here are twenty stories written from 1909 to 2008. You can see the evolution of anthropomorphic animals from the lone cat in 1909 to the animals-as-humans of the last half of the 20th century and early 21st century, both in general fiction and genre fiction written by furry fans for themselves. Twenty stories, for your enjoyment and education.

What may be most fascinating about "Tobermory" today is not the cat who learns to talk, but Saki's savage portrayal of Britain's Edwardian upper classes. This was the period when the average "gentleman" was expected to sleep all day, and go to his exclusive club in the evening to drink port and play cards all night, only to go to bed the next morning and sleep all day to get ready for the next night. If he wanted to know what was happening in the world, he sent his gentleman's gentleman (his butler) out to buy a newspaper. Well, he didn't always sleep all day. Sometimes he went to the races, or out riding to hounds (fox hunting); or to the opera in the evening. If he was a she, she played tennis or the pianoforte, or "did good deeds". Work? Gentlemen didn't work! That was for the lower classes who needed to earn money. Work was what servants were for.

In "Tobermory", "Esmé", "The Toys of Peace", "Mrs. Packletide's Tiger", and similar short stories (many of which feature Clovis Sangrail as a sardonic guest), Saki lampooned the deliberately effete pre-World War I upper classes. In "Tobermory", they go to endless house parties at the estates of people of class, and do almost anything to escape boredom. Teaching a cat to talk goes a bit too far. (If anyone today wonders what was so special about an Axminster carpet, look it up on Wikipedia.)

Tobermory, whether he can talk or not, is haughty, supercilious, condescending, and self-centered. He couldn't care less for anyone else— very feline, in other words. Few authors since Saki have better described the personality of a housecat.

Tobermory

by Saki

It was a chill, rain-washed afternoon of a late August day, that indefinite season when partridges are still in security or cold storage, and there is nothing to hunt—unless one is bounded on the north by the Bristol Channel, in which case one may lawfully gallop after fat red stags. Lady Blemley's house-party was not bounded on the north by the Bristol Channel, hence there was a full gathering of her guests round the tea-table on this particular afternoon. And, in spite of the blankness of the season and the triteness of the occasion, there was no trace in the company of that fatigued restlessness which means a dread of the pianola and a subdued hankering for auction bridge. The undisguised openmouthed attention of the entire party was fixed on the homely negative personality of Mr. Cornelius Appin. Of all her guests, he was the one who had come to Lady Blemley with the vaguest reputation. Some one had said he was "clever," and he had got his invitation in the moderate expectation, on the part of his hostess, that some portion at least of his cleverness would be contributed to the general entertainment. Until tea-time that day she had been unable to discover in what direction, if any, his cleverness lay. He was neither a wit nor a croquet champion, a hypnotic force nor a begetter of amateur theatricals. Neither did his exterior suggest the sort of man in whom women are willing to pardon a generous measure of mental deficiency. He had subsided into mere Mr. Appin, and the Cornelius seemed a piece of transparent baptismal bluff. And now he was claiming to have launched on the world a discovery beside which the inventions of gunpowder, of the printing-press, and of steam locomotion were inconsiderable trifles. Science had made bewildering strides in many directions during recent decades, but this thing seemed to belong to the domain of miracle rather than to scientific achievement.

"And do you really ask us to believe," Sir Wilfrid was saying, "that you have discovered a means for instructing animals in the art of human speech, and that dear old Tobermory has proved your first successful pupil?"

"It is a problem at which I have worked for the last seventeen years," said Mr. Appin, "but only during the last eight or nine months have I been rewarded with glimmerings of success. Of course I have experimented with thousands of animals, but latterly only with cats, those wonderful creatures which have assimilated themselves so marvellously with our civilization while retaining all their highly developed feral instincts. Here and there among cats one comes across an outstanding superior intellect, just as one does among the ruck of human beings, and when I made the acquaintance of Tobermory a week ago I saw at once that I was in contact with a 'Beyond-cat' of extraordinary intelligence. I had gone far along the road to success in recent experiments; with Tobermory, as you call him, I have reached the goal."

Mr. Appin concluded his remarkable statement in a voice which he strove to divest of a triumphant inflection. No one said "Rats," though Clovis's lips moved in a monosyllabic contortion which probably invoked those rodents of disbelief.

"And do you mean to say," asked Miss Resker, after a slight pause, "that you have taught Tobermory to say and understand easy sentences of one syllable?"

"My dear Miss Resker," said the wonderworker patiently, "one teaches little children and savages and backward adults in that piecemeal fashion; when one has once solved the problem of making a beginning with an animal of highly developed intelligence one has no need for those halting methods. Tobermory can speak our language with perfect correctness."

This time Clovis very distinctly said, "Beyond-rats!" Sir Wilfrid was more polite, but equally sceptical.

"Hadn't we better have the cat in and judge for ourselves?" suggested Lady Blemley.

Sir Wilfrid went in search of the animal, and the company settled themselves down to the languid expectation of witnessing some more or less adroit drawing-room ventriloquism.

In a minute Sir Wilfrid was back in the room, his face white beneath its tan and his eyes dilated with excitement.

"By Gad, it's true!"

His agitation was unmistakably genuine, and his hearers started forward in a thrill of awakened interest.

Collapsing into an armchair he continued breathlessly: "I found him dozing in the smoking-room, and called out to him to come for his tea. He blinked at me in his usual way, and I said, 'Come on, Toby; don't keep us waiting;' and, by Gad! he drawled out in a most horribly natural voice that he'd come when he dashed well pleased! I nearly jumped out of my skin!"

Appin had preached to absolutely incredulous hearers; Sir Wilfrid's statement carried instant conviction. A Babel-like chorus of startled exclamation arose, amid which the scientist sat mutely enjoying the first fruit of his stupendous discovery.

In the midst of the clamour Tobermory entered the room and made his way with velvet tread and studied unconcern across to the group seated round the tea-table.

A sudden hush of awkwardness and constraint fell on the company. Somehow there seemed an element of embarrassment in addressing on equal terms a domestic cat of acknowledged dental ability.

"Will you have some milk, Tobermory?" asked Lady Blemley in a rather strained voice.

"I don't mind if I do," was the response, couched in a tone of even indifference. A shiver of suppressed excitement went through the listeners, and Lady Blemley might be excused for pouring out the saucer full of milk rather unsteadily.

"I'm afraid I've spilt a good deal of it," she said apologetically.

"After all, it's not my Axminster," was Tobermory's rejoinder.

Another silence fell on the group, and then Miss Resker, in her best district-visitor manner, asked if the human language had been difficult to learn. Tobermory looked squarely at her for a moment and then fixed his gaze serenely on the middle distance. It was obvious that boring questions lay outside his scheme of life.

"What do you think of human intelligence?" asked Mavis Pellington lamely.

"Of whose intelligence in particular?" asked Tobermory coldly.

"Oh, well, mine for instance," said Mavis, with a feeble laugh.

"You put me in an embarrassing position," said Tobermory, whose tone and attitude certainly did not suggest a shred of embarrassment. "When your inclusion in this house-party was suggested Sir Wilfrid protested that you were the most brainless woman of his acquaintance, and that there was a wide distinction between hospitality and the care of the feeble-minded. Lady Blemley replied that your lack of brain-power was the precise quality which had earned you your invitation, as you were the only person she could think of who might be idiotic enough to buy their old car. You know, the one they call 'The Envy of Sisyphus,' because it goes quite nicely up-hill if you push it."

Lady Blemley's protestations would have had greater effect if she had not casually suggested to Mavis only that morning that the car in question would be just the thing for her down at her Devonshire home.

Major Barfield plunged in heavily to effect a diversion.

"How about your carryings-on with the tortoiseshell puss up at the stables, eh?"

The moment he had said it every one realized the blunder.

"One does not usually discuss these matters in public," said Tobermory frigidly. "From a slight observation of your ways since you've been in this house I should imagine you'd find it inconvenient if I were to shift the conversation on to your own little affairs."

The panic which ensued was not confined to the Major.

"Would you like to go and see if cook has got your dinner ready?" suggested Lady Blemley hurriedly, affecting to ignore the fact that it wanted at least two hours to Tobermory's dinner-time.

"Thanks," said Tobermory, "not quite so soon after my tea. I don't want to die of indigestion."

"Cats have nine lives, you know," said Sir Wilfrid heartily.

"Possibly," answered Tobermory; "but only one liver."

"Adelaide!" said Mrs. Cornett, "do you mean to encourage that cat to go out and gossip about us in the servants' hall?"

The panic had indeed become general. A narrow ornamental balustrade ran in front of most of the bedroom windows at the Towers, and it was recalled with dismay that this had formed a favourite promenade for Tobermory at all hours, whence he could watch the pigeons—and heaven knew what else besides. If he intended to become reminiscent in his present outspoken strain the effect would be something more than disconcerting. Mrs. Cornett, who spent much time at her toilet table, and whose complexion was reputed to be of a nomadic though punctual disposition, looked as ill at ease as the Major. Miss Scrawen, who wrote fiercely sensuous poetry and led a blameless life, merely displayed irritation; if you are methodical and virtuous in private you don't necessarily want every one to know it. Bertie van Tahn, who was so depraved at seventeen that he had long ago given up trying to be any worse, turned a dull shade of gardenia white, but he did not commit the error of dashing out of the room like Odo Finsberry, a young gentleman who was understood to be reading for the Church and who was possibly disturbed at the thought of scandals he might hear concerning other people. Clovis had the presence of mind to maintain a composed exterior; privately he was calculating how long it would take to procure a box of fancy mice through the agency of the EXCHANGE AND MART as a species of hush-money.

Even in a delicate situation like the present, Agnes Resker could not endure to remain too long in the background.

"Why did I ever come down here?" she asked dramatically.

Tobermory immediately accepted the opening.

"Judging by what you said to Mrs. Cornett on the croquet-lawn yesterday, you were out for food. You described the Blemleys as the dullest people to stay with that you knew, but said they were clever enough to employ a first-rate cook; otherwise they'd find it difficult to get anyone to come down a second time."

"There's not a word of truth in it! I appeal to Mrs. Cornett—" exclaimed the discomfited Agnes.

"Mrs. Cornett repeated your remark afterwards to Bertie van Tahn," continued Tobermory, "and said, 'That woman is a regular Hunger Marcher; she'd go anywhere for four square meals a day,' and Bertie van Tahn said—"

At this point the chronicle mercifully ceased. Tobermory had caught a glimpse of the big yellow Tom from the Rectory working his way through the shrubbery towards the stable wing. In a flash he had vanished through the open French window.

With the disappearance of his too brilliant pupil Cornelius Appin found himself beset by a hurricane of bitter upbraiding, anxious inquiry, and frightened entreaty. The responsibility for the situation lay with him, and he must prevent matters from becoming worse. "Could Tobermory impart his dangerous gift to other cats?" was the first question he had to answer. It was possible, he replied, that he might have initiated his intimate friend the stable puss into his new accomplishment, but it was unlikely that his teaching could have taken a wider range as yet.

"Then," said Mrs. Cornett, "Tobermory may be a valuable cat and a great pet; but I'm sure you'll agree, Adelaide, that both he and the stable cat must be done away with without delay."

"You don't suppose I've enjoyed the last quarter of an hour, do you?" said Lady Blemley bitterly. "My husband and I are very fond of Tobermory— at least, we were before this horrible accomplishment was infused into him; but now, of course, the only thing is to have him destroyed as soon as possible."

"We can put some strychnine in the scraps he always gets at dinner-time," said Sir Wilfrid, "and I will go and drown the stable cat myself. The coachman will be very sore at losing his pet, but I'll say a very catching form of mange has broken out in both cats and we're afraid of it spreading to the kennels."

"But my great discovery!" expostulated Mr. Appin; "after all my years of research and experiment—"

"You can go and experiment on the shorthorns at the farm, who are under proper control," said Mrs. Cornett, "or the elephants at the Zoological Gardens. They're said to be highly intelligent, and they have this recommendation, that they don't come creeping about our bedrooms and under chairs, and so forth."

An archangel ecstatically proclaiming the Millennium, and then finding that it clashed unpardonably with Henley and would have to be indefinitely postponed, could hardly have felt more crestfallen than Cornelius Appin at the reception of his wonderful achievement. Public opinion, however, was against him—in fact, had the general voice been consulted on the subject it is probable that a strong minority vote would have been in favour of including him in the strychnine diet.

Defective train arrangements and a nervous desire to see matters brought to a finish prevented an immediate dispersal of the party, but dinner that evening was not a social success. Sir Wilfrid had had rather a trying time with the stable cat and subsequently with the coachman. Agnes Resker ostentatiously limited her repast to a morsel of dry toast, which she bit as though it were a personal enemy; while Mavis Pellington maintained a vindictive silence throughout the meal. Lady Blemley kept up a flow of what she hoped was conversation, but her attention was fixed on the doorway. A plateful of carefully dosed fish scraps was in readiness on the sideboard, but sweets and savoury and dessert went their way, and no Tobermory appeared either in the dining-room or kitchen.

The sepulchral dinner was cheerful compared with the subsequent vigil in the smoking-room. Eating and drinking had at least supplied a distraction and cloak to the prevailing embarrassment. Bridge was out of the question in the general tension of nerves and tempers, and after Odo Finsberry had given a lugubrious rendering of "Melisande in the Wood" to a frigid audience, music was tacitly avoided. At eleven the servants went to bed, announcing that the small window in the pantry had been left open as usual for Tobermory's private use. The guests read steadily through the current batch of magazines, and fell back gradually, on the "Badminton Library" and bound volumes of PUNCH. Lady Blemley made periodic visits to the pantry, returning each time with an expression of listless depression which forestalled questioning.

At two o'clock Clovis broke the dominating silence.

"He won't turn up to-night. He's probably in the local newspaper office at the present moment, dictating the first instalment of his reminiscences. Lady What's-her-name's book won't be in it. It will be the event of the day."

Having made this contribution to the general cheerfulness, Clovis went to bed. At long intervals the various members of the house-party followed his example.

The servants taking round the early tea made a uniform announcement in reply to a uniform question. Tobermory had not returned.

Breakfast was, if anything, a more unpleasant function than dinner had been, but before its conclusion the situation was relieved. Tobermory's corpse was brought in from the shrubbery, where a gardener had just discovered it. From the bites on his throat and the yellow fur which coated his claws it was evident that he had fallen in unequal combat with the big Tom from the Rectory.

By midday most of the guests had quitted the Towers, and after lunch Lady Blemley had sufficiently recovered her spirits to write an extremely nasty letter to the Rectory about the loss of her valuable pet.

Tobermory had been Appin's one successful pupil, and he was destined to have no successor. A few weeks later an elephant in the Dresden Zoological Garden, which had shown no previous signs of irritability, broke loose and killed an Englishman who had apparently been teasing it. The victim's name was variously reported in the papers as Oppin and Eppelin, but his front name was faithfully rendered Cornelius.

"If he was trying German irregular verbs on the poor beast," said Clovis, "he deserved all he got."

Amazing Stories, *the first science-fiction magazine, started in April 1926. Early magazine s-f (also known today as "primitive s-f") was touted at the time as educational, by* Amazing's *editor Hugo Gernsback and the other s-f magazine editors. The stories were considered to be sugar-coated science lessons for the adolescents who were believed to be the s-f pulps' readers.*

"Dr. Lu-mie" (Astounding Stories, *July 1934), is a "horror story" in which Robert Warrington, a businessman visiting Colombia, is invited by the mysterious Dr. Lu-mie to his home. He learns that he is in a disguised termitarium, and Dr. Lu-mie is a disguised giant termite, bred by the other termites to be their agent among humans. Warrington spends the rest of the story running all through the termites' jungle nest, trying to escape. Actually, the story is a thinly-disguised tour inside a termite nest, for the edification of the reader. Today's reader is more likely to be amused by the description of the tall and incredibly thin "man" with gloved hands and a long, face-covering black beard: Dr. Lu-mie, the giant talking termite disguised as a human.*

Dr. Lu-mie

by Clifton B. Kruse

On the morning of the 17th of April, the regular passenger plane flying from Barranquilla to Bogota, Republic of Colombia, settled upon the landing field two hours before sunup. It had been a monotonous trip with but one passenger besides myself, and neither of us had felt inclined to address a word to the other. Indeed, I had been so predisposed to a bitter brooding silence that the voice of a fellow man would have been an irritation.

Though I was on my way to bury myself completely and forever upon the plantation operated by Seville, Duncan, Ltd., some forty miles in the wilds north of Bogota, yet my heart and' soul were left behind in London—in London with a beautiful English girl whom I must now think of as Lady N—. To me this flying journey across this strange, new, and yet indescribably old country of Colombia was the end of all adventure.

Immediately upon alighting from the plane an official came hurrying with a cablegram for Mr. Robert Warrington. My hands shook as I received and opened it. Could it be from Mae? No; I must remember to say Lady N— now. However, to my utter amazement I found the message to be a succinct cancellation of my contract with Seville, Duncan, Ltd. The plantation was no longer to be operated by my employers. It had been sold to a French firm almost within the hour of my departure in the plane from Barranquilla.

"You may return by the evening plane, señor," the courteous official consoled me. "Your return passage has already been arranged, as you will note, and you will have the entire day to devote to our beautiful Bogota."

Naturally I resigned myself to the return; although I assured the obliging official that I was in no mood for sightseeing. I elected to remain and brood out the hours about the landing field.

"Pardon me, señor, will you?" For the first time my fellow passenger spoke to me. "But seeing that you have a day upon your hands here in Bogota, why not accept my hospitality?"

I glanced up at him, for he was tall and truly incredibly thin. His words came from the depths of a luxurious black beard above which extended his amazingly long, pointed brown nose. His eyes, too, were shielded by thick, heavily smoked lenses, though nevertheless seeming actually to glisten through this translucent protection.

"I am not a stranger here," the man went on. "My villa lies but a few miles outside the city. You may make it yours for the day, and I shall return you within ample time to board tonight's flyer."

Indeed, why not?

"Excellent!" And the stranger beamed, although I had not yet agreed. "Just check your baggage. My car will be along shortly. And may I introduce myself?"

His card bore the mysterious name: "Dr. Lu-mie, Bogota, Colombia."

"And I am Robert Warrington," I replied in acquiescence, "with Seville, Duncan, Ltd. of London. I was to manage one of their plantations near here until this"—I indicated the London cablegram—"came to wreck my plans for isolation."

"You are so unhappy, then?"

"Well, rather, or perhaps I should say completely indifferent to life."

"With civilization, then?" Dr. Lu-mie pursued pleasantly as we sauntered a bit beyond the flying field's station.

"There are occasions," I ruminated, "which create a bitterness within the human heart, my friend."

A native in a car of surprisingly late vintage soon arrived, and shortly we were leaving civilization's rather feeble imprint in this, to me, incipient world of Latin America and were speeding on our way south and west of Bogota. All the while my odd though genially understanding host listened as I talked.

Was it tact, I wondered when I thought of it, or was this strange Dr. Lu-mie actually interested in me as a newfound friend?

Dr. Lu-mie had a decided taste for isolation, or so I fancied, as we wound continually in and about the prolific growths of Colombia's torrid vegetation. It was already beyond the break of day before the chauffeur drove into the walled enclosure of the doctor's estate. A large iron-gray mansion stood out like a glaring outcropping of rock amid a vast garden of tropical fungi.

I shuddered with a premonition of disaster at the tomblike structure sticking up so unbeautifully in the center of such a grotesque garden. In truth, the home of Dr. Lu-mie was as different from any other human habitation I had seen as the tall, lean doctor himself differed from other men.

No serving man welcomed us to this home; although I marveled at the noiseless swing of doors as we entered the house and passed down the gray-cemented hall to the reception room, situated, as I judged, near the center of this uninviting house. Dr. Lu-mie bade me seat myself upon the leather divan as he excused himself to see to the arrangements for our breakfasting.

What an odd room! Gray walls, smooth as polished steel and utterly devoid of either pictures or other decoration. The floor, too, was of the same smooth cement and quite without a vestige of any covering. A single round globe suspended from the ceiling gave forth a sickly yellowish illumination.

Besides the divan upon which I now rested, the room boasted but a single marble-topped, iron-legged table and one large lounging chair, finished in the same brown leather as was the divan. Before me an indentation in the wall suggested a fireplace, although no blaze flared up to cheer me. Not that any fire was necessary, for certainly the room was almost uncomfortably warm. But windowless! It seemed a veritable prison, and I shook with some uncanny feeling of unreality about all of this.

To shake off my sudden spell of fear I arose and walked to the "fireplace." There, sure enough, was a pile of rubbish like material. To my complete amazement the thing actually exuded a perceptible bit of heat, fetid and with a slight odor of decaying vegetation, yet unmistakably heat radiations.

"Uncanny," I thought, and went back to the divan.

I listened for Dr. Lu-mie, now. Being here in this deuced gray hole alone was an agony to the spirit. All I could hear was a faint, scarcely audible, rustling sound which seemed to emanate from the very substance of the walls.

"You are comfortable, my friend Warrington?" Dr. Lu-mie suddenly appeared before me bearing a small tray which he lowered to my lap.

I nodded, attempting a smile to hide my keen mystification.

"It is odd to you, no doubt." Dr. Lu-mie, still with cloak, hat, beard, and spectacles sat down opposite me. "But first you must eat."

I regarded my bowl of grayish-colored porridge and sniffed hungrily at the steam from the small stone teapot. At least the tea seemed real enough.

"But you also, Dr. Lu-mie, are you not breakfasting?"

He shook his head slowly, the gleaming lights of his eyes showing through the masklike spectacles. "I am not eating now" he said; "later you will understand."

So saying, he sat down and left me to sip my tea. The odious porridge I could not touch.

Nevertheless I must make the best of my bargain, so excusing my want of hunger I poured myself a cup of tea and sat back to sip and revive my downcast spirits in its warm fragrance. I really wanted a bit of sugar, but as my host seemed not to sense the natural union of tea and sugar I would do without it.

Scarcely had I finished half a cup when my strange host, seated as he was quite near the indenture which I called a fireplace, reached to an almost invisible ledge along the top of the place and drew out a long, gray strip of tubing, one end of which he stuck through the massive beard into his mouth. So doing, he proceeded to relax and suck slowly from the thing. My tea chilled as I observed, open mouthed. The fellow was actually drinking in some substance through the hose which I now noted extended on through the wall.

Mad! Unquestionably I was in the house of no usual eccentric. Chills struck my spine until I quaked. With determined force I checked a wild impulse to get up and run. Possibly the fact that I realized how deeply buried in this South American jungle we were caused me to get a hold on my fidgety nerves.

I began to drop a few pointed remarks about an earlier return to Bogota than we had first planned. I even suggested that my host permit me to entertain him at one of Bogota's finest restaurants. I even mentioned a suddenly acquired grip of nausea, suggesting that a dash of open air would be a most essential restorative.

To all of this the incalculable Dr. Lu-mie only shook his head. He said nothing, yet his eyes—what I could see of them—beamed steadily upon me.

"Dr. Lu-mie," I arose impatiently, "I must implore you to excuse me."

Dr. Lu-mie arose, stepped toward me. "I cannot." His words fell softly yet with fearful penetration.

"What manner of man are you?" I cried in sudden desperation. I was feeling a prickly, suffocating heat pressing over my entire body. My lungs were beginning to gasp for oxygen.

Dr. Lu-mie seemed to shrug his narrow shoulders. "Perhaps it is better that you know, after all."

"Know? Know what? Dr. Lu-mie, I find you utterly incomprehensible!"

"I am sorry, Robert Warrington," he was rubbing his long bony hands together and for the first time I noted that he wore thin, tight-fitting gloves of flesh color, "but I had hoped to meet you and know you as man to man."

He paused. He seemed to be groping for words. "The truth is—I am not man."

"What?"

He nodded. "I don't wish to frighten you. But you have asked for it. I repeat, I am not man."

"Not—not a man?"

For an answer he slowly lifted his hands, grasped the bushy black beard and with a few deft twists pulled it free of his face.

Face did I say? Not face truly! My blood seemed to congeal with horror. I was paralyzed at the ghostly awfulness of it with beard and spectacles gone.

Long, narrow, and glistening brown. A snout-like thing for a mouth where a chin should have been. And the eyes! Indescribable disks without pupil or iris as we think of the eye parts. Compound eyes, they were, with glinting refractions from thousands of points.

Next he pulled off the skin-like gloves, disclosing long, saw-edged paws. He reached up to part his cloak. I covered my eyes and cried out in sheer terror. The thing was awful to behold. My senses reeled. I became ill. The thing which called itself Dr. Lu-mie carried me to the divan. From the hideous snout the same soft voice attempted to console me.

"I am sorry, Robert Warrington, but you are not to fear."

My attempted replies were incoherent.

Dr. Lu-mie now removed his outer garments while I looked on in dumb horror.

The body was long, truncated, and with the lower portion not two feet above the ground. His legs were chitinous, gray-brown appendages starting from a juncture of his body well above the middle. He was four handed, if I may term the upper appendages hands. One pair had been completely withdrawn during his masquerade as a human being. Then beneath his wig the smooth, coppery head bore two long antennae. The thing had neither nose nor ears as we understand them.

"You are—" I gasped.

"Lu-mie," the thing answered me; "The termite who became a man."

"Termite!"

Lu-mie nodded, his myriad-faceted eyes gleaming down upon me. He now appeared as the man-sized insect which he truly was.

"Then this," I came to my feet, is not a house. It is a termitarium."

I understood the gray-cemented walls, the absence of windows, the stifling, humid atmosphere so nearly devoid of oxygen.

Like one insane I whirled from the spot and dashed for the door, shoved it open violently, and ran with fear-inspired impulse down the hallway.

But where was the outer door? The passage was without sign of a single crevice and would have been quite without light were it not for the opened door from the lighted room. Lu-mie stood in the doorway, showing no indication of haste or impatience save for the slight wavering of his two antennae which now stood erect above the broad, shining forehead.

Deliberately he approached me, but now he had ceased to walk erect. His body dropped to a horizontal position, and he moved forward upon four bony appendages in true termite fashion. He was no longer Dr. Lu-mie the man, but Lu-mie the termite of human proportions.

I felt the long, hard forearms about me. They bound me rigidly to the soft, pulpy body. I was lifted and carried back to the one lighted room. Lu-mie laid my trembling form upon the divan, held me there. I became aware of an almost inaudible sibilation followed by the soft scurry of millions upon millions of tiny feet. My body tingled with the movement of countless tiny insect beings crawling over me. After a while Lu-mie released his hold.

I tried to spring up, but could not budge from the spot. I was literally glued to the divan, helpless to do anything save move my eyes and lips. Cold sweat exuded profusely, and I shook with convulsive chills despite the uncomfortable warmth of the place. Lu-mie stood before me looking down with that utterly expressionless face of the termite. The eyes glittered in the yellowish light, and the tubular mouth vibrated fishlike as he formed the low pitch of human speech.

"I have brought you here to teach me more of the ways of men," he was saying. "It is for you to choose whether you will do so or not."

"I'll not do it," and I cursed him in my anguish.

Lu-mie gently shrugged the collar-like shield around his body which corresponded to his narrow shoulders. "Very well. Think it over, and while doing so remember that your body is merely a substance—not a being—to my little people."

"Eaten alive!" I shrieked in horror.

"But no," Lu-mie continued; "to them you would be merely a fungus bed, the soil of their gardens. Do I make myself clear?"

Was it hours or days that I lay there? I could not tell. I knew only that life was bitterest agony. My mind swirled in fiery flights, yet my body weakened. I longed, even prayed, for death. Yet I could not die. Gradually the tempest of my individuality waned. I grew apathetic, a senseless, seemingly incorporeal and irrational consciousness.

I remember that Lu-mie came and went with periodic frequency. Now and then he would place a hard tube in my mouth. Sweet, sticky drops of some pungent substance would pass from it down my throat without effort upon my part. At first the aromatic stuff was nauseating, though as the operation was repeated again and again I felt an increasing longing for it. Fortunately I neither dared nor cared to think what the stuff might be. Though I possessed eternal consciousness yet had I ceased really to be.

As my strength and reason gradually returned under these forced feedings of Lu-mie and his termite brethren, I was permitted to sit up, though with my feet still glued to the divan in a cast of the gray termite cement. It became increasingly clear to me why I was imprisoned. At periodic intervals Lu-mie would come to me with his endless questions. I am tempted to say "daily," despite the fact that within termitaria the terms day and night are meaningless, for the termites live in eternal darkness save those higher castes of the creatures which are capable of reproduction.

Though the normal termitarium is a social state comprising up to a million workers, soldiers, and the three orders of kings and queens, this community ruled by the termite king Lu-mie must have numbered many millions. Of course up to this time I knew scarcely anything of my captors save the regular attention paid to my physical needs by an organized army of the blind, soft, and unpigmented little workers. At those times the single light would be extinguished and not relighted until the thousands of extraordinary small creatures had departed for other duties in this gigantic old termitarium.

Lu-mie and I were fast becoming pupil and teacher. He would question and I answer to the best of my ability. I gathered from these interviews that he had made but few excursions out into the odious world of light and humankind. Finding me and deciding, as he did, on the spur of the moment, to abduct me as a teacher to save many future trips to the outside world was in Lu-mie's mind a truly fortunate affair. The driver of the car, I learned, was an illiterate Indian who lived in the jungle nearby and occasionally served Dr. Lu-mie without suspecting his employer's identity.

What about my country of England? Why did we employ the types of social and political assemblage common to homo sapiens? What were the eventual aims of human nations? Oh, the countless questions, the innumerable angles of human life to be divined by the indefatigable Lu-mie!

"But your purpose, Lu-mie," I was provoked at last to question him, "why are you as you are?"

"You learn so little," Lu-mie mused as he replied. "Homo sapiens—sapiens indeed! What does your kind know of wisdom? Do you realize, Robert Warrington, that your type of beings can never rule the world?"

"But we—"

"No, no!" Lu-mie interrupted. "I grant that mankind is at present supreme. But hear me. The termites have lived on this world for uncounted ages. Your own scientists have discovered the fossil remains of my ancestors who lived as far back as the Tertiary period. And we have evolved from the simple cockroach characters to the great social units of the Metatermitidae. Now heed this. I tell you much because you yourself are slowly becoming one of us, my friend. We are not individuals as you man-beings conceive of individuality. Begin with that. It is your first clue to understanding both Lu-mie and the regular or normal termites of the patiently conquering Metatermitidae.

"Every termitarium is a true individualism, Robert Warrington. We termites are but the units of a whole. This particular termitarium is not the kingdom of Lu-mie as you fancy it, but rather is itself one individual being of which Lu-mie is but a part. Do you follow? See how we live, work, eat! Our workers and soldiers do not themselves consume one drop of our diet of cellulose and fungi! It is given for only the larvae and the kings and queens of the three upper orders of life to consume such raw food.

"From our bodies we exude the food in proper form, plus the delectable exudates of our own persons and the glandular secretions of our completely adult bodies. This partially digested food and the exudations of termite bodies circulate from pore to mouth continually, even as your ownbody cells pass on the superior food material from body cell to body cell. A termite, you see, is not an individual; he is merely a body cell of that true individuality which is the whole of our completely socialized organization known as a termitarium."

I nodded in stupefaction. "But you, Lu-mie, are so different. You yourself are one individual." Lu-mie's truculent body quivered with some indefinable termite emotion. Perhaps it was amusement at my human stupidity.

"Yes, Robert Warrington; I am different. In ways I am an individual. Nevertheless it is for a purpose. Generations ago, how many I dare not suggest, the august ancestors of this termitarium conceived in their collective will the desire to conquer this world and let it be solely the habitation of termites with only our domesticated beetles and termitophilus flies. So it was that after the nuptial flight of the first-order king and queen who established this termitarium, a certain particularly promising egg was set aside and especially fed for the singular purpose of producing individuality.

"The emerging larva was never permitted to taste the common exudate of his fellow termites. His food was especially prepared from certain fungi and never recharged with the common fluid. Also certain skillful operations were performed and a special silk spun so that this larva slept in the nymphal state for ten of the seasonal changes which you humans call years.

"Thus the larva grew to giant proportions due to the glandular changes, and because of this lack of exudations of his fellow termites he failed to become an integral part of the great termite body. Thus Lu-mie was given partial individuality."

"Unbelievable," I exclaimed.

"Only to the limited individual mind of a human creature," Lu-mie resumed, "for to a termite nothing is impossible once the common mind of the termitarium has willed it to be. Only time is required, and to us time is nothing. Our little cells may be born and die, but the termite mind, incased not in one fragile little brain but in millions and millions yet to come—does not cease to be."

For minutes we sat in silence while my numbed brain sought frantically to assimilate the incomprehensible. A thousand questions flared up in my mind. Where should I begin my questioning?

Suddenly the room resounded with the scurrying feet of thousands of termites. The walls whispered. A tense, awe-inspiring air of uncertainty pervaded us.

Lu-mie had suddenly become taut. His long antennae rose stiff. He poised upon his steel like appendages. What message of the greater individual, the terrnitarium, was he receiving?

Lu-mie stood before me tensely, his myriad-faceted eyes gleaming strangely. "I must go," he was speaking; "danger threatens. Our enemy, the great red ants of the fields, are invading our fungi gardens."

"Let me go!"

For a moment he hesitated. His soft snout scented over my body a moment. "Your word?" "I am bound: How could I escape, anyway?"

"Perhaps it is the taint of individuality which provokes me; nevertheless I call you friend. Yes, you may come—But wait!"

He seemed to call. The light went out. Soon the rush of thousands of worker termites made their whispering rustle over the floor. Lu-mie was commanding them, though in a pitch of voice I could not quite understand. The creatures covered my body. Now I felt myself covered with a sticky, aromatic stuff from head to foot. The termites had left. Lu-mie was cutting away the plaster which bound my feet.

"Come," he whispered.

I grasped an arm like appendage and followed Lu-mie out of the room and down the long passageway to a doorway. At his command I dropped to my hands and knees and crawled many feet along a tortuously winding tunnel.

We were somewhere deep in the labyrinthine caverns and tunnels beneath the room of my imprisonment. Though I could not see I could hear and at times feel the hurried movements of termite soldiers. We went on and on, but not alone. Before and behind us marched the robot-like fighters with soft, crunching tread and the tense, excited clicking of thousands of mandibles. It was a march to war.

The passageway lightened. I could now see, though indistinctly. In regular masses the fighters moved forward, keeping an even pace and maintaining definite fighting groups of two to three hundred termites. Save Lu-mie alone these fearless warriors were no larger than small ants, yet in that determined assemblage they appeared invincible.

Now the sounds of struggle—shrieks and shrill battle cries. Antennae were rigid. The steel against steel clash and clank of metallic mandibles gave the ringing sound of ten thousand swords. My nerves tingled. Now the scene of battle! A broad passageway, thick with fungi, gleamed a bluish white under the first radiance of the sun it had ever known. Scarcely twenty feet before us appeared a huge gap nearly a yard in width through which poured row upon row of shining red bodies. Great creatures were they with flying mandibles. The warrior ants charged with a fury no human might feel. Utterly fearless was the charge and with a determination far more fervid than any man-against-man attack.

The red invaders were nearly three times the size of the termite defenders. Their huge, knifelike mandibles were hurled with skillful hate. A convulsive wave of thousands upon thousands of fighting creatures toiled, shrieked, and died, cut beyond recognition. Now came the charge of those brigades which we had accompanied. Mandibles flung high and chopping savagely they tore straight for the slowly advancing roll of battle. Now the line tightened. The carnage became incredible. For a moment the line wavered; now it assumed new strength; was pushing back again toward the broken wall.

The gap between us and the frenzied soldiers cleared. The termites were holding their adversaries by sheer strength of numbers and even more reckless savagery than that displayed by the red ants.

With the line holding, thousands of the blind, defenseless termite workers now rushed madly around and over us. Their bodies formed a pallid, moving carpet. On to a point midway between us and the line of battle they advanced and stopped. Their work was just beginning. With a zeal no human worker could show, they emptied their bodies upon a line running straight across the passageway. Millions of droplets of excreta were poured forth. Thousands of jaws chewed and spat a thick, viscous fluid.

Now inch by inch a wall was raised—inch by heart-breaking inch as the thousands of warrior termites out there beyond thrust and cut and held the ravaging red ants to the line. An hour passed and yet another. Now only a tiny gap loomed at the top of the wall. Still the workers gave their all. Now came total darkness. Silence. Intense weariness.

The termitarium had been saved. But at what a cost! How many thousands of brave, determined soldiers had died on that howling, maddening, cutting line of battle! I shuddered as I followed Lu-mie back on our crawling, twisting journey up to our room. For me Lu-mie's words had become vividly real. No individuality this!

As we made our slow way back, I felt hundreds of the blind worker termites crawling upon my body. Nearly exhausted from their arduous task of wall building against time and with stomachs and intestines now quite empty, they fell to eating the viscous fluids smeared over my own body. This I knew was chiefly exudate, saliva, and even bits of partially digested food particles which Lu-mie had seen fit to have put upon me. Had this not been done many of the frenzied fighters might have turned upon me as an enemy. Now my defense had become a delicacy to my starved captors.

Lu-mie turned off. We were now moving in a different direction. The passageway sloped downward again. Not long after, we entered a large cavern. To my gratification as well as amazement I could see. About the room fetid piles of rubbishlike substance gave off, it seemed, faint radiations. Not much, yet quite enough to enable my eyes, accustomed to absolute night, to see clearly.

Then I saw the queens. Five masses of whitish pulp, each nearly half a foot in length, lay helplessly accepting the ministrations of the workers. The blind termites fed the queens, coming in a constant file with their droplets of food which they regurgitated into the gaping mouths. Hundreds of the workers lapped in trembling ecstasy the luscious exudations pouring from the huge pores in the puffy, queenly bodies.

Then I saw the lines of workers going to and from each queen. Going, they were burdenless, but coming from her each bore an egg. Among the Metatermitidae, of whom Lu-mie was so proud, the gigantic, utterly helpless queens lay eggs with clocklike rhythm at the rate of one a second.

"New soldiers for those who died back there!" Lu-mie whispered with the pride of an unconquerable people.

It was a veritable factory. Terrifying in its prolific output, ominous in its threat to other living beings.

We returned to our quarters, both completely exhausted. Although Lu-mie's face was incapable of expression, yet I could tell by the quivering appendages and the drooping antennae that he was more shaken by the recent turmoil than he cared to admit.

Nevertheless I felt a new surge of strength and hope within my mind. Today's adventure had given me an idea. Alone I was helpless. But now, I thought, might I not enlist the aid of the termitarium's greatest foe? If I could only make myself understood to the red ants, let them know that I was an ally, could we not together destroy this hellish place? Despite the fact that during the moments of battle I had no thought of escaping, for indeed my numbed senses had actually rejoiced at the courage and resourcefulness of the defenders; nevertheless I felt myself now more nearly rational.

But why hadn't I made a dash for liberty through that break in the wall? For a long while I could not understand my utter lack of wit.

Gradually I saw the truth. What had Lu-mie mentioned about the common mind of the whole group being formed in the circulation of exudates, digested food particles, and ejecta from body to body? I sickened as I reasoned my way out of the dilemma. The feeding tube which had been regularly stuck in my mouth. The sweetish, pungent syrup which had poured through it into my own system. And Lu-mie's own remark about my becoming more termite than human.

My blood curdled with the ugly thought of it. I had been fed upon the common stuff of the termitarium. I had been filled with it, \and my own mind had been dulled by the powerful exudates. I shuddered. I vowed never again to touch it. But what else could I eat?

My fate was clearly before me. Obviously I dared no longer consume the stuff from the bodies of my captors lest my own free mind and human individuality be completely warped. This meant immediate action. Whatever I would do must be done before my body should become hopelessly weakened by lack of any food at all.

Lu-mie was in the room with me now, his weary body slumped upon the floor with deadening fatigue. He had sipped of the tube and fallen into a lethargy which rendered him unconscious. Just how lost to the world he might be I feared to think. None the less I had to chance all. It was life or a living death for me.

I arose slowly, my eyes held to the still figure of the giant termite. My first thought was to leave the room undetected. Deliberately, step by step, I moved to the doorway. Here I paused. Lu-mie had not stirred. Once in the hall I made frantic plans. Which way should I turn? I thought of the scene of battle. That way doubtlessly led to some long tunnel extension used for food forages. Without definite plans I started on, dropping to my hands and knees as I entered the low-ceilinged cavern and tremblingly felt my way on and on through the thick, hot darkness of the place.

Turn after turn, through tunnel after tunnel and cavern after cavern I burrowed for hours. My back ached and the palms of my hands as well as my kneecaps became raw. Still I crawled on with a delirious hope and a growing fear. Darkness and fear! Heat and stench! Suddenly I came upon an apparently straight tunnel leading out I knew not where. My heart leaped with new hope. Clearly this must lead somewhere away from the termitarium.

I had to lie down to catch my breath and ease my throbbing muscles. I rolled the ragged bits of my trousers up over my knees. My shirt went for hand bandages. The air was so rare that my heart pounded and my lungs burned for more oxygen.

Scurrying feet! A tense charge of something in the air! Approaching termites! I recognized the heavy rustle of innumerable tiny feet. I was on my hands and knees. I shook convulsively with nauseating fear. But I crawled on, exerting every atom of my strength now in a frenzied dash on and on through the narrow, black tunnel.

Suddenly I crashed headlong into a wall. The tunnel had ended. Frantically I threw out my hands. I felt myself in a small cavern. But I could stand up. My knees cracked with fiery pain as I raised myself. I stretched my hands upward. Still nothing above.

Yet the room was not black dark but only shadowy gray. And I drew sweet, oxygen-filled air into my lungs. But where was the outlet? Somewhere above surely. I strained my eyes. Yes; there appeared a ledge above me, and beyond it extended another tunnel which seemed to give out a few feeble rays of light. That was indeed the way to the outer world.

Behind me the horde was advancing. I could hear them distinctly now. "Robert Warrington!" It was Lu-mie's voice calling. I braced myself with back to the wall. Above me, beyond my reach, was the way to freedom. Tears of rage and despair flooded my eyes. Bitterest irony!

But I would never go back! My fists were clenched. I would sell my life dearly-though futilely as I knew too well.

Then Lu-mie stood before me. Behind him the tunnel teemed with warriors and workers in brigade after brigade. But Lu-mie did not advance. He stood there, great termite that he was, and surveyed me.

"Robert Warrington!" His voice was oddly low. I tensed myself for the struggle which I thought inevitable. Still we stood there, motionless, tense, each of us trembling with the mysterious emotions of our separate kinds.

I prayed in awe. "Were you but a man, Lu-mie!"

A moment of silence.

"And you!" Lu-mie's voice choked with emotion. "Were you but a termite—my friend!"

"Lu-mie," I gasped, "you understand?"

"I understand," he replied simply.

Suddenly one of his hand-like appendages stuck out. "Like men, my friend."

I reached out, grabbed the claw. We held the clasp, our eyes fixed steadily upon each other.

Now Lu-mie came forward. "Above you is human freedom." He spoke with effort. "Follow the way and you will come to the house of the man-being Juan. He will give you clothing, human needs—and take you to Bogota." He lifted me bodily so that my hands reached over the ledge. I crawled up. Ahead of me I could see the faint, bluish light of day.

I turned to call farewell to my strange captor-friend. "You are a man—a real man—Dr. Lu-mie!" I gasped out.

"And you," the sad voice returned, "are indeed a true termite of the first blood, oh, my brother!"

Thus we parted; I to my human world from which I now felt so inexplicably apart; and Lu-mie? What of him? Truly both termite and man in that moment of revelation learned that life itself—the nobler life—is greater than any earthly kind.

The gene-altering effects of radiation gradually became known during the early 20th century, and were popularized by the 1930s. Radiation for random mutations began to appear in science fiction about then; at first neutrally or humorously as in "The Blue Giraffe" by L. Sprague de Camp (1939), then horrifically after the nuclear destruction of Hiroshima and Nagasaki in 1945. Controlled genetic breeding was first described (as plasto-biology) in "Jerry Was a Man" by Robert A. Heinlein (1947) and as "genetic engineering" in Dragon's Island by Jack Williamson (1951). Despite this, random radiation-caused mutations were still the fictional norm for decades, as in Twilight World by Poul Anderson (1961): "Another band of children went by, as dirty and tattered as the first, but—not human. Mutant. No two alike. A muzzled beast face. A finger less or a finger more than five. Feet like toeless, horny-skinned hoofs, twisted backs, grotesque limping gait. Pattering dwarfs. Acromegalic giants, seven feet tall at six years of age. A bearded six-year-old. And worse." (p. 38) Shortly after the Chernobyl Nuclear Power Plant disaster of April 26, 1986 near Pripyat, Ukraine, which resulted in the complete evacuation and quarantine of the 49,000-population city (still in effect; scientists today study how nature has reclaimed an abandoned city), a Ukrainian politician blamed the Soviet government for the accident that he claimed (without evidence, unfortunately) had resulted in mutant six-legged foxes running through the nearby forests.

"The Blue Giraffe" seems to imply that its radiation-caused mutations will not breed true, except (for story purposes) for the baboon-people. Of course, all the animal anthropomorphizations in the furry fiction of the 1980s to the present always breed true.

The Blue Giraffe

by L. Sprague de Camp

Athelstan Cuff was, to put it very mildly, astonished that his son should be crying. It wasn't that he had exaggerated ideas about Peter's stoicism, but the fact was that Peter never cried. He was, for a twelve-year-old boy, self-possessed to the point of grimness. And now he was undeniably sniffling. It must be something jolly well awful.

Cuff pushed aside the pile of manuscript he had been reading. He was the editor of *Biological Review*; a stoutish Englishman with prematurely white hair, prominent blue eyes, and a complexion that could have been used for painting box cars. He looked a little like a lobster who had been boiled once and was determined not to repeat the experience.

"What's wrong, old man?" he asked.

Peter wiped his eyes and looked at his father calculatingly. Cuff sometimes wished that Peter wasn't so damned rational. A spot of boyish unreasonableness would be welcome at times.

"Come on, old fella, out with it. What's the good of having a father if you can't tell him things?"

Peter finally got it out. "Some of the guys—" He stopped to blow his nose. Cuff winced slightly at the "guys." His one regret about coming to America was the language his son picked up. As he didn't believe in pestering Peter all the time, he had to suffer in silence.

"Some of the guys say you aren't really my father."

It had come, thought Cuff, as it was bound to sooner or later. He shouldn't have put off telling the boy for so long.

"What do you mean, old man?" he stalled.

"They say," *sniff*, "I'm just a 'dopted boy."

Cuff forced out, "So what?" The despised Americanism seemed to be the only thing that covered the situation.

"What do you mean, 'so what'?"

"I mean just that. What of it? It doesn't make a particle of difference to your mother or me, I assure you. So why should it to you?"

Peter thought. "Could you send me away some time, on account of I was only 'dopted?"

"Oh, so that's what's worrying you? The answer is no. Legally you're just as much our son as if… as anyone is anybody's son. But whatever gave you the idea we'd ever send you away? I'd like to see that chap who could get you away from us."

"Oh, I just wondered."

"Well, you can stop wondering. We don't want to, and we couldn't if we did. It's perfectly all right, I tell you. Lots of people start out as adopted children, and it doesn't make any difference to anybody. You wouldn't get upset if somebody tried to make fun of you because you had two eyes and a nose, would you?"

Peter had recovered his composure. "How did it happen?"

"It's quite a story. I'll tell you, if you like."

Peter only nodded. "I've told you," said Athelstan Cuff, "about how before I came to America I worked for some years in South Africa. I've told you about how I used to work with elephants and lions and things, and about how I transplanted some white rhino from Swaziland to the Kruger Park. But I've never told you about the blue giraffe—"

* * *

In the 1940's the various South African governments were considering the problem of a park that would be not merely a game preserve available to tourists, but a completely wild area in which no people other than scientists and wardens would be allowed. They finally agreed on the Okvango River Delta in Ngamiland, as the only area that was sufficiently large and at the same time thinly populated.

The reasons for its sparse population were simple enough: nobody likes to settle down in a place when he is likely to find his house and farm under three feet of water some fine morning. And it is irritating to set out to fish in a well-known lake only to find that the lake has turned into a grassy plain, around the edges of which the mopane trees are already springing up.

So the Batawana, in whose reserve the Delta lay, were mostly willing to leave this capricious stretch of swamp and jumble to the elephant and the lion. The few Batawana who did live in and around the Delta were bought out and moved. The Crown Office of the Bechuanaland Protectorate got around its own rules against alienation of tribal lands by taking a perpetual lease on the Delta and surrounding territory from the Batawana, and named the whole area Jan Smuts Park.

When Athelstan Cuff got off the train at Francistown in September of 1976, a pelting spring rain was making the platform smoke. A tall black in khaki loomed out of the grayness, and said: "You are Mr. Cuff, from Cape Town? I'm George Mtengeni, the warden at Smuts. Mr. Opdyck wrote me you were coming. The Park's car is out this way."

Cuff followed. He'd heard of George Mtengeni. The man wasn't a Chwana at all, but a Zulu from near Durban. When the Park had been set up, the Batawana had thought that the warden ought to be a Tawana. But the Makoba, feeling chesty about their independence from their former masters, the Batawana, had insisted on his being one of their nation. Finally the Crown Office in disgust had hired an outsider. Mtengeni had the dark skin and narrow nose found in so many of the Kaffir Bantu. Cuff guessed that he probably had a low opinion of the Chwana people in general and the Batawana in particular.

They got into the car. Mtengeni said: "I hope you don't mind coming way out here like this. It's too bad that you couldn't come before the rains started; the pans they are all full by now."

"So?" said Cuff. "What's the Mababe this year?" He referred to the depression known variously as Mababe Lake, Swamp, or Pan, depending on whether at a given time it contained much, little, or no water.

"The Mababe, it is a lake, a fine lake full of drowned trees and hippo. I think the Okavango is shifting north again. That means Lake Ngami it will dry up again."

"So it will. But look here, what's all this business about a blue giraffe? Your letter was dashed uninformative."

Mtengeni showed his white teeth. "It appeared on the edge of the Mopane Forest seventeen months ago. That was just the beginning. There have been other things since. If I'd told you more, you would have written the Crown Office saying that their warden was having a nervous breakdown. Me, I'm sorry to drag you into this, but the Crown Office keeps saying they can't spare a man to investigate."

"Oh, quite all right, quite," answered Cuff. "I was glad to get away from Cape Town anyway. And we haven't had a mystery since old Hickey disappeared."

"Since who disappeared? You know me, I can't keep up with things out in the wilds."

"Oh, that was many years ago. Before your time, or mine for that matter. Hickey was a scientist who set out into the Kalahari with a truck and a Xosa assistant, and disappeared. Men flew all over the Kalahari looking for him, but never found a trace, and the sand had blown over his tire tracks. Jolly odd, it was."

The rain poured down steadily as they wallowed along the dirt road. Ahead, beyond the gray curtain, lay the vast plains of northern Bechuanaland with their great pans. And beyond the plains were, allegedly, a blue giraffe, and other things.

* * *

The spidery steelwork of the tower hummed as they climbed. At the top, Mtengeni said: "You can look over that way... west... to the other side of the forest. That's about twenty miles."

Cuff screwed up his eyes at the eyepieces. "Jolly good 'scope you've got here. But it's too hazy beyond the forest to see anything."

"It always is, unless we have a high wind. That's the edge of the swamps."

"Dashed if I see how you can patrol such a big area all by yourself."

"Oh, these Bechuana they don't give much trouble. They are honest. Even I have to admit that they have some good qualities. Anyway, you can't get far into the Delta without getting lost in the swamps. There are ways, but then, I only know them. I'll show them to you, but please don't tell these Bechuana about them. Look, Mr. Cuff, there's our blue giraffe."

Cuff started. Mtengeni was evidently the kind of man who would announce an earthquake as casually as the morning mail. Several hundred yards from the tower half a dozen giraffes were moving slowly through the brush, feeding on the tops of the scrubby trees.

Cuff swung the telescope on them. In the middle of the herd was the blue one. Cuff blinked and looked again. There was no doubt about it; the animal was as brilliant a blue as if somebody had gone over it with paint. Athelstan Cuff suspected that that was what somebody had done. He said as much to Mtengeni.

The warden shrugged. "That, it would be a peculiar kind of amusement. Not to say risky. Do you see anything funny about the others?"

Cuff looked again. "Yes... by Jove, one of 'em's got a beard like a goat; only it must be six feet long, at least, now look here, George, what's all this leading up to?"

"I don't know myself. Tomorrow, if you like, I'll show you one of those ways into the Delta. But that, it's quite a walk, so we'd better take supplies for two or three days."

* * *

As they drove toward the Tamalakane, they passed four Batawana, sad-looking reddish-brown men in a mixture of native and European clothes. Mtengeni slowed the car and looked at them suspiciously as they passed, but there was no evidence that they had been poaching.

He said: "Ever since their Makoba slaves were freed, they've been going on a… decline, I suppose you would call it. They are too dignified to work."

They got out at the river. "We can't drive across the ford this time of year," explained the warden, locking the car, "But there's a rapid a little way down, where we can wade."

They walked down the trail, adjusting their packs. There wasn't much to see. The view was shut off by the tall soft-bodied swamp plants. The only sound was the hum of insects,

The air was hot and steamy already, though the sun had been up only half an hour. The flies drew blood when they bit, but the men were used to that. They simply slapped and waited for the next bite.

Ahead there was a deep gurgling noise, like a foghorn with water in its works. Cuff said: "How are your hippo doing this year?"

"Pretty good. There are some in particular that I want you to see. Ah, here we are."

They had come in sight of a stretch of calm water. In the foreground a hippopotamus repeated its foghorn bellow. Cuff saw others, of which only the eyes, ears, and nostrils were visible. One of them was moving; Cuff could make out the little V-shaped wakes pointing back from its nearly sub-merged head. It reached the shallows and lumbered out, dripping noisily.

Cuff blinked. "Must be something wrong with my eyes."

"No," said Mtengeni. "That hippo she is one of those I wanted you to see."

The hippopotamus was green with pink spots.

She spied the men, grunted suspiciously, and slid back into the water.

"I still don't believe it," said Cuff. "Dash it, man, that's impossible."

"You will see many more things," said Mtengeni. "Shall we go on?"

They found the rapid and struggled across; then walked along what might, by some stretch of the imagination, be called a trail. There was little sound other than their sucking footfalls, the hum of insects, and the occasional screech of a bird or the crashing of a buck through the reeds.

* * *

They walked for some hours. Then Mtengeni said: "Be careful. There is a rhino near."

Cuff wondered how the devil the Zulu knew, but he was careful. Presently they came on a clear space in which the rhinoceros was browsing.

The animal couldn't see them at that distance, and there was no wind to carry their smell. It must have heard them, though, for it left off its feeding and snorted, once, like a locomotive. It had two heads.

It trotted toward them sniffing.

The men got out their rifles. "My God!" said Athelstan Cuff. "Hope we don't have to shoot him. My God!"

"I don't think so," said the warden. "That's Tweedle. I know him. If he gets too close, give him one at the base of the horn and he... he will run."

"Tweedle?"

"Yes. The right head is Tweedledum and the left is Tweedledee," said Mtengeni solemnly. "The whole rhino I call Tweedle."

The rhinoceros kept coming. Mtengeni said: "Watch this." He waved his hat and shouted: "Go away! *Footsack!*"

Tweedle stopped and snorted again. Then he began to circle like a waltzing mouse. Round and round he spun.

"We might as well go on," said Mtengeni. "He will keep that up for hours. You see Tweedledum is fierce, but Tweedledee, he is peaceful, even cowardly. So when I yell at Tweedle, Tweedledum wants to charge us, but Tweedledee he wants to run away. So the right legs go forward and the left legs go back, and Tweedle, he goes in circles. It takes him some time to agree on a policy."

"*Whew!*" said Athelstan Cuff. "I say, have you got any more things like this in your zoo?"

"Oh, yes, lots. That's what I hope you'll do something about."

Do something about this! Cuff wondered whether this was touching evidence of the native's faith in the white omniscience, or whether Mtengeni had gotten him there for the cynical amusement of watching him run in useless circles. Mtengeni himself gave no sign of what he was thinking.

Cuff said: "I can't understand, George, why somebody hasn't looked into this before."

Mtengeni shrugged. "Me, I've tried to get somebody to, but the government won't send anybody, and the scientific expeditions, there haven't been any of them for years. I don't know why."

"I can guess," said Cuff. "In the old days people even in the so-called civilized countries expected travel to be a jolly rugged proposition, so they didn't mind putting up with a few extra hardships on trek. But now that you can ride or fly almost anywhere on soft cushions, people won't put themselves out to get to a really uncomfortable and out-of-the-way place like Ngamiland."

Over the swampy smell came another, of carrion. Mtengeni pointed to the carcass of a waterbuck fawn, which the scavengers had apparently not discovered yet.

"That's why I want you to stop this whatever-it-is," he said. There was real concern in his voice.

"What do you mean, George?"

"Do you see its legs?"

Cuff looked. The forelegs were only half as long as the hind ones.

"That buck," said the Zulu. "It naturally couldn't live long. All over the Park, freaks like this they are being born. Most of them don't live. In ten years more, maybe twenty, all my animals will have died out because of this. Then my job, where is it?"

* * *

They stopped at sunset. Cuff was glad to. It had been some time since he'd done fifteen miles in one day, and he dreaded the morrow's stiffness. He looked at his map and tried to figure out where he was. But the cartographers had never seriously tried to keep track of the changes in the Okavango's multifarious branches, and had simply plastered the whole Delta with little blue dashes with tufts of blue lines sticking up from them, meaning simply "swamp." In all directions the country was a monotonous alternation of land and water. The two elements were inextricably mixed.

The Zulu was looking for a dry spot free of snakes. Cuff heard him suddenly shout "*Footsack!*" and throw a clod at a log. The log opened a pair of jaws, hissed angrily, and slid into the water.

"We'll have to have a good fire," said Mtengeni, hunting for dry wood. "We don't want a croc or hippo wandering into our tent by mistake."

After supper they set the automatic bug sprayer going, inflated their mattresses, and tried to sleep. A lion roared some-where in the west. That sound no African, native or Africander, likes to hear when he is on foot at night. But the men were not worried; lions avoided the swampy areas. The mosquitoes presented a more immediate problem.

Many hours later, Athelstan Cuff heard Mtengeni getting up.

The warden said: "I just remembered a high spot half a mile from here, where there's plenty of firewood. Me, I'm going out to get some."

Cuff listened to Mtengeni's retreating steps in the soft ground; then to his own breathing. Then he listened to something else. It sounded like a human yell.

He got up and pulled on his boots quickly. He fumbled around for the flashlight, but Mtengeni had taken it with him.

The yell came again.

Cuff found his rifle and cartridge belt in the dark and went out. There was enough starlight to walk by if you were careful. The fire was nearly out. The yells seemed to come from a direction opposite to that in which Mtengeni had gone. They were highpitched, like a woman's screams.

He walked in their direction, stumbling over irregularities in the ground and now and then stepping up to his calves in unexpected water. The yells were plainer now. They weren't in English. Something was also snorting.

He found the place. There was a small tree, in the branches of which somebody was perched. Below the tree a noisy bulk moved around. Cuff caught the outline of a sweeping horn, and knew he had to deal with a buffalo.

He hated to shoot. For a Park official to kill one of his charges simply wasn't done. Besides, he couldn't see to aim for a vital spot, and he didn't care to try to dodge a wounded buffalo in the dark. They could move with racehorse speed through the heaviest growth.

On the other hand, he couldn't leave even a poor fool of a native woman treed. The buffalo, if it was really angry, would wait for days until its victim weakened and fell. Or it would butt the tree until the victim was shaken out. Or it would rear up and try to hook the victim out with its horns.

Athelstan Cuff shot the buffalo. The buffalo staggered about a bit and collapsed.

The victim climbed down swiftly, pouring out a flood of thanks in Xosa. It was very bad Xosa, even worse than the Englishman's. Cuff wondered what she was doing here, nearly a thousand miles from where the Maxosa lived. He assumed that she was a native, though it was too dark to see. He asked her if she spoke English, but she didn't seem to understand the question, so he made shift with the Bantu dialect.

"*Uveli phi na?*" he asked sternly. "Where do you come from? Don't you know that nobody is allowed in the Park without special permission?"

"*Izwe kamafene wabantu,*" she replied.

"What? Never heard of the place. Land of the baboon people, indeed! What are you?"

"*Ingwamza.*"

"You're a white stork? Are you trying to be funny?"

"I didn't say I was a white stork. Ingwamza's my name."

"I don't care about your name. I want to know what you *are*."

"*Umfene umfazi.*"

Cuff controlled his exasperation. "All right, all right, you're a baboon woman. I don't care what clan you belong to. What's your tribe? Batawana, Bamangwato, Bangwaketse, Barolong, Herero, or what? Don't try to tell me you're a Xosa; no Xosa ever used an accent like that."

"*Amafene abantu.*"

"What the devil are the baboon people?"

"People who live in the Park."

Cuff resisted the impulse to pull out two handfuls of hair by the roots. "But I tell you nobody lives in the Park! It isn't allowed! Come now, where do you really come from and what' s your native language and why are you trying to talk Xosa?"

"I told you, I live in the Park. And I speak Xosa because all we *amafene abantu* speak it. That's the language Mqhavi taught us."

"Who is Mqhavi?"

"The man who taught us to speak Xosa."

Cuff gave up. "Come along, you're going to see the warden. Perhaps he can make some sense out of your gabble. And you'd better have a good reason for trespassing, my good woman, or it'll go hard with you. Especially as it resulted in the killing of a good buffalo." He started off toward the camp, making sure that Ingwamza followed him closely.

* * *

The first thing he discovered was that he couldn't see the light of any fire to guide him back. Either he'd come farther than he thought, or the fire had died altogether while Mtengeni was getting wood. He kept on for a quarter of an hour in what he thought was the right direction. Then he stopped. He had, he realized, not the vaguest idea of where he was.

He turned. "*Sibaphi na?*" he snapped. "Where are we?"

"In the Park."

Cuff began to wonder whether he'd ever succeed in delivering this native woman to Mtengeni before he strangled her with his bare hands. "I know we're in the Park," he snarled. "But *where* in the Park?"

"I don't know exactly. Somewhere near my people's land."

"That doesn't do me any good. Look: I left the warden's camp when I heard you yell. I want to get back to it. Now how do I do it?"

"Where is the warden's camp?"

"I don't know, stupid. If I did I'd go there."

"If you don't know where it is, how do you expect me to guide you thither? I don't know either."

Cuff made strangled noises in his throat. Inwardly he had to admit that she had him there, which only made him madder. Finally he said: "Never mind, suppose you take me to your people. Maybe they have somebody with some sense."

"Very well," said the native woman, and she set off at a rapid pace, Cuff stumbling after her vague outline. He began to wonder if maybe she wasn't right about living in the Park. She seemed to know where she was going.

"Wait," he said. He ought to write a note to Mtengeni, explaining what he was up to, and stick it on a tree for the warden to find. But there was no pencil or paper in his pockets. He didn't even have a match safe or a cigarette lighter. He'd taken all those things out of his pockets when he'd lain down.

They went on a way, Cuff pondering on how to get in touch with Mtengeni. He didn't want himself and the warden to spend a week chasing each other around the Delta. Perhaps it would be better to stay where they were and build a fire—but again, he had no matches, and didn't see much prospect of making a fire by rubbing sticks in this damned damp country.

Ingwamza said: "Stop. There are buffalo ahead."

Cuff listened and heard faintly the sound of snapping grass stems as the animals fed.

She continued: "We'll have to wait until it gets light. Then maybe they'll go away. If they don't, we can circle around them, but I couldn't find the way around in the dark."

They found the highest point they could and settled down to wait. Something with legs had crawled inside Cuff's shirt. He mashed it with a slap.

He strained his eyes into the dark. It was impossible to tell how far away the buffalo were. Overhead a nightjar brought its wings together with a single startling clap. Cuff told his nerves to behave themselves. He wished he had a smoke.

The sky began to lighten. Gradually Cuff was able to make out the black bulks moving among the reeds. They were at least two hundred yards away. He'd have preferred that they were at twice the distance, but it was better than stumbling right on them.

It became lighter and lighter. Cuff never took his eyes off the buffalo. There was something queer about the nearest one. It had six legs.

Cuff turned to Ingwamza and started to whisper: "What kind of buffalo do you call—" Then he gave a yell of pure horror and jumped back. His rifle went off, tearing a hole in his boot.

He had just gotten his first good look at the native woman in the rapidly waxing dawn. Ingwamza's head was that of an overgrown chacma baboon.

The buffalo stampeded through the feathery papyrus. Cuff and Ingwamza stood looking at each other. Then Cuff looked at his right foot. Blood was running out of the jagged hole in the leather.

"What's the matter? Why did you shoot yourself?" asked Ingwamza.

Cuff couldn't think of an answer to that one. He sat down and took off his boot. The foot felt numb, but there seemed to be no harm done aside from a piece of skin the size of a sixpence gouged out of the margin. Still, you never knew what sort of horrible infection might result from a trifling wound in these swamps. He tied his foot up with his handkerchief and put his boot back on.

"Just an accident," he said. "Keep going, Ingwamza."

Ingwamza went, Cuff limping behind. The sun would rise any minute now. It was light enough to make out colors. Cuff saw that Ingwamza, in describing herself as a baboon-woman, had been quite literal, despite the size, general proportions, and posture of a human being. Her body, but for the greenish-yellow hair and the short tail, might have passed for that of a human being, if you weren't too particular. But the astonishing head with its long bluish muzzle gave her the appearance of an Egyptian animal-headed god. Cuff wondered vaguely if the *'fene abantu* were a race of man-monkey hybrids. That was impossible, of course. But he'd seen so many impossible things in the last couple of days.

She looked back at him. "We shall arrive in an hour or two. I'm sleepy." She yawned. Cuff repressed a shudder at the sight of four canine teeth big enough for a leopard. Ingwamza could tear the throat out of a man with those fangs as easily as biting the end off a banana. And he'd been using his most hectoring colonial-administrator tone on her in the dark!

He made a resolve never to speak harshly to anybody he couldn't see.

* * *

Ingwamza pointed to a carroty baobab against the sky. "*Izwe kamagene wabantu.*" They had to wade a little stream to get there. A six-foot monitor lizard walked across their path, saw them, and disappeared with a scuttle.

The *'fene abantu* lived in a village much like that of any Bantu people, but the circular thatched huts were smaller and cruder. Baboon people ran out to peer at Cuff and to feel his clothes. He gripped his rifle tightly. They didn't act hostile, but it gave you a dashed funny feeling. The males were larger than the females, with even longer muzzles and bigger tusks.

In the center; of the village sat a big *umfene umntu* scratching himself in front of the biggest hut. Ingwamza said, "That is my father, the chief. His name is Indlovu." To the baboon-man she told of her rescue.

The chief was the only *umfene umntu* that Cuff had seen who wore anything. What he wore was a necktie. The necktie had been a gaudy thing once.

The chief got up and made a speech, the gist of which was that Cuff had done a great thing, and that Cuff would be their guest until his wound healed. Cuff had a chance to observe the difficulties that the *'fene abantu* had with the Xosa tongue. The clicks were blurred, and they stumbled badly over the lipsmack. With those mouths, he could see how they might.

But he was only mildly interested. His foot was hurting like the very devil. He was glad when they led him into a hut so he could take off his boot. The hut was practically unfurnished. Cuff asked the *'fene abantu* if he might have some of the straw used for thatching. They seemed puzzled by his request, but complied, and he made himself a bed of sorts. He hated sleeping on the ground, especially on ground infested with arthropodal life. He hated vermin, and knew he was in for an intimate acquaintance with them.

He had nothing to bandage his foot with, except the one handkerchief, which was now thoroughly blood-soaked. He'd have to wash and dry it before it would be fit to use again. And where in the Okavango Delta could he find water fit to wash the handkerchief in? Of course he could boil the water. In what? He was relieved and amazed when his questions brought forth the fact that there was a large iron pot in the village, obtained from God knew where.

The wound had clotted satisfactorily, and he dislodged the handkerchief with infinite care from the scab. While his water was boiling, the chief, Indlovu, came in and talked to him. The pain in his foot had subsided for the moment, and he was able to realize what an extraordinary thing he had come across, and to give Indlovu his full attention. He plied Indlovu with questions.

The chief explained what he knew about himself and his people. It seemed that he was the first of the race; all the others were his descendants. Not only Ingwamza but all the other *amafene abafazi* were his daughters. Ingwamza was merely the last. He was old now. He was hazy about dates, but Cuff got the impression that these beings had a shorter life span than human beings, and matured much more quickly. If they were in fact baboons, that was natural enough.

Indlovu didn't remember having had any parents. The earliest he remembered was being led around by Mqhavi. Stanley H. Mqhavi had been a black man, and worked for the machine man, who had been a pink man like Cuff. He had had a machine up on the edge of the Chobe Swamp. His name had been Heeky.

Of course, Hickey! thought Cuff. Now he was getting somewhere. Hickey had disappeared by simply running his truck up to Ngamiland without bothering to tell anybody where he was going. That had been before the Park had been established; before Cuff had come out from England. Mqhavi must have been his Xosa assistant. His thoughts raced ahead of Indlovu's words.

Indlovu went on to tell about how Heeky had died, and how Mqhavi, not knowing how to run the machine, had taken him, Indlovu, and his now numerous progeny in an attempt to find his way back to civilization. He had gotten lost in the Delta. Then he had cut his foot somehow, and gotten sick, very sick. Cuff had come out from England. When Mqhavi had gotten well he had been very weak. So he had settled down with Indlovu and his family. They already walked upright and spoke Xosa, which Mqhavi had taught them. Cuff got the idea that the early family relationships among the *'fene abantu* had of necessity involved close inbreeding. Mqhavi had taught them all he knew, and then died, after warning them not to go within a mile of the machine, which, as far as they knew, was still up at the Chobe Swamp.

Cuff thought, that blasted machine is an electronic tube of some sort, built to throw short waves of the length to affect animal genes. Probably Indlovu represented one of Hickey's early experiments. Then Hickey had died, and—left the thing going. He didn't know how it got power; some solar system, perhaps.

Suppose Hickey had died while the thing was turned on. Mqhavi might have dragged his body out and left the door open. He might have been afraid to try to turn it off, or he might not have thought of it. So every animal that passed that doorway got a dose of the rays, and begat monstrous off-spring. These super-baboons were one example; whether an accidental or a controlled mutation, might never be known.

For every useful mutation there were bound to be scores of useless or harmful ones. Mtengeni had been right: it had to be stopped while there was still normal stock left in the Park. He wondered again how to get in touch with the warden. He'd be damned if anything short of the threat of death would get him to walk on that foot, for a few days anyhow.

* * *

Ingwamza entered with a wooden dish full of a mess of some sort. Athelstan Cuff decided resignedly that he was expected to eat it. He couldn't tell by looking whether it was animal or vegetable in nature. After the first mouthful he was sure it was neither. Nothing in the animal and vegetable worlds could taste as awful as that. It was too bad Mqhavi hadn't been a Bamangwato; he'd have really known how to cook, and could have taught these monkeys. Still, he had to eat something to support life. He fell to with the wooden spoon they gave him, suppressing an occasional gag and watching the smaller solid particles closely. Sure enough, he had to smack two of them with the spoon to keep them from crawling out.

"How it is?" asked Ingwamza. Indlovu had gone out.

"Fine," lied Cuff. He was chasing a slimy piece of what he suspected was waterbuck tripe around the dish. "I am glad. We'll feed you a lot of that. Do you like scorpions?"

"You mean to *eat?*"

"Of course. What else are they good for?"

He gulped. "No."

"I won't give you any then. You see I'm glad to know what my future husband likes."

"What?" He thought he had misunderstood her.

"I said, I am glad to know what you like, so I can please you after you are my husband."

Athelstan Cuff said nothing for sixty seconds. His naturally prominent eyes bulged even more as her words sank in. Finally he spoke.

"*Gluk,*" he said. "

What's that?"

"*Gug. Gah.* My God. Let me out of here!" His voice jumped two octaves, and he tried to get up. Ingwamza caught his shoulders and pushed him gently, but firmly, back on his pallet. He struggled, but without visibly exerting herself the *'fene umfazi* held him as in a vise.

"You can't go," she said. "If you try to walk on that foot you will get sick."

His ruddy face was turning purple! "Let me up! Let me up, I say! I can't stand this!"

"Will you promise not to try to go out if I do? Father would be furious if I let you do anything unwise."

He promised, getting a grip on himself again. He already felt a bit foolish about his panic. He was in a nasty jam, certainly, but an official of His Majesty didn't act like a frightened schoolgirl at every crisis.

"What," he asked, "is this all about?"

"Father is so grateful to you for saving my life that he intends to bestow me on you in marriage, without even asking a bride price." "But... but... I'm married already," he lied.

"What of it? I'm not afraid of your other wives. If they got fresh, I'd tear them in pieces like this." She bared her teeth and went through the motions of tearing several Mistresses Cuff in pieces. Athelstan Cuff shut his eyes at the horrid sight.

"Among my people," he said, "you're allowed only one wife."

"That's too bad," said Ingwamza. "That means that you couldn't go back to your people after you married me, doesn't it?"

Cuff sighed. These *'fene abantu* combined the mental outlook of uneducated Maxosa with physical equipment that would make a lion think twice before attacking one. He'd probably have to shoot his way out. He looked around the hut craftily. His rifle wasn't in sight. He didn't dare ask about it for fear of arousing suspicion.

"Is your father set on this plan?" he asked.

"Oh, yes, very. Father is a good *umntu*, but he gets set on ideas like this and nothing will make him change them. And he has a terrible temper. If you cross him when he has his heart set on something, he will tear you in pieces. *Small* pieces." She seemed to relish the phrase.

"How do *you* feel about it, Ingwamza?"

"Oh, I do everything father says. He knows more than any of us."

"Yes, but I mean you personally. Forget about your father for the moment."

She didn't quite catch on for a moment, but after further explanation she said: "I wouldn't mind. It would be a great thing for my people if one of us was married to a man."

Cuff silently thought that that went double for him.

Indlovu came in with two other *amafene abantu*. "Run along, Ingwamza," he said. The three baboon-men squatted around Athelstan Cuff and began questioning him about men and the world outside the Delta.

When Cuff stumbled over a phrase, one of the questioners, a scarred fellow named Sondlo, asked why he had difficulty. Cuff explained that Xosa wasn't his native language.

"Men do speak other languages?" asked Indlovu. "I remember now, the great Mqhavi once told me something to that effect. But he never taught me any other languages. Perhaps he and Heeky spoke one of these other languages, but I was too young when Heeky died to remember."

Cuff explained something about linguistics. He was immediately pressed to "say something in English." Then they wanted to learn English, right then, that afternoon.

Cuff finished his evening meal and looked without enthusiasm at his pallet. No artificial light, so these people rose and set with the sun. He stretched out. The straw rustled. He jumped up, bringing his injured foot down hard. He yelped, swore, and felt the bandage. Yes, he'd started it bleeding again. Oh, to hell with it. He attacked the straw, chasing out a mouse, six cockroaches, and uncounted smaller bugs. Then he stretched out again. Looking up, he felt his scalp prickle. A ten-inch centipede was methodically hunting its prey over the underside of the roof. If it missed its footing when it was right over him—He unbuttoned his shirt and pulled it up over his face. Then the mosquitoes attacked his midriff. His foot throbbed.

A step brought him up; it was Ingwamza. "What is it now?" he asked.

"*Ndiya kuhlaha apha,*" she answered.

"Oh no, you're not going to stay here. We're not... well, anyway, it simply isn't done among my people."

"But Esselten, somebody must watch you in case you get sick. My father—"

"No, I'm sorry, but that's final. If you're going to marry me you'll have to learn how to behave among men. And we're beginning right now."

To his surprise and relief, she went without further objection, albeit sulkily. He'd never have dared to try to put her out by force.

When she had gone, he crawled over to the door of the hut. The sun had just set, and the moon would follow it in a couple of hours. Most of the *'fene abantu* had retired. But a couple of them squatted outside their huts, in sight of his place, watchfully.

Heigh ho, he thought, they aren't taking any chances. Perhaps the old boy is grateful and all that rot. But I think my fiancé let the cat out when she said that about the desirability of hitching one of the tribe to a human being. Of course the poor things don't know that it wouldn't have any legal standing at all. But that fact wouldn't save me from a jolly unpleasant experience in the meantime. Suppose I haven't escaped by the time of the ceremony. Would I go through with it? *Br-r-r!* Of course not. I'm an Englishman and an officer of the Crown. But if it meant my life... I don't know. I'm dashed if I do. Perhaps I can talk them out of it... being careful not to get them angry in the process.

* * *

He was tied to the straw, and enormous centipedes were dropping off the ceiling onto his face. Then he was running through the swamp, with Ingwamza and her irate pa after him. His feet stuck in the mud so he couldn't move, and there was a light in his face. Mtengeni—good old George!—was riding a two headed rhino. But instead of rescuing him, the warden said: "Mr. Cuff, you must do some-thing about these Bechuana. Them, they are catching all my animals and painting them red with green stripes." Then he woke up.

It took him a second to realize that the light was from the setting moon, not the rising sun, and that he therefore had been asleep less than two hours. It took him another second to realize what had wakened him. The straw of the hut wall had been wedged apart, and through the gap a *'fene umntu* was crawling. While Cuff was still wondering why one of his hosts, or captors, should use this peculiar method of getting in, the baboon-man stood up. He looked enormous in the faint light.

"What is it?" asked Cuff.

"If you make a noise," said the stranger, "I will kill you."

"What? What's the idea? Why should you want to kill me?"

"You have stolen my Ingwamza."

"But… but—" Cuff was at a loss. Here the gal's old man would tear him in pieces— *small* pieces—if he didn't marry her, and a rival or something would kill him if he did. "Let's talk it over first," he said, in what he hoped was a normal voice. "Who are you, by the way?"

"My name is Cukata. I was to have married Ingwamza next month. And then you came."

"What… what—"

"I won't kill you. Not if you make no noise. I will just fix you so you won't marry Ingwamza." He moved toward the pile of straw.

Cuff didn't waste time inquiring into the horrid details. "Wait a minute," he said, cold sweat bedewing not merely his brow, but his whole torso. "My dear fellow, this marriage wasn't my idea. It was Indlovu's, entirely. I don't want to steal your girl. They just informed me that I was going to marry her, without asking me about it at all. I don't want to marry her. In fact there's nothing I want to do less."

The *'fene umntu* stood still for a moment, thinking. Then he said softly: "You wouldn't marry my Ingwamza if you had the chance? You think she is ugly?"

"Well—"

"By u-Qamata, that's an insult! Nobody shall think such thoughts of my Ingwamza! Now I will kill you for sure!"

"Wait, wait!" Cuff's voice, normally a pleasant low baritone. became a squeak. "That isn't it at all! She's beautiful, intelligent, industrious, all that a 'ntu could want. But I can never marry her." Inspiration! Cuff went on rapidly. Never had he spoken Xosa so fluently. "You know that if lion mates with leopard, there are no offspring." Cuff wasn't sure that was so, but he took a chance. "It is that way with my people and yours. We are too different. There would be no issue to our marriage. And Indlovu would not have grandchildren by us to gladden his old age."

Cukata, after some thought, saw, or thought he did. "But," he said, "how can I prevent this marriage without killing you?"

"You could help me escape."

"So. Now that's an idea. Where do you want to go?"

"Do you know where the Hickey machine is?"

"Yes, though I have never been close to it. That is forbidden. About fifteen miles north of here, on the edge of the Chobe Swamp, is a rock. By the rock are three baobab trees, close together. Between the trees and the swamp are two houses. The machine is in one of those houses."

He was silent again. "You can't travel fast with that wounded foot. They would overtake you. Perhaps Indlovu would tear you in pieces, or perhaps he would bring you back. If he brought you back, we should fail. If he tore you in pieces, I should be sorry, for I like you, even if you are a feeble little *isipham-pham*." Cuff wished that the simian brain would get around to the point. "I have it. In ten minutes I shall whistle. You will then crawl out through this hole in the wall, making no noise. You understand?"

When Athelstan Cuff crawled out, he found Cukata in the alley between two rows of huts. There was a strong reptilian stench in the air. Behind the baboon-man was something large and black. It walked with a swaying motion. It brushed against Cuff, and he almost cried out at the touch of cold, leathery hide.

"This is the largest," said Cukata. "We hope some day to have a whole herd of them. They are fine for traveling across the swamps, because they can swim as well as run. And they grow much faster than the ordinary crocodile."

The thing was a crocodile but such a crocodile! Though not much over fifteen feet in length, it had long, powerful legs that raised its body a good four feet off the ground, giving it a dinosaurian look. It rubbed against Cuff, and the thought occurred to him that it had taken an astonishing mutation indeed to give a brainless and voracious reptile an affection for human beings.

Cukata handed Cuff a knobkerry, and explained: "Whistle loudly, when you want him to come. To start him, hit him on the tail with this.

To stop him, hit him on the nose. To make him go to the left, hit him on the right side of the neck, not too hard. To make him go to the right, hit him—"

"On the left side of the neck, but not too hard," finished Cuff. "What does he eat?"

"Anything that is meat. But you needn't feed him for two or three days; he has been fed recently."

"Don't you use a saddle?"

"Saddle? What's that?"

"Never mind." Cuff climbed aboard, wincing as he settled onto the sharp dorsal ridges of the animal's hide.

"Wait," said Cukata. "The moon will be completely gone in a moment. Remember, I shall say that I know nothing about your escape, but that you go out and stole him yourself. His name is Soga."

* * *

There were the baobab trees, and there were the houses. There were also a dozen elephants, facing the rider and his bizarre mount and spreading their immense ears. Athelstan Cuff was getting so blasé about freaks that he hardly noticed that two of the elephants had two trunks apiece: that another of them was colored a fair imitation of a Scotch tartan; that another of them had short legs like a hippopotamus, so that it looked like something out of a dachshund breeder's night-mare.

The elephants, for their part, seemed undecided whether to run or to attack, and finally compromised by doing nothing. Cuff realized when he was already past them that he had done a wickedly reckless thing in going so close to them unarmed except for the useless kerry. But somehow he couldn't get excited about mere elephants. His whole life for the past forty-eight hours had had a dreamlike quality. Maybe he was dreaming. Or maybe he had a charmed life. Or something. Though there was nothing dreamlike about the throb in his foot, or the acute soreness in his gluteus maximus.

Soga, being a crocodile, bowed his whole body at every stride. First the head and tail went to the right and the body to the left; then the process was reversed. Which was most unpleasant for his rider.

Cuff was willing to swear that he'd ridden at least fifty miles instead of the fifteen Cukata had mentioned. Actually he had done about thirty, not having been able to follow a straight line and having to steer by stars and, when it rose, the sun. A fair portion of the thirty had been hugging Soga's barrel while the croc's great tail drove them through the water like a racing shell. No hippo or other crocs had bothered them; evidently they knew when they were well off.

Athelstan Cuff slid—almost fell—off, and hobbled up to the entrance of one of the houses. His practiced eye took in the roof cistern, the solar boiler, the steam-electric plant, the batteries, and finally the tube inside. He went in. Yes, by Jove, the tube was in operation after all these years. Hickey must have had something jolly unusual. Cuff found the main switch easily enough and pulled it. All that happened was that the little orange glow in the tube died.

The house was so silent it made Cuff uncomfortable, except for the faint hum of the solar power plant. As he moved about, using the kerry for a crutch, he stirred up the dust which lay six inches deep on the floor. Maybe there were notebooks or something which ought to be collected. There had been, he soon discovered, but the termites had eaten every scrap of paper, and even the imitation-leather covers, leaving only the metal binding rings and their frames. It was the same with the books.

Something white caught his eye. It was paper lying on a little metal-legged stand that the termites evidently hadn't thought well enough of to climb. He limped toward it eagerly. But it was only a newspaper, *Umlindi we Nyanga*—"The Monthly Watchman"— published in East London. Evidently, Stanley H. Mqhavi had subscribed to it. It crumbled at Cuff's touch.

"Oh, well," he thought, "can't expect much. We'll run along, and some of the bio-physicist chappies can come in and gather up the scientific apparatus."

He went out, called Soga, and started east. He figured that he could strike the old wagon road somewhere north of the Mababe, and get down to Mtengeni's main station that way.

* * *

Were those human voices? Cuff shifted uneasily on his Indian fakir's seat. He had gone about four miles after leaving Hickey's scientific station.

They were voices, but not human ones. They belonged to a dozen *'fene abantu*, who came loping through the grass with old Indlovu at their head.

Cuff reached back and thumped Soga's tail. If he could get the croc going all out, he might be able to run away from his late hosts. Soga wasn't as fast as a horse, but he could trot right along. Cuff was relieved to see that they hadn't brought his rifle along. They were armed with kerries and spears, like any of the more savage *abantu*. Perhaps the fear of injuring their pet would make them hesitate to throw things at him. At least he hoped so.

A familiar voice caught up with him in a piercing yell of "Soga!" The croc slackened his pace and tried to turn his head. Cuff whacked him unmercifully. Indlovu's yell came again, followed by a whistle. The croc was now definitely off his stride. Cuff's efforts to keep him headed away from his proper masters resulted in his zigzagging erratically. The contrary directions confused and irritated him. He opened his jaws and hissed. The baboon-men were gaining rapidly.

So, thought Cuff, this is the end. I hate like hell to go out before I've had a chance to write my report. But mustn't show it. Not an Englishman and an officer of the Crown. Wonder what poor Mtengeni'll think.

Something went *whick* past him; a fraction of a second later, the crash of an elephant rifle reached him. A big puff of dust ballooned up in front of the baboon-men. They skittered away from it as if the dust and not the bullet that made it were something deadly. George Mtengeni appeared from behind the nearest patch of thorn scrub, and yelled, "Hold still there, or me, I'll blow your heads off." If the *'fene abantu* couldn't understand his English, they got his tone.

Cuff thought vaguely, good old George, he could shoot their ears off at that distance. But he has more sense then to kill any of them before he finds out. Cuff slid off Soga and almost fell in a heap.

The warden came up. "What... what in the heavens has been happening to you, Mr. Cuff? What are these?" He indicated the baboon-men.

"Joke," giggled Cuff. "Good joke on you, George. Been living in your dashed Park for years, and you never knew—Wait, I've got to explain something to these chaps. I say, Indlovu... hell, he doesn't know English. Got to use Xosa. You know Xosa, don't you George?" He giggled again.

"Why, me, I... I can follow it. It's much like Zulu. But my God, what happened to the seat of your pants?"

Cuff pointed a wavering finger at Soga's sawtoothed back. "Good old Soga. Should have had a saddle. Dashed outrage, not providing a saddle for His Majesty's representative."

"But you look as if you'd been skinned! Me, I've got to get you to a hospital... and what about your foot?"

"T'hell with the foot. 'Nother joke, Can't stand up, can't sit down. Jolly, what? Have to sleep on my stomach. But, Ind-lovu! I'm sorry I had to run away. I couldn't marry Ingwamza. Really. Because... because—" Athelstan Cuff swayed and collapsed in a small, ragged pile.

* * *

Peter Cuff's eyes were round. He asked the inevitable small-boy question: "What happened then?"

Athelstan Cuff was stuffing his pipe. "Oh, about what you'd expect. Indlovu was jolly vexed, I can tell you, but he didn't dare do anything with George standing there with the gun. He calmed down later after he understood what I had been driving at, and we became good friends. When he died, Cukata was elected chief in his place. I still get Christmas cards from him."

"Christmas cards from a baboon?"

"Certainly. If I get one next Christmas, I'll show it to you. It's the same card every year. He's an economical fella, and he bought a hundred cards of the same pattern because he could get them at a discount."

"Were you all right?"

"Yes, after a month in the hospital. I still don't know why I didn't get sixteen kinds of blood poisoning. Fool's luck, I suppose."

"But what's that got to do with me being a 'dopted boy?"

"Peter!" Cuff gave the clicks represented in the Bantu languages by *x* and in English by *tsk*. "Isn't it obvious? That tube of Hickey's was on when I approached his house. So I got a full dose of the radiations. Their effect was to produce violent mutations in the germ-plasm. You know what that is, don't you? Well, I never dared have any children of my own after that, for fear they'd turn out to be some sort of monster. That didn't occur to me until afterward. It fair bowled me over, I can tell you, when I did think of it. I went to pieces, rather, and lost my job in South Africa. But now that I have you and your mother, I realize that it wasn't so important after all."

"Father—" Peter hesitated.

"Go on, old man."

"If you'd thought of the rays before you went to the house, would you have been brave enough to go ahead anyway?"

Cuff lit his pipe and looked off at nothing. "I've often wondered about that myself. I'm dashed if I know. I wonder… just what would have happened—"

Running rats and mice through mazes began in the early 20th century, and were a well-known stereotype for scientific experiments on or with animals by 1950. They were often used to breed for increased intelligence. Barney is a rat that has become too intelligent, without the experimenters noticing it.

Barney

by Will Stanton

August 30th. We are alone on the island now, Barney and I. It was something of a jolt to have to sack Tayloe after all these years, but I had no alternative. The petty vandalisms I could have forgiven, but when he tried to poison Barney out of simple malice, he was standing in the way of scientific progress. That I cannot condone.

I can only believe the attempt was made while under the influence of alcohol, it was so clumsy. The poison container was overturned and a trail of powder led to Barney's dish. Tayloe's defense was of the flimsiest. He denied it. Who else then?

September 2nd. I am taking a calmer view of the Tayloe affair. The monastic life here must have become too much for him. That, and the abandonment of his precious guinea pigs. He insisted to the last that they were better suited than Barney to my experiments. They were more his speed, I'm afraid. He was an earnest and willing worker, but something of a clod, poor fellow.

At last I have complete freedom to carry on my work without the mute reproaches of Tayloe. I can only ascribe his violent antagonism toward Barney to jealousy. And now that he has gone, how much happier Barney appears to be! I have given him complete run of the place, and what sport it is to observe how his newly awakened intellectual curiosity carries him about. After only two weeks of glutamic acid treatments, he has become interested in my library, dragging the books from the shelves, and going over them page by page. I am certain he knows there is some knowledge to be gained from them had he but the key.

September 8th. For the past two days I have had to keep Barney confined and how he hates it. I am afraid that when my experiments are completed I shall have to do away with Barney. Ridiculous as it may sound there is still the possibility that he might be able to communicate his intelligence to others of his kind. However small the chance may be, the risk is too great to ignore. Fortunately there is, in the basement, a vault built with the idea of keeping vermin out and it will serve equally well to keep Barney in.

September 9th. Apparently I have spoken too soon. This morning I let him out to frisk around a bit before commencing a new series of tests. After a quick survey of the room he returned to his cage, sprang up on the door handle, removed the key with his teeth, and before I could stop him, he was out the window. By the time I reached the yard I spied him on the coping of the well, and I arrived on the spot only in time to hear the key splash into the water below.

I own I am somewhat embarrassed. It is the only key. The door is locked. Some valuable papers are in separate compartments inside the vault. Fortunately, although the well is over forty feet deep, there are only a few feet of water in the bottom, so the retrieving of the key does not present an insurmountable obstacle. But I must admit Barney has won the first round.

September 10th. I have had a rather shaking experience, and once more in a minor clash with Barney I have come off second best. In this instance I will admit he played the hero's role and may even have saved my life.

In order to facilitate my descent into the well I knotted a length of three-quarter inch rope at one foot intervals to make a rude ladder. I reached the bottom easily enough, but after only a few minutes of groping for the key my flashlight gave out and I returned to the surface. A few feet from the top I heard excited squeaks from Barney, and upon obtaining ground level I observed that the rope was almost completely severed. Apparently it had chafed against the edge of the masonry and the little fellow perceiving my plight had been doing his utmost to warn me.

I have now replaced that section of rope, and arranged some old sacking beneath it to prevent a recurrence of the accident. I have replenished the batteries in my flashlight and am now prepared for the final descent. These few moments I have taken off to give myself a breathing spell and to bring my journal up to date. Perhaps I should fix myself a sandwich as I may be down there longer than seems likely at the moment.

September 11th. Poor Barney is dead an soon I shell be the same. He was a wonderful ratt and life without him is knot worth living. If anybody reeds this please do not disturb anything on the island but leeve it like it is as a shryn to Barney, espechilly the old well. Do not look for my body as I will caste myself into the see. You mite bring a couple of young ratts an leeve them as a living memorial to Barney. Females—no males. I sprayned my wrist is why this is written so bad. This is my laste will. Do what I say and don't come back or disturb anything after you bring the young ratts like I said. Just females.

Goodby

Philip K. Dick burst upon the s-f scene (not counting over four dozen mostly-forgettable short stories) in the mid-1950s with five Ace Books novels: Solar Lottery *(1955),* The World Jones Made *(1956),* The Man Who Japed *(1956),* The Cosmic Puppets *(1957), and* Eye in the Sky *(1957). Nobody at the time knew who Dick was, but judging from the themes of these and others (*Time Out of Joint, *1959; the Hugo Award-winning* The Man in the High Castle, *1962), he was seriously paranoid.*

Dick's 1953 short story "Expendable" prefigures these. The unnamed narrator is the only man in the world who has found out that all other life forms—the ants, birds, caterpillars, and spiders at least—are sentient and have been keeping humans in blissful ignorance. Of course, now that he has found out, he will have to be killed …

Expendable

by Philip K. Dick

The man came out on the front porch and examined the day. Bright and cold—with dew on the lawns. He buttoned his coat and put his hands in his pockets.

As the man started down the steps the two caterpillars waiting by the mailbox twitched with interest.

"There he goes," the first one said. "Send in your report."

As the other began to rotate his vanes the man stopped, turning quickly.

"I heard that," he said. He brought his foot down against the wall, scraping the caterpillars off, onto the concrete. He crushed them.

Then he hurried down the path to the sidewalk. As he walked he looked around him. In the cherry tree a bird was hopping, pecking bright-eyed at the cherries. The man studied him. All right? Or—The bird flew off. Birds all right. No harm from them.

He went on. At the corner he brushed against a spider web, crossed from the bushes to the telephone pole. His heart pounded. He tore away, batting the air. As he went on he glanced over his shoulder. The spider was coming slowly down the bush, feeling out the damage to his web.

Hard to tell about spiders. Difficult to figure out. More facts needed— No contact, yet.

He waited at the bus stop, stomping his feet to keep them warm.

The bus came and he boarded it, feeling a sudden pleasure as he took his seat with all the warm, silent people, staring indifferently ahead. A vague flow of security poured through him.

He grinned, and relaxed, the first time in days.

The bus went down the street.

Tirmus waved his antennae excitedly.

"Vote, then, if you want." He hurried past them, up onto the mound. "But let me say what I said yesterday, before you start."

"We already know it all," Lala said impatiently. "Let's get moving. We have the plans worked out. What's holding us up?"

"More reason for me to speak." Tirmus gazed around at the assembled gods. "The entire Hill is ready to march against the giant in question. Why? We know he can't communicate to his fellows—It's out of the question. The type of vibration, the language they use, makes it impossible to convey such ideas as he holds about us, about our—"

"Nonsense." Lala stepped up. "Giants communicate well enough."

"There is no record of a giant having made known information about us!"

The army moved restlessly.

"Go ahead," Tirmus said. "But it's a waste of effort. He's harmless—cut off. Why take all the time and—"

"Harmless?" Lala stared at him. "Don't you understand? He knows!"

Tirmus walked away from the mound. "I'm against unnecessary violence. We should save our strength. Someday we'll need it."

The vote was taken. As expected, the army was in favor of moving against the giant. Tirmus sighed and began stroking out the plans on the ground.

"This is the location that he takes. He can be expected to appear there at period-end. Now, as I see the situation—"

He went on, laying out the plans in the soft soil.

One of the gods leaned toward another, antennae touching. "This giant. He doesn't stand a chance. In a way, I feel sorry for him. How'd he happen to butt in?"

"Accident." The other grinned. "You know, the way they do, barging around."

"It's too bad for him, though."

It was nightfall. The street was dark and deserted. Along the sidewalk the man came, newspaper under his arm. He walked quickly, glancing around him. He skirted around the big tree growing by the curb and leaped agilely into the street. He crossed the street and gained the opposite side. As he turned the corner he entered the web, sewn from bush to telephone pole. Automatically he fought it, brushing it off him. As the strands broke a thin humming came to him, metallic and wiry.

"...wait!"

He paused.

"...careful... inside... wait..."

His jaw set. The last strands broke in his hands and he walked on. Behind him the spider moved in the fragment of his web, watching. The man looked back.

"Nuts to you," he said. "I'm not taking any chances, standing there all tied up."

He went on, along the sidewalk, to his path. He skipped up the path, avoiding the darkening bushes. On the porch he found his key, fitting it into the lock.

He paused. Inside? Better than outside, especially at night. Night a bad time. Too much movement under the bushes. Not good. He opened the door and stepped inside. The rug lay ahead of him, a pool of blackness. Across on the other side he made out the form of the lamp.

Four steps to the lamp. His foot came up. He stopped.

What did the spider say? Wait? He waited, listening. Silence.

He took his cigarette lighter and flicked it on.

The carpet of ants swelled toward him, rising up in a flood. He leaped aside, out onto the porch. The ants came rushing, hurrying, scratching across the floor in the half light.

The man jumped down to the ground and around the side of the house. When the first ants came flowing over the porch he was already spinning the faucet handle rapidly, gathering up the hose.

The burst of water lifted the ants up and scattered them, flinging them away. The man adjusted the nozzle, squinting through the mist. He advanced, turning the hard stream from side to side.

"God damn you," he said, his teeth locked. "Waiting inside—"

He was frightened. Inside—never before! In the night cold sweat came out on his face. Inside. They had never got inside before. Maybe a moth or two, and flies, of course. But they were harmless, fluttery, noisy—

A carpet of ants!

Savagely, he sprayed them until they broke rank and fled into the lawn, into the bushes, under the house.

He sat down on the walk, holding the hose, trembling from head to foot.

They really meant it. Not an anger raid, annoyed, spasmodic; but planned, an attack, worked out. They had waited for him. One more step.

Thank God for the spider.

Presently he shut the hose off and stood up. No sound; silence everywhere. The bushes rustled suddenly. Beetle? Something black scurried—he put his foot on it. A messenger, probably. Fast runner. He went gingerly inside the dark house, feeling his way by the cigarette lighter.

Later, he sat at his desk, the spray gun beside him, heavy-duty steel and copper. He touched its damp surface with his fingers.

Seven o'clock. Behind him the radio played softly. He reached over and moved the desk lamp so that it shone on the floor beside the desk.

He lit a cigarette and took some writing paper and his fountain pen. He paused, thinking.

So they really wanted him, badly enough to plan it out. Bleak despair descended over him like a torrent. What could he do? Whom could he go to? Or tell. He clenched his fists, sitting bolt upright in the chair.

The spider slid down beside him onto the desk top. "Sorry. Hope you aren't frightened, as in the poem."

The man stared. "Are you the same one? The one at the corner? The one who warned me?"

"No. That's somebody else. A Spinner. I'm strictly a Cruncher. Look at my jaws." He opened and shut his mouth. "I bite them up."

The man smiled. "Good for you."

"Sure. Do you know how many there are of us in—say—an acre of land. Guess."

"A thousand."

"No. Two and a half million: Of all kinds. Crunchers, like me, or Spinners, or Stingers."

"Stingers?"

"The best. Let's see." The spider thought. "For instance, the black widow, as you call her. Very valuable." He paused. "Just one thing."

"What's that?"

"We have our problems. The gods—"

"Gods!"

"Ants, as you call them. The leaders. They're beyond us. Very unfortunate. They have an awful taste—makes one sick. We have to leave them for the birds."

The man stood up. "Birds? Are they—"

"Well, we have an arrangement. This has been going on for ages. I'll give you the story. We have some time left."

The man's heart contracted. "Time left? What do you mean?"

"Nothing. A little trouble later on, I understand. Let me give you the background. I don't think you know it."

"Go ahead. I'm listening." He stood up and began to walk back and forth.

"They were running the Earth pretty well, about a billion years ago. You see, men came from some other planet. Which one? I don't know. They landed and found the Earth quite well cultivated by them. There was a war."

"So we're the invaders," the man murmured.

"Sure. The war reduced both sides to barbarism, them and yourselves. You forgot how to attack, and they degenerated into closed social factions, ants, termites—"

"I see."

"The last group of you that knew the full story started us going. We were bred"—the spider chuckled in its own fashion—"bred some place for this worthwhile purpose. We keep them down very well. You know what they call us? The Eaters. Unpleasant, isn't it?"

Two more spiders came drifting down on their webstrands, alighting on the desk. The three spiders went into a huddle.

"More serious than I thought," the Cruncher said easily. "Didn't know the whole dope. The Stinger here—"

The black widow came to the edge of the desk. "Giant," she piped, metallically. "I'd like to talk with you."

"Go ahead," the man said.

"There's going to be some trouble here. They're moving, coming here, a lot of them. We thought we'd stay with you awhile. Get in on it."

"I see." The man nodded. He licked his lips, running his fingers shakily through his hair. "Do you think—that is, what are the chances—"

"Chances?" The Stinger undulated thoughtfully. "Well, we've been in this work a long time. Almost a million years. I think that we have the edge over them, in spite of the drawbacks. Our arrangements with the birds, and of course, with the toads—"

"I think we can save you," the Cruncher put in cheerfully. "As a matter of fact, we look forward to events like this."

From under the floorboards came a distant scratching sound, the noise of a multitude of tiny claws and wings, vibrating faintly, remotely. The man heard. His body sagged all over.

"You're really certain? You think you can do it?" He wiped the perspiration from his lips and picked up the spray gun, still listening.

The sound was growing, swelling beneath them, under the floor, under their feet. Outside the house bushes rustled and a few moths flew up against the window. Louder and louder the sound grew, beyond and below, everywhere, a rising hum of anger and determination. The man looked from side to side.

"You're sure you can do it?" he murmured. "You can really save me?"

"Oh," the Stinger said, embarrassed. "I didn't mean that. I meant the species, the race... not you as an individual."

The man gaped at him and the three Eaters shifted uneasily. More moths burst against the window. Under them the floor stirred and heaved.

"I see," the man said. "I'm sorry I misunderstood you."

"The Conspirators" was not the first s-f story told from the uplifted animals' viewpoint, but it was still very rare in 1954 to make the animals rather than humans the protagonist. An exploratory starship, crewed by humans with several laboratory animals and a cat aboard, experiences something (radiation? the lack of gravity?) that increases the animals' intelligence and makes them telepathic. They don't want to be used for experimental purposes. Felix the ship's cat, now telepathic, realizes how wrong it would be to eat intelligent mice. The animals hope to leave the starship and make their new home on the planet that's just been discovered. But first they must escape from the humans' starship…

James White was known for featuring friendly aliens in his stories, and for his ability to see things from a non-human viewpoint. Most of his early s-f was published in the British New Worlds *magazine, after being constantly rejected by John W. Campbell, the* human-über-alles *editor of* Astounding Science-Fiction *who preferred stories about heroic humans outsmarting the stupid aliens.*

The Conspirators

by James White

Something had gone wrong. It was outside his range, but Felix caught a sharp, incoherent sensation of mingled shock, loss, and panic in the instant that it happened. He floated, outwardly unconcerned, in the middle of the corridor which led to the Biology Section, and waited for the details to come down the line.

A few minutes later the relay who was clinging to the wall-net at the end of the corridor began sending him the facts. The news was very bad.

It seemed that the Small One whose job it was to damage certain tiny but important circuits in the Communications Room for purposes connected with the Escape had had an accident. Singer had seen it happen—Felix had guessed it was Singer. Even on the fourth leg of a relay the thought pattern was unmistakable; all emotion and not enough fact— the Small One had jumped for cover when he heard the crew-man coming, misjudged, and landed on a live section. It was only a couple of hundred volts, but that was an awful lot to a Small One—he was very thoroughly dead. What was left of him was floating in plain sight, and Singer was rapidly killing himself with his frenzied attempts at holding the crew-man's attention, because if the man noticed the body, and the disconnected wiring beside it, he might be suspicious. Singer wanted somebody to do something, quick. The message ended with a sense-free garble of fear, urgency and panic that was almost hysteria.

To another Small One concealed in a ventilator at the other end of the Corridor, Felix relayed the message exactly as he'd received it. But he had an addition to make. He sent, "Include this. Felix to Whitey. I think I can handle this. Send someone to replace me—I'm on relay duty halfway along corridor Five-C—I'm going to Communications." He wriggled furiously until he made contact with the wall-net, then launched himself down the corridor towards the intersection leading to the scene of the accident.

Usually Felix left important decisions to the Small Ones. They had the brains. He didn't know why he'd taken the initiative this time. Whitey, he thought, might not be pleased.

He was able to enter the Communications Room and get to the Small One's body without the crew-man seeing him. Singer, though impractical in many ways, could create quite a diversion when he wanted to. Singer was fluttering around the man's head in tight circles, and the man was making ineffectual grabs at him and wondering loudly what had got into the blasted thing. He had eyes and thoughts, Felix knew, only for Singer. Good.

The fur on the body was badly scorched, and Felix's nose told him that parts of the underlying flesh were cooked, too. Suddenly a raw, animal hunger stirred inside him and began to grow, but he fought it down. Since the Change had begun, satisfaction of that nature was not for him. Felix batted the tiny corpse towards the opposite corner of the room, well away from those all-important circuits, then launched himself after it.

When he'd retrieved it and had it settled between his paws, he told Singer, "All right, bird-brain. You can relax. Better leave now—you're supposed to be afraid of me."

A bright yellow streak of motion, Singer flew out the door and down the corridor. Before he was out of range he returned, "I *am* afraid of you... you... *savage!*"

Seconds later the crew-man caught sight of Felix. Pleased, he said, "Felix! Where've you been hiding yourself?" He grabbed Felix by the neck with one hand and pulled himself into a seat with the other. Clipping in and settling Felix on his lap, he went on, "So you caught a mouse, eh, Felix? But what have you been doing with it? Having a barbecue or something?" He stopped talking then, but his mind was busy. He began to stroke the back of Felix's neck.

Felix didn't feel at all like purring, but he knew that it was expected of him. After a while he began to enjoy it in spite of himself, but that didn't stop him from reading the crew-man's thoughts.

A sharp, clear thought—characteristic of the Small Ones—brought him abruptly to full attention. Felix couldn't see the other, but he knew that the Small One was within thirty feet of him—that was the maximum effective range of their telepathy—probably in the emergency spacesuit hanging outside the door that Felix had noticed coming in. The thought said, "Felix, your replacement is in position. Whitey wants you to report."

"Right. Relay this. Felix to Whitey..."

For a moment Felix felt awed as he thought of Whitey in Bio-Lab Three—more than half the length of the great Ship away—surrounded by Big Ones, and the Small Ones who weren't on relay duties, and all of them working on the Escape. And of the other telepathic relays that linked Lab Three with places like Seed Storage, Central Control, and Engines... Catching an impatient thought from the Small One out in the corridor, Felix hastily brought his mind back to the report.

"... This Human is not suspicious," he sent. "The Small One was so badly scorched that the Lab markings have been obliterated, and he thinks it is a Wild One from Seed Storage section. He thinks that I have knocked it against some live wires while playing with it, and that I'm very lucky I didn't meet the same fate myself—there's that old 'nine lives' concept again—but he is wondering why I didn't eat the thing..."

Felix knew that a feeling of shocked revulsion was left in the wake of his message as it went down the line. Felix did not share the deep sorrow that the accident had caused among the more intelligent and highly-sensitive Small Ones. He took a perverse pleasure in shocking them sometimes. Without meaning to they made him feel inferior, envious. Felix wasn't proud of these feelings, but there wasn't much he could do about them. The Change was very slow in him.

"... He is not interested in checking any of the room's equipment," Felix continued, "but is impatient to rejoin the bulk of the crew who are packed into Astronomy section all trying to get a closer view of the new planet. He is feeling rebellious at having to stand watch here at a time like this, and is wondering sarcastically if the Captain is expecting natives—if any—of the planet below to just ring him up.

"At the back of his mind he is feeling angry because the scoutship is unable to make a landing. But neither he nor anyone else suspects that we were responsible for damaging its Planetary Drive coils. The fact that the replacements are also missing they blame on a clerical error in storing or checking the equipment back home. They don't know we've hidden them."

The Human stopped his stroking of Felix and pushed him gently off his lap. Felix ended, "He intends trying to sleep now. Nobody will be coming here, he knows, and he's a light sleeper anyway." He waited a little anxiously for Whitey's reply.

"You've done well, Felix."

Even though colored by the personalities of nearly a score of the relay entities, the thought was still warm, congratulatory. Then it changed subtly. "Come to the Lab at once, Felix. There is a transport problem."

"Right," Felix answered. "But before I go; the Human is asleep now. If you send somebody to arrange those disconnected wires so's they'll pass visual inspection, nothing can go wrong here."

He intercepted the reply when he was already halfway to the Lab. He'd been hurrying. It was:

"Thanks, Felix. It is already being done."

* * *

When he reached the Lab two of the Big Ones had the ventilator grill moved aside for him. The door was never used for the reason that the Humans kept it fastened, so that opening it would have aroused their suspicions. Felix wriggled through. As he kicked himself across the small anteroom leading into the lab proper he heard the Big Ones sliding the grill back into position. *Nothing*—especially now that they were so near to success—must be allowed to make the crew-men suspect anything wrong. Even the Big Ones, who weren't too bright, understood that.

Felix hadn't been "reaching" with his mind—too much telepathy was still inclined to tire him—so he had no warning of what to expect. Weightless, unable to stop himself, he sailed gracefully into the Lab—right smack into the middle of it.

He was hit five times and sent spinning, his nicely timed dive ruined, by flying Big Ones. And he lost track of how often young Small Ones rammed him. Everybody in the place—*and* their young, too, if any—were in rapid motion, sailing from wall to wall, floor to ceiling, and even corner to corner. It looked like a furry snowstorm. When he succeeded at last in reaching a wall-net, he directed a thought at the white mouse clinging to the fur of a Big One on the other side of the room. The thought was wordless, incoherent, an all-embracing question mark.

"They're practicing for the evacuation, Felix," Whitey explained. "And that is the problem I mentioned. Some of them—the young, especially—won't be able to make it." Whitey stopped to give instructions to a Big One who was floundering helplessly out in the middle of the lab. He resumed, "Come over here, Felix. We can 'talk' better at short range."

Felix was again hit several times on the way across by flying Big Ones. But being in collision with a guinea-pig wasn't painful, merely disconcerting, and he hadn't enough dignity left for that to be hurt. He had just settled beside the Big One bearing Whitey when Singer flew in and joined them. The canary hung, wings folded and turning slowly in the draft from the air-conditioner, just six inches from Felix's nose. Felix wondered suddenly what it would be like to bite his head off.

Radiating shock and panic, Singer flapped desperately out of range. "Stop that, Felix!"

Whitey was really angry at him, with the helpless frustrated anger that is inspired by the constant misbehavior of a backward child. Ashamed, Felix addressed Singer.

"Sorry, I didn't mean that. I wouldn't hurt you for anything. Come on back."

Singer fluttered back nervously, thinking about horrid, insensitive brutes, and great hairy cannibals. He wasn't completely reassured.

Whitey, his anger gone as quickly as it had come, began to state the problem.

"You two know that we intend to evacuate everyone, and you also know how we're going to leave the Ship—in one of the radio-controlled testing rockets. But we've misjudged badly. The distance from the Lab here to the launching slips is a little over five hundred feet, and now we find that there won't be enough time to get everybody to the rocket.

"You see, several trips will have to be made for the young, and the Big Ones are slow and awkward. They've never had a chance to practice long-distance weightless travel like us, and they're much worse at it than we'd expected. And they're so slow to learn, some of them…"

So slow to learn, Felix thought sadly. Just like me.

He knew that all three of them were thinking about the Change, and how it had affected them personally, as well as the way it affected their species as a whole.

Not one of them knew for sure just why the Change had come about, but there were theories. The generally accepted one was that the prolonged absence of gravity occasioned by the operation of the Ship's overdrive or the freedom from their home planet's gravitation, or the removal of some hypothetical radiation given off by the home sun, either singly or taken together had caused a change in the cell structure of the small, relatively simple brains of the animals aboard the Ship. Its result was a steady Increase In their IQ.

The Change, however, did not occur at a uniform rate, but varied with the size of the brain concerned.

The small-brained mice were affected first. They developed a high intelligence quickly, and with it the faculty for communicating telepathically. And, as well as reading each other's thoughts, they were able to tap the mind of the crew-man who came to the Lab at weekly intervals to replenish the automatic food dispenser which kept them fed.

They learned a lot from him; his duties, his background, what he thought about the other members of the crew, and, most important, the purpose of the Expedition. Also, because he vocalized his thoughts, they learned the language. This increased their understanding of their environment, but it also caused them to make an important assumption based, although they didn't know it, on too little data. Because the Ship had only been gone from Earth barely four months, and the awful boredom had not yet set in, this particular Human was full to bursting with the glorious thoughts of this first exploration among the stars, the possible colonization of newly discovered planets, and a warm, brotherly feeling towards everybody in general. And he was naturally kind to animals. He was also the only Human whose mind was available to the animals for reading—no other crew-man came within the thirty-foot radius of the Small Ones' telepathy. Their assumption, therefore, was justified.

For six weeks the community of Small Ones existed in the Lab, with servo-mechanisms attending to their every need, happy, contented, and very excited.

They thought they were the Ship's colonists.

Then one day Singer had been put in the Lab. Singer was a completely new species to the Small Ones.

He was bright yellow in color, had "wings" which made it easy for him to move about in the weightless condition of the Ship, and he produced audible vibrations which were very pleasant to hear. Though he wasn't as bright as the Small Ones, the Change had made him telepathic. He had a lot more information to impart about the Ship and its crew, information that left the Small Ones shocked and horrified. He was able to tell them of their true status aboard the Ship, and of the fate that experimental animals could expect when the time came to test the atmosphere, plant-life, and bacteria of a new planet. Singer also told of a ferocious black monster the Humans called "Felix" that roamed the Ship, and how the Humans had put him in here to keep the beast from killing him.

Living was suddenly a grim business. They would try to escape, of course, but the Small Ones knew enough about the operation of the Ship now to realize how small was the opportunity of doing that. And they couldn't leave the Lab even, because of this thing called Felix. If that had been possible they might have been able to create an opportunity for escape, by sabotage or some other means. But the only thing they could do was wait, and hope that the Big Ones, who also lived in the Lab, would be able to take care of "Felix" when they became further advanced.

But the Big Ones had been slow, Felix knew, and their bigness was only relative. Luckily they never had to try taking care of him; a scrap between a guinea-pig—or even several guinea-pigs—and a full grown cat would have been no contest at all.

Felix had been nosing about outside the Lab one day, hoping to catch himself some food "on the hoof," when he suddenly realized that the animals inside were "talking" to him. The reason for the strange ability he'd noticed in himself in being able to understand the Humans—even when they didn't speak aloud—was explained to him, and very soon he had more important things on his mind than a craving to eat Small Ones. All at once he had become an important person, an *invaluable* person. The way the Small Ones explained it, his wider knowledge of the Ship and its crew, together with his aid in guiding them to certain key spots, would make an escape not only possible, but highly probable…

* * *

"Pay attention, Felix," Whitey radiated sharply.

Felix came hastily out of his day-dream, conscious that if he'd been a Human, his face would have been very red.

"I was saying that the Big Ones are slow," Whitey went on, "and awkward. That's partly because we haven't allowed them outside the Lab much; they'd be spotted too easily. But that's the problem now, moving them quickly.

"At the moment I can see no solution. But you two being 'pets,' and having the freedom of the Ship, might be able to suggest something." Whitey paused, and the ghastly wordless images they all knew so well surged up from the back of his mind. Experimentation, vivisection, *murder*. Grimly, he went on, "I don't want to leave anybody behind to *that*—"

He broke off as two reports came, almost simultaneously, from opposite ends of the great Ship.

"Relay from Secondary Engines. Quarter G deceleration has been ordered for three minutes."

"Relay from Control-room. Captain has ordered quarter G deceleration…" It was practically a duet.

The telepathic link-ups that ran from all the key points on the Ship to the Lab were fast, efficient, and accurate. But they were just a little slower than the Ship's inter-com system. Some of the animals were able to act on the information before the deceleration hit them, and hang on. The rest dropped, an uneven, struggling layer of grey and brown, onto the forward wall.

Felix landed the way he always did, crouching, and on his feet. Unfortunately he also landed on a group of eight very young Small Ones. The resultant blast of fear and raw, uninhibited anger from their underdeveloped minds nearly curdled his brain before he was able to reel off. Then he had to counter the bolts of the outraged parent concerned, even though the adult Small One was intelligent enough to realize that none of it was Felix's fault. There were some things that didn't depend on intelligence, Felix realized, and mother love was one of them.

Abruptly Felix felt awed at himself. He was the muscle man around here—he'd never had thoughts like that before. But the feeling left him just as quickly.

While the deceleration lasted Felix listened to the ranting of the Small One, and tried to keep the amusement he felt from showing too much in his mind. He hadn't hurt the youngsters, of course, just frightened them. They were extraordinarily strong for their size, and they were so light that they could take a knocking about that would probably kill Felix. He began to wonder about their toughness, and about the evacuation problem. Suppose…

The Small One caught his half-formed thought and radiated a horrified negative. Felix tried to reassure her, but just then weightlessness returned and he launched himself towards Whitey again.

When Felix was still airborne Whitey sent, "I heard some of that, too, Felix. Would you expand on that thought about ferrying the young to the rocket?"

Felix took the mental equivalent of a deep breath. He was acutely conscious of the fact that his thinking, when compared with that of the Small Ones, was slow and almost incoherent at times. But he did his best.

"It is this. I suggest we ferry the young to the launching slips *before* the adults go, instead of at the same time. That way the Big Ones would have only one trip to make, and no matter how inexperienced they are, there would be plenty of time for the journey. With Singer here to help me as look-out, I can transfer them six or eight at a time to the test rocket. And even if the crew-man should see me—"

Whitey interrupted: "*How* are you going to move them, Felix?" Every mind in the room was giving him full attention now.

"By pretending to play with them," Felix answered.

Hesitantly, he began to explain. "In the old days, before I knew all about the Change, the crew used to give me things to play with. It was great fun…" He stopped suddenly, feeling ashamed and embarrassed at the confession he'd just made. Hastily, he went on, "That was before I met you, of course.

"But what I want to say is that I know where some of those playthings are. They are soft, spherical, and their fabric is easily opened. The young ones can hide inside them while I push the things along.

"The Humans won't be suspicious of a cat playing with an old rag ball."

Almost before he had completed his thought the objections were coming thick and fast. Felix found it a little frightening; he had never had so many minds thinking at him all at once before like this. But somehow, after the first few minutes, it didn't scare him anymore. It was a strange feeling. He still felt awed by their vastly greater intelligence, but not as much as before. Now he respected them—and almost liked them—as equals. Possibly it was the nature of the thoughts they were thinking that brought about the change in him. Felix could understand their feelings, but those thoughts hurt.

Impatiently, he interrupted the constant stream of protest. They were beginning to repeat themselves.

"Whitey! Tell them I'm not going to eat the things..."

They didn't believe him.

Oh, the Small Ones knew that he meant what he said, Felix realized, but they didn't trust his—impulses. The less intelligent Big Ones still thought of him as a semi-domesticated carnivore, and wouldn't trust him with their young farther than they could see him. But, he knew if he could convince the Small Ones that his plan would work, they could win over the Big Ones.

Whitey hadn't taken sides in the argument yet, so that left it up to himself. He signaled sharply for attention and felt pleasantly surprised when he got it at once. He began his sales-talk.

"This is the position as I see it at the moment," he sent. "The Ship is in the process of taking up an eight-hour orbit around the first apparently habitable planet to be discovered. The planet, not yet named, is referred to by the crew as Epsilon Aurigae VII, and they are very excited about finding it during the first seven months of their three-year exploratory voyage.

"From our telepathic relay lines to the Ship's control centers we know that this orbiting maneuver will be complete in just under three hours, after which most of the crew will be engaged in mapping the planetary surface, studying its weather, or just looking at it through telescopes. Roughly an hour after the Ship takes up its orbit, two of the big testing rockets will be sent down under remote control to the surface, for the purpose of collecting samples of air, soil and liquid from as many widely separate points on the planet as possible. These rockets will be guided automatically, and if everything goes off according to plan, we will be on one of them."

Felix paused. He was thinking about the Small One who had died so recently in the Communications room.

"We have been able," he went on, "to fix the alarm circuits here on the Ship so that the rocket containing us will apparently behave normally, though actually it will be disabled by us at the first suitable landing point so that we can disembark. But we have only an hour—*less* than an hour, to allow for slip-ups—when the crew will be too busy to notice our movements; and during this period all the animals must be got aboard the test rocket. That means that everyone here, all the Small Ones in Seed Storage, and all the relays scattered about the Ship will have to reach the launching slip and find their places aboard in that short time. And most of them will have to make several trips back and forwards for their young, or—" Felix regarded the untrained and clumsy Big Ones—the people who haven't been able to practice weightless travel.

"Whitey says that this is impossible."

The Small Ones knew all this, Felix thought, and the Big Ones should know it, too. But everybody had developed the habit of explaining things' several times to the Big Ones—they weren't very bright yet… Felix got control of himself quickly. That last thought had been tactless. He hoped the Big Ones had been too busy with their own thoughts to notice his slip.

"Now my idea is that we evacuate the young of both species first, and before the orbiting maneuver is completed. That way even the clumsiest" —Felix would have liked to use a kinder word, but it was impossible to lie with the mind,—"Big Ones will be able to make their way to the slip in the hour remaining before the test rocket leaves. Also, with everybody making just one trip, the risk of discovery by a crew-man will be practically nil. I think I can handle it, but I'll need a lot of help."

Felix was trying to give them the idea that he'd be under their observation all the time, and that even if he had wanted to, he couldn't pull anything. It was the only way, he knew, to get them to agree to his plan.

"There will have to be Small Ones at both ends of the line to load and unload the young, and I'll need Singer to create a diversion should a crew-man wander by and want to play with me. And I'll need help with other things, too…"

Abruptly he wondered why he was taking all this trouble for them. A short time ago he wouldn't have bothered. What was happening to him?

He ended simply, "I don't see any other way of doing it in time."

Later, as he was propelling a lumpy, brightly-colored ball filled with eight struggling baby guinea pigs along the corridor towards the rocket, Felix thought how close it had been. When Whitey agreed to his plan Felix had thought everything would be settled—after all, he was their leader. But it hadn't been like that. There had almost been a civil war before they finally agreed to his plan, and they had wasted more than half an hour with their arguing. They just didn't trust Felix, it seemed.

At the intersection leading to the launching slip Felix let his load collide with the wall-net, landing partly on top of it to keep the springy mesh from bouncing it back again. His passengers immediately shrieked that they were being murdered and they wanted their mothers. Luckily, Felix thought, it was on the telepathic frequency; had it been audible, men would have come running from all over the Ship. Hastily he reassured the Small One on relay duty in the corridor who was radiating anxiety like a fluorescent light tube. At the other end of the corridor he saw Singer fluttering around in a slow loop. That was the all-clear signal. Felix settled his burden solidly between his fore-paws and chest and kicked himself off again.

He couldn't really blame them for not trusting him, he thought, as the corridor walls drifted slowly past. There was still quite a lot of the savage in him. Much of it was due to the slowness of his Change, but a lot was due also to the crew-men who had brought him aboard as the Ship's mascot. They were the non-specialists on the Ship. They did most of the donkey work, and they were, to put it mildly, decidedly uncouth. From their minds Felix had learned practically everything he knew until the time of his meeting up with the Small Ones. The result was that he was inclined to think and act like his erstwhile "masters." The idiom he used when trying to express his thoughts, and his general air of tough cynicism, made it difficult for the others to trust him completely. It was very hard to convince them that his ideas had changed.

Still, even though he wasn't a nice character, the Small Ones were lucky to have him. They were intelligent, Felix knew; the most intelligent and highly-civilized beings on the Ship—and that included the crew. If they'd only had hands, and a more practical approach to solving their problems, they could have taken over the running of the Ship themselves months ago, and got rid of the Humans. But they weren't tough enough, or practical. When there was any time to spare they used their high intelligence to get into philosophical discussions among themselves, and they were, Felix thought pityingly, terribly unrealistic—soft, even. Like Singer in many ways.

Why, when Whitey had begun planning the Escape he'd told Felix— seriously—that nobody was to be hurt, *not even crew members*.

Felix had thought that very funny.

* * *

Just before he made contact with the bulkhead at the end of the corridor a sudden surge of acceleration sent him skidding into the wall.

Clinging to a section of wall-net he watched his load roll for several yards, then lodge itself none too gently in a corner. The mental uproar from the passengers nearly drowned out the message from a relay somewhere in the vicinity who reported, "Captain has ordered half G acceleration for three seconds."

Now, Felix thought disgustedly, they tell me.

Singer, who was fluttering his wings slowly to compensate for the half G, hovered a few yards away. Anxiously, he asked, "How many more, Felix? There isn't much time left..."

"About a dozen Small Ones, and five of the others," Felix replied as the engines stopped and he began pushing his load through the open air-lock of the Test Rocket blister. "Relax. Two more trips should do it."

But Singer was the worrying type. Supposing Felix was caught at the wrong end of a corridor during a burst of acceleration. A fall of a hundred or more feet, even under quarter weight, would be bad for his passengers...

And it would be bad for him, too, Felix thought grimly. Possibly it would be fatal. He told Singer rather sharply to be quiet. Felix didn't like being reminded of all the unpleasant things that could happen to him. Both test rockets lay in their slips. Blunt, grey torpedoes, their access panels lay open, and their stiffly extended antennae made them resemble twenty-foot beetles. Streamlining was unnecessary; the things weren't designed to break speed records, but to cruise about in the atmosphere of the planet being surveyed at a speed that wouldn't damage their sensitive testing gear, and possibly the even more delicate samples they would pick up from time to time. It was this low speed factor that had made the Escape possible. An ordinary missile, or even a message rocket, with an acceleration of fifty or sixty G's would have made a thin stew out of its passengers five seconds after blast-off. He thought the whole thing had depended on luck right from the start. The animals, apart from odd instances like the Communications Room death, seemed to get all the breaks.

Felix didn't like that. He was distrustful of too much good luck.

He gave his load a gentle nudge in the direction of the nearer rocket. It appeared deserted, innocuous, but Felix knew that inside it was a hive of activity. Most of the Small Ones from the nearby Seed Storage section— the "wild" brethren of the Laboratory mice whose job was the provisioning of the rocket—were already in their positions. The rest were hidden at the open access panels waiting to take care of Felix's passengers.

"Here's another bunch of them," Felix thought at the apparently empty hull. He added lightly, "Fragile. Handle with care."

"Right," came the curt response. "We see them."

These particular Small Ones had no sense of humor at all where Felix was concerned, and with good reason. Before the Change had made them too smart to be caught, and before that same Change made Felix a reluctant vegetarian where live meat was concerned, he had hunted them a lot. During the early part of the voyage the carnage in Seed Storage had been shocking. They had never forgotten it, or forgiven him. Felix thought sometimes that living on a planet with the Small Ones wouldn't be much fun with a thing like that between them—he was becoming strangely sensitive about his bloody past—but when he thought of what the human minds were like at times...

Angry with himself for some reason, Felix kicked off on the first leg of his return journey to the Lab. He kept telling himself that he didn't care what the Small Ones thought of him. He didn't care at all. But he was an awful liar, he knew.

Transferring the remaining young to the test rocket was a simple, if strenuous job. There was only one point on the route that was dangerous—an intersection visible to anyone who might be standing in the entrance to the Control Room. But there had been too much going on in there for anyone to be hanging about the door, so they hadn't been spotted. Luck was still with them.

Felix waited beside Whitey, with an almost imperceptible weight pressing them against the wall. All around, the animals waited, too; not communicating, but thinking their own personal thoughts. He took what he hoped was his last look around the Lab. One of his cloth balls, he saw, had been stuffed with food from the robot dispenser—even though the Seed Storage people were supposed to handle the food supply end. Somebody was taking no chances. All the cages were open, and both of the ventilator grills above the door had been moved aside. As he watched, the door swung suddenly outwards and hung open under its own weight. The Small One who had been working at the latch jumped free and fell slowly across the room. They were almost ready to go.

If a Human should look in here now, Felix thought, it would be just too bad.

Weight disappeared again as the gentle deceleration ceased. Seconds later a Small One in the tensely-waiting crowd announced. "Relay from Control Room. Captain has ordered kill engines. Orbiting maneuver completed."

To everyone in the room Whitey sent. "You know the drill. Nothing can go wrong if we're careful, and if we keep our heads. The relays will give warning if a crew-man intends coming too close to our escape route, minutes before he arrives." Whitey was obviously thinking at the Big Ones as he went on. "There are lots of places to hide along the route if a Human should come—inside the crew's life-suits, for instance—so there is no real danger if you don't panic. Get to the rocket as quickly as possible. And remember, you're on your own.

"The way is clear now. Move off!"

He added, "You first, Felix."

Felix sprang neatly through the Lab door, caught the corridor wall net, and sprang again. An almost solid mass of dun-colored animals erupted behind him and began to pile up against the wall facing the door. He caught the sharp, clear thought of Whitey cutting through the growing confusion, trying to sort the mess out and get it moving again. Felix didn't envy him his job.

Felix took up his assigned position—at the intersection in sight of the Control Room—and waited. There were men in there—he could hear low voices—but the range was too great for him to catch their thoughts. They couldn't have been important anyway, or the relay in there would have passed them on. With a whole new planet to examine, the crew were far too busy to think about the laboratory animals—*yet*.

Eleven Small Ones came sailing along the corridor.

They landed against the wall-net almost as one, then launched themselves on the next leg of their journey, still in that tight formation. It was beautiful, Felix thought, but then the Small Ones had had plenty of practice at weightless maneuvering; besides, one of their greatest sources of pleasure was the execution of the most highly-complicated aerobatics to mind music. They were thinking serious, personal thoughts, but when he asked how the Big Ones were making out, one of them came out of it long enough to send him the mental equivalent of a snort of derision.

When Felix looked back along the corridor he saw what the other had meant.

A kicking, madly-struggling mass of Big Ones had just reached the end of the passage. A few Small Ones were trying to control the resultant pile-up, but without much success. It looked, Felix thought in awe, rather like a cloud of leaves being blown slowly up the corridor by a whirlwind. The Big Ones were moving fast, but they'd no sense of direction at all—they kept bouncing *between* the walls, rapidly, and with a violence that made Felix wince. For every foot they moved forward, they travelled yards sideways, and even at this distance he could hear their panicky squeaking. Some of them definitely weren't keeping their heads. Suddenly worried, Felix sent to the relay near him, "Tell them to stop that noise, or the Humans will *hear* them."

There wasn't much danger of that just yet, of course. His ears were more sensitive than any Human's, but Felix didn't want to take any chances at all.

One of the Big Ones, more by luck than by judgment, came sailing up the middle of the corridor to land on the wall opposite Felix. Pleased, Felix began to radiate grudging approval, then caught what the other was thinking. "Don't," he warned desperately. "Not that way—"

But he was too late. The Big One, disoriented and frightened by his trip, had already taken off from the wall, *and he was headed down the corridor leading to the Control Room!* Felix made some hurried calculations of direction and velocity, hoped fervently they were right, and took off after him.

Even with his stronger muscles giving him greater impetus, they were half-way to the Control Room door before Felix caught up with the other—and then he thought he was going to pass him. But with a series of convulsions that nearly broke his back he got close enough to grab a furry leg in his teeth. He hung on desperately as their different masses and velocities sent them spinning rapidly about their common center of gravity. They smacked hard against the wall, only a few yards from the Control Room. Ignoring the frenzied struggles of the Big One, who was sure his leg was bitten off, Felix transferred his hold to the fur at the back of the other's neck and leapt back the way they'd come. He anchored himself solidly at the intersection.

"*That* way, stupid," he sent angrily, and with a strong jerk of his neck muscles he flung the Big One into the corridor leading to the launching slips.

Abruptly he was sorry. There'd been no time for gentleness, of course, but he'd almost enjoyed mauling the unfortunate Big One back there. The other had been lost, confused, never been outside the Lab before. He shouldn't have... Felix didn't quite know what he shouldn't have done.

"The thought does you credit, Felix."

Whitey had left the brown maelstrom that was boiling past the intersection, and was clinging to the net beside Felix. He had been in the thick of it, trying to keep the Big Ones moving—in the right direction, if possible—and he looked decidedly ruffled. He had been in collision with inanimate walls and over-animated animals alike more times than he could remember and his nerves were beginning to suffer, too. Felix got all that from his mind in the brief pause before Whitey continued.

"That was fast, accurate thinking back there, Felix," he complimented. "You did very well—you can be proud of it. And when we reach the planet, you're going to do a lot better..."

Suddenly uncomfortable and vaguely frightened at some formless meaning that was behind the other's thought, Felix interrupted hastily.

"Is that the lot?" He indicated a few stragglers floundering after the main group along the corridor leading to the rocket blister.

"Yes, that's all of the Big Ones," Whitey replied.

"But the others have been told to wait for a bit. There's enough crowding and confusion as it is, and they, being Small Ones, can move quickly and hide more easily if they're spotted. They'll wait in the Lab until the Big Ones are safely aboard."

But Whitey wasn't to be put off by questions. Returning to his praising of Felix, he said, "You don't have to feel uncomfortable, Felix. Or frightened, either... but tell me, what do you think of the Big Ones? And what, in your opinion, makes them think and behave as they do?"

Felix thought that this was a fine time to start a philosophical discussion, but Whitey tactfully ignored that thought, so he began trying to explain how he felt about the slow, unbelievably impractical, but somehow likeable Big Ones. He didn't take long over it as he'd never really thought about them very much.

"You should have thought about them, Felix. You're wrong, completely wrong, in everything, you think about them—" Whitey broke off as a straggler came crashing into the wall beside him. He reassured the frightened Big One, told him to take it easy, and sent him on his way again. Then he returned to Felix.

"They're definitely *not* stupid, Felix. Just slow to develop," he explained. "The Change is very gradual in them. With us Small Ones it was different— we Changed and reached our peak very quickly—in a few months, in fact. But now we've found indications that the Big Ones have a much greater potential I.Q. than we have—they are still changing. In a few months' time, Felix, they will be our intellectual equals, *then they will pass us.*" There was no sign of rancor in the thought—Whitey was too highly intelligent and civilized for that—only a great and burning excitement. "Think what this means, Felix. The size of their brains compared with ours..."

"*No!*" Felix was frightened, scared. He didn't want to think about it.

"But *yes*, Felix," the other contradicted. He stated solemnly, "You can't avoid the obvious. I am now certain that, barring accidents, you will eventually outstrip all of us. You will be the leader.

"If only," Whitey ended wistfully, "you weren't the only one of you..."

Felix felt suddenly that his brain had turned into a bubbling porridge and was about to squeeze from his ears. Fear and disbelief gradually gave way to belief, and an even greater fear—the fear of *responsibility*. But before he could form a coherent reply, another interruption drove everything else from his mind.

"Observation Room to Whitey," the relay in the corridor reported. "A Human has just left here. Intends walking in direction of launching slips. No fixed purpose—thinks he's in way of specialist crew members." The Small One stopped, waiting instructions.

Three long, agonizing seconds later, he was still waiting.

Felix had never known Whitey to behave like this before. The other's mind was a tight knot of fear and panic. It was an unforeseen and possibly tragic turn of events—just a sheer piece of filthy luck, but, Felix thought with a sudden feeling of pity, Whitey was behaving almost like one of the guinea-pigs.

Suddenly Felix remembered something; he took the initiative.

"Singer! Where's Singer?"

"Here, Felix." Singer was close by, only a few yards around the turn of the corridor.

"You heard that report." It was a statement, not a question. "You've got to intercept that Human, and stop him. Do the same as you did in Communications this morning—but get to him *quickly*. Follow the relay line to Observation, they'll give you his movements.

"And Singer, that is the most important job you ever had. Everything depends on it. You've got to stop that Human from coming here. The Big Ones aren't all aboard the rocket yet, and half the Small Ones are scattered over the Ship on relay duty." He ended grimly, "Stop him, Singer, if you've to peck his eyes out."

"*Felix!*" Singer was shocked again, but he got moving. Felix addressed Whitey:

"Better call in the relays. Singer may not be able to stop that Human, but if he delays him enough to get everyone to the launching compartment…"

To the relay beside him Whitey commanded, "Send this. To all Small Ones on relay duty and those waiting in the Lab. Move as quickly as possible to the launching slips—*now*. This supersedes all previous instructions." He paused, then went on to Felix alone, "You really meant that? About blinding the Human?" Horror, and a great sorrow was in the thought. "I cannot allow that, Felix, no matter what happens."

"You can't allow it!" Felix was exasperated. Angry, yet somehow pitying, he went on, "Listen. You tell me I'm going to be boss eventually. Well, I'm taking over *now*—temporarily. You people aren't equipped to fight your way out of this, or anything else. I don't know how you'll be able to exist on the planet if one of its life-forms decides to put up an argument— brains aren't everything, you know. You're just too civilized for your own good. You wouldn't hurt a fly, even if not hurting it was to kill you." Felix became more and more heated as he continued, "With me its different. You need someone like me to protect you. Someone who knows Humans well enough to be able to fight them. I ask you, would you let all our friends be caught and killed in lots of unpleasant ways, just to keep a Human from being messed up a little?

"Before I'd allow *that* to happen, I would kill that Human." He ended viciously, "There are ways an intelligent, trusted cat could do just that."

"Felix, you wouldn't... you *can't* take a life—even a Human life—like that." Horror, revulsion, and a terrible shocked urgency were in the other's thought. "Please don't think like that, Felix. Even injuring him..."

In ones and twos, Small Ones were passing them, landing on the wall, and leaping towards the rocket compartment. They were the relays from all over the Ship, making for safety, escape. None of them paid any attention to the argument; they were too busy with their own thoughts.

"... You wouldn't be able to live with a thing like that on your mind," Whitey went on desperately. "You think you could, now. But later, when you've grown more intelligent, more sensitive... You're still a baby, Felix, a young savage, even if—"

One of the Small Ones passing broke in urgently, "Whitey. Singer's in trouble. Couldn't get details, the relay line is breaking up too fast, but it seems the Human got scared and took a swat at him. Broke his wing. Now the Human is taking him to Sick Bay to patch him up."

The Small One hurried on.

Felix used some thought vocalizations that his old "masters" would have envied. Then—

"To all Small Ones who can hear me," he sent as strongly as he could. "If you can get to the rocket within one minute, *move!* If you can't, *take cover!*"

Sick Bay was next door to the launching slips.

The corridor was suddenly empty as the Small Ones scurried for cover or the launching compartment. Felix knew that less than fifteen minutes remained before the rocket took off. And seconds before that happened, the access panels would close, the inner air-lock would seal itself, and a section of the Ship's hull would swing outwards—all automatically, and pre-timed to a second. If anyone wasn't aboard by that time, it would be just too bad. Felix knew what his own chances of making it were now that this latest crisis had been sprung on them, but he also knew that somebody should take control of the situation at the test rocket. Somebody smart— or in the confusion only a handful would get away...

He had no need to finish the thought. Whitey knew what was required.

"I'll go, Felix. But try to make it yourself. We're going to need you." Whitey tried to be commanding, but there was uneasiness in his thought as he reiterated, "And remember, Felix. I won't allow anyone to be hurt."

"I'll try," Felix replied hastily. "And there'll be no rough stuff unless it's necessary. Get going, Whitey. Luck."

* * *

The soft slap of sandals on the wall at the end of the corridor announced the arrival of the Human. The Man didn't notice the rapidly moving Whitey against the light grey paintwork, he came Sailing nearer, still unsuspicious. As the other drew level with him, Felix leapt alongside with just enough power in his spring to keep pace with him. He was getting an idea.

The man reacted as expected.

"Uh-uh, Felix," the Human said harshly, "Don't touch," and hastily he transferred the unconscious Singer from his hand to the safety of the inside of his blouse. He was thinking that if Felix tried any tricks with the injured canary he would kick Felix the length of the Ship. The man didn't like cats.

So the crew-man thought he wanted to get at the bird. Good; that was exactly what Felix wanted him to think.

As they drifted nearer the launching compartment, an urgent thought from Whitey told him that there were still a lot of animals milling about outside the rocket. Felix had expected that. He made contact with the wall-net and, just as the Human was approaching the open lock of the launching compartment, he sprang hard at the Human's chest.

He landed with considerable force beside the bulge that was the unfortunate Singer, sunk his claws into the fabric, and began screeching and spitting for all he was worth. Startled and angry, the Human tried to knock him off, all the time thinking of sneaking, treacherous cats trying to eat poor, defenseless birds. When Felix fastened his teeth into the other's sleeve—and into a piece of his arm, too—the Human began to get rough. It was quite a melee.

It ended when a vicious, open-handed smack sent Felix against the wall with a thump that nearly shook his teeth loose. But it had served its purpose; they'd floated past the open air-lock without the Human seeing what was going on inside.

Feeling more dead than alive, Felix watched the crew-man halt himself neatly at the door of Sick Bay. Once in there, Felix knew, even though the launching slips were only yards away, the animals would be safe, because the Human intended to be busy working over Singer for some time. Maybe Felix would be able to make it to the rocket after all. The thought that Singer and some of the Small Ones still in hiding about the Ship would not make it had a dampening effect on his sudden rise in spirits. But, he told himself, he couldn't do anything about that.

The Human had the door open slightly, and was looking backwards over his shoulder to see that Felix wasn't going to sneak in, too, when he stared suddenly along the corridor. His jaw dropped open.

Felix felt the fur rise along his back. There was no need for him to follow the startled crew-man's gaze—he saw what was happening with shocking vividness in the other's mind.

About twenty Small Ones had landed at the intersection at the other end of the corridor. Felix had forgotten about them; they were the ones Whitey had told to stay in the Lab, and because the relays had been called in, they'd had no knowledge of Singer's failure to stop the Human. Watched by the startled crew-man, they took off again as they'd landed—in a tight, geometrically exact formation—in the direction of the launching room's air-lock. They must have seen the Human half-concealed in the door-way as soon as they jumped, but while rushing along the center of the corridor in weightless flight there was nothing they could do about it.

Of all the blind, senseless, *lousy* luck. If it had happened just one second later the Human would have been safely in Sick Bay. But no. Bitter rage, born of despair, flared suddenly in Felix as he thought how near they'd been to escape—the gentle, impractical, too-intelligent Small Ones, and their slow, apparently stupid, but likeable big brothers. But some of them could be saved yet—the ones already aboard the rocket—if Felix could force himself to act quickly enough.

The initial surprise in the crew-man's mind had given way to an intense curiosity, and there was a slowly gathering suspicion as well. Felix knew he had to act fast. Deliberately he let his rage take root in his mind and grow. He could have controlled it at the start, but instead he fed it with memories, painful and humiliating incidents, anything at all that would fan it to greater heat. For what he knew he had to do Felix would have to be in the proper mood. He no longer trusted himself—or the soft, sentimental way he'd begun to think lately.

From inside the launching compartment Whitey's thought beat at him, desperately urging him to stop, to *think*. But it was like a cup of water on a forest fire. His rage mounted. Hazily he knew that the crowd of Small Ones had landed at the air-lock and that Whitey was giving them orders, but the thoughts didn't register. His rage grew to a blazing, white-hot fury, and his eyes never left the crew-man.

The Human hung about ten yards away, with one hand holding the door and the other inside his blouse, defenseless. Vaguely, Felix knew that all the Small Ones were thinking at him now, but it had no effect at all.

For an instant he tensed for the spring, calculating, watching the Human's face. Then, with black murder in his heart, he leapt at the other's eyes.

He never reached them.

The mass and inertia of a moving Small One is inconsiderable, but twenty of them, leaping together and hitting him as one, was more than enough to deflect his dive towards the Human. Felix crashed into the wall-net amid a cloud of Small Ones, two feet away from the crew-man. He was too shocked by the turn of events to move, but the Human wasn't. Kicking himself free of the doorway he drifted up the corridor, thinking that if he didn't get out of here quick he'd be drowned in living mice; and then thinking that mice shouldn't behave like that, and that Felix shouldn't...

Suddenly the Human's thoughts began to jump around. Instances, apparently unrelated, were linking up in his mind. Wires gnawed through, small components missing, tiny but important gadgets sabotaged. Could it be... Just then his jump carried him past the open lock of the launching compartment. He saw what was happening inside.

Felix hadn't realized how quiet it had been until the General Alarm siren blared out. Senses dulled with despair, he watched the crew-man jabbering into a wall phone and holding the Alarm button down with a hard-pressed palm. Voices began approaching from all over the Ship; excited, slightly frightened voices. Thoughts followed them as the crew-man at the intercom broadcast his suspicions—the wary, coldly-implacable thoughts born in the brains of the most ferocious and deadly beast of all, *man*.

But, Felix knew, these beasts were logical. They would realize that they still needed experimental animals for the planets they hoped to find. They would not, he hoped fervently, slaughter all his friends right away.

But if they were too angry, they wouldn't behave logically.

* * *

Through the direct observation port Captain Ericsson watched a star that blazed like a gorgeous sapphire against a background of scattered silver dust. Home. He could almost see it coming closer. Smiling, he stroked the cat that sat on his shoulder, serenely following his gaze.

"Good thing your friends didn't make it to that first planet, Felix," he said reminiscently. "That virus... They wouldn't have lasted a week. But they should do all right on the world we picked for them. No animal life to speak of, but a semi-intelligent plant-life to keep them from getting too lazy. Unless…"

Unless the gravity of their new planet brought about a reversal in the Change that had taken place in space, he was thinking. Even he didn't know for certain whether it was the prolonged absence of weight that had caused it, or some enigmatic radiation given off by their home sun, Sol. That was why Felix had elected to remain on the Ship. A cat among a colony of mice and guinea-pigs, and all of them degenerating… It wasn't a pretty thought.

As he addressed the others in the room, the tremendous being that Captain Ericsson had become used spoken words. They would be orbiting Earth in three days, and he wanted to become accustomed to communicating non-telepathically again. He said, "We are not going to like the Earth, even though it is our home. We've… outgrown it. The Change in us humans, with our larger and more complex brain structure, was very slow indeed—it took almost two years before our maximum development was attained. But even Felix here, who looks on us as near deities, is incapable of realizing just how much we have matured." He paused, shaking his head gravely. "No. It is our duty to report the habitable planets we've found, the Change that takes place in space, everything. And they will want some of us for psychological testing. But we will not like Earth. On Earth they fight, and hate, and do violence. They… they *kill*.

"I think we will want to leave again as quickly as we can."

Is Willow Beeman really a human? Or a hairless dog? Or some sort of everyanimal?

Don't try to figure it out. Just accept "Sic Transit... ?" as an existentialist "shaggy dog" fable about evolution.

Sic Transit… ? A Shaggy Hairless-Dog Story

by Steven Utley and Howard Waldrop

There never was another man like Willow Beeman.

There never would be, either, because Willow was the very last one in the whole world. His heart was closed out to the memory of men; and he did quite well without that memory, thinking of himself only as a large dog without hair.

He could recall a time, long, long ago, when he had been not a dog but a gorilla, or something close to it, at any rate. But he had forgotten all the parts about being a man and living in Sumer, in Babylon, and Tyre, and Rome. He even disremembered about Cheyenne and Bismarck and Bayonne, and about women, cigarettes, automobiles, ice cream, God, spaceships, books, and underarm deodorants. He would not even have remembered being a gorilla were it not for his friend Patrox, who was something very like a Galapagos tortoise and who had lived quite a long time. "Longer than you, anyway," Patrox was fond of reminding Willow.

Patrox was also fond of telling stories. Willow found these stories disturbing. They were full of esoteric references that got into his skull and nibbled at his brains. "What is *suburb?*" Willow would demand, seizing upon an odd word in one of Patrox's incomprehensible yarns, and Patrox would shrug and say that he didn't really know. "Then why do you tell these stories?" Willow would ask, and Patrox would shrug again and say that he didn't really know that, either. "I think you're making it all up," Willow would declare, by way of closing the subject, and stomp away in a sulk, irritated as all get-out by the nibbling going on in his head.

Willow Beeman was not singular in his disbelief in both men and his own man-ness. Once he had cast off the memories, to say nothing of the overbearing swaggers, of *Homo sapiens*, it was easy for the animals to take his presence among them for granted. And, excepting Patrox, who had his doubts, they, too, thought of Willow only as a large dog without hair. Willow drank with them at the water holes and licked salt with them at the salt lick. He slept on the ground when he was tired, and he ate crawdads and wild berries when he was hungry. So he had all of the animal comforts and pleasures.

Except one. Willow kept noticing animals copulating.

"What makes them do that?" he wondered aloud, one mellow day of a mellow spring.

"There's a story about it," Patrox murmured at his side. "But it's a dirty one, and my mother would spin in her grave if I told it."

Willow frowned, perplexed by the oddness of the words *dirty* and *grave*. His head began to throb with nibblings. He turned Patrox over onto his shell and left him kicking there for a day or two, just to pay him back.

As the mellow spring passed into a mellow summer, Willow noted that all of the animals who had previously been copulating were now birthing lots of little animals which resembled them somewhat, despite a certain largeness of skull and a marked clumsiness of foot. Willow devoted no small amount of thought to the matter and, by and by, put together a fantastic theory, which he then presented to Patrox.

Patrox listened, nodded sagely, and said, "See, Willow, I told you it was dirty."

"You mean, I'm right?" said Willow, awed by his own hitherto unsuspected brilliance.

"You hit the *nail* squarely on the head," Patrox affirmed.

Willow winced and rubbed his temples. A little more time passed, and Willow Beeman forgot all his newly gained knowledge of reproduction. Or, rather, he placed the information in that portion of his mind which contained all the rest of the useless information he had accumulated about the way the world was. Like how the leaves kept coming off the trees at a certain time of year. Like how that big, useless, white thing in the night skies sometimes was round and sometimes was only a curved line of light with pointy ends and sometimes was not there at all.

But another mellow spring came along eventually, and Willow looked around at the copulating animals, sighed, sat down on Patrox's back, and said, "I'm lonely. I think."

"You have me, don't you?" asked Patrox.

"Well, it occurs to me that this thing the animals do must be a lot of fun, since all of the animals do it at least once a year. And they always seem to be in great spirits afterward."

"How well I remember!" Patrox snorted. There was a note of longing in his snort.

"Really, Patrox? You've done it, too?"

"Yes, but it was a long time ago, when I was young and limber and full of juice, so don't get any ideas. Besides, we're both boys."

"What's *boys*?"

"Never mind, Willow."

Willow ground his teeth with frustration for a few seconds. Then: "Patrox, the more I think about it the more I'd like to have some little animals that look like me. So I'm just going to have to find somebody with whom to do this wonderful copulation thing."

And he did, too.

It took Willow Beeman five weeks to completely recover from the wounds he suffered at the claws of the she-wolverine. He kept wondering where he had gone wrong.

"As I remember it," Patrox offered, "animals only copulate with other animals of the same kind."

"I'll have to find another big, hairless dog in that case," said Willow. *Or*, he added to himself, *if that doesn't pan out, at least a gorilla.*

"I tend to doubt that you'll find another big, hairless dog out here in the woods, Willow."

"Maybe I should go to one of those places that don't look like the woods." And, six days later, Willow pulled into just such a place.

It was actually all that was left of a city, but Willow didn't know this. He was, on the other hand, rather sore of foot and had begun to ache peculiarly in the groin, which is how it goes when notions about copulation take root in one's brains. Willow searched through the City, looking at disintegrating hulks of automobiles, rust-eaten shards of tin cans, a Lacrosse missile launcher, and the like—though, to Willow, these things were just some sort of strange plant life that couldn't be eaten.

Willow began to lose heart after a while. "This isn't getting me anywhere," he muttered to himself. "I do believe I've been everywhere in this place, and I haven't seen a single dog. Or even any gorillas. Maybe it'd be better if I just went on back to the woods and spent my time crawfishing with my hands in some pool."

It was as he was about to leave the place that he came upon the low, stone edifice with a door ajar and a sign that read CRYOGEN, INC.

Willow couldn't read the sign, reading being one of the things that Patrox had never quite gotten around to showing him how to do. But the door was half-open; and Willow, who was now feeling rather ferocious with frustration, barged in furiously. What happened next you would not believe, even if we told you. Suffice it for explanation that there was still some power running this or that arcane machine when Willow entered.

Willow stayed inside for a long, *long* time. When this or that arcane machine finally did sputter and give up the ghost, thereby releasing Willow from his protracted sleep, the low, stone edifice had been worn away to the level of the ground. The door and the sign were gone, too.

Willow sat up, looked around, and immediately saw that the strange, inedible plant life had given way to salt marshes and mud flats. There were a few stunted, scraggly trees, several of whom regarded him with baleful equivalents of eyes. Their attitude toward him appeared to be, "Hmpf, and what is *this?*"

Willow scratched his skull bemusedly and asked, "Where've all the animals gotten off to?"

"Dead and gone, most of them!" snapped one of the trees." And good riddance, I say."

Willow recalled the purpose of his coming to the place. "You haven't seen any big, hairless dogs around here, have you? Or any gorillas?"

"No dogs or gorillas," the tree answered irritably.

"Just something that looks very like a Galapagos tortoise."

"That must be Patrox!"

"Yes, I believe he did say his name was Patrox. And, now that I think about it, he spoke of some animal that looks the way you look. He said that he had known this animal a long time ago and had always thought highly of it." The tree peered at Willow closely. "I can't say as I find much in you to think highly of."

Willow was dejectedly surveying the new landscape. "So everything is gone," he muttered dismally.

"What did you expect?" the tree demanded. "I've been listening to your infernal snoring ever since I can remember, and my mother says you were here when *she* came to the area. You've been asleep for some time, and things have a natural tendency to change with time. Even people, though they generally resist that change."

"What is *people?*"

"Why, now that most of the animals are gone, people are the dominant form of life on the earth today. Look, I can't stand here all day and explain things to you, so why don't you walk around and sort of acclimate yourself to stuff. It stands to reason that you've got some catching up to do."

"What is *reason?*"

"Never you mind. Now run along."

Willow Beeman ran along, still considerably confounded. The world seemed drabber, uglier. The air tasted funny. Frankly, Willow was fairly well put out with it all after he had acclimated himself to only a few square miles of stuff. He parked his fanny on a smooth, green rock and said, "On top of everything else, I still haven't gotten to do what the animals do to make little animals like themselves."

"Eh?" said the rock, who was actually Patrox, who had been taking a nap. "Why, Willow! It's you! Long time, no see."

"I'm mighty glad to see you again," Willow confessed.

"Need help?" Patrox inquired solicitously.

"What is *help?*"

"What do you want more than anything else right now?"

"I want to copulate," said Willow. "I want to make little animals like myself. I came looking for another, big, hairless dog. Or a gorilla, if I couldn't find a dog. I never found either. There must be something with which I can copulate."

"Have you tried it with people?"

"I wouldn't know people if I saw one."

Patrox squinted toward the salt marshes. "People hang around over there. As long as you're determined to do this, you may as well give them a try, Willow."

"Well, if you say so." Frowning deeply, Willow went over to the salt marshes. He returned one minute later, and he was frowning more deeply than before. "They're *frogs*, Patrox. I know frogs when I see them."

"They're people now," Patrox insisted.

"But when I lived in the woods, they used to keep me awake at night going *breedeep breedeep breedeep*. They're frogs."

"They're the best I can offer," Patrox stated flatly. "Take them or leave them."

"Oh, all right."

Willow walked back to the salt marsh and tried to get the frogs to copulate with him, but whenever he made a lunge at one of them, it would vanish in a puff of pale blue smoke.

Not like frogs at all, Willow thought disgustedly. He squatted in the muck, feeling very sorry for himself. The ache in his groin was worse now, his stomach was rumbling with hunger, and his throat was raw with thirst. He did not look up when Patrox settled into the mud at his side.

"What now?" Patrox asked softly.

"I don't know," Willow admitted. "I was doing just fine in the woods. But now everything's so depressing. Where'd all the grass and ferns go? Where are the birds and deer and wolverines? I miss them. Everything's been a mess ever since I decided to make little animals like myself."

"Well, maybe that's *why* everything got messed up," Patrox suggested. "Weren't you happy being a big, hairless dog in the woods?"

Willow nodded forlornly.

"You probably could've gone right on being a big, hairless dog if you hadn't gone off looking for someone like yourself. When the time came for all the dogs to go away, you would simply have become something else. An ostrich, maybe. You'd have been an ostrich for as long as you could, then something else, then something else again. That's how you managed to hang on as long as you did back there in the woods, Willow."

"I'm not sure I quite follow you," Willow said. "And, besides, what's that got to do with everything going away?"

"It has everything to do with it," Patrox replied. "Willow, I've always been pretty certain that you were a gorilla before you were a dog, even though I didn't know you personally before then. You yourself apparently suspect as much. Before you were a gorilla, who knows? At any rate, the point is that you, being the only one left of your kind, managed to stay alive by not being whatever it is that you really are. And as long as there was only one of you, Mother Nature could pretend not to notice you and go along with the idea of you being a gorilla or a dog or whatever.

"But then," Patrox continued, "Mother Nature got panicky when you decided to try and make little animals like yourself. Don't you see? You were safe in the woods as long as you were content to remain one of a kind, a unique exception to the rules. If you wanted to be a gorilla, fine, Mother Nature let you be a gorilla for as long as there were real gorillas in the world. The same goes for dogs. But there just wasn't—and *isn't*—a place for more than a single Willow Beeman creature. While you were away, Mother Nature was making everything become extinct. She was looking for you, trying to keep you from upsetting her apple cart, but she didn't find you. The more she didn't find you, the more panicky she became, and the more things she made become extinct. So now just about everything is gone, except for the trees and the people—and my kind. And you're in terrible danger, Willow. I suggest that you decide, but *fast*, what you intend to become now. You can't stay a dog, because there aren't any dogs left. You're too soft to make a good tree, even if they'd have you. And the people don't seem to care for you at all."

Patrox got to his four feet, turned, and started to amble away. "Be something quickly," he said over his shoulder. "Otherwise, Willow, you're extinct."

"But what else is there to be," Willow called after the departing Patrox, "if not a tree or a people?"

Patrox paused and shrugged within his shell.

Willow Beeman got up out of the muck and walked over to him. "Say, Patrox, why don't I be whatever you are?"

Patrox laughed. "Now *that* might be interesting. But what would you do for a shell? Your camouflage has to be good if you don't want to die off."

"I—I could make a shell out of dried mud." Willow walked around Patrox several times, examining him closely, "Yes, I think it can be done. I'll be one of your kind. Uh, Patrox? Just what *are* you, anyway? I mean, in case anybody asks."

"Don't you think that I look very like a Galapagos tortoise?" Patrox inquired slyly.

"But what are you *really*?"

Patrox looked around and asked, in a lowered voice, "You promise you won't ever tell anyone?"

"I promise, Patrox," said Willow.

"*Tyrannosaurus rex*, at your service, Willow."

The earliest story of professional quality in furry fandom was "Rat's Reputation" by Michael H. Payne, the first in his "Around About Ottersgate" series, in FurVersion #16, May 1989. Since then, Rat, Crow, Fisher, Bobcat, Skink, Judge Owl and their mortal neighbors, plus the twelve Curials (animal Gods) like Lady Raven and Lord Lion who rule the mortal world—plus everyone's enemy, the Blood Jaguar—have been appearing in short fiction and the novel The Blood Jaguar *(Tor Books, December 1998; reprinted by Sofawolf Press, June 2012). Payne's sequel to* The Blood Jaguar *is due from Sofawolf Press soon.*

There is no collection yet of the "Around About Ottersgate" short fiction, so here is the story "Crow's Curse" from twenty-four years ago. This will introduce Crow, Fisher, Doctor Swift and the gypsy squirrels, and refer to others. Welcome to one of the oldest fiction series in furry fandom.

Crow's Curse

by Michael H. Payne

The wind whipped through Crow's feathers as he crouched at the edge of the cliff, a black wind, cold and sharp in the pre-dawn darkness. The forest far below rustled uncomfortably, and Crow stared, his eyes intent on the eastern horizon. He was waiting for the moon to come up.

His mind skittered and jumped, but Crow did his best not to think about the way the satchel leaning against his side clattered whenever he shivered. He shivered often, though, clamped between the cold black above and the hard gray below with darkness swirling all around him.

At last, over the long straight edge of the horizon, Crow saw the red tip of the thin crescent moon rising. He stood and clasped his wings together, pointing toward the growing spike until the sliver of moon had risen entirely and was balancing blood-red on the horizon.

Crow closed his eyes then and whispered, "Lady Raven, please hear me and have pity on me. I have done a terrible, terrible thing; I don't know if you can ever understand, but I had to come and explain."

He knelt down and felt the satchel cold against him. "I don't really know how it happened, but what else could I have done? The poor thing was dying, was nearly dead when I heard it crying out. Its parents shouldn't've let it out of the nest; it was just too young to be out by itself. There was nothing I could've done to help it, nothing at all, and it was nearly dead when I found it. I couldn't let it suffer, could I? Could I? Please try to understand, Lady Raven, please try. Sometimes things just happen; it was luck, that's all, bad luck, yes, but, I mean, it wasn't anyone's *fault* is all, and I just wanted to try to explain how... how it happened..."

Crow gathered the satchel up and held it against his chest. "I... I brought his—*its*, its bones, here in my satchel. I thought I should bury him—*it, it*, bury it up here where you could see and understand." Crow scraped a shallow pit in the loose dirt at the cliff's edge and carefully laid the contents of his satchel at the bottom. His wings were shaking. "Why did it have to be out alone? It shouldn't've happened, not ever..." He stared at the bones for a second, bright points flashing in the dark earth, then covered them over with dirt and small stones.

When he was done, he turned back to the moon. Its brightness was beginning to fade as the coming morning made gray the sky around it. Crow clasped his wings and bowed. "Please, Lady Raven, don't let it happen again. Please do everything you can not to let it happen again." Then he brushed the ground with his wing tips to hide the traces of his digging, gathered up his satchel and, stepping over the cliff edge, glided out over the forest, the sun starting to spark at the horizon. Crow winged his way home and curled exhausted into bed.

The sun rose, slid across the sky, and settled into late afternoon before Crow finally stirred and awoke.

He wasn't really feeling any better, though; his head ached and his back was stiff and wooden. A nice flight over the forest, he was sure, and he'd feel like his old self again. The acorns in the pantry didn't appeal to him, and it was too early for dinner anyway, so he just gathered up his satchel and took off into the autumn afternoon sunlight.

Below him, the forest rustled with reds and golds. The sky was a deep, sharp blue, and Crow turned lazily through it, his mind doing its best to stay away from memories of yesterday and this morning. He managed to concentrate on riding the winds, diving and climbing, and the cold gusts washing through his wings.

He drifted north and east with no real destination in mind until he became aware of an odd sort of piping floating along through the breeze from off to his left. It sounded like calliope music.

Crow wheeled left, his ears intent on the snatches of piping that danced around him in the wind. The music got louder and more coherent as Crow approached Valder's Clearing, and he could tell now for sure that it *was* calliope music.

But who would be out in these woods playing a calliope? It had to be a gypsy caravan. It was autumn after all, and the gypsy squirrel families always held their Autumn Festival in Ree's Meadow just about a month after the equinox. This had to be some northern gypsy squirrels on their way down to the Festival.

Crow winged over Valder's Clearing, and there, set out in a crescent beside the little spring, were the wagons of a gypsy caravan. Crow could see strings of gray and burgundy flags fluttering in the breeze and various mice and sparrows and other such folk walking about between the booths set up in front of the wagons. The long afternoon shadows were lying deep throughout the clearing, and the music steamed and gushed up from the calliope parked at the end of the wagon row.

Crow circled the clearing and flapped to the ground next to the machine. Its pipes stretched tall and bright into the autumn sky, a massive fan of pipes into which a bronze frieze had been pressed showing the Twelve Curials. The detail was incredible, the smooth strength of the Lady Lioness, the august bearing of the Lord Tiger, the flashing fire of the Lady Squirrel's eyes, all captured more perfectly than Crow had ever seen, right down to the dark sheen of the Lady Raven's feathers. The whole instrument was a marvel, gleaming with brass and ivory and marked in places with the same gray and burgundy as the flags.

The squirrel playing the calliope was thin and rather tall for a squirrel, his burgundy vest hanging loose from his shoulders. He was lunging back and forth over the keyboard, the tempo of the piece climbing and soaring, the music rushing louder and louder. The squirrel's claws flashed through one final cadenza, and, with a grand flourish, he leaned into the keyboard and drove the last chord bursting out into the air.

The squirrel fell back onto his stool as the chord sped into the sky and was gone. Crow began applauding and was surprised when no one else joined in. Looking around, he saw that the other folk were all further along the caravan, all engrossed in the items for sale.

'Hmmph!' Crow thought. Still applauding, he said aloud, "Bravo, sir, bravo! Absolutely wonderful! There's nobody can play a calliope like a gypsy squirrel, I always say."

The squirrel turned around in his seat and flashed a broad smile, his golden front tooth catching the rays of the setting sun. "Ah, Corvine!" The squirrel leaped down from the calliope and bowed low. "I have always said there is no one appreciates the calliope like a corvine. She is a misunderstood instrument, eh, Corvine?"

"Too true, sir, and it's really too bad. There's nothing in the world like it. But this machine of yours! It's fantastic! I've never seen anything like it! And your playing, sir! I haven't heard playing like that for many a Festival."

"She's a special one, she is. It takes a special squirrel to play such as her." His smile flashed through the clearing again. "And a special someone to hear her the right way." He stuck out a paw. "I am Alphonse Karakchik, and you will do me a great kindness, Corvine, if you will allow me to buy you a drink or two."

Crow wrapped some feathers around the squirrel's paw. "It will be an honor, sir, if you will let me buy you a few."

The squirrel laughed and seized a gray and burgundy checked bandana from beneath the calliope. "Come then, my friend! We will toast one another!"

"Oh, and the calliope as well, sir."

"Of course! We shall both buy her drinks, yes?"

They made their way along the row of wagons, Karakchik stopping at the various booths and introducing Crow to just about everybody in the camp. By the time the two arrived at the wagon where tables were being laid out with gray and burgundy tablecloths and red candles were being lit in wax encrusted bottles, they had amassed quite a following of squirrels, mice, sparrows, wrens, all of them invited by Karakchik to share some wine and to toast the calliope.

It was just getting on toward evening as they settled down at the tables and the squirrels began bringing dusty bottles out of the wagon. They toasted the calliope, Karakchik toasted Crow, Crow toasted Karakchik and all the gypsies, a mouse at one of the tables toasted the autumn sunset, and the wine and the laughter flowed freely throughout the camp. The sun settled below the horizon; logs were set out and a huge bonfire started, around which the toasting continued.

Things began running together in Crow's mind, the flash of the firelight off Karakchik's gold tooth, the singing of the squirrels in languages Crow was certain he didn't know but which he sang in nonetheless, the hot spicy taste of the wine they were serving, the heavy scent of the smoke from the bonfire, everything spinning and whirling his head around and around until he felt sleep's warm darkness settle over him and wrap itself thick about him.

The smoke and the songs and the wine were still floating and humming through his head when there was a sudden cold wet slap at his face, and he sputtered awake, freezing water dripping through his feathers.

Crow shook his head and tried to raise a wing to wipe the water from his eyes, but something held him back. He strained to move his wing again, and this time he could feel the cords tighten as he tried to lift it.

Cords? Was he tied down? Crow opened his eyes.

He was lying on his back, his wings spread out, tied and staked to the ground. He could feel cords tight across his chest and abdomen, too, and, struggle as he might against them, he remained rooted to the spot.

With some difficulty, he raised his head and looked down the length of his body. The bonfire was still burning there, but he couldn't see anyone around it. He could hear muffled whisperings, though, and as he let his head drop back down, he turned to his right to see if anyone was there.

The night was thick all around, but by the light of the fire, Crow could see a shadowy figure; as it began to move toward him, Crow could see that it was Alphonse Karakchik, the calliope player. The squirrel now wore a black bandana over one ear, and a long black cloak billowed from his shoulders, making him look even taller and more gaunt than before. Karakchik stopped a few steps from Crow's head, the cloak swirling to close around the squirrel's thin frame.

"Alphonse," Crow managed to cough out, "why am I tied up? What's going on here?"

"Going on?" The squirrel's face was strange and stark in the bonfire's light. "It is your Doom, Corvine."

Crow could only stare into the gypsy's deep and unblinking eyes. The whispering stopped, and the only sound in the clearing was the crackle of the fire. "My… my Doom?" Crow managed to get out.

"Just so," the squirrel replied. He threw back his head and let out a high-pitched wail that was immediately taken up by voices in the darkness around Crow. Karakchik brought his eyes back down to Crow's. "For what you have done."

In the darkness, the voices began a low, deep chanting, and Crow suddenly knew what Karakchik meant. "No! No, wait! I already prayed to the Lady Raven! I dedicated the bones to her! She… she's given me her blessing, don't you see? She won't let it happen again!" The chanting continued, and Karakchik did not move, his eyes still burning deep into Crow's mind. "No! It's all right now! She understands! I already explained to her!"

Karakchik blinked once. "There are other powers, Corvine, powers who are not so understanding. We come to serve *their* judgment upon you."

"No! No! You don't—"

"Silence!" roared Karakchik. He sprang forward, tearing open his cloak, and something thin and sharp flashed in his paws. Before Crow could react, the squirrel thrust down and across, and a long metal spike crashed through Crow's beak, piercing it from bottom to top. Crow tried to scream, but the spike held his beak tightly clamped; he strained at the ropes and slammed his head from side to side, pain wracking through him, but all he got was weaker and weaker.

He lay still at last, his mind skipping and jittering, and panted through his nostrils while the roaring in his head sank to a hard rumbling. Only then could he turn to look at Karakchik. The squirrel still stood there, his face still hard in the fire's flickering shadows.

"Your Doom, Corvine," he said again, and the chanting rose in pitch and volume. Karakchik took a step closer and stood staring directly down into Crow's eyes. He drew his arms slowly out of the cloak, and two more thin spikes gleamed in his paws. The chanting came to a peak and stopped.

"Understand, Corvine," Karakchik said into the silence, the firelight glowing dully off his gold tooth, "we do not ask you to bring the dead back to life. You cannot do this, for the dead are the dead. But the lost you can find, and the found you can return, a life for a life. A life for a life."

Crow wanted to stop him, ask him what he meant, plead with him to listen, try to explain himself, but the spike held his beak closed. He could only stare at the squirrel and at the long flashing spikes in his paws.

Karakchik called out something in a language Crow didn't understand, and voices chorused back from beyond the bonfire. Karakchik took a step back, held the spikes high in the air, and cried out, "The Doom is the Doom of the Senseless! One spear serves to shackle the tongue; no more shall anyone, creature, folk, or otherwise, hear a word that falls from your beak!"

The voices chanted again, and Crow felt his beak throb. Karakchik continued.

"One spear serves to pierce the heart!" And Karakchik leaped into the air and slammed one of the spears straight into Crow's chest. Crow heard ribs snap, but he couldn't move, couldn't scream, couldn't feel or think of anything but the spike ripping through his body. Karakchik's voice rang in his ears: "No more shall anyone, creature, folk, or otherwise, feel the stroke of your wing nor the grip of your claw!"

Crow couldn't tell if his eyes were open or shut. Fire shot through him, raging and twisting his insides. Then Karakchik came into sight right above him once again. "And one spear serves to shatter the mind!" The squirrel raised the last spear in both paws and drove it down between Crow's eyes. Crow's vision burst into a jagged babble of sharp reds, burning golds, and engulfing blacks as he heard Karakchik's voice chanting, "No more shall anyone, creature, folk, or otherwise, see your face, your form, nor even your shadow! You are now a beast of dust and oblivion, the smallest whisper of the passing breeze! So it is, and so it will be!" The blackness snarled up, slashing at him and crushing him till he had to scream, had to fly, had to escape.

And then he was leaping into the air, the screams bursting from him. He careened wildly, wings flailing, spinning over and over, around and around, shrieking and shrieking, until he slammed into the branches of a willow tree and fell tangled to the ground. He clawed his way free of the willow branches and leaped to his feet beneath the canopy of the tree, his breath coming fast and his mind still spinning and whirling.

After a while, his breath slowed, his mind wound down, and a cloudy sort of calm settled over him. He realized that he was standing and staring at the trunk of a willow tree. Then he realized that he was very tired. So he *sat* and stared at the trunk of the willow tree. After another while, the fog in his head began to bother him a little; he thought maybe he'd better sort a few things out.

It was early morning and seemed to be overcast. OK so far. He was sitting in the dirt under the branches of a willow tree. Yes, that seemed to be right. He had been in a gypsy camp in Valder's Clearing. That, he'd better check.

He looked out through the branches of the willow. A little stream was flowing past outside, and looking up along it, Crow could see the clearing, gray and quiet under the morning clouds. But there weren't any wagons or gypsies, no colorful flags or streamers, no calliope music, nothing.

Crow shivered and thought about this. Maybe his memory was playing tricks. He tried to remember what *else* had happened to him last night.

The memory hit him then, all sharp and burning and awful. He grabbed his beak and ran his wings up and down, over and under, feeling his beak and his chest and his forehead.

Again, nothing. No spikes, no holes, no blood. But there had been! Hadn't there? All that was left now was an ache throughout his entire body. But he also remembered drinking a great deal without eating anything. Could he have dreamed the whole thing?

But if he *had* dreamed the gypsy caravan, where had he gotten all the wine? And if he *hadn't* dreamed the gypsies, where were they now? His head felt all thick; everything was just too hazy, all the flashing of lights and the strange chanting and singing and the terrible pain of those spikes…

Crow was rubbing his beak again when there was a tiny click at the base of the willow trunk, and a small door swung open. A bleary-eyed mouse carrying two wooden buckets stepped out and, yawning mightily, started walking down toward the stream. He didn't seem to notice Crow sitting just off to the left of his door.

"Excuse me, sir," Crow called out, "but were you perhaps at the gypsy camp last night?"

The mouse kept on walking, heading for the stream outside the willow canopy.

"Sir? Excuse me, sir?" Crow heaved himself to his feet and half hopped, half stumbled after the mouse. "Sir?"

The mouse kept on walking, the buckets hanging from his arms rattling with each step.

"Sir?" Crow caught up to the mouse with only a few hops. "Sir? Please, I have to know about the gypsies!"

The mouse kept on walking, going right past Crow and only yawning again.

"Sir?!" Crow jumped forward and grabbed at the mouse. He had to stop him, spin him around, find out what had happened.

The mouse kept on walking, passing right through Crow's clenched wing as he might through a thin fog.

Crow stared at the mouse's retreating back. 'No,' he told himself. 'I'm just not quite awake yet.' He hopped again, over the mouse's head, and planted himself right in the mouse's path. "Sir? Please stop. Please! I've got to—"

The mouse kept on walking, and Crow felt a cold chill as the mouse's head and shoulders met and passed right into Crow's chest. Crow bent down and watched the mouse's feet and the two buckets as they moved along the feathers between his legs. Crow straightened up and looked back just in time to see the mouse pop out from his tail feathers and continue on toward the willow branches.

Crow stood in that same position, just blinking and blinking, as the mouse went out through the branches, down to the stream, dipped his buckets in, turned around, and headed back. Crow stood and stared, and the mouse, his buckets sloshing over as he staggered slightly, walked right up to Crow's tail and walked right through. Crow swung his head around and watched as the mouse emerged from his chest feathers. Crow stood and watched as the mouse walked up to the door, went through, put one of the buckets down, reached out, and pulled the door closed with a tiny click.

Crow stood that way for a long time.

Finally, he started moving his head from side to side. "No," he whispered. "No. No. No." His Doom. It was all coming back to him. And it was all coming true.

"No!" he shouted, leaping into the air. "No!" He slammed out through the willow branches and beat against the air with his wings. "No!" He couldn't close his eyes, couldn't *let* them close, not with those sights in his mind; the fire and the spears and the Doom all boiled behind his eyelids, and a mouse that walked right through him as if he was less than a shadow. He had to fly, to pound and pound and pound his way into the sky, up and up to where things were understandable.

He heard magpies calling to each other in the trees below and shouted out to them. They didn't respond. A flock of geese flapped by overhead, but they didn't return his greeting. He careened madly through the sky, shouting and screaming, but no one looked up, no one called out, no one noticed him flying by. He perched on a branch next to a group of finches and yelled every insult he could think of, but not a one even ruffled a feather. He plummeted right through the small formation of Mr. and Mrs. Sparrow and their family, plunged down without a whisper or a shout from any one of them, and barely missed slamming into the treetops.

Crow shouted and shouted and shouted till his voice was in shreds, and he whipped back and forth over the forest till his wings felt like stone. He didn't know where he was or where he was going; it didn't matter anyway. Everywhere, it was the same, but Crow wheeled and screamed around and around while the sun strode on into late afternoon again.

And so Crow dropped through the trees as his wings gave out and fell panting and heaving to the forest floor. What else could he do? He was Doomed. Karakchik had said it, and it had happened. No one would ever see or hear him again.

With effort, he brought his wings around and clasped them together. His throat was raw, but straining his voice, he rasped, "Lady Raven! You've got to hear me! Even if no one else can, you still can! And all you Curial powers, please! Lord and Lady Leopard, Lord Kit Fox, Lady Squirrel, you've got to still hear me! Yes, I killed him! He was small and lost and hurt and scared and cold and crying and sick and alone and I killed him! And then… oh, gods! I can't say it; how can I say it? It's too late, all too late. Please believe me, if I could do anything now, I would, but there's nothing! Nothing!"

Crow couldn't hold himself up anymore, so he slumped forward and lay aching and quivering in the fallen leaves. "All I can do," he whispered after a minute, "is say I'm sorry, and that's less than nothing. Lady Raven, I… I… oh, gods…"

His vision blurred, and he felt the feathers around his eyes become wet. He was lost now forever, and it was exactly what he deserved. A life for a life, Karakchik had said: Crow's life for the life he had destroyed.

So Crow lay in the leaves and waited for the cold touch of nightfall to whisk him away.

After a while, though, he thought he heard a soft, chirping cry from somewhere nearby. It struck something in his clouded mind, but he couldn't tell what. Then there was a cough and a choke and another cry. Crow lifted his head and looked around.

Something twitched among the leaves at the base of the next tree. As Crow watched, a tiny wing rose out of the leaves and then dropped back down.

A shiver ran through him, a violent one that snapped his beak shut. The leaves had stopped twitching, but Crow's eyes were locked on the place where he had seen the wing rise. He pushed himself to his feet and stumbled over to the tree.

She was lying there, half covered by brown leaves, her eyes closed but her chest still moving with a quick, shallow flutter. She was a barn swallow, very young and a terrible, pallid gray color.

Crow could only stare for a few moments, his mind not quite turning over. It was only after her head gave a quick twitch and she let out another thin cough that Crow could make himself move again. He unslung his satchel and squatted down next to the little swallow.

"I'll do it... do it right this time," he whispered, reaching out his wings. "I will. It's into the satchel, and then... then to Doctor Swift down in Ottersgate..." Crow cradled his wings around her, gently cupped them together, and lifted.

And the little swallow slipped through his wings as if she wasn't even there.

"No!" Crow hissed. "I'm trying to *help* her this time!" He tried again to lift her from the leaves, and again she seemed to slip right through his wings. He stood up and tried to wrap a claw around her, but it was like trying to grab empty air. "No, no, no, no, no!" he croaked, hopping up and down. "Lady Raven! This is my chance! I... I..."

Crow could only stare as the little swallow shivered among the brown leaves, her wings wracked with sharp little spasms. Crow tried to move her a few more times but only ended up hopping up and down again.

"I won't!" he managed to croak out. "I won't kill you again! I... I... I... don't know!" He hopped around some more. "I'll have to go to Ottersgate and get Doctor Swift somehow. Somehow." He looked back down at the swallow. "Don't worry," he whispered. "I'll get help. I will." He threw his satchel over his back and took off.

Once airborne, Crow got his bearings and realized he was just north and west of Ottersgate. His wings were still solid and heavy and aching from his tearing around all day, so he had to try gliding. The winds were all wrong, though, coming up from the south, and he sank closer and closer to the treetops. After only five minutes, his feet were scraping the highest branches, and his wings felt about ready to lock up. He forced them to flap once, twice, a third time, thinking of the small gray body back in the leaves.

He strained into a fourth flap, his shoulders bursting and his back knotting up, when a tangle of branches reared up in his path. It caught around his claws, grabbed him up and twisted him down, around, and hard into the tree's canopy. He crashed through, bounced off one branch, and fell to rest in a fork, his wings pounding and burning.

Crow wriggled himself free of the branches' grip, his wings hanging like slabs from his back. It couldn't be too much further to Ottersgate; he could hear the River already. He would just have to get to the top of the tree and glide from treetop to treetop. His head spinning, he sighted on the branch above him and was about to try a jump when he heard a voice behind him say, "Whoa, Crow, whoa! Where're you going?"

There was a thump on the branch beside him, and something long and black and furry appeared out of the leaves. Crow blinked at her. "Fisher?" he whispered.

"That was a nasty fall." Fisher was looking up through the broken branches. "Maybe you better just sit a while…"

"Fisher!" Crow's voice was a rasp. "You can see me!"

Fisher blinked at him. "Yeah. Yeah, I can see you, Crow."

"And… and you can *hear* me!"

"Just barely. You don't look so good, Crow. The blackfire's going around, y'know; you gotta cold, you shouldn't—"

"But you can hear me! You can see me!"

"Uhhh, sure…"

"Well of *course* you can!" Crow shook his head. "I'm not thinking! You know the ways of the Curial powers!"

"I what?"

"Yes, of course! I see it now!" Crow stepped closer to her on the branch. "Fisher," he hissed, "you've got to come with me; you're the only one who can help me!"

Fisher ran a paw over Crow's head. "I think you cracked yourself pretty good coming down just now. How 'bout we sit here and talk for a while, okay?"

"No, you don't understand! Back in the forest north of here there's a poor sick little swallow child. I was trying to get to Ottersgate to get Doctor Swift, but my wings, I've just done so much flying today, I guess I lost control. But you, Fisher, you're a sorceress, right?" He remembered she was; he knew she was.

Fisher was looking very worried. "Well, 'shaman' would be a better word, but—"

"But you'd know what to do! You can see me and hear me! You could help her! You've got to come with me!"

"Okay, Crow, okay; calm now, calm, okay? Just calm…"

Crow tried to take some deep breaths, but he was too jittery. "We've got to hurry!" he croaked.

"I just don't want you falling apart on me." She moved her paws along the sides of his neck. "Crumbs," Crow heard her say under her breath, then quickly out loud, "can you lead me to where she is?"

"I've got to." Crow could barely hear himself. "I've *got* to."

"Uh-huh. You just fly there, OK? I'll follow down here in the trees. You sure you can fly, now?"

"I've got to." And Crow knew it was true. He understood now. It was a life for a life, *not* a death for a death. "Follow me." He saw Fisher nod, and then he leaped upward through the hole he had made coming down.

His wings felt better for the brief rest, and knowing that Fisher was below him in the trees reassured him no end. And heading north, he had the winds with him, so he could glide to the spot where he had left the little swallow. The branches rustled and snapped below him, and occasionally Crow would catch a glimpse of Fisher flashing between the trees, her dark fur catching the rays of the setting sun.

"To the left!" Crow croaked out as loudly as he could manage. "Then follow me down!" Let his head pound all it wanted, this was one spot he could never forget. He flapped down through the tree canopy and landed at the foot of the tree where he had left the swallow. It was darker now under the branches, but he could still see her chest fluttering wildly. He started hopping as Fisher scrambled down the trunk to his side.

Fisher bent down close and put one paw to the side of the bird's head. "Gods!" she whispered. "It's the blackfire all right."

"But," Crow whispered, "you know what to do? You can... can save her?"

Fisher clicked her tongue. "Maybe. First thing, though, we gotta keep her warm." She turned to Crow. "You gotta hold her, Crow, up in your wings and close to your chest while I go after some plants I need, okay? You can do that?"

Crow felt a cold chill. "I don't know. I'll try..."

"It's easy. Here, hold your wings out, one on top of the other, crossed, yeah, like that. Now just hold still a minute..." And Fisher slowly and gently lifted the swallow out of the leaves and started to place her in Crow's wings.

"Wait!" Crow hissed. "What if she falls through?"

"Just hold her close; trust me." Fisher let the little bird down into Crow's wings. And she didn't fall through. "Hold her close," Fisher said again, "up to your chest. That's right."

His eyes wide, Crow drew the little swallow close, and the bird coughed and snuggled into his feathers.

Fisher chuckled. "Well, that's a good sign."

Crow looked over at Fisher. "She... she didn't fall through..." he somehow managed to say.

"No, she didn't. Now you just hold her like that." She reached around him and unfastened his satchel. "I saw some frialn over there as we came in. I'll be right back." The leaves crunched under her feet, and Fisher was gone.

Crow cradled the little swallow in his wings. "You didn't fall through," he whispered, touching his beak gently to hers. "Fisher can see me, and it'll all be all right. Just hold on. Hold on." He felt the swallow shiver against him, and he hunched himself around her closer, his silent 'thank you's going up to every Lord and Lady of the Curia.

Soon there was a scuffling along the leaves, and Fisher came up beside him with the satchel full of some sort of plant. "This'll do for now," she said, pulling a leaf out and grinding it up in her paws, "but we've gotta get her to Ottersgate. Doc Swift'll have frialn compound, and that's what she needs. Hold her up, Crow."

Crow unfolded himself from the swallow. Fisher worked her beak open, sprinkled some of the powdered leaf in, and started stroking the little bird's throat. The swallow shuddered, her wings twitching up and down, and Crow was afraid she might cough the powder out. But her neck rolled shakily under Fisher's soft stroking, and her tongue darted out of her beak a few times. Fisher blew out a breath. "OK, she's got it down."

"She'll be all right then?" Crow croaked out as he felt the little bird relax into his wings.

"If we can get her to Ottersgate." Fisher was pulling another leaf out of the satchel. She held it up to Crow. "Now you. Eat up, the whole thing."

Crow blinked at her. "Me? What for?"

"High fever, glassy eyes, swollen nodes, raw throat, stiffness, et cetera, et cetera. You got the blackfire, my friend, one of the worst adult cases I've seen in years."

Crow stared at her and didn't quite understand what she was saying. "The blackfire? Me?"

"Eat the leaf, Crow."

Crow opened his beak to protest, and Fisher stuffed the leaf in. "Chew it up, now," she said.

It was dry and bitter and dissolved against his tongue. Crow swallowed the stuff down. "Me? The blackfire? But... but how? And—"

"Later, Crow, later. Right now, you gotta fly this little one down to Ottersgate and get the both of you to Doc Swift."

The paste of the frialn stuck to Crow's tongue and made his mouth sour. "Me? Fly her to Ottersgate?" He thought for a minute. "Yes, I suppose I must. That leaf, it was magic? To make me solid again?"

Fisher looked sideways at him. "Magic? Yeah, OK, magic. Look, I've lined your satchel with frialn leaves. We wrap her up in 'em, strap the satchel on you, and you fly her to Doc Swift. I'd take her, but bouncing through the trees is *not* what she needs right now and running'd just take too long. I know you're not feeling all that well, but you can get her there

121

faster'n I can even if you take it easy. So take it easy, but get her there. You got it?"

Crow nodded. "I understand. It's the only way. I see that now. I can't bring the dead back, but the lost can be found, and the found, returned, a life for a life. That's what he said; I remember now. And then I'll be found again. It all makes sense." He looked over at Fisher. She was staring at him. "But you're a sorceress; you know this already."

There was a pause. "Uhh, right," Fisher said. "Now just come over here, Crow, and lay her real gentle in the satchel."

The frialn Crow had swallowed was numbing his various aches, and his wings already felt lighter. He walked over to where Fisher was standing by the satchel and, with her help, laid the little bird in among the leaves. Fisher then lifted the satchel and helped Crow strap it on, lodging it close in the feathers under his right wing.

"Take it easy," Fisher said again. "Fly straight for the Bailey Oak. Doc Swift or Mallard or Tara Wren or *somebody* oughtta be there; they'll know what to do, and I'll be right behind you, okay?"

Crow nodded again. "I will not fail this time."

"And make sure they—no, I'll take care of *you* when I get there. You just stay put till I show up, got it?"

"I will."

"Good. Let's go." Fisher sprang up the trunk, and Crow took off, climbing slowly through the darkening trees. He came out over the treetops and forced his mind to start thinking, very conscious of the small warm bundle pressing against his side.

The wind was still coming up from the south, so Crow decided on a long south-eastern tack. He couldn't head straight to Ottersgate without flapping more than either he or his passenger could take. With a tack, though, he could glide south-east on the wind halfway, then glide back south-west. He'd get to the Bailey Oak with very little wing movement overall, and he wouldn't have to get too high above the treetops.

Yes, that sounded good. He was sure that's what he would do if his mind was working properly. So he set his wings to catch the wind and began gliding south and eastward.

He kept wracking his brain, trying to remember the landmarks he always navigated by. That was the River below him now, that dark stripe flashing with the orange of the setting sun. The trees whipped by beneath him, and Donal's Lake stood out ahead. He would want to keep that on his left. That's right; he remembered that.

Crow turned his eyes westward and squinted into the sun. Something would happen over there, something about trees... Yes, the trees would stop at the northern edge of Ree's Meadow. He would want to cut west, keeping his southward momentum, and glide right over Ottersgate to the Bailey Oak.

That was it. And there, the trees were starting to thin out. A slight shift of his tail, the smallest flap of his wings, and he was wheeling to the west.

The satchel bumped against him, and Crow thought he could feel the swallow stirring inside. The cold of the wind was biting deep through his feathers, and his back was cramping up again. Crow hoped the little one was warm enough, but it wasn't much further. It couldn't be much further.

Crow scanned the landscape, and there, ahead and to his left, a tall old oak rose up, its branches spreading out above the forest canopy. The Bailey Oak. It had to be. He knew it was. Crow called out silently to the Lady Raven and concentrated on his wings, on not letting them cramp up, on just caressing the air and sliding through it.

Doctor Swift's office was on the eighth level of the Bailey Oak, Crow remembered, at about canopy level. Crow dipped his wings just the slightest bit, the wind digging into them, and dropped down, down, gradually down till he spotted the branch that was outside the doctors' office.

Crow glided in and grabbed the branch with tired claws. From a twig above the lighted hole in the trunk, a sign was hanging: Dr. Swift—Dr. Mallard, General Practitioners. Crow hopped down the branch, his wing tucked around the precious bundle in his satchel.

Through the hole was a waiting room, and just coming out of a door behind a small desk was Doctor Swift, yawning and straightening a plaid hat over his head. "See you in a few hours, Tara," the doctor was calling as he closed the door.

"Doctor!" Crow managed to croak out. "Wait!"

Doctor Swift's head jerked up, and he blinked at Crow a few times. "Crow!" he said after a moment. "I'm sorry; I didn't hear you come in." His brow wrinkled as he looked at Crow. "I think you'd better sit down."

Crow shook his head. "Not me, Doctor; this little one here…" Crow raised his wing and opened his satchel. "Fisher said it's the blackfire. You've got to help her, Doctor, you've *got* to…"

Doctor Swift hopped forward, his eyes wide, and touched his wings to the swallow child's head. Crow heard his sharp intake of breath followed by his shout of "Tara! Tara, out here! Quick!"

The door behind the desk opened, and a tired looking wren stuck her head out. "Doc? What…" Her voice trailed off as she saw Crow. "What in the—"

"Hot water bottles, a glucose IV set up, and a quarter cc of pure frialn compound." Doctor Swift's voice was calm but cracked a little as he lifted the swallow child out of Crow's satchel. "Room three's empty, and get a rosewood inhaler in there."

The wren was gone in a flash, and Doctor Swift was carrying the little swallow toward the still open door.

"Will she be all right?" Crow hissed, unable to stop jumping from foot to foot.

"If we hurry." Doctor Swift turned and backed through the doorway. His eyes snapped up to meet Crow's. "You stay put, Crow. Stay right here."

Crow nodded, and the doctor was through the doorway and gone.

Crow sank to the floor. He couldn't move his wings, he noticed, so he just let them flop beside him. His head buzzed and his eyes hurt. It was going to be all right, though. He had gotten her here in time. He knew he had. It was all going to be all right now…

There was a scuffling at the front door, and Fisher slid into the room. "Crow! Did you… ?"

He nodded. "She's inside. Doctor said to wait…"

"Good." Fisher opened a larger door in the wall to Crow's left. She went through and came out a moment later with a large dark bundle. The bundle unfolded into a blanket, and Fisher wrapped it around Crow's back, tucking it over his wings and tail and closing it around his chest. "How're you feeling?" she asked as she smoothed the blanket around him.

Crow wasn't really sure. "Tired," he managed to whisper, "very tired, Fisher."

Fisher nodded. "You think you can walk, just upstairs? There'll be beds up there; you can take a good rest."

"Will *she* be up there?" Crow was having a hard time focusing on Fisher's face. "I can't leave her, Fisher."

"She'll be fine. C'mon, now; you're not gonna do her any good keeling over out here. I'll help you, if you want."

Crow tried to open his eyes, but found they already were. "Yes," he got out at last. "Thank you."

Crow felt Fisher slide under his right wing. "It's just upstairs," she said. "You'll be all right."

Crow leaned onto her and managed to move his feet. They seemed so far away, and his beak was so heavy he couldn't raise his head. After a long while, he heard Fisher's voice say from off somewhere, "OK, just lie down now…" Then it swirled away from him and was lost in the cold misty darkness.

But there were things in the darkness, huge silent things that sat very still and waited. And Crow knew why. "Please, she's got to live! I don't care what you do to me anymore, but she's got to live! Give me my Doom back if that's what it takes, but please, please, don't let me kill this one, too…"

He begged and pleaded, pouring everything out of himself, promising and praying and hoping that they would listen. At long, long last, something somewhere seemed to click, and the shapes began to fade into the mist, the shifting shadows closing up around them. Crow fell back then, and, sprawling on the ground, he finally let himself sleep.

It was a deep and quiet sleep this time, and Crow came out of it slowly, drowsily, feeling numb and spent. Fisher lay curled on a padded lounge chair to his left, her dark fur matted and dull, a half-eaten roll nestled between her arms. She looked like she needed the sleep, so Crow rested against his pillows and watched the patterns the afternoon sun cast through the shutters onto the floor.

After a bit, Fisher stirred and sat up, catching the roll before it hit the floor. She set it on the chair and smiled at Crow. "You're looking better."

"What about the swallow child?" Crow's voice was so soft, he wasn't sure if he'd actually spoken. He cleared his throat. "How is she?"

"She went home yesterday." Fisher put a paw to his forehead. "Classic two day recovery. *You* had us more worried than she did."

"Then she's all right?"

Fisher laughed quietly. "She's fine. Her parents invited you, me, and the doc over for dinner soon as you feel up to it. They thought they'd lost her for sure."

Crow closed his eyes. "Thank the Lady Raven."

"Blackfire's like that," Fisher went on, leaning back against the end of the lounge chair. "It strikes so fast, the kids wander off before anyone knows they're sick, and it's even worse with these baby birds. They just fly away, and by the time anyone finds 'em, it's usually too late. Sometimes they don't even find the bodies." She closed her eyes and rubbed them. "But you get 'em frialn compound in time, and they're up again in two days, ready to go."

"How long have I been out?"

"Three days now. Your fever broke just this morning. You had it *bad*." She stopped and looked away from him. "Look, Crow," she said after a minute, "I—" She stopped again.

Crow blinked at her and was about to ask what was wrong when she turned back to him and said, "Before your fever broke, you talked a lot. Some of it was just gibberish, but some of it, well, some of it answered a few questions I'd had, and… and, well, we gotta talk about it. Sooner, the better."

Crow blinked some more. "Well, I feel all right now. A bit shaky still, but if it's important—"

"It is."

"Ah. All right. And if it gets to be too much for me, I'll—"

"It *is* gonna be too much for you; I already know that. But it's gonna be too much three weeks from now too, maybe even more than it is now."

Fisher stopped again, and Crow could only stare at her. She looked away. "The thing is," she went on, "there's not a whole lotta ways an adult can get the blackfire, and a case as bad as yours, well, there's even fewer. I'd been wondering how you managed to catch it, and then, last night," her eyes met his, "last night, you *told* me. It's one of the severest forms of blackfire because it's transmitted by the… by the ingestion of diseased tissue—"

"Don't." Crow turned away. His head felt tingly, and he went cold all over. "Please don't."

"It's true, then."

Crow couldn't look at her. "It's all over now. I did my penance, and they lifted the Doom. It's over, and it won't happen again. Ever again."

"How d'you know?"

Crow glanced over at her. "What?"

"The urge, Crow. It isn't the sorta thing that just hits once and then goes away, y'know. You've never given in before, but I'll bet this isn't the first time you've wanted a little meat in your diet."

"Stop it, Fisher, stop it! It's sick, warped, immoral! You shouldn't even say it!"

"Why? Just 'cause it's true?"

"It isn't true! It isn't true at *all*!"

"It isn't?"

Crow was shaking all over. He pulled the blanket up around his neck. What business was it of hers anyway? "I'm sick. You shouldn't say those kinds of things to sick folk."

"You gotta face up to it, Crow, or it'll just get worse. Trust me; I don't go after trout everyday 'cause I especially like the flavor, y'know."

Crow stared at her. "What? You mean… you too?"

Fisher spread her paws. "I think it's in most of us larger folk. You just gotta learn to deal with it. I mean, there's plentya creatures out there that aren't folk: fish and insects and the like. If it can't talk to you, it's fair game, I always say."

The blanket was too hot around him. Crow lowered it a little and rested his eyes on its rough weave. "I… I don't know what to say. I always thought, well, that… that it was just *me*…"

"Naw. You just can't turn your back on it is all. If you hide it, bottle it up and ignore it, it'll come bursting out when you're least ready to deal with it."

"But… but what do I *do*? I can't just give in to it. I mean, we're folk; this is all so, I don't know, so bestial."

Fisher shrugged. "Sure you resist it; you have to. Otherwise you end up drooling on your neighbors. But if you just ignore it, it's gonna blow up on you, and you're gonna do something that'll either drive you crazy or get you locked up or maybe even killed. That's *not* the way to deal with it."

"So how do you deal with it?"

"You use your head. There's always fish and all the insects we got around here, like I said. And you can always go out to the deep woods and hunt up some pygmy shrews. You just wanna do it away from Ottersgate or you're liable to snatch up some mouse family's pet."

Crow had to smile a little. "You've done that?"

Fisher waved a paw at him. "Don't get me started. But I mean it, Crow." Her voice got quiet. "I've seen folk go crazy 'cause they can't deal with it. They go Wilding, and you just gotta hunt 'em down…" Her eyes were dark and far away. Then she blinked a few times, shook her head and gave a half grin. "So anytime it gets to be too much for you, you come see me. Don't just hope it'll go away, 'cause it won't. I'll show you some good spots along the River, OK? Anytime."

Crow rubbed at the ache behind his eyes. "I don't know, Fisher," he said after a minute. "I just don't know. So much has happened in the last few days…" He looked over at her. "I'll think about it. That's all I can promise you."

"I can't ask for more than that." Fisher got to her feet. "You feel like some soup?"

So Crow ate and slept and woke the next morning ready to try his wings again. Doctor Swift and Fisher both looked him over and pronounced him fit to go home.

"Just take it easy for a couple of days," Doctor Swift told him, "at least till you get my bill."

"I will," Crow said, "and thank you for everything."

The doctor tucked his stethoscope into his white vest. "See you at the Swallows' tonight then." And he hopped out the door.

Fisher handed Crow his satchel. "Remember what I said, Crow. Anytime."

"I'll remember." Crow slowly buckled his satchel on. "I'd like to talk all this over with you, all that's happened to me and everything, if you wouldn't mind."

"Anytime," she said again. She pulled open the shuttered balcony door. Faint snatches of music drifted in on the breeze. "Calliopes," Fisher said, stepping out onto the balcony. "Guess the Autumn Festival's starting up."

Crow joined her and peered out over the rail. Across the roofs of Ottersgate, over the River on the grassy hills of Ree's Meadow, stood tents and wagons, all adorned with flags and streamers and the wafting music of the calliope. "I think I'll go have a look," he said to Fisher. "Shall I be at your place before sundown? I don't know where the Swallows live."

"Sure, why not? See you then." Fisher poked his shoulder and went back into the room.

Crow stepped off the balcony and let the morning breeze carry him over Ree's Meadow. The flags fluttered in every color and pattern, he noticed, except for gray and burgundy checks. He drifted over the field three times without spotting that combination, so he flapped over and settled to the ground next to the seven tired old calliopes, all gathered in a circle to the west of the Festival's midway.

There was one young squirrel seated at one of the calliopes, her skirt a bright red and yellow plaid. She was just finishing a slow, waltzing tune as Crow winged down.

Crow waited until she turned around before he asked, "Excuse me, but could you perhaps help me? I'm looking for a calliope player called Karakchik, Alphonse Karakchik."

The squirrel only looked at Crow. He repeated the name. The squirrel looked at him some more. Then she said, "He was saying a corvine might come looking for him. You are that?"

Crow nodded. The squirrel jumped down from the calliope and pulled a satchel out from underneath. She began undoing the buckles. "He said to give you this if you came looking." She lifted the flap and brought out something wrapped in black velvet. It seemed heavy, this something, and it flashed in the morning sun as she folded the velvet back. She held the something up, and Crow could see it was a silver calliope, intricately formed and embellished with ivory, brass, and gray and burgundy stones.

Crow reached out and took the calliope. "It's… oh, it's…" He couldn't find the words. It shone and sparkled like the full moon off the rapids of the River and laughed and danced as only the music of the calliope can.

Crow looked down at the squirrel. "Will you… will you be seeing him any time soon?"

The squirrel shrugged. "Maybe so, maybe not."

"Could you tell him, the next time you see him—" Tell him what? Thank you? Crow thought he understood what Karakchik had done, but he wasn't sure he was ready to *thank* the squirrel for it yet. But there was so much he wanted to say to him, to ask him. "Tell him... tell him I hope we will meet again someday under more pleasant circumstances. Would you please tell him that?"

"If I see him, I'll tell him."

"Thank you." Crow tucked the calliope gently into his satchel and leaped into the air. The sky was clear and the winds soft. Crow set his wings and glided north, heading home at last.

Reincarnation fantasies, of a dead human being reborn as an animal but remembering his or her human life, are rare. The best-known examples may be from outside the s-f or furry genres. There is the 1951 fantasy-comedy motion picture You Never Can Tell, starring Dick Powell as King, a poisoned German Shepherd who is reincarnated as Rex Shepherd, a human private detective to investigate his murder (with the ghost of a racehorse, Golden Harvest, reincarnated as Goldie, his sassy secretary). Or the 1977 dramatic novel Fluke by James Herbert, adapted into a major 1995 motion picture, about Fluke, a dog who becomes aware he is a reincarnated man. He grows obsessed with finding out more about his human life and family, and how he died. The 1990-2003 French-language Billy the Cat comic-book series by Stéphane Colman (artist) and Stephen Desberg (writer), about a young human brat who is killed by a car and reincarnated as a kitten, was notoriously considered too dark for children when it was turned into a 1996-2001 TV cartoon series; Billy became a boy who is enchanted into a cat by a magician. And who can forget (although we've tried!) the 1965-66 TV sitcom series My Mother the Car?

The theme has been most popular with authors who write novels and short stories about murdered people reincarnated as cats for vengeance. "Nine Lives to Live" by Sharyn McCrumb is slightly different and more humorous in giving her human soul a cat's instincts. Philip Danby plots revenge on his killer—if he can just resist taking long naps, obsessively grooming himself, or being sidetracked by female cats in heat.

Nine Lives To Live

by Sharyn McCrumb

It had seemed like a good idea at the time. Of course, Philip Danby had only been joking, but he had said it in a serious tone in order to humor those idiot New Age clients who actually seemed to believe in the stuff.

"I want to come back as a cat," he'd said, smiling facetiously into the candlelight at the Eskeridge dinner table. He had to hold his breath to keep from laughing as the others babbled about reincarnation. The women wanted to come back blonder and thinner, and the men wanted to be everything from Dallas Cowboys to oak trees. *Oak trees?* And he had to keep a straight face through it all, hoping these dodos would give the firm some business.

The things he had to put up with to humor clients. His partner, Giles Eskeridge, seemed to have no difficulties in that quarter, however. Giles often said that rich and crazy went together; therefore, architects who wanted a lucrative business had to be prepared to put up with eccentrics. They also had to put up with long hours, obstinate building contractors, and capricious zoning boards. Perhaps that was why Danby had plumped for life as a cat next time. As he had explained to his dinner companions that night, "Cats are independent. They don't have to kowtow to anybody; they sleep sixteen hours a day; and yet they get fed and sheltered and even loved—just for being their contrary little selves. It sounds like a good deal to me."

Julie Eskeridge tapped him playfully on the cheek. "You'd better take care to be a pretty, pedigreed kitty, Philip." She laughed. "Because life isn't so pleasant for an ugly old alley cat!"

"I'll keep that in mind," he told her. "In fifty years or so."

It had been more like fifty days. The fact that Giles had wanted to come back as a shark should have tipped him off. When they found out that they'd just built a three-million-dollar building on top of a toxic landfill, the contractor was happy to keep his mouth shut about it for a mere ten grand, and Giles was perfectly prepared to bury the evidence to protect the firm from lawsuits and EPA fines.

Looking back on it, Danby realized that he should not have insisted that they report the landfill to the authorities. In particular, he should not have insisted on it at six p.m. at the building site with no one present but himself and Giles. That was literally a fatal error. Before you could say "philosophical differences," Giles had picked up a shovel lying near the offending trench, and with one brisk swing, he had sent the matter to a higher court. As he pitched headlong into the reeking evidence, Danby's last thought was a flicker of cold anger at the injustice of it all.

* * *

His next thought was that he was watching a black-and-white movie, while his brain seemed intent upon sorting out a flood of olfactory sensations. *Furniture polish ... stale coffee ... sweaty socks ... Prell shampoo ... potting soil ...* He shook his head, trying to clear his thoughts. Where was he? The apparent answer to that was: lying on a gray sofa inside the black-and-white movie, because everywhere he looked he saw the same colorless vista. A concussion, maybe?

The memory of Giles Eskeridge swinging a shovel came back in a flash. Danby decided to call the police before Giles turned up to try again. He stood up, and promptly fell off the sofa.

Of course, he landed on his feet.

All four of them.

Idly, to keep from thinking anything more ominous for the moment, Danby wondered what *else* the New Age clients had been right about. Was Stonehenge a flying saucer landing pad? Did crystals lower cholesterol? He was in no position to doubt anything just now. He sat twitching his plume of a tail and wishing he hadn't been so flippant about the afterlife at the Eskeridge dinner party. He didn't even particularly like cats. He also wished that he could get his paws on Giles in retribution for the shovel incident. First he would bite Giles's neck, snapping his spine, and then he would let him escape for a few seconds. Then he'd sneak up behind him and pounce. Then bat him into a comer. Danby began to purr in happy contemplation.

The sight of a coffee table looming a foot above his head brought the problem into perspective. At present Danby weighed approximately fifteen furry pounds, and he was unsure of his exact whereabouts. Under those circumstances avenging his murder would be difficult. On the other hand, he didn't have any other pressing business, apart from an eight-hour nap which he felt in need of. First things first, though. Danby wanted to know what he looked like, and then he needed to find out where the kitchen was, and whether Sweaty Socks and Prell Shampoo had left anything edible on the countertops. There would be time enough for philosophical thoughts and revenge plans when he was cleaning his whiskers.

The living room was enough to make an architect shudder. Clunky Early American sofas and clutter. He was glad he couldn't see the color scheme. There was a mirror above the sofa, though, and he hopped up on the cheap upholstery to take a look at his new self. The face that looked back at him was definitely feline, and so malevolent that Danby wondered how anyone could mistake cats for pets. The yellow (or possibly green) almond eyes glowered at him from a massive triangular face, tiger-striped, and surrounded by a ruff of gray-brown fur. Just visible beneath the ruff was a dark leather collar equipped with a little brass bell. That would explain the ringing in his ears. The rest of his body seemed massive, even allowing for the fur, and the great plumed tail swayed rhythmically as he watched. He resisted a silly urge to swat at the reflected movement. So he was a tortoiseshell, or tabby, or whatever they called those brown-striped cats, and his hair was long. And he was still male. He didn't need to check beneath his tail to confirm that. Besides, the reek of ammonia in the vicinity of the sofa suggested that he was not shy about proclaiming his masculinity in various corners of his domain.

No doubt it would have interested those New Age clowns to learn that he was not a kitten, but a fully grown cat. Apparently the arrival had been instantaneous as well. He had always been given to understand that the afterlife would provide some kind of preliminary orientation before assigning him a new identity. A deity resembling John Denver, in rimless glasses and a Sierra Club T-shirt, should have been on hand with some paperwork regarding his case, and in a nonthreatening conference they would decide what his karma entitled, him to become. At least, that's what the New Agers had led him to believe. But it hadn't been like that at all. One minute he had been tumbling into a sewage pit, and the next, he had a craving for Meow Mix. Just like that. He wondered what sort of consciousness had been flickering inside that narrow skull prior to his arrival. Probably not much. A brain with the wattage of a lightning bug could control most of the items on the feline agenda: eat, sleep, snack, doze, dine, nap, and so on. Speaking of eating…

He made it to the floor in two moderate bounds, and jingled toward the kitchen, conveniently sign posted by the smell of lemon-scented dishwashing soap and stale coffee. The floor could do with a good sweeping, too, he thought, noting with distaste the gritty feel of tracked-in dirt on his velvet paws.

The cat dish, tucked in a corner beside the sink cabinet, confirmed his worst fears about the inhabitants' instinct for tackiness. Two plastic bowls were inserted into a plywood cat model, painted white, and decorated with a cartoonish cat face. If his food hadn't been at stake, Danby would have sprayed *that* as an indication of his professional judgment. As it was, he summoned a regal sneer and bent down to inspect the offering. The water wasn't fresh; there were bits of dry cat food floating in it. Did they expect him to drink *that*? Perhaps he ought to dump it out so that they'd take the hint. And the dry cat-food hadn't been stored in an airtight container, either. He sniffed contemptuously: the cheap brand, mostly cereal. He supposed he'd have to go out and kill something just to keep his ribs from crashing together. Better check out the counters for other options. It took considerable force to launch his bulk from floor to countertop, and for a moment he teetered on the edge of the sink fighting to regain his balance, while his bell tolled ominously, but once he righted himself he strolled onto the counter with an expression of nonchalance suggesting that his dignity had never been imperiled. He found two breakfast plates stacked in the sink. The top one was a trove of congealing egg yolk and bits of buttered toast. He finished it off, licking off every scrap of egg with his rough tongue, and thinking what a favor he was doing the people by cleaning the plate for them.

While he was on the sink, he peeked out the kitchen window to see if he could figure out where he was. The lawn outside was thick and luxurious, and a spreading oak tree grew beside a low stone wall. Well, it wasn't Albuquerque. Probably not California, either, considering the healthy appearance of the grass. Maybe he was still in Maryland. It certainly looked like home. Perhaps the transmigration of souls has a limited geographic range, like AM radio stations.

After a few moments' consideration, while he washed an offending forepaw, it occurred to Danby to look at the wall phone above the counter. The numbers made sense to him, so apparently he hadn't lost the ability to read. Sure enough, the telephone area code was 301. He wasn't far from where he started. Theoretically, at least, Giles was within reach. He must mull that over, from the vantage point of the window sill, where the afternoon sun was marvelously warm, and soothing… zzzzz.

* * *

Danby awakened several hours later to a braying female voice calling out, "Tigger! Get down from there this minute. Are you glad Mommy's home, sweetie?"

Danby opened one eye, and regarded the woman with an insolent stare.

Tigger? Was there no limit to the indignities he must bear? A fresh wave of Prell shampoo told him that the self-proclaimed *mommy* was chatelaine of this bourgeois bungalow. And didn't she look the part, too, with her polyester pants suit and her cascading chins! She set a grocery bag and a stack of letters on the countertop, and held out her arms to him. "And is my snookums ready for din-din?" she cooed.

He favored her with an extravagant yawn, followed by his most forbidding Mongol glare, but his hostility was wasted on the besotted Mrs.—he glanced down at the pile of letters—Sherrod. She continued to beam at him as if he had fawned at her feet. As it was, he was so busy studying the address on the Sherrod junk mail that he barely glanced at her. He hadn't left town! His tail twitched triumphantly. Morning Glory Lane was not familiar to him, but he'd be willing to bet that it was a street in Sussex Garden Estates, just off the bypass. That was a couple of miles from Giles Eskeridge's mock-Tudor monstrosity, but with a little luck and some common sense about traffic he could walk there in a couple of hours. If he cut through the fields, he might be able to score a mouse or two on the way.

Spurred on by the thought of a fresh, tasty dinner that would beg for its life, Danby/Tigger trotted to the back door and began to meow piteously, putting his forepaws as far up the screen door as he could reach.

"Now, Tigger!" said Mrs. Sherrod in her most arch tone. "You know perfectly well that there's a litter box in the bathroom. You just want to get outdoors so that you can tomcat around, don't you?" With that she began to put away groceries, humming tunelessly to herself.

Danby fixed a venomous stare at her retreating figure, and then turned his attention back to the problem at hand. Or rather, at paw. That was just the trouble: *Look, Ma, no hands!* Still, he thought, there ought to be a way. Because it was warm outside, the outer door was open, leaving only the metal storm door between himself and freedom. Its latch was the straight-handled kind that you pushed down to open the door. Danby considered the factors: door handle three feet above floor, latch opens on downward pressure, one fifteen-pound cat intent upon going out. With a vertical bound that Michael Jordan would have envied, Danby catapulted himself upward and caught onto the handle, which obligingly twisted downward, as the door swung open at the weight of the feline cannonball. By the time gravity took over and returned him to the ground, he was claw-deep in scratchy, sweet-smelling grass.

As he loped off toward the street, he could hear a plaintive voice wailing, "Ti-iii-gerrr!" It almost drowned out the jingling of that damned little bell around his neck.

* * *

Twenty minutes later Danby was sunning himself on a rock in an abandoned field, recovering from the exertion of moving faster than a stroll. In the distance he could hear the drone of cars from the interstate, as the smell of gasoline wafted in on a gentle breeze. As he had trotted through the neighborhood, he'd read street signs, so he had a better idea of his whereabouts now. Windsor Forest, that pretentious little suburb that Giles called home, was only a few miles away, and once he crossed the interstate, he could take a shortcut through the woods. He hoped that La Sherrod wouldn't put out an all-points bulletin for her missing kitty. He didn't want any SPCA interruptions once he reached his destination. He ought to ditch the collar as well, he thought. He couldn't very well pose as a stray with a little bell under his chin.

Fortunately, the collar was loose, probably because the ruff around his head made his neck look twice as large. Once he determined that, it took only a few minutes of concentrated effort to work the collar forward with his paws until it slipped over his ears. After that, a shake of the head—jingle! jingle!—rid him of Tigger's identity. He wondered how many pets who "just disappeared one day," had acquired new identities and gone off on more pressing business.

He managed to reach the bypass before five o'clock, thus avoiding the commuter traffic of rush hour. Since he understood automobiles, it was a relatively simple matter for Danby to cross the highway during a lull between cars. He didn't see what the possums found so difficult about road crossing. Sure enough, there was a ripe gray corpse on the white line, mute testimony to the dangers of indecision on highways. He took a perfunctory sniff, but the roadkill was too far gone to interest anything except the buzzards.

Once across the road, Danby stuck to the fields, making sure that he paralleled the road that led to Windsor Forest. His attention was occasionally diverted by a flock of birds overhead, or an enticing rustle in the grass that might have been a field mouse, but he kept going. If he didn't reach the Eskeridge house by nightfall, he would have to wait until morning to get himself noticed.

In order to get at Giles, Danby reasoned, he would first have to charm Julie Eskeridge. He wondered if she was susceptible to needy animals. He couldn't remember whether they had a cat or not. An unspayed female would be nice, he thought. A Siamese, perhaps, with big blue eyes and a sexy voice.

Danby reasoned that he wouldn't have too much trouble finding Giles's house. He had been there often enough as a guest. Besides, the firm had designed and built several of the overwrought mansions in the spacious subdivision. Danby had once suggested that they buy Palladian windows by the gross, since every nouveau-riche home-builder insisted on having a brace of them, no matter what style of house he had commissioned. Giles had not been amused by Danby's observation. He seldom was. What Giles lacked in humor, he also lacked in scruples and moral restraint, but he compensated for these deficiencies with a highly developed instinct for making and holding on to money. While he'd lacked Danby's talent in design and execution, he had a genius for turning up wealthy clients, and for persuading these tasteless yobbos to spend a fortune on their showpiece homes. Danby did draw the line at carving up antique Sheraton sideboards to use as bathroom sink cabinets, though. When he also drew the line at environmental crime, Giles had apparently found his conscience an expensive luxury that the firm could not afford. Hence, the shallow grave at the new construction site, and Danby's new lease on life. It was really quite unfair of Giles, Danby reflected. They'd been friends since college, and after Danby's parents died, he had drawn up a will leaving his share of the business to Giles. And how had Giles repaid this friendship? With the blunt end of a shovel. Danby stopped to sharpen his claws on the bark of a handy pine tree. Really, he thought, Giles deserved no mercy whatsoever. Which was just as well, because, catlike, Danby possessed none.

* * *

The sun was low behind the surrounding pines by the time Danby arrived at the Eskeridge's mock-Tudor home. He had been delayed en route by the scent of another cat, a neutered orange male. (Even to his color-blind eyes, an orange cat was recognizable. It might be the shade of gray, or the configuration of white at the throat and chest.) He had hunted up this fellow feline, and made considerable efforts to communicate, but as far as he could tell, there was no higher intelligence flickering behind its blank green eyes. There was no intelligence at all, as far as Danby was concerned; he'd as soon try talking to a shrub. Finally tiring of the eunuch's unblinking stare, he'd stalked off, forgoing more social experiments in favor of his mission.

He sat for a long time under the forsythia hedge in Giles's front yard, studying the house for signs of life. He refused to be distracted by a cluster of sparrows cavorting on the birdbath, but he realized that unless a meal was coming soon, he would be reduced to foraging. The idea of hurling his bulk at a few ounces of twittering songbird made his scowl even more forbidding than usual. He licked a front paw and glowered at the silent house.

After twenty minutes or so, he heard the distant hum of a car engine, and smelled gasoline fumes. Danby peered out from the hedge in time to see Julie Eskeridge's Mercedes rounding the corner from Windsor Way. With a few hasty licks to smooth down his ruff, Danby sauntered toward the driveway just as the car pulled in. Now for the hard part: how do you impress Julie Eskeridge without a checkbook?

He had never noticed before how much Giles's wife resembled a giraffe. He blinked at the sight of her huge feet swinging out of the car perilously close to his nose. They were followed by two replicas of the Alaska pipeline, both encased in nylon. Better not jump up on her; one claw on the stockings, and he'd have an enemy for life. Julie was one of those people who air-kissed because she couldn't bear to spoil her makeup. Instead of trying to attract her attention at the car (where she could have skewered him with one spike heel), Danby loped to the steps of the side porch, and began meowing piteously. As Julie approached the steps, he looked up at her with wide-eyed supplication, waiting to be admired.

"Shoo, cat!" said Julie, nudging him aside with her foot.

As the door slammed in his face, Danby realized that he had badly miscalculated. He had also neglected to devise a backup plan. A fine mess he was in now. It wasn't enough that he was murdered and reassigned to cathood. Now he was also homeless.

* * *

He was still hanging around the steps twenty minutes later when Giles came home, mainly because he couldn't think of an alternate plan just yet.

When he saw Giles's black sports car pull up behind Julie's Mercedes, Danby's first impulse was to run, but then he realized that, while Giles might see him, he certainly wouldn't recognize him as his old business partner. Besides, he was curious to see how an uncaught murderer looked. Would Giles be haggard with grief and remorse? Furtive, as he listened for police sirens in the distance?

Giles Eskeridge was whistling. He climbed out of his car, suntanned and smiling, with his lips pursed in a cheerfully tuneless whistle. Danby trotted forward to confront his murderer with his haughtiest scowl of indignation. The reaction was not quite what he expected.

Giles saw the huge, fluffy cat, and immediately knelt down, calling, "Here, kitty, kitty!"

Danby looked at him as if he had been propositioned.

"Aren't you a beauty!" said Giles, holding out his hand to the strange cat. "I'll bet you're a pedigreed animal, aren't you, fella? Are you lost, boy?"

Much as it pained him to associate with a remorseless killer, Danby sidled over to the outstretched hand, and allowed his ears to be scratched. He reasoned that Giles's interest in him was his one chance to gain entry to the house. It was obvious that Julie wasn't a cat fancier. Who would have taken heartless old Giles for an animal lover? Probably similarity of temperament, Danby decided.

He allowed himself to be picked up and carried into the house, while Giles stroked his back and told him what a pretty fellow he was. This was an indignity, but still an improvement over Giles's behavior toward him during their last encounter. Once inside Giles called out to Julie, "Look what I've got, honey!"

She came in from the kitchen, scowling. "That nasty cat!" she said. "Put him right back outside!"

At this point Danby concentrated all his energies toward making himself purr. It was something like snoring, he decided, but it had the desired effect on his intended victim, for at once Giles made for his den and plumped down in an armchair, arranging Danby in his lap, with more petting and praise. "He's a wonderful cat, Julie," Giles told his wife. "I'll bet he's a purebred Maine coon. Probably worth a couple of hundred bucks."

"So are my wool carpets," Mrs. Eskeridge replied. "So are my new sofas! And who's going to clean up his messes?"

That was Danby's cue. He had already thought out the pièce de résistance in his campaign of endearment. With a trill that meant "This way, folks!," Danby hopped off his ex-partner's lap and trotted to the downstairs bathroom. He had used it often enough at dinner parties, and he knew that the door was left ajar. He had been saving up for this moment. With Giles and his missus watching from the doorway, Danby hopped up on the toilet seat, twitched his elegant plumed tail, and proceeded to use the toilet in the correct manner.

He felt a strange tingling in his paws, and he longed to scratch at something and cover it up, but he ignored these urges, and basked instead in the effusive praise from his self-appointed champion. Why couldn't Giles have been that enthusiastic over his design for the Jenner building, Danby thought resentfully. Some people's sense of values was so warped. Meanwhile, though, he might as well savor the Eskeridges' transports of joy over his bowel control; there weren't too many ways for cats to demonstrate superior intelligence. He couldn't quote a little Shakespeare or identify the dinner wine. Fortunately, among felines toilet training passed for genius, and even Julie was impressed with his accomplishments. After that, there was no question of Giles turning him out into the cruel world. Instead, they carried him back to the kitchen and opened a can of tuna fish for his dining pleasure. He had to eat it in a bowl on the floor, but the bowl was Royal Doulton, which was some consolation. And while he ate, he could still hear Giles in the background, raving about what a wonderful cat he was. He was in.

"No collar, Julie. Someone must have abandoned him on the highway. What shall we call him?"

"Varmint," his wife suggested. She was a hard sell.

Giles ignored her lack of enthusiasm for his newfound prodigy. "I think I'll call him Merlin. He's a wizard of a cat."

Merlin? Danby looked up with a mouthful of tuna. Oh well, he thought, Merlin and tuna were better than Tigger and cheap dry cat food. You couldn't have everything.

* * *

After that, he quickly became a full-fledged member of the household, with a newly purchased plastic feeding bowl, a catnip mouse toy, and another little collar with another damned bell. Danby felt the urge to bite Giles's thumb off while he was attaching this loathsome neckpiece over his ruff, but he restrained himself. By now he was accustomed to the accompaniment of a maniacal jingling with every step he took. What was it with human beings and bells?

Of course, that spoiled his plans for songbird hunting outdoors. He'd have to travel faster than the speed of sound to catch a sparrow now. Not that he got out much, anyhow. Giles seemed to think that he might wander off again, so he was generally careful to keep Danby housebound.

That was all right with Danby, though. It gave him an excellent opportunity to become familiar with the house, and with the routine of its inhabitants—all useful information for someone planning revenge. So far he (the old Danby, that is) had not been mentioned in the Eskeridge conversations. He wondered what story Giles was giving out about his disappearance. Apparently the body had not been found. It was up to him to punish the guilty, then.

Danby welcomed the days when both Giles and Julie left the house. Then he would forgo his morning, midmorning, and early afternoon naps in order to investigate each room of his domain, looking for lethal opportunities: medicine bottles or perhaps a small appliance that he could push into the bathtub.

So far, though, he had not attempted to stage any accidents, for fear that the wrong Eskeridge would fall victim to his snare. He didn't like Julie any more than she liked him, but he had no reason to kill her. The whole business needed careful study. He could afford to take his time analyzing the opportunities for revenge. The food was good, the job of house cat was undemanding, and he rather enjoyed the irony of being doted on by his intended victim. Giles was certainly better as an owner than he was as a partner.

An evening conversation between Giles and Julie convinced him that he must accelerate his efforts. They were sitting in the den, after a meal of baked chicken. They wouldn't give him the bones, though. Giles kept insisting that they'd splinter in his stomach and kill him. Danby was lying on the hearth rug, pretending to be asleep until they forgot about him, at which time he would sneak back into the kitchen and raid the garbage. He'd given up smoking, hadn't he? And although he'd lapped up a bit of Giles's scotch one night, he seemed to have lost the taste for it. How much prudence could he stand?

"If you're absolutely set on keeping this cat, Giles," said Julie Eskeridge, examining her newly polished talons, "I suppose I'll have to be the one to take him to the vet."

"The vet. I hadn't thought about it. Of course, he'll have to have shots, won't he?" murmured Giles, still studying the newspaper. "Rabies, and so on."

"And while we're at it, we might as well have him neutered," said Julie. "Otherwise, he'll start spraying the drapes and all."

Danby rocketed to full alert. To keep them from suspecting his comprehension, he centered his attention on the cleaning of a perfectly tidy front paw. It was time to step up the pace on his plans for revenge, or he'd be meowing in soprano. And forget the scruples about innocent bystanders: now it was a matter of self-defense.

* * *

That night he waited until the house was dark and quiet. Giles and Julie usually went to bed about eleven-thirty, turning off all the lights, which didn't faze him in the least. He rather enjoyed skulking about the silent house using his infrared vision, although he rather missed late-night television. He had considered turning the set on with his paw, but that seemed too precocious, even for a cat named Merlin. Danby didn't want to end up in somebody's behavior lab with wires coming out of his head.

He examined his collection of cat toys, stowed by Julie in his cat basket because she hated clutter. He had a mouse-shaped catnip toy, a rubber fish, and a little red ball. Giles had bought the ball under the ludicrous impression that Danby could be induced to play catch. When he'd rolled it across the floor, Danby lay down and gave him an insolent stare. He had enjoyed the next quarter of an hour, watching Giles on his hands and knees, batting the ball and trying to teach Danby to fetch. But finally Giles gave up, and the ball had been tucked in the cat basket ever since. Danby picked it up with his teeth, and carried it upstairs. Giles and Julie came down the right side of the staircase, didn't they? That's where the bannister was. He set the ball carefully on the third step, in the approximate place that a human foot would touch the stair. A trip wire would be more reliable, but Danby couldn't manage the technology involved.

What else could he devise for the Eskeridges' peril? He couldn't poison their food, and since they'd provided him with a flea collar, he couldn't even hope to get bubonic plague started in the household. Attacking them with tooth and claw seemed foolhardy, even if they were sleeping. The one he wasn't biting could always fight him off, and a fifteen-pound cat can be killed with relative ease by any human determined to do it. Even if they didn't kill him on the spot, they'd get rid of him immediately, and then he'd lose his chance forever. It was too risky.

It had to be stealth, then. Danby inspected the house, looking for lethal opportunities. There weren't any electrical appliances close to the bathtub, and besides Giles took showers. In another life Danby might have been able to rewire the electric razor to shock its user, but such a feat was well beyond his present level of dexterity. No wonder human beings had taken over the earth; they were so damned hard to kill.

Even his efforts to enlist help in the task had proved fruitless. On one of his rare excursions out of the house (Giles had gone golfing, and

Danby slipped out without Julie's noticing), Danby had roamed the neighborhood, looking for... well... pussy. Instead he'd found dimwitted tomcats, and a Doberman pinscher, who was definitely Somebody. Danby had kept conversation to a minimum, not quite liking the look of the beast's prominent fangs. Danby suspected that the Doberman had previously been an IRS agent. Of course, the dog had *said* that it had been a serial killer, but that was just to lull Danby into a false sense of security. Anyhow, much as the dog approved of Danby's plan to kill his humans, he wasn't interested in forming a conspiracy. Why should he go to the gas chamber to solve someone else's problem?

Danby himself had similar qualms about doing anything too drastic— such as setting fire to the house. He didn't want to stage an accident that would include himself among the victims. After puttering about the darkened house for a wearying few hours, he stretched out on the sofa in the den to take a quick nap before resuming his plotting. He'd be able to think better after he rested.

The next thing Danby felt was a ruthless grip on his collar, dragging him forward. He opened his eyes to find that it was morning, and that the hand at his throat belonged to Julie Eskeridge, who was trying to stuff him into a metal cat carrier. He tried to dig his claws into the sofa, but it was too late. Before he could blink, he had been hoisted along by his tail, and shoved into the box. He barely got his tail out of the way before the door slammed shut behind him. Danby crouched in the metal carrier, peeking out the side slits, and trying to figure out what to do next. Obviously the rubber ball on the steps had been a dismal failure as a murder weapon. Why couldn't he have come back as a mountain lion?

Danby fumed about the slings and arrows of outrageous fortune all the way out to the car. It didn't help to remember where he was going, and what was scheduled to be done with him shortly thereafter. Julie Eskeridge set the cat carrier on the backseat and slammed the door. When she started the car, Danby howled in protest.

"Be quiet back there!" Julie called out. "There's nothing you can do about it."

We'll see about that, thought Danby, turning to peer out the door of his cage. The steel bars of the door were about an inch apart, and there was no mesh or other obstruction between them. He found that he could easily slide one paw sideways out of the cage. Now, if he could just get a look at the workings of the latch, there was a slight chance that he could extricate himself. He lay down on his side and squinted up at the metal catch. It seemed to be a glorified bolt. To lock the carrier, a metal bar was slid into a socket, and then rotated downward to latch. If he could push the bar back up and then slide it back...

It wasn't easy to maneuver with the car changing speed and turning corners. Danby felt himself getting quite dizzy with the effort of concentrating as the carrier gently rocked. But finally, when the car reached the interstate and sped along smoothly, he succeeded in positioning his paw at the right place on the bar, and easing it upward. Another three minutes of tense probing allowed him to slide the bar a fraction of an inch, and then another. The bolt was now clear of the latch. There was no getting out of the car, of course. Julie had rolled up the windows, and they were going sixty miles an hour. Danby spent a full minute pondering the implications of his dilemma. But no matter which way he looked at the problem, the alternative was always the same: do something desperate or go under the knife. It wasn't as if dying had been such a big deal, after all. There was always next time.

Quickly, before the fear could stop him, Danby hurled his furry bulk against the door of the cat carrier, landing in the floor of the backseat with a solid thump. He sprang back up on the seat, and launched himself into the air with a heartfelt snarl, landing precariously on Julie Eskeridge's right shoulder, and digging his claws in to keep from falling.

The last things he remembered were Julie's screams and the feel of the car swerving out of control.

* * *

When Danby opened his eyes, the world was still playing in black-and-white. He could hear muffled voices, and smell a jumble of scents: blood, gasoline, smoke. He struggled to get up, and found that he was still less than a foot off the ground. Still furry. Still the Eskeridges' cat. In the distance he could see the crumpled wreckage of Julie's car.

A familiar voice was droning on above him. "He must have been thrown free of the cat carrier during the wreck, officer. That's definitely Merlin, though. My poor wife was taking him to the vet."

A burly policeman was standing next to Giles, nodding sympathetically. "I guess it's true what they say about cats, sir. Having nine lives, I mean. I'm very sorry about your wife. She wasn't so lucky."

Giles hung his head. "No. It's been a great strain. First my business partner disappears, and now I lose my wife." He stooped and picked up Danby. "At least I have my beautiful kitty-cat for consolation. Come on, boy. Let's go home."

Danby's malevolent yellow stare did not waver. He allowed himself to be carried away to Giles's waiting car without protest. He could wait. Cats were good at waiting. And life with Giles wasn't so bad, now that Julie wouldn't be around to harass him. Danby would enjoy a spell of being doted on by an indulgent human, fed gourmet cat food, and given the run of the house. Meanwhile he could continue to leave the occasional ball on the stairs, and think of other ways to toy with Giles, while he waited to see if the police ever turned up to ask Giles about his missing partner. If not, Danby could work on more ways to kill humans. Sooner or later he would succeed. Cats are endlessly patient at stalking their prey.

"It's just you and me, now, fella," said Giles, placing his cat on the seat beside him.

And after he killed Giles, perhaps he could go in search of the building contractor that Giles bribed to keep his dirty secret. He certainly deserved to die. And that nasty woman Danby used to live next door to, who used to complain about his stereo and his crabgrass. And perhaps the surly headwaiter at Chantage. Stray cats can turn up anywhere.

Danby began to purr.

John Gregory Betancourt's novel Rememory *(Popular Library/Questar, October 1990) is a fast-moving cyberpunk thriller set in a depressing future. Many people are so depressed that they use futuristic technology to opt out of humanity and turn themselves into animalforms—catmen, dogmen, penguinmen, or whatever their chosen totem animals are. There are bodyshops such as Animen-R-Us, where humans can get themselves converted. Conversion used to be an individual adult choice, but now that animal communities have developed, parents have their children converted as soon after birth as possible. Catmen and dogmen can transform themselves at will, were-animal style, between a human bipedal posture and an animal quadrupedal stance. Animen adults have enhanced muscles and steel claws; children have plastic practice claws. Bioengineered body forms establish the basic feline or canine structure, including head-shape, fangs, claws, tail, and so on; but the skin and body-fur are easily interchangeable. A catman can appear as a tiger, a leopard, a cougar, a cheetah, a man-sized Siamese cat, or just about any other feline almost as easily as a human can change clothes. There can also be hybrids, such as a dogman smuggler with the head of a Doberman and the body of a wolf or a husky.* Rememory *is available on Kindle today.*

In 1994, Esther Friesner & Martin Greenberg edited an anthology, Alien Pregnant By Elvis. *Authors were asked to write a humorous story that might be inspired by a lurid tabloid headline. Betancourt wrote "Vole", a spinoff from* Rememory, *as a collection of newspaper clippings about animen conversions, classified ads by sleazy conversion shops advertising their services, and people wanting to turn into something besides humans—even voles. This may seem desirable to us, but Betancourt's story was introduced by the editors as, "Here follows something… bizarre, even for this book."*

Vole

by John Gregory Betancourt

From the *New York Sun-Tribune*

VOLE MEN—A NEW MEDICAL MUTILATION?
By Ari J. Hermann
Staff Writer

Dozens of patients flock to "animen doctors" each week to be surgically reconstructed into their favorite animals. Societies of elite "catmen," "dogmen," and other breeds of animal-men are developing throughout New York and Los Angeles as a result.

"The so-called 'animan surgery' is neither safe nor sensible," according to Dr. Bruce Athwait of the County General Hospital. "It appeals to the baser, animal instincts in man," Athwait says. "If you need an outlet for your animal agressions, see a licensed psychiatrist. Do not mutilate your body!"

New York's most celebrated animan surgeon, Dr. Ferret, disagrees. "Man is past the point of needing just one body," he alleges. "New limbs and vital organs can be cloned in nutrient tanks for amputees. Why not graft on whole new bodies?" Dr. Ferret, a six-year animan himself (ferretman), further claims to have performed "over eight hundred successful operations over the last three years, for animan bodies ranging from cats to dogs to, yes, even penguins."

As new animalform bodies are developed and commercially marketed, Dr. Ferret runs advertisements in local papers offering specials on these new bodies. The latest animalform is "vole" — and over fifty people have already signed up for the new "voleman" surgical operations.

Legislation is pending in Congress to make animalforms either illegal or harder to get for most Americans. Several southern states have already passed laws against human-body mutilation aimed at curbing the animalform practice, and a test case is currently with the Supreme Court. Battle lines seem drawn between pro-animalform and anti-animalform groups.

Only time will tell whether animen are the wave of the future—or a bizarre affectation of the present.

John Gregory Betancourt

From the
NEW YORK POST-DISPATCH
PERSONANIMALS Column

ROOST WANTED
Pigeonman seeks birdlover for coos and cuddles. Send photo of coop. Reply Box 2022

SNAKEMAN S-S-SOUGHT
Slinky snakewoman seeks sensuous snakeman for long oil baths, mooshoo mice, sunning on stones. Adders preferred. Reply Box 9298.

TIGER BY THE TAIL?
B-I-G tigerman seeks ferocious mate. Claws sharp, teeth ready, here I am. G-R-O-W-L! Reply Box 3832.

VAMPIRE BAT
Bloodsucker seeks victims for midnight feasts. I use anaesthetic for all bloodletting. Reply Box 8281.

VOLES ANONYMOUS
Abandonned? Friendless? Try Voles Anonymous support group for volemen and volewomen. Don't be alone any more! Call 9992-93842 (recorded message).

VOLE SEEKS SAME
Lonely voleman seeks volewoman for skulks in the park, nibbles of celery, and romantic evenings. Desperate for affection. Reply Box 4492.

WANTED: CATWOMAN
Catman seeks feline friend for frisky feline frolics. No fleas. Reply Box 4523.

WOLF CUB SEEKS MATE
Up for a howl at the moon? Young, cute, no fleas wolfman seeks wolf- or dog-woman for fun and twilight explorations. Sincere. All messages answered. Reply

WOLF WOMAN WANTED
Animan-curious SWM seeks wolfgirl of dreams. I'll hold your paw in times of joy or trouble. Send picture, letter. Box 1002

WOLFPACK FORMING
Meet like-minded, swinging wolfpeople. Sunday pack meetings, group activities. Run with the best. Reply Box 2933

YELLOWJACKET WOMAN
One of a kind?! Hot honeyqueen looking for swarm to serve her. Give me a bzzzz. Reply Box 4589

ZEBRAMAN
Me: honest, sincere, and hot-to-trot through the NY nightlife. You: light-on-hooves, enjoy love nips, hay. Recently reshod. Reply Box 2351

The first stories about transformations were 1920s and '30s s-f/horror tales about Mad Scientists or Mad Surgeons turning people into animals or vice versa by surgically switching their brains, always against their screaming victims' wills. Stories about pseudoscientific and supposedly safe transformations showed up during the last quarter of the 20th century, but it was invariably a one-time and one-way transformation. Edd Vick's "Choice Cuts" in the furry APA Rowrbrazzle *was one of the first to depict changing bodies, including genders and species, as something as easy and blasé as changing your clothes, and—except to those not used to it—not horror at all.*

But changing species was still a bit too much for editors and readers outside furry fandom in 1995. Vick had to rewrite "Choice Cuts" to remove the non-humans to make a sale. It appeared in the small-press Electric Velocipede #6, *Spring 2004, as still a s-f "horror story". This is the first republication of the original story.*

Choice Cuts

by Edd Vick

"I believe I've chosen. Bring me the tenderloin, a Caesar salad, a glass of your house white, and make me female. A squirrel, I think."

"Yes, ser, and how would you like that steak cooked? Oh, and what color fur? We have a special on black tonight."

Robin finished ordering and set aside his menu. The skunk had ordered much more than usual, as Changers often did. It wasn't like he'd be saddled with the extra kilos.

As always, it would take a little time for the machinery to engineer the Change. It wasn't like he'd imagined, so many times, as a depressed teen. Down would come the magic, and touch him, and up would sweep the Change, from toes to scalp, narrowing his feet, denuding his legs—he'd somehow thought women weren't subject to leg hair—widening his hips, inhaling his penis, budding his breasts, and so on up to hair that would be long, lush, and full. The fur… well, that hadn't been part of his dreams. Not then, anyway.

On the contrary, the Change was surprisingly mechanical. Make the order, wait for a vat-grown body to be altered according to taste, and squirt his mind into it. It was almost like putting on a form-fitting leotard, if you didn't mind stripping down to your psyche.

A sudden hush washed across the restaurant, and Robin looked up. Two people, a man and a woman, humans, stood backlit in the doorway. The woman was obviously pregnant. A sudden wave of nausea hit Robin then, and he heard the scraping of chairs as other diners edged away from the obscenity.

The headwaiter stepped forward and motioned them to one side, into the hallway leading to the restrooms. Conversations resumed, but to

Robin's trained ear it sounded artificial, strained. An otter at the next table said, "What do you get when you cross an unChanged man with anything?"

"That one's a hundred years old," said his companion. "Babies." They both laughed.

Robin saw his server approaching, and stood to meet her. She was nervous, he could see that in the set of her ears, and before she could say anything he held up a hand and nodded. She looked relieved, then turned to lead him back toward the hall. Once there, she tapped at a side door marked 'Private' and opened it for him.

The humans were there in the office with the restaurant's owner, a heavyset rhino of indeterminate gender, who scowled at Robin in obvious distaste.

"Robin Coope? You're a Teacher?"

That took Robin back. It had been years since he'd been called a Teacher. For the last nine decades, since the end of birthing, he'd gotten by with Change Therapy, with Group Sects seminars, with whatever he could to make ends meet.

Robin nodded. "Did they ask for one?" Then, before the ser could answer, he turned to the male—he couldn't quite force himself to face the pregnant female—and asked, "Were you looking for a teacher?"

The human nodded. "We just wanted to find someone who could help us." His accent was Outworldish, decipherable but rustic, reminding Robin of preChange movies. "I'm sorry, this is the first place that would even let us in the door. We, Molly and me, we were up on Ganymede Colony. They—they weren't going to let us keep the baby. They said the chance of it having a learning disorder was more than ten percent, and so they wouldn't even let us try again, and we'd heard how Earth was but we thought maybe we'd have a chance here, that maybe you'd let us birth it, so we stowed away on an H3 tanker and—" The words ran out and he sat, trembling, clutching the arm of the female, reminding Robin of an old flat photograph he'd seen long ago of an aboriginal couple on their first airplane ride.

The restaurant owner hauled serself out of ser's chair and loomed over Robin. "I want them out of here."

There came a rapping on the door, and Robin's server poked her head into the room. "Your order is ready, ser."

Robin sighed, then turned back to the owner. "I haven't Changed in— well, in quite a while. You know how it is."

The rhino—Robin realized the owner was male—nodded reluctantly. "We'll expedite your Change on the house, but you can forget about the food. It'd be wasted on that body, anyway. Just be quick about it." He beckoned the server. "Hook him up at my terminal."

Robin turned back to the couple, forcing himself to look at both of them. "Molly and—I'm sorry, I don't know your name."

"John. John Farmer."

"John and Molly. Well, John and Molly, I'm about to go through a Change. You know what that is?" He waited for their hesitant nods. "It's really nothing, like putting on a new set of clothes, but I'll be different when you see me again. Just sit on the couch, don't get in the way, and I'll be back to help you as soon as I can." That said, he followed his server to the owner's desk and watched as she skillfully passed her hands over a series of sensors.

"Sit back," she said, "and this will all be over in a few moments."

Robin felt his usual anticipation preceding a Change. He stared at the mandala pulsing in the air before him. Its projectors subtly sensed his mood and matched its beats to his alpha rhythm. Then it came, the snapping, tearing sensation, and he cried out briefly.

When Robin came back to herself, she was an elfin, dark-furred naked squirrel girl. She dressed, then hurried to meet her new clients. Something had changed then, in her perceptions of the couple, and she found herself smiling. It would be nice to exercise the skills she'd been trained to use, and getting paid wouldn't hurt, either.

She waved cheerily to the other Changed guests she met, turned once more into the hallway, rapped briefly at the door, and entered the office to find two servers wrestling Robin Coope's old body out of the owner's chair.

"Be done here in a sec," one of them wheezed.

The Farmers watched, aghast. Robin walked over to them, and suddenly she found herself smiling again: at them, at Molly, and at John, and at the obvious bulge that was their baby.

"Molly? John? It's me, Robin Coope. Again."

* * *

It took the better part of the afternoon to get the Farmers registered with the Web as immigrants. Robin arranged for living quarters, paid for by one of the few anthropological societies extant on the Web. She got their Ident cards fabbed at a public printer, listed them with emergency services, and bought a muumuu for Molly. She felt livelier than she had in decades.

She even wangled a stipend from the anthro team to hold her over while introducing the Farmers to 22nd Century Earth.

The next morning, Robin entered her brand new office. The room was spacious, almost four meters square. The cameras were innocuous, the couches low and inviting. The only intrusion was the invisible pattern of nanites riding in Robin's inner ear and passing on comments, questions, instructions, and judgments from her patrons.

"The Farmers are at the door," announced the room.

Robin ushered the couple into the room. "I hope you slept well," she said.

"Oh, we did," said Molly. "Thank you, Missus- Miss Robin." She blushed.

"Just Robin will do." She offered them seats and showed them the automenu on which they could order breakfast. "Just press any key, and the kitchen will deliver it to you. Are you comfortable? I mean, with talking about your situation?" She waited for a nod. "Ganymede cut all ties with Earth right after Changing became popular, so I'm not sure exactly where to start."

"We know about NullPop," offered John. "You don't birth anybody until somebody dies. I mean, really *dies*."

"That's right, we stabilized the population at twelve billion, and we don't allow pregnancies any more. We use the same technology that we use in Changing, except we allow a personality to grow in a vatbody."

"Why didn't anybody meet us when we landed?" Molly asked. "If one'a you had flown all the way out to Ganytown we'd have turned out the whole place to welcome you."

Robin cocked her head, listening to a dozen voices, then stilled them all by saying, "We don't like surprises. Suppose—suppose you're somebody who's lived a hundred and fifty years, and you know that, by jumping from body to body—by Changing—you can live as long as you want. You do one of two things: either you go out and do everything, experience as much of life as you can; or you shut down the part of you that wants to do novel things, because there's too much of a chance that you'll run out of new things to do, or one of those things might kill you. And, sure enough, over a century and a half, most of the more adventurous people ran out of luck, leaving the rest of us." Robin had distant memories of windsurfing, of mountain-biking, but they were slippery, almost intangible, as if they had happened to someone else. Which, when she thought about it, they had.

Molly shifted uneasily on her cushion, studying the menu. "I'm gettin' a chocolate milk. You want a chocolate milk, hon?"

John shook his head.

"Over the years," Robin continued, "we started to value a lack of curiosity. None of us look around at our neighbors, much less up at the sky. About the only change that's acceptable is *the* Change, because that's what keeps us alive."

"What happened to your body?" asked Molly. "Your other body, I mean."

"Oh, that?" Robin waved a hand. "It was just meat." A strangled noise came through her link, and she winced. "That was insensitive of me," she added quickly. "We don't have much respect for flesh and fur, I suppose, considering we put it on and take it off so readily. I was in that male body for twelve years, and was a female mink before that. But we really don't have the resources to bury or waste good flesh like that, even when it was a little on the old side."

Molly's drink had arrived, and she made a production of sniffing it and setting it aside before turning a half-frightened, half-determined glare on Robin. "You all are very different, but it all comes down to this." She put both hands on her belly. "Do you have respect for this baby of ours? Can we bring it into the world, and love it like we ought to?"

Robin chose her words carefully, aware she was trying to span the vast void between worlds. "We understand your attraction to your… offspring. While we have no intention or desire to interfere with familial attraction—"

"What?"

Robin sighed. "We know you love your baby. We will certainly allow you to bring it to term. To birth it, as you say."

"And after?"

"Population Control, NullPop, is not a flexible agency. They have rules for immigration; they'll just delay two personality implants for you and your husband. But there is no option open for natural births; it's not just illegal, it's unheard of." She didn't say 'repugnant'. "Everyone on Earth is made allergic to embryos."

John was standing, folding his fingers into the palms of his hands in a way that made Robin uneasy. From behind him, Molly said, "They can make a—an option, can't they? Make it so another person doesn't implant, right?"

Robin stood and walked toward the couple, intent on calming them. "Maybe, sure, maybe. Look, if you're so concerned about your baby, we can try to find somebody who'd want to Change into its body. I couldn't guarantee it, but—"

The movement was sudden, caught only in Robin's peripheral vision, then the man's folded hand caught her on the side of her head and neck, knocking the much smaller squirrel into the menu console, off which she crumpled to the floor.

That's something else we've gotten rid of in the last century, noted a voice in her ear she barely heard before chasing darkness down to nothing.

* * *

"They call it a 'fist.'" The capybara doctor was hesitant, obviously as rusty at his skill as she was at teaching. "He appears to have used it to break a vertebra in your neck. I don't believe you will be able to move anything from there down. At one time there were mechanical remedies for these types of injuries, but of course with Changing they've gone out of style."

Robin stared at the ceiling. "Where are they?"

"The Farmers? Oh, they were Changed. Some kind of law having to do with violent offenders." The doctor shone a light in one of Robin's eyes, then flicked it away. "They're much happier now. Are you ready to Change?" The question was a formality; already the mandala was forming in the air above Robin's eyes.

"I suppose," she said. "I suppose I'm ready now. Would you make me a male, please? Perhaps a lynx, if there's a mature one available." As the doctor refocused the mandala, Robin's last thoughts moved back to her teenage years, when she had been suicidal, sure that her wish to be the opposite sex was perverse. She remembered, keenly, imagining the magic coming down and changing her: sprouting hair on her face, flattening her chest, narrowing her hips, and so on. The thoughts, newly minted, were yet ones she remembered from all the female bodies she'd had. It was comforting.

"What happened to the Farmers' baby?"

The capybara wheeled a portable terminal to the bedside and ran a sure hand over its diagnostic lightbuttons. "I'm not sure. I could check for you."

"No," said Robin. "Don't bother." She knew what had happened to it.

Then the snapping, the tearing, and soon Robin came back to himself.

In 1997, there was a short-lived online website, Mark Phaedrus' *Transformation Stories Contests*, for several contests to write a story involving transformations around set themes. One of them was as follows:

> Come up with a game, or a sport, that involves shapeshifting. The game doesn't have to be friendly; it could be a way of resolving duels, for example. It can involve violence, but it shouldn't be violent to the degree that death of a player is likely. It can involve sex, if your tastes run that way. :-)
>
> Creativity is key here; just taking an existing game and tacking shapeshifting on it, like the story with the poker game where the losers were turned into bimbos, probably won't do the trick.
>
> The game doesn't have to exclusively involve shapeshifting—if the players were wizards, for example, it could involve other kinds of magic as well. But shapeshifting should play a major role; otherwise the story is on the wrong list. :-)
>
> If you just write down the rules of your game, that's all you need to do. But you'll get major extra credit if you can also write an interesting story about the game.

"Transmutational Transcontinental" by Phil Geusz was the winner. When we asked a few months ago if we could republish it here, he said that he had forgotten all about it long ago! It was one of the first ten stories that he wrote as an adult.

Transmutational Transcontinental

by Phil Geusz

Always Think Outside the Box!

That was the slogan engraved on the cover of my laptop, and I did my absolute best to live by it. A transmutational racer must at heart be an optimist, and that went double for me. I spent hours and sometimes even days before every event poring over the rules, seeking out loopholes, oversights and inspiration. Such large purses were well worth a little skull-sweat! But this year's North American Classic regulations seemed entirely bulletproof. The race looked to be a straight run for the money. I scowled in frustration and scratched an itchy ear with a hindpaw. Damnit! I'd won more than a few easy victories in the past by outthinking race committees, but they were catching on fast. This year it looked like I'd have to win the hard way if I wanted to remain champion.

I *hated* the hard way. It was too much work!

The year's biggest competition (and largest purse!) was a toughie— New York to San Francisco by paw, hoof or whatever; racer's choice. We were permitted to set our own courses, choose our own forms, and take our own chances. All the transcontinentals worked like that. Humans have always raced against each other by every means available. Cars, carriages, pogo sticks... If miles can be made with it, it's been raced. Most likely with great intensity and enthusiasm. So when transmutation technology became both widespread and cheap, new forms of racing quite naturally followed. At first it was human horses, but soon there were cheetahs, pigeons, hawks, frogs, whales, baboons...

Since the sport was a natural for tridee, high profile events quickly grew both intense and frequent. Serious prize money and endorsement contracts were on the line almost weekly. Once you hit the pro level, well... I rarely had time to become human between competitions anymore. Even as I prepared for the second annual North American Classic, I was still wearing the jackrabbit's body that'd carried me to a very respectable second-place finish in the Outback Dash. The winner made the obvious choice of camel form, as did the third, fourth, fifth, sixth, seventh, eighth, ninth and tenth-place finishers. My schtick was to put on more of a show via not choosing the obvious while still remaining a serious contender. Second place was plenty good enough to keep me well up in the point standings for the year. Besides, the sponsors paid a lot better for something different. Especially, they paid well for a form that just might not survive the event. At the finish line of the Outback I actually drew more media attention than the winner. In the long run I expected to earn considerably more than she did as well.

Sighing, I used the pencil in my mouth to press the "page back" key repeatedly on my machine until once again ready to begin at the beginning. Most of the rules were pretty straightforward. The race was to run from the foot of the Empire State Building to the Golden Gate Bridge. Except for defined paths through the cities at both ends of the course, travel by road or rail right-of-way was forbidden. Competitors were required to live entirely off the land—trashcan-raiding was specifically prohibited, though farms and household gardens were fair game—and weren't allowed any contact with humans except for the media's filming and officially-supervised interviews en-route. Sign-reading was permitted - one could hardly avoid the things, after all. And water and shelter were where you found them, natural or otherwise. Mostly, however, racers were forbidden from utilizing any human-built infrastructure. The race was meant to be all about we competitors and the forms we'd chosen versus time, distance and the local ecology, pretty much the standard package on the transmutational circuit these days. We weren't even allowed to speak; if we used our vocal implants for anything but sanctioned interviews we'd be disqualified.

This particular competition was relatively open in regard to permissible forms. We could compete as any mammal, reptile, or flightless bird known to be extant in the year 1900. I smiled at this last requirement, or would've were a jackrabbit's face designed that way. Last year I'd taken advantage of the "any reptile" loophole to become a pteranodon with a forty-foot wingspan and win the event in an easy glide. But it wasn't going to be so easy this time around. Try as I might, I couldn't find a way to cheat the system. Sighing quietly—hares habitually sigh in near silence, lest they become something's dinner—I turned off the computer and laid down on the carpet. Reading the screen through jackrabbit eyes was giving me a headache, and I wasn't learning anything new.

In transmutational racing form selection is *everything*. Species choice is the key to both winning and making boatloads of money alike. Everything else is secondary, driven by this most vital of all decisions. A competitor has to be able to easily find nourishment and avoid danger, all the while moving as quickly as possible through the various terrains and biomes. But this event was unique in that there were so *many* biomes! First there came the East Coast suburbs, then the Appalachians, the cornfields of the Midwest, the plains, the Rockies... It was awesome to contemplate. A competitor could easily (and sometimes did) end up starving, being eaten, falling off a cliff, drowning, getting shot, or even end up as road kill. And weighing these risks was just the *first* step—after that, it was time to think about winning!

Personally, I always worried more about river crossings than anything else. We carried an internal electric shocker-thingie that— usually at least—deterred predators, though using it meant automatic disqualification. But you can't shock an angry river into submission! This particular event featured far too many oversized waterways for my taste. The only way to avoid major crossings was to select a far-north routing and do an end-around of the entire Mississippi Valley. Most of my competitors would probably end up doing exactly that. It was also a pretty safe bet that almost everyone else would choose some long-legged deer or equine or perhaps even antelope form to compete in. That way, finding food would be relatively simple and long-distance running would come naturally. Which in turn meant that these obvious options were closed to me. I had a reputation for originality to maintain, after all!

A cougar, perhaps? No, predators never worked out. Hunting took too long.

I sat back and gnawed at my pencil some more. *Hmm...*

A buffalo? I'd have no predation worries, plus the advantage of being in historically-correct natural habitat practically all the way. And a good ol' American Bison could make pretty decent time. I'd have to avoid the river crossings like everyone else, though...

Then I scowled. It just wasn't original enough. Let the also-rans take that route. True victory—*profitable* victory!—would lie in figuring out a way to both take the most direct route *and* be different while doing it.

What about that Chinese water buffalo I'd once read about—the kind that was bred long ago to pull small barges in canals by swimming in front of them? The species could handle the river crossings sure enough, but would be slow, slow, slow over land…

It was really too bad about those rivers. If it weren't for them I'd have been half tempted to remain a jackrabbit. I was well adapted to being a hare; the form suited me, particularly well in psychological terms. It'd also save me time in the tank, freeing me up for more extensive route research than any of the other competitors would be able to manage. The individuals I was most worried about were all still camels at the moment and would certainly spend weeks changing forms in order to meet the demands of North America. Jackrabbits were surprisingly capable of covering ground, and easy to feed as well. Even in the heart of the Australian desert I'd eaten almost every single day. Since the race was being held in summer, the form could survive easily anywhere on the continent…

…except in the rivers. I shivered at the very *thought* of facing all that water as a hare. There were limits to the risk-level that even someone as crazy as me could accept, and swimming the Mississippi as a bunny rabbit was well off the chart. We competitors were equipped with built-in panic buttons and tracers, of course. But one could drown *awfully* fast…

I sighed again and put the hare-brained idea aside. Permanently.

Then I had another thought. Perhaps I had my priorities backwards? Raccoons could swim. And they were native almost everywhere along the way too. I just might manage the Big Muddy as a 'coon. But could I cover the rest of the distance quickly enough? I had a deadline to beat, one set by galloping horses and swift deer…

No. I'd still be far too slow, even with the others traveling so much further. Damnit!

Well, then! Perhaps I could use all that water to my advantage? What if I took some sort of otter form? Then I'd swim most of the way; the Ohio, Mississippi and Missouri would become highways instead of barriers. And that wasn't even considering the minor streams that might allow me to work my way even closer to my goal. After all, the western slope of the Rockies was pretty wet—probably the only long stretch I'd have to walk would be over the Divide itself, plus a few other little portages here and there. I could fish as I traveled, live predator free, and let the current help me along a good part of the way…

…while also having the same current work against me for even more miles, I realized suddenly. Plus, I'd also have to travel all the curves of the rivers instead of taking a straight shot.

Hell *and* damnation!! This was *tough*!

Last year's contest had been much easier. Before the race I'd mapped out a series of cliffs and river bluffs to overnight on. In the mornings I simply let the warming air lift me effortlessly to altitude. Then I'd glide effortlessly west to my next roost, expending little to no energy along the way. My reptilian metabolism was extremely efficient, though I was forced to hunt a bit from time to time. A couple deer, along with some carrion here and there, proved plenty enough to see me through. (Fortunately, carrion tasted just fine while I was a pteranodon.) The rivers had been nothing, no trouble at all…

Which was precisely *why* the officials had ensured there'd be no flying forms this time around. They didn't *like* it when people thought outside of their little boxes.

Then I blinked, and a little light bulb lit up just above my long ears.

I switched my machine back on and carefully looked over the rules again. No species extinct before 1900. Avian forms allowable, but must be flightless. Reptiles were also legal. As well as all mammals…

I stood up on all fours and kicked my hind legs over and over again in sheer joy, then frolicked to and fro about my apartment as I poured out my feelings in hare-bodied fashion. I had them, I had them, I had them! I was going to win again, and nothing could stop me! They'd left another loophole!

After kicking the air one last time for the sheer joy of it, I headed back to the study. Though my panting would make keyboarding even more difficult than usual, I settled in to do some serious research. It was all *so* much fun!

What kind of bat was I going to be? I couldn't wait to find out!

Metamor Keep *is one of the oldest shared-world fiction series in furry fandom. It was created by Copernicus (Kevin Deenihan) in November 1997 with a story of the same title on the online TSA (Transformation Story Archive)-Talk mailing list. In a fantasy medievalish world, Metamor Keep castle and its nearby civilian town are attacked by Nasoj, a powerful human black wizard, and his army of Lutins (basically gremlins). Nasoj casts a complex spell on MK, with the result (grossly simplified) of transforming all its inhabitants into either anthropomorphic animals, age-regressed people (adults in children's bodies), or reversed genders (men into women and vice-versa). Nasoj is defeated, but his spell is permanent. What's more, it also affects anyone who spends more than a week in MK and its surrounding lands. After writing the original story, Copernicus allowed others to write their own sequels. Today, the MK website is run by a committee headed by Christian O'Kane, and has over 570 stories by over 80 authors, from short-short stories to massive novels. (http://metamorkeep.com/)*

For An Anthropomorphic Century, we have concentrated on stories featuring the anthro animal "Keepers" only. "Daylight Fading" by Chris Hoekstra is one of the best of these. (Also, frankly, one of the few that does not require an extensive familiarity with the series as a whole). The focus is upon just two characters; Rickkter, a warrior turned into an anthro raccoon, and Kayla, an upper-class lady turned into an anthro skunk. How their transformations have affected them is a good example of the Metamor Keep *world.*

Daylight Fading

by Chris Hoekstra

Kayla reached down and took the white rook, replacing it with her bishop. "You're not on your game tonight, Rick. What's the matter? You've lost six already."

The raccoon seated across from her reached up to massage his neck. His movements had a kind of lethargic motion to them that had been prevalent all evening. She watched as he slowly rubbed the muscles under his thick gray fur, eyes closed and lost in the shadows of his face as the lamplight highlighted the white on his face and nose.

"I'm sorry," he murmured in a gravelly voice. "I guess I'm just not very good company tonight."

Reaching across the table, Kayla gave his arm a quick rub, dragging her small claws through his fur. She knew how much he liked that. The fact that his eyes opened and a smile came to his face was proof enough of that. "Bad day?"

Rickkter gave a half-hearted murr and looked into her eyes. The light from the many candles glinted from his brown eyes. "You could say that, my dear," he said with a small smile. "I spent the afternoon with Caroline."

"Ah, I see. Is she getting better?"

"Some. Physically, she's doing remarkably well. I figure that she might be able to start using her hands again within the next week. Mentally?" He shook his furry head. "That I couldn't tell you."

"I do hope she feels better soon," muttered Kayla. She had picked up one of Rick's bishops she had captured earlier and was turning it end over end between her fingers. "I like her, and it hurts to see her like that."

A small smile came to the raccoon's lips. "She likes you, too. Claims it's nice to talk to someone who isn't a soldier, just another woman. She also told me you're invited to stop in and see her sometime this week. Something about planning a 'surprise' for her man."

Kayla snickered, still toying with the chess piece. "Oh, I wouldn't doubt that. Are you going to ever make a move?" she asked with a nod of her head to the board.

"Yes I am." He stood up and walked across the room to the door, stopping half way and turning back to her. "I'm going to get a late dinner. Would you care to join me?"

"Hum, let me think about that." Kayla leaned back in her chair a little and tapped a claw on the game board. "I could either go with you and get some food, alleviating that pesky feeling of starvation I've been having for the last few hours. Or I could sit here and hold intimate conversations with a bunch of wooden game pieces, hoping to divine the answers to the universe."

Rick's ears perked up to full attention. "Really? Well, let me know what all of you finally figure out, then."

The skunk's sharp, barking laugh brought a smile to the raccoon's face. "Just for that one, you're taking me someplace good. For a change," said Kayla as she sauntered over, her lush tail swishing around behind her. "And you're paying for it all," she emphasized with a poke to his chest.

Rickkter chuckled as he slipped on his coat and put an arm around Kayla as she wrapped her tail around his waist and snuggled up against his chest. "Well, considering it's you, I suppose I can." As he looked down at Kayla, it struck her that he seemed to want to do something else. Instead, he just gave her shoulder a little squeeze and started out of the room.

Kayla kept close to the raccoon's side, and was pleased that he left his arm where it was. It was so nice to have someone that wanted her close like that. So long had she been nearly alone, with just Jessica and some of the gang from The Tavern's Heath for comfort, only now to have two people interested in her. Muri was easy enough to explain to her mind. He was a skunk, he had never been around any other morphs before, and he looked to her for guidance. After all, he had that mink, whom his heart seemed to belong to.

The thought of Llyn sent a small shiver though her. Like so many others, Llyn seemed to possess an irrational hatred of Kayla. Normally such behavior would have been written off to the fact that she was a skunk. But Muri was a skunk and Llyn didn't seem to have a problem with him. Which, of course, left the fact that she was a female skunk. Jessica was probably right; Llyn viewed Kayla as competition for Muri's affections.

Drawing her companion closer, causing Rickkter to sway a little as they walked, Kayla murred contentedly to herself. She had her own man, what did she need with anyone else's? Of course she couldn't understand Rickkter's motivations. From the first time they had met, he had always been something of a mystery. Why they were drawn to each other, she didn't know. But based on the results, she didn't much care. The smell of new leather filling her nostrils was enough for that. Rickkter had had no reason to ask her to help him select the jacket he was wearing, and while she had been surprised at first by his request, she had enjoyed the trip. That had been a few days ago, and this was only the second time she had to see how handsome he looked in it.

And handsome he did look. It was times like this that Kayla noticed just how much the curse had changed some of his extremities. The body was still humanoid, retaining much of its original shape and build. Unlike Brian Coe, Rickkter's arms and legs had retained their human proportion instead of acquiring the squatter animalistic ones some keepers had. That feature was one of the few they had in common. Rickkter walked with his tail swishing behind him near his feet, unlike Kayla who carried hers up against her back to keep from catching it on anything. There was nothing remarkable about his face; the muzzle was slightly elongated as opposed to her own, but it fit his raccoon profile. As did the black mask and grayish ears. Unlike the thin layer of her own, his were covered with thick, grey fur.

A smile came to her lips at the memory of playing with them several days back. They had been out at the Mule along with Misha the fox, Caroline the otter, and other Long Scouts. She had left for a moment to freshen up, and when she came back she had walked behind him. It was probably her good mood resulting from the good wine that gave her reason to reach out and lightly touch one his ears. She had only touched the guard hairs, where they stuck up just above the rest of the fur, and laughed at the erratic flicking it produced. So did the rest of the table, though Rickkter was quick to hunch his head down and glare back at her. But his eyes shone with a good humor that kept the grin on her face.

"What are you smiling at?" Rickkter asked.

Kayla snapped back to the present then looked up at him. She snuggled up against his arm. "Oh, nothing really. Just remembering Misha's face the other day, when you dumped that whole pitcher of mead over his head when he kept teasing you about being sprayed by Muri."

Rickkter shook his head. "I don't know which I want to hurt more, the skunk or the fox."

"I suggest the fox. Safer that way."

"I think so, too," Rickkter admitted as he squeezed her arm. "So have you decided on where to go for this expensive dinner of yours?"

"Jolly Collie, I think. From what I remember from the reports on that whole incident with Bolva, it sounds like a nice place."

"At least we know the food can't be half bad if Long Scouts can survive it."

Kayla burst into laughter. "Longs can live on bark and dirt and *like* it."

"Let us hope they have first class bark here, then!"

The skunk and raccoon both dissolved into laughter and sauntered down the street, arm in arm, in a mildly drunken manner, looking for their restaurant.

* * *

The main room of the Jolly Collie was only sparsely populated with various keepers and a few traders and teamsters staying for the night. There were other couples at the tables and several groups occupying the long table with benches near the one wall. A few solitary drinkers dotted the bar. Kayla and her raccoon had a table near the hearth, where a small fire glowed.

Their orders had been placed with the serving girl several minutes ago, and they were just passing time now. Kayla had made good on her threat of ordering an expensive meal; she would be dining on a dish of thrushes braised in wine sauce, stuffed with figs. At least the cup of wine she ordered to go with that wasn't too much more.

"You know, that sounds good," Rickkter commented. Never the less, he chose something a little easier on his funds for the evening; he ordered pheasant with a cup of mead.

Jessica had been right, Kayla reflected. She was lucky to have Rickkter. But it was then she realized she didn't really know anything about him. Like much of the Keep, she knew the regions he was from and what he used to do. But she didn't really know anything about him.

"I've been wondering, Rick. How old are you?"

He turned back from gazing at the fireplace. The flames from the fragrant wood that was burning reflected brilliant amber off the white around his nose and mask, and Rickkter's eyes flashed gold for an instant as they caught the light just right. "Thirty-four, why?"

Oh, not as old as she had expected at first. They weren't that far apart then. "As of when?"

Rickkter shrugged. "Some time in the summer."

Blinking once, the skunk frowned at him. "What do you mean?"

Sighing, Rickkter put his elbows up on the table and leaned across from her. By his tone, she could tell he had done this before. "I mean, that

I don't know an exact date when I was born. I don't even know a season for certain. It's just that each summer I feel older, so I decided that's when it would be. Heck, even age is an estimate. Where I grew up, seasons don't change much, so I had few benchmarks to go by, resorting to comparing myself to other people. How about yourself?"

Kayla was a little taken aback by that. "Um, twenty-nine. Born late June. Rick, what about your parents? I'd be interested in what kind of a family you had before coming here."

It was obvious she had touched something there, for Rickkter's expression hardened and his whiskers drooped down to over his hands where they rested beneath his chin. "Perhaps you should go first with that one."

Kayla looked down at the table and ran her tongue over her jowls. "Well, where to begin?" she said, wuffing a laugh. "You already know my grandfather, so I don't know what I could say there." Kayla's grandfather was Elijhah Tremayne, a renowned tactician famous for advocating unconventional tactics over more accepted battlefield manoeuvres. She had found earlier that Rickkter was an admirer of the man. "That just leaves my immediate family, then.

"I really don't know my mother. She died when I was very young and my father rarely spoke of her. I often wonder if my father ever really loved her. His name was Andrew. You see, my grandfather had acquired a good deal of wealth during the wars and never really did anything to manage it. On the other hand, while my father never really took to games of war, he did have quite a head for money. Over several years he took a small fortune and had made it a very modest one by the time he met my mother. From what I gather— from what my grandfather told me—it was a marriage of alliance and power. After two years of that, I was born. A year later my mother was dead; she caught some dreadful disease that they couldn't cure. After that, we moved around a lot, eventually winding up in Chantry.

"Have you ever been there, Rick?" she asked. He shook his head. "It's a wonderful city. Very cultured. You can feel the ages past when you walk the streets. The houses have a good bit of charm to them, and the temples and gardens are often breathtaking. You'd be amazed at the amount of marble in some of them. And that is where I spent most of my years growing up."

The mephit shook her head and leaned back, the firelight dancing off the white markings of her face. In the old days, it would have danced off the gold at her neck and in her hair. Briefly she lost herself in the memories of another time, a time when she had been beautiful. Rickkter's rather deep dislike of nobility came to her mind as she started with the next part. "I spent those years enjoying the privileges that wealth brought. In Chantry the Tremayne name held influence. Oh, not too much, but enough. I had no worries, no cares, none of what the average woman my age had to contend with. My grandfather was still a large part of my life. In fact, he basically took over the role of father for me, as my real one was now occupied almost full time with his money. He kept up the role of banker and a moneylender, much to his father's disapproval. Grandpa always wanted him to carry on the family tradition of military service, even if he was just an officer. My father didn't want any of that, he was more interested in managing the money and reaping the rewards there. Eventually my father won out."

Her eyes lowered to the table top, and she started picking at a groove in the grain with a claw. "And so I grew up in a life of pleasure and privilege. Until he died when I was nineteen, my grandfather was about the only

man I had to learn from. After his death, my father and I moved up here. He had heard there were some new trade routes opening up and figured he could get in on some good business opportunities. That was… god, that was ten years ago now." She sighed, remembering.

"So I take it you had a great deal of suitors, then?" asked Rick. His voice was so quiet that Kayla almost missed hearing it. She looked up briefly and noticed that he was lounging back in his seat, one arm over the back. His posture was casual, but she could see in his expression that he was listening to everything she said.

"You might say that," she admitted as a small smile played on her muzzle. "They weren't exactly beating my door down, but they were there. I wasn't the most beautiful woman, but I had my charms. They were attracted to those, but mostly it was the money, I think. And after the Battle of the Gates, that was all gone." Kayla's smile quickly turned bitter. "Over the course of several days I lost everything. The raiders destroyed our home just outside the Keep, smashing anything they couldn't take. Metamor needed all the warriors they could get, so my father and the man whom I loved then went out to try and hold the Lutins off." A single tear rolled over the black fur of her cheek as she squeezed her eyes shut. "Nasoj took them both from me. And then he took the last thing I had; my body. And gave me this," she concluded with a disgusted flick of her paw.

"But you made it," Rickkter said. Leaning forward, he reached, grasping Kayla's other one where it lay on the table. He squeezed it between his own. "You made it through that and you're here now. You can't ask much more."

Kayla was still focused on the past and the gesture was lost on her. "You think so, do you?" she asked sarcastically. "After the Battle, I was left with next to nothing. For the first time in my life I was left without family and the support it and its money provided. Most of my father's assets were tied up in business ventures and the Lutins had stolen much of the rest. After the Gates, most of his creditors didn't think they had to pay a dead man, and so didn't. I spent a day going through what was left of my home, picking out things that might be of value and looking for any currency they may have missed. I didn't find a lot in either case. The friends that I thought I had? Gone. Either dead, uninterested in a poor girl, or repulsed by my form.

"I was abandoned by everyone!" she growled, snatching her hand away. "I had never worked a day in my life and had no idea what to do. The money I had, what little there was, only lasted for eight months in rent and food. I even had to skip meals to stretch that out as it was." She decided to skip over the whole affair with John Glass. "About the only one I had at that time was Jessica. That was it.

"Do you know it was her who got me that job with intelligence? Even so, I practically begged for the job." She shook her head. "At least I had my father's memory for facts and my grandfather's ability to out-think the enemy, or I never would have lasted. At least when Phil finally took over about a year later it got better." Rick knew that Phil, due to his rather permanent, high-degree change into a rabbit, was unable to write for himself, so he often dictated things to her when he needed it done quickly. "And that's pretty much where I've been ever since."

Her timing for the conclusion was perfect, as it coincided nicely with the arrival of their food. Rickkter graciously accepted his plate of pheasant, starting to pick at it almost as soon as he had it down. Kayla paused over her meal inhaling the sensuous aromas. It had been a very long time indeed since she had indulged in this particular taste. Picking up one of the small birds with her fingers, she tore off a wing, the skin and cartilage tearing wetly. The skunk's sharp teeth made quick work of the morsel, sucking the tender meat from the bone. It had been far too long since she had experienced this. When she was done with the wing, she looked over at her companion. He was resolutely working on his own dish, giving her no regard.

"You still haven't answered my question, Rick."

Rickkter shrugged and looked up at her. "Not a lot to tell."

"Well, just tell me what there is." She licked some of the sauce from her muzzle. "It's only fair. Believe it or not, you're the first person, besides Jessica—since the Curse—whom I've told my story to. So, come on."

"Well, where to start? You already know I don't have an exact birth date. Would it surprise you to learn I also don't have any real family name?" Kayla's brow shot up and her eyes grew a little wider. "Heh, I guess it did. It's true, though; I have no family name, no kingdom, and no place to call home. My physical characteristics mark me—er, marked me as northeastern, yet my earliest memories are of the Southlands, with my father. Unlike you, I don't know my father's name. If any of the people we ever met used it, I can't recall. All I know, was that he looked like me, called me his son, and taught me some magic. The last I saw of him was when I was a little over seven, when he left me with a sect of warriors to become one of them. I can't tell you why he did it, only I think he might have been suffering from the same thing I was when I came here. Either way, I was never told and doubt I'll ever find out."

Between mouthfuls of pheasant, he retold of his history with the Kankoran, Ebon, and after. His early life was kept as vague as he could manage, no names being used. He gave different details, mostly of his travels, during other parts. The only part he kind of stumbled over was

Deanna. Of course he always stumbled there. She had been the best thing in his life and he had been responsible for destroying her. At least the pretense of the food allowed him to gloss over the parts he didn't want to or couldn't talk about.

"Wow. I don't think I've heard anything like that before. Ever since you showed me around your apartment that one day, I've been wondering where a person like you would learn to play the violin. And you do a wonderful job of it, too."

He smiled at her, his hands coming together beneath his chin. "Thank you. Oh, you remember how I told you I spent the afternoon with Caroline? Well, it seems she's decided to take up the flute. She's been practicing a bit overmuch now, but when her hands have healed some more she'll attack it with vigor."

"If she's as good at that as she is at archery, than I look forward to hearing some of her playing. Perhaps you and her could get together, have a little duet?"

With a smile and a nod, the raccoon across from her agreed it was a distinct possibility. They then quietly resumed their dinners, trying to finish the meals before they went completely cold. Kayla mulled over in her mind what he had told her, trying to see how both the story and the man across from her fit the image she knew. It was an odd combination, and a fascinating one all the same. But there was one more thing she wanted to know.

"So what are your feelings about being changed into a raccoon morph, Rick?"

"What are my feelings about the transformation?" repeated Rickkter. He raised his paws, resting his chin on his thumbs, and idly clicked his index fingers together. "I think I've come to accept that I'm stuck like this forever. But... I've realized it's not so bad. I've always been here, I've always looked out from behind these eyes. Nothing can change that." He closed his eyes and sighed. "It feels like it's taken me a lifetime to realize that."

"So what finally made you do it?"

Much to Kayla's surprise, Rickkter's hand snaked out and took hold of hers. "My friends helped a lot. They've dealt with it for years." He raised both their paws off the table a few inches and imparted a small lick on her knuckles. "I think you've helped the most. A... lovely lady who has spent time with me by her own choice."

Kayla was quite taken aback by such a comment. Oddly enough, she found herself laughing over the whole notion while her cheeks burned red underneath their black fur. "You're glad I spent time with you? Why do you say that?"

Letting go of her hand, Rickkter withdrew his own, looking away and flicking his eye ridges. "Well… because it's true. All of my other friends are either warriors or mages. Misha, Caroline, Kershaw, even Muri… but, uh, I like to think you're different." He snickered. "At least you're certainly a sight prettier than Misha."

If she didn't have her mouth full, Kayla might have laughed. As it was, she only managed to snort, then giggled around her food as she tried to chew. "Is that a compliment?" she finally managed to get out.

Rickkter smirked. "I would advise taking it at one, yes."

Kayla laughed, then returned to her food, working to finish her meal of the thrushes. It was the most luxurious meal she had eaten in years and probably more than she should have asked of Rick. He could certainly have objected had it bothered him, yet he hadn't. She was secretly glad for that. She felt like something special tonight, something extravagant. Something to make her feel like her old self again.

Her mind drifted back to what he had said to her. Rick had been spending time with her for, what? A couple of months now? At least since the summer solstice festival. That had been the first time he had asked her to join him for anything. Heck, it had been the first time anyone had asked her to join them for anything like that in far too long. Of course she was reminded of Glass and had shied away. But still, there was… something about him, and she had realized that after their evening in The Tavern's Hearth. During their time together she had also gotten to know his friends better, especially Caroline. She had known the Long Scout from reports, but had never really gotten to know her. She could empathize with the otter over what had happened to her…

A cry of indignation caused the skunk to look up from her meal and across the tavern. There, near the far end of the bar, was a man dressed in the garb of a trader who had his hand locked on the arm of one of the wenches. The server was a young girl, probably not quite eighteen, and wasn't taking the advances of the trader well. From the look of things, the girl probably still wasn't totally comfortable with her female form. Kayla looked over the bar wondering where the owner was and why he wasn't doing anything about it, and why no one else was helping. But considering the man was about six-foot-four and most of his over two-hundred pound frame was muscle, it was unlikely anyone would want to even try and stop him. He also looked to be almost twice as old as the young girl he was trying to take.

"Aren't you going to do something about that, Rick?"

The raccoon looked up from his food and over at the small commotion. "Not my business," he mumbled around a bite.

Kayla shot him an incredulous look.

Rickkter looked up at her and saw the look on her face. He cringed and stopped eating. "Okay, okay. I'll go over there and see if I can do anything."

He didn't know why he said that, as he got up from their table and started over across the tavern. As he had told Kayla, this wasn't his business; if the girl really was unwilling, then her boss could sort it out. Besides, this was a natural thing in bars all over the world.

So why was he doing it?

The answer was surprisingly simple; because she had asked. Well, because she had more or less demanded it of him. If it had been anyone else he would have argued the point or told them to go do it themselves. Not her. No, she was something different, someone… special? to him. And now here he was, standing behind a large, obnoxious, foul smelling trader.

"Hey," Rickkter barked. "Lady doesn't appear interested. Let her go."

"And I say that all she needs is a little persuading," growled back the man as he moved his face a few inches closer to the squirming tavern waitress. Rickkter could tell by his thick accent he was Fassitian. "Now be a good little raccoon and leave me be."

Okay, the direct approach was for naught, so Rickkter tried something else. "Do you have a thing for men? You do know she used to be a man, didn't you? We're all cursed here, even those that don't appear to be."

"And I don't think you heard ME," snarled the trader as he turned his face to Rickkter. "Leave us. Now. Before you regret it."

Subtle humor wasn't working, so onto something more drastic. "Look, you ugly cretin, I'm sure you're not as stupid as you look. Nobody could be. Now, since you're obviously depriving a village somewhere of its idiot. Let the girl go and get out of here."

The man's face was an ugly scowl as he inched it closer to Rickkter. "Or what?"

Rickkter's rabbit punch hit the man solidly on his stubble-covered jaw. When subtly didn't work, more often than not, hostility did. Or so the raccoon had found.

The face of the trader went from surprise to rage in an instant. Rickkter had guessed right; this man was a bully. And like any bully, he was shocked to discover that someone would actually stand up to him, let alone physically strike him. Getting to his feet, the man all but threw the girl to the ground as he towered over Rickkter, trying to use his bulk to intimidate the Keeper. Considering he had over half a foot and about eighty pounds on the raccoon, there was a good chance of that happening. Or so his imposing stance seemed to indicate he believed. Their exchange was drawing looks from all over the Jolly Collie.

"You flea ridden, piece of shit," the man growled in his native tongue. "You'll pay for that. Your hide is going to be lining my wagon seat when I leave here tomorrow."

Rickkter had never been impressed by bullies and that had led to a lot of fights in his youth. Of course, he had won most of them and against people who were larger than this hulking trader. This was a man whom experience taught that he could get others to do anything he wanted simply by pressing them hard enough. Well, Rickkter wasn't one to bend under such pressure.

"Hey, look," he said, answering in the common tongue despite being able to understand what the other man had said perfectly well. He wanted to keep that for later. "I don't think either of us wants any trouble here, do we?"

"Your kind make me sick," snarled Rick's opponent in a drunken manner. "When I'm done with you, then I'm going to have fun with both the girl *and* that fucking stinking girlfriend of yours." He sneered down at the raccoon. "Not that someone like you could get anything better than that smelly bitch."

Rickkter's expression cooled instantly and he let the loud, drunken trader see exactly how large a mistake he had made. " Oh. Now you shouldn't have said that," he muttered.

Whatever the man was going to say when he opened his mouth would never be known, as Rickkter drove his fist deep into the man's gut. The trader let out a loud grunt as he was rocked back by the blow. His face went pale and his hands folded over his stomach by reflex.

Which allowed Rickkter to get a hold of the man's hair and smash his face against the top of the bar. The sharp, wet crack as the man's nose was crushed and several of his front teeth were knocked out drew the attention of the rest of the bar. The trader began to slide backwards, leaving a smeared trail of blood on the dark, scarred wood of the bar top. Pulling the man's head up, Rickkter put his muzzle next to the stunned trader's ear.

"You boke ma nose," the man muttered as he dabbed at his ruined face.

Rickkter shook his head to get the man's attention. "I'll break a hell of a lot more if I ever hear you speak that shit about her or any other Keeper again, understand?" he snarled in the man's ear.

The trader nodded dumbly.

"Good." Rickkter released him to slump against the bar, then delivered a swift chop to the back of the trader's bull neck. That crumpled the obnoxious human like the sack of shit he was.

When Rickkter looked up as he resettled his jacket on his shoulders, he noticed that the bar had gone silent and everyone in the place was looking at him. He adjusted the coat on his shoulders a little more and turned to a pair who were dressed similar to the man at his feet. "I believe your friend here has had a little too much to drink tonight. I suggest you take him back up to his room and see that he stays there for the rest of the night." The two nodded dumbly and came over to retrieve their unconscious friend.

Kayla sat in her chair looking rather stunned at the whole affair. She hadn't known what to expect when she asked Rickkter to go over there, but it wasn't that! The language the two had spoken had been unintelligible to her, but actions spoke louder than words. It was only now, while the two men were hauling out their friend, that fur on Rickkter's neck and tail was lying down. He watched the two men depart, then went to talk to the serving girl. By this time normal conversation had resumed, and they were talking in tones too low for her to hear anyway. Rickkter spent a few minutes in conversation with the girl before returning.

"So what did she have to say?" Kayla asked after Rickkter had seated himself and resumed his dinner.

The raccoon moved his eyes to look up at her, tearing off a bite of meat and swallowing it. "I just wanted to know if she was alright; she said she was. I also asked about those men. Apparently they're part of a convoy that will be heading out tomorrow morning."

"You're not worried that those three might try something?"

Rickkter shook his head. "Nah. I've been around people like that for years. They won't try anything tonight and they're leaving tomorrow. Anyway, if they did, I could handle them. His kind are nothing."

"Well, I hope you're right." Kayla went back to her meal, taking a bite off the breast of her remaining thrush. "What did he say to you?"

Rickkter eerfed at her.

"Just before you… bounced his face off the bar, what did he say to you?"

After swallowing his bite of pheasant Rickkter licked his chops. "Oh, that. That was just something inappropriate that I didn't believe should have been said in front of ladies." Without further explanation, Rickkter returned to his meal.

Kayla "Oh"ed as well and went back to her dinner. But something about the way Rickkter had said it, the look he had given her, told her that there was perhaps something more to that. She didn't know what it was, but only hoped she could find out soon.

* * *

Rickkter's distant mood carried over during their trip back to the Keep. He made conversation with Kayla readily enough, but never kept it going or initiated any of it on his own. Kayla tried to keep it up at first, but as their journey wore on she let it go and they walked in silence. Instead, she turned her thoughts inwards, trying to figure out what was making him act like this.

It wasn't the fight that was on his mind, that was certain. She had been out with him on a number of occasions to the Mule, where they had spent evenings at tables of Long Scouts, and he could match tales of bar fights with the best of them. Kayla also doubted that his tales were as blown out of proportion as a few she had heard, so it wasn't that.

But it was connected to that fight, somehow, of that she was certain. The only thing that it could have been was what the man said. When the man had starting going on the second time, in that guttural language of his, she had seen Rickkter's ears go flat against his head. Moments after that he had delivered two extraordinary fast blows, then was holding the man's beard while snarling viciously at him. Never had she seen Rickkter lose control like that.

They were ascending a wide, circular staircase with an open centre when the raccoon finally said something to her. "We still have that chess game, you know. Do you want to go back to my place and finish it?"

Kayla looked up at him and smiled. She squeezed his paw. "Sure."

When they walked into the room, Rickkter waved his paw causing the various lamps and candles to burst into flame. Such displays had at first taken Kayla by surprise, but she was used to it by now. Rickkter went over to his seat at the chess table and took his seat, perching over the pieces and wiggling his fingers as he tried to decide which piece to move.

But the female skunk wasn't ready for the game yet. Instead, she decided to examine some of the other things Rickkter's apartment held. As she was walking through the main room, passing the bookcase, something caught her attention at the corner of her eye. Stopping, she moved over to the small pile of papers where they sat upon their portfolio on the shelf. A small smile came to her face when she saw the top picture. She loved looking though such things, especially when it was Rickkter who had drawn them. The first time she had seen his drawings had been when she had stumbled upon him in the gardens one afternoon. They had spent that lunch looking over the different sketches and having such a good time in general that she wound up being late in getting back to work.

"Um, what are you looking at?" said Rick as he rose from his chair.

Kayla shuffled the top picture—Saroth basking in the new dawn light—to the bottom as she picked up the pile and moved closer to a stand of candles. "Your pictures. You didn't tell me you did any today." She moved past a portrait of another dragon, one named Gornul if memory served. "I don't know why. You know how I love these things, Rick."

"Kayla, I don't think…" he began, only to trail off when the skunk pulled free the next picture. From the look on her face, her wide eyes and her muzzle hanging open a few centimetres, he could tell exactly what picture she was looking so closely at. The silence dragged on as she stared at the picture, eventually lowering it and the rest to her side. Neither of them had anything to say.

"Rick," Kayla eventually ventured, "why did you do this? It… it's exquisite, but why did you do it? Why me?"

It was an inner battle for Rickkter, trying to reconcile what he should tell her. "Why does a painter paint what they do? Or a writer write? They do so because they have to, they feel a need to create what their muses demand they do. I am a slave to my muse, and you were the inspiration, the same as the rest." Well, that wasn't entirely a lie. The others were inspiration. Her picture, and the time invested to capture the details his mind's eye knew so well, that was something else. Something more.

"Oh, I see," replied the skunk as she put her picture back with the rest and returned the stack to its place on the shelf. Rickkter's eyes never left her, despite the fact that her gaze was directed somewhat at the floor and had a very nervous quality to it as she turned and headed out. "Good night," she whispered upon reaching the exit.

"Good night, my dear."

Kayla abruptly turned back though she still couldn't look at him. "Tell me something, Rick," said the mephit as she held out the sides of her skirt a little, her thick monochromatic tail swishing around behind her as she slowly danced from foot to foot. "Tell me… tell me if you think I'm pretty?"

Rickkter stood there, the light from a candelabra playing shifting patterns of candlelight where it showed on the lighter sections of his fur. The silence stretched, his eyes roving over her form several times, taking it in as though it were the first time he had ever really seen her. "No, I don't," was his eventual response.

The blue eyes of the female skunk across from him rose to meet his, something akin to shock and hurt welling up in them. Her tail drooped and her ears laid back flat against her skull.

Rickkter could scarcely believe the words that came to his lips next. He couldn't believe he was admitting this to her. "You are not pretty, you're beautiful. Very, very beautiful."

The smile that came to her face, her lovely, round black ears perking up at his words. They, along with the look in her eyes, made it all worth it.

Rickkter felt as though a weight had been lifted from his heart. "Do you mean that?" she whispered.

He nodded. "I do. Pretty is not beautiful. Pretty changes. Beautiful is what the mind arranges. And you are beautiful."

Kayla rushed up to him, wrapping her arms around his neck and pulling him close to her as she buried her face in his shoulder. Rickkter's hands slowly rose behind her back and as returned the embrace, he finally let go of all the inhibitions he had concerning her. And for the first time since they had first met, he savored contact with her. Slowly rubbing the bottom of his chin against the top of her head, he worked his way down until he was nestling his nose against the base of her neck. Even with the spell field of her talisman, he could detect a faint hint of her musk.

"That is something I've had to relearn since I arrived here," he murmured into her thick black fur. "What somebody looks like, what somebody is externally, isn't important. It's what that individual is on the inside that counts. I once heard it said that there is no beauty that hath not some strangeness in the proportion." Pulling her away from him, Rickkter regarded her meticulously in the room's candlelight. "And to my eyes you are beautiful."

Kayla's paws were resting on the raccoon's sides as his slid up to her shoulders, the right one cupping her cheek and rubbing gently at the abundance of soft fur there. That brought another small smile to her lips and a purring deep within her chest. From the look in Rickkter's eyes, it appeared like he was trying to figure out what to do next. As time drew out, the two stood there in the room that was silent aside from the sounds made by the skunkette. She was about to question this when his expression broke and he started to chuckle.

His eye ridges pulled together in a sort of embarrassed cast, his chuckling intensified until he was actually laughing. Kayla wore a puzzled frown, her eyes open wide as she nervously laughed along. Of all that Rickkter had done that evening, this puzzled her the most. She was about to ask but he beat her to it.

"It just occurred to me," he confessed. "I have no idea how one is supposed to kiss with a muzzle."

Kayla wuffed, smiled, then laughed as openly as he, the tension of the whole situation broken. She raised her eye ridges in an "Are you serious?" expression, a huge grin on her open muzzle. Rickkter only nodded and laughed harder, his brown eyes never leaving hers. The remaining tension of the encounter left the two of them in a rush as they were both caught up in the laughter. Rickkter actually had to back off, one hand on his knee for support, the other clutching his side.

But that little interlude didn't last long and their mutual laughter slowly died. The apartment resumed its quiet candlelit façade, the dancing light playing off the white fur of the two animal morphs. Kayla and Rickkter both looked up from their bent over positions, their eyes meeting and locking as they straightened up together. The tension that had existed between before ignited into a passion that caused the two morphs to once more come into an embrace.

Kayla reached up, ruffling the fur on the back of Rickkter's neck before sliding her hand down to the side of his chin. The other rested on his left shoulder. "Come here, you silly raccoon," she murmured as she guided his head to one side.

He leaned down to meet her kiss. Kayla leaned up, feeling his breath on her muzzle as it came from his slightly open mouth. And then their muzzles touched and pressed together, their heads turning further to the side to allow better access. Rickkter seemed hesitant at first, tensing at the first contact, but the feeling of Kayla's warm tongue brushing over his lips and muzzle made him quickly relax. Their muzzles opened a little more, their tongues meeting and entwining, probing each other's mouths. Kayla felt Rickkter's larger canines with her tongue, his own playing alongside hers. Their whiskers quivered and brushed together, Rickkter's longer ones tickling Kayla's muzzle and adding to the thrill of the moment as they explored each other with all of their senses. The kiss went on and on, until at last they had to separate and come up for air.

"Rick, how long has it been since you were with someone?" she panted as he moved his nipping down to the side of her neck.

"Don't know. Can't say. A while," he mumbled as his teeth pricked the loose flesh at the nape of her neck. Her smell, the feel of her fur on his paw, her taste; it was intoxicating. "You?"

"Far too long."

"Then we'll have to do something about that," he rumbled as he brought his head up and pressed his muzzle to hers once more.

It had finally happened. One of Rickkter's arms went around behind her shoulders, the other going to her waist. Their tongues continued to play with each other and he pulled her close, reveling in the feel of the skunk's lithe body against his own. And for the first time in months, he felt all the burdens go away only to be filled with his feelings for her.

It was glorious.

* * *

It was… morning. Or so the pale light that came in through the open doorway and the fireplace told the still sleepy raccoon. He squished his eyes closed and murred deeply as he stretched his body. But his eyes snapped back open when his foot touched something behind him. Rolling his head back, he saw what was in his bed.

Kayla.

Rickkter was careful when he rolled the rest of himself over, as the last thing he wanted to do right then was to disturb her. She looked beautiful, so beautiful, lying there. The blanket had tented a bit when he had moved, revealing her chest to him. It was a lovely white, the coloration starting at the underside of her jaw, travelling down the front of her neck where it spread out to cover her front. Her breasts, not very large but still ample, were covered in that fine white fur, except for the area around the nipples. The fur around them still held a matted look from their activities the night before. The fur on her stomach was a little longer, Rickkter observed, as he ran his paw up her front, rubbing it in slow, small circles. His paw came to rest deeply entwined with the lush fur at her side.

The events of the night before came to his mind, the first time he had had his hand on her furred side like this. They had just made it to his bedroom and just finished disrobing, and were admiring each other's form.

"This is the first time you've done this since you changed?" she had asked.

"How did you know?" he had answered her with an embarrassed grin.

"A guess," she replied. She then ran her hands up his chest, twining some of the lighter gray fur she found there around one clawed digit. "Yet considering your profession, I find it surprising. I know the other soldiers here tend to frequent the prostitutes in town. I've even heard it said that some of them prefer the animal morphs."

Rickkter was still running his hand through the fur at her hip, working it through the layer of fur to the skin beneath. He couldn't believe how wonderful it felt and couldn't help but wonder why he hadn't wanted to do this earlier. The answer to her question was an uncomfortable one. "Because I was ashamed. Of what I had become."

"Ashamed?" she had whispered. He heard what could only be surprise overlaying a heartfelt comfort. She backed off until she was at the very end of his arm's length. "How could you be ashamed of this?" she had wanted to know, running her claws through the fur over his muscular chest.

His reply had been simple. Taking his paw off her hip, he brought it to the white under his chin, running it forward to the edge as he tipped her head up to meet his gaze. "How could you be ashamed of this?" he whispered. Her response was to give him another passionate kiss, one of many that night.

The skunk beneath his slowly rubbing paw stirred, drawing Rickkter back to the present. Kayla's pirr intensified greatly as she came around and stretched her body from fingers to toes and tail. But when her hands were coming down, the right one coming to rest on Rickkter's shoulder, her eyes flew open in surprise.

"Good morning, Kayla," was the first thing that came to his lips. He lay there for several seconds, taking in the black and white form of the female skunk across from him. While having appeared nervous and unsure at first, she seemed to have calmed down, her blue eyes large and roving over the exposed parts of his body. "So what do you think of your decision now? In the cold light of morning?"

The mephit was silent a while longer, and Rickkter began to get worried over what her reaction might be. Then she moved beneath his gentle touch and slipped forward a few inches, her mouth opening to reveal the rows of small, sharp teeth and a pink tongue inside. That tongue darted out and gave Rickkter a quick lick on the nose. "Good morning, lover," she burred.

"The Good Sport" by Bill "Greyflank" Kieffer is a second Metamor Keep *tale. This shows how, a few years after their transformation, MK's teenagers have been affected by growing up as anthro animals. Some have tried to reject their physical form and remain as human as possible. Others have embraced their new animal natures and instincts. How does this affect a group of young friends, some of whom are now passive herbivores, and others of whom are aggressively predatory carnivores?*

"The Good Sport" was a finalist for the first Ursa Major Award for Best Anthropomorphic Short Fiction of 2001.

The Good Sport

by Bill Kieffer

Lars sprang through the woods; his impala body a blur in and out of the trees.

He was naked, of course. His parents shunned magic and, even if he didn't believe magic was inherently evil, it also made him uneasy. Beside, he really could not afford armor or clothing that could magically fit both his near human morph form and his full impala form. There was no avoiding the curse, however, so Lars was intent on enjoying as much of it as he could.

He was safe enough in the woods on this side of the Keep. Wicker and his father had patrolled this area yesterday, so they knew that the Lutins were inactive in this area. The woods were thick with his friends. He reveled in his speed and his freedom.

A huge orange and black blur appeared out of nowhere and Lars' heart stopped, but he managed to turn himself at a right angle and leap over the tiger-boy gracefully. Lars zig-zagged with a breathy laugh and left the tiger cursing behind him.

Lars transformed back as closely to human form as he could and leaned against a tree to catch his breath. He was still covered with fur, but his nose was wider, his eyes facing forward, and each hand sported five fingers in a white glove of fur so fine you could see pink skin underneath. "Can't get me!" It would be nice to be able to be fully human someday, to leave the Keep and see the world, but it wasn't to be. He tried to concentrate on the fun he was having.

Of course, he was supposed to have outgrown the need for playing, too, according to his father. The paper mill was a terribly boring place; bad enough to be cursed to live out the rest of his life hiding from the world, did he have to spend his life making sure that bits of wood and cloth were pulped finely enough to go through the mangler? He hated the mangler. He hated the paper mill. He hated his parents.

He blamed his parents for coming to Metamor Keep. Of course, there was no curse on the place then, but couldn't they see what a target the mountain community was to the very forces they opposed? They were just plain stupid. Lars was only 16 and he could see that this was no place to raise children, curse or no curse. Sure, maybe the library was impressive and, maybe, some of the finest minds did live here, but they were all Mages, which they hated more than the families that had run their church out of the country.

Those people they had forgiven. Stupid!

And they wondered why he had no respect for them.

Thank god for friends like Custard, Carnage, and Wicker, otherwise he'd have gone crazy. They understood him… for the most part.

Hearing the brush rattle, Lars morphed back into his impressively fast impala form and darted off. He loved the way it felt, letting the curse loose, twisting his body, finding form that allowed no frustrations. The impala was built to run; although the real impalas did that running in the savannahs of Heartland on the other side of the world. The trees and underbrush slowed him down.

Sometimes he wished he'd become something else. The only other impala was his father and that old man couldn't be dragged away from the paper mill short of a life or death situation. Be nice, if there was a girl impala. His destiny would have at least been decided. Or even a boy impala to play with… to talk to. Maybe, if he'd become a wolf or some other canine… certainly, Wicked would have more respect for him.

Wicked was younger, but so much bigger than any of the other boys. He was a tiger morph and Lars suspected that he only hung around with them because he was a bit of a rough-houser and kids his own age were too fragile, especially the few still soft and pink. Lars had trouble looking at Wicked and seeing a 14-year-old.

Clay, the tiger morph's older brother, was like that too, before he got all moody and withdrawn. When Clay got "artistic," as the gang liked to call it. Too bad, really, Lars kind of liked rough-housing with Clay. Clay was still mostly unchanged, and there was something about feeling the fur-less arms grab him roughly in a tackle that made him feel good… Not that he ever let Clay tackle him. That would be stupid. He was just a good sport, that was all.

The best thing about having Wicked, as they called the tiger-morph, hanging out with the group was that Lars was no longer the youngest. Lars was still the designated "prey" in most of their predator and prey games, but he was all right with that. After all, he was a herbivore and that put him in a certain place within the food chain. Not that it really mattered to any of the Keepers, but for the game it did. And, it wasn't like the others didn't sometimes take his place, but Lars actually found stalking someone to be a bit boring. And the first time someone had said, "Oh, no, save me from the wild, man-eating gazelle!" he had felt incredibly silly.

Wicked won at least half the games and was getting better all the time. Sometimes Lars won, escaping the designated hunting area, but that was getting rarer, too. Which was good; Lars always felt he was cheating them if one of the hunters didn't win. He liked to see the other guys happy.

This time the orange and black blur nailed him, dragging him to the ground. This tackle was different, harder than even Wicked had ever hit him before: something was wrong. Wicked morphed from animal to his "normal" fuzzy form before the impala was down and cupped a hand over Lars' muzzle. "Shhhhhh," the tiger morph growled quietly, urgently. "We found Lutins."

Lars gasped. He morphed back to his normal, almost human, form and grabbed at Wicked's loose fur. "We have to get back to the Keep! We have no weapons! We don't even have clothes, for Eli's sake!"

"We have claws and teeth, Meat!" Wicked had his own nicknames for the guys. Thankfully, he never used them in front of the grown-ups or the faux kids. Who knew what they'd make of that. There were already rumors that Clay was what his parents called "fancy."

"You do! Not me!" He flinched to hear the whining in his voice.

Wicked smiled evilly. "Listen to me, Meat, we won. *We won*. We killed the Lutins."

Wicked helped him up as Lars sputtered questions. He could see that Wicked was covered in blood now, and his heart raced as he wondered just how close he had come to leaping in a group of the little green nasty creatures. "Sweet Yahshua! Look at you." The white apron of fur that covered his chest and stomach were matted with blood so thickly no wonder he hadn't seen the tiger coming.

"You should see the other guys." Wicked was so solid and proud of himself, yet Lars could barely keep his knees from shaking. "Custard ran right into them! A group of ten, gathering bones it looked like, probably for some magic spell." Wicked's eyes glittered with delight as he would tell a bit of the tale, take a few steps and then tell some more. "Custard called out for the others, Meat, and then Carnage and Evil were there and then I got there in time to rip into some of them. It was glorious. It was what I was made for, Meat. Ripping, tearing, I was lightning and thunder!"

Wicked roared with delight, "*I was death!*"

Lars was awed and confused, and glad that his inhuman muzzle made reading his face hard. He had no idea what emotions a human face would have betrayed in him. The impala morph had never seen the young tiger like this. Amused. Angry. Bored. Aggravated. Yes. Now, for the first time, Wicked was truly happy and it scared Lars on levels he couldn't comprehend. His instinct was to run, but that was just the animal in him talking. Wicked was a friend. "I'm… I'm sorry I missed that."

Wicked smiled and hugged Lars, without embarrassment. Lars was shocked! Their stomachs touched and he had to quickly turn his hip to make sure nothing else did. But as quickly as it happened, his brute friend held him at arm's length and smiled a grin that could have swallowed him whole. "That's the best part, Meat. We saved one for you!"

Wicked's eyes glittered like diamonds as he led Lars back to the others. When they got close, Wicked called out that he had Lars with him and the other three guys started chanting, "Fresh meat! Fresh meat!" Fresh Meat had always been the name of the newest kid, but Lars had been the newest and youngest member of the gang for such a long time, that the name had stuck. Lars didn't mind. In fact, he kind of liked it; it was not only a little suggestive but it was the last thing his parents would ever want him to be called.

When he walked into the clearing he found the three young Keepers guarding a young—not full grown, at all—Lutin male. He was crying in the middle of a circle drawn into the ground… the bodies of about a dozen different Lutins littered the ground around him in plain view for the goblin kid to see. The three other guys, all of who had their fur covered in Lutin blood, growled at him whenever the poor kid moved.

Lars felt incredibly sorry for the little monster. He tried not to imagine what it had seen, and how it must feel to be surrounded and overpowered by fur-covered monstrosities. An albino bear. A custard-colored wolf thing from another continent. A black dragon that walked like a man. All naked and covered with the blood of one's friends. Maybe even family. "Wicked, he's just a kid!"

Wicked smiled and shrugged. "Work your way up, Meat."

Lars felt sick to his stomach. "I can't."

"You have to," Wicked turned Lars so that he could avoid the tiger-morph's eyes. It wasn't fair that such pretty eyes should be in such a nasty cat. "Look, Lars, for all you know, we saved you from these things. Okay? Do your part. Be a good sport."

Lars opened his mouth but nothing came out. What could he say? Wicked was right. He knew that almost any other Keeper would see this for the gift it was. His parents had ruined him. That thought gave him fortitude. "All right. What do I do?"

Wicked clapped him on his tawny back and then pushed him gently towards the circle. "Kick him to death. You've got hooves. Use them." So matter of fact. So simple. So brutal. God forgive him, but he wanted it all so badly.

Lars could feel all four of them looking at him. Custard—a young coyote morph who had just joined the civil guard. Evil—a demonic-looking dragon morph who probably hated his parents more than Lars did (they had come here on purpose, after the curse). Carnage—a white bear morph that wanted to be a writer and was hot for Wicked's sister, Tina (who used to be the boy, Tinker). They all stood as close to human as they could get. In Carnage's case, it was very, very close. They were all chanting his name. Meat. Meat. Meat. And then he heard Wicked's voice take up the chant and he knew he was going to have to do it.

They had saved the Lutin for him, after all.

He entered the ring and the young Lutin wouldn't even look at him. It simply stared at the fallen members of its kin and sobbed pitifully. The gang cheered at him to kick, but Lars could not bring himself to simply put his hoof through a defenseless creature. He pushed him, instead. He'd seen countless fights start with a simple push. Usually, the fight instantly took up a life all its own. The little goblin child just sobbed.

Custard booed and then so did Evil. Wicked just yelled, "Harder, get his attention!"

So, that was exactly what Lars did. He pushed the kid nearly out of the circle before he got the damn thing to really notice him. It just cried at him and continued to back up as if Lars was still pushing it. It wasn't even aware that there was a two-horned monster in the circle with it. Lars was a bit insulted. He stepped his form back a bit. Letting his horns grow and his fingers merge into a hoof and a sharp thumb at each wrist. The little green kid gave him the same pathetic look his younger brothers gave him when they wanted to be picked up. Lars roared at him, offended that this little monster should seem so much more human than any of his friends.

The kid stepped out of the circle and suddenly Carnage's bear form was nipping at the young Lutin's bloodied feet. It hopped back in, eyes wide, and then stopped and then stared at Lars as if seeing the bipedal impala for the first time. Carnage growled a laugh as the Lutin emptied his bladder onto the floor of the battle circle. Lars swore and then felt himself blush under his fur.

He kicked at the thing in disgust and then it just lay on the ground sobbing hysterically. Lars screamed in frustration and then turned to Wicked. "I can't do this. It acts like a real person too much!"

Wicked did not look too happy about that and marched over to the circle. He shoved Lars gently back into place and grabbed a long knife from one of the dead Lutins. For a moment, Lars thought Wicked was going to slit the little thing's throat as it laid belly up on the ground. Instead, the tiger morph roughly grabbed the creature by its head and jerked it upright. He bounced it a few times until it got the idea Wicked wanted it to stand.

It did and Wicked's friends laughed, reminded of puppets on strings.

Wicked patted its head and hunkered down in mock parental attitude. "Now, listen up," the tiger morphed growled. "If you kill him, you get to go free. Understand? You kill him… you go free." Wicked wrapped the knife handle in the young Lutin's right hand and then pointed it at Lars and then hooked his thumbs together and flapped his finger claws in unison. He'd made a white dove from his monstrous paws. It was the most absurd thing to hear and see, that Lars was certain his younger friend couldn't possibly be giving the little green creature permission to kill him. "Free? Understand?"

Wicked smiled at him as the message sunk into the little monster's skull. Bright cat eyes locked with Lars' dark chestnut eyes as his friend stood and stepped back.

"You see, I bet you can kill him now."

Suddenly, it was Lars' bladder that needed release. "Wicked!"

Wicked stepped out of the circle without looking away from Lars. "Aw, c'mon. Kill him. He'd kill you." He spread his paws almost comically. "He *will* kill you." The other boys chuckled.

As if on cue, the little Lutin sprang forward with the knife. Lars' training kept him from being cut too badly. He felt the blade bounce roughly off his upper arm, and then catch a bit of skin on his forearm as he dodged. He spun and kicked, letting himself slip a little further into the impala within, so that his leg—his hind leg—carried more force than it would have otherwise. The Lutin was flung nearly completely out of the dirt circle.

All Keepers underwent some form of combat training, as all Keepers were expected to defend the Keep and even go out on patrol, but Lars hadn't been sure if he could count on his own training to surface when he needed it. It was… satisfying… knowing it was there when he needed it, just as Jack deMule said it would be.

Lars morphed back into his full humanoid form just as Custard and Evil threw the half conscious Lutin child back into the circle. It was child's play to snap the knife from its hand. In fact, the impala heard the bone snap as his fist struck its forearm. It shrieked in pain and terror and Lars couldn't bear it any longer. And he knew Wicked and the others would never let him walk away from this... not when they had saved this Lutin for him to kill.

So he screamed in frustration and forced himself to wade into the tiny monster. He struck with his fists and with his hooves and he no longer saw a green, scared child.

He saw his father's face, his human face before the battle, self-righteous, and too stubborn to see when he'd failed.

He saw his mother's face, her jaw distending into a beak even as she huddled with her children and promised the Eli would protect them... even as her own prayers failed.

He saw Clay's pink pretty peeking out onto the street the day the curse had changed Lars into something less than human, as they all knew it would someday... everyone changed eventually, except Clay Potter who looked away and shut a door between them, forever.

But then it was over and Lars stood over the broken Lutin, his fury spent. With infinite misery, Lars saw that it wasn't dead, not yet. It would only take a little force to end its suffering. That would be the humane thing to do. But even that rationale could not move Lars to do further violence. As wide and as expansive as his rebellious and angry river of resentments within him had seemed, it did not seem to run very deep. He was empty.

"I can't, Wicker." The impala morph said softly, "I just can't..."

"That's all right," the tiger morph said as he brushed past Lars. "I knew you couldn't do it, Meat." Then with a casualness that shocked Lars, Wicker Potter—brother to Lars' one-time best friend—leaned over as if picking up a rock and speared the claws of his left paw into the throat of the little Lutin and then flung it into the underbrush ten feet away. Custard laughed like a hyena as the body fell rag-doll-limp into the bushes.

Wicked turned around and Lars was vaguely aware that he was alone in the circle with Wicked, not that there was any circle left. The scuffle with the little green monster had completely obliterated the line in the dirt. Lars had a panicky thought that the missing boundaries meant something symbolic, and he wanted to ask Carnage what that might mean... but a glance in the polar bear's direction didn't encourage any questions. His humanity had withdrawn and only the arctic bear remained.

"You're covered in blood, Lars." Wicked remarked softly.

"I couldn't do it. I wanted to, Wicked, but I couldn't!"

Wicked stood inches from Lars. While the impala morph was slightly taller and much older than the tiger morph, Wicked's presence was overpowering. Naked, the two young men faced each other as Lars began to feel the heady effect of the adrenaline wear off. He began to shake. He wanted to sit down, but Wicked's eyes held him fast. He could not read them... or he did not want to.

"In life," the tiger morph said, "you have to choose between being prey and being predator. I gave you that choice. You made it."

"I wanted to..."

"The evil... vile creatures that infest this forest for leagues in every direction... Creatures responsible for making us outcasts amongst our own kind."

"I wanted to..."

"I know." Wicked clasped Lars on both shoulders and held him. The tiger's eyes burnt into his and Lars could not believe how weak he'd been. Out of the corner of his eyes, he saw the other three slink off. He'd disappointed all of them. None of them were Followers, none of them understood. "You tried, but none of us can overcome our natures, can we?"

"No," Lars said miserably. "No, we are wh-wh... what we are."

The tiger morph slid the curse within. He grew larger with the mass of a jungle cat piling onto his frame. Even as his nose flattened and his jaws extended, he seemed to become more masculine. Lars could feel Wicked's hot breath on his neck, the white and cream hairs tickled by the moist breeze. "I just want you to know, I'm not mad at you, Meat," The tiger said and then leaned forward and began licking Lars' blood covered chest.

The impala gasped as a dozen odd and unwanted sensations filled him and he was filled with a sinful shame that buried his other, more recent shame instantly. It felt good. It felt wrong, evil, and, in front of the other guys... what was Wicked thinking!? Lars tried pushing his naked body away but Wicked held him in an iron grip, his claws digging into the impala morph's shoulders with just enough force to hold him there. He could see the others watching them from the woods in their animal forms.

"Lutin blood tastes like crap," the tiger morph mumbled as his rough tongue moved to Lars' injured shoulder. Lars' mouth moved and he started hitting Wicked on his shoulders, as he could feel his body begin to react. This wasn't right! Not at all! It wasn't supposed to be like this, not in front of everyone!

Lars' mind was overwhelmed as he tried to make sense of what was happening. As Wicked's claws dug painfully into him, he began to cry. Somehow, the guys had gotten drunk and then the Lutins found them. Or maybe the Lutins tried defending themselves with magic... everyone knew how they had changed Christopher into a full bear. Maybe they were acting like animals because of that. But whatever the reason, it was wrong! It was so damn wrong! And in front of the guys!

Wicked found the slash and began licking that with his rough tongue. At first, it felt pleasant and Wicked made a mewling sound as he cleaned the wound of fur and dirt with his tongue. Lars whimpered, "Wicked, please don't!" He needed his friend to stop before he noticed the hardness, the third horn that grew out of him, twisted obscenely into a red stick too long and too thin to be of any use.

Wicked pulled him in tighter, crossing his arms across Lars' furry back, claws sinking into the meat under his shoulder blades. Lars bit his lips so as not to cry out in pain. It was bad enough that he had to beg, that he wasn't strong enough to make Wicked stop. He could feel his body reacting sinfully to the younger boy's pressure, to the fur brushing on his naked tool. He balled his fists up and shoved them in his eyes and whimpered, No. No. No. No. The tongue now lapped painfully at his wound and Lars knew he'd have to scream or all would be lost.

And then Wicked said something strange. Something that erased everything out of his mind and made him forget the Lutins and the other guys. Something that even made the pain vanish in the very second Wicked spoke to him.

Wicked said, softly, almost lovingly, "Change. It'll be easier that way, Meat."

The words were cold water to his nightmare. In all his time playing with Wicked, Lars had never guessed how truly evil the tiger-morph was until that moment. Not just bad. Not misunderstood, and certainly not just another rebellious teenager, but evil.

In that one second of clarity, Lars did the only thing he could do. He prayed.

When Wicked sank his fangs into Lars' neck, it was too late to scream. The windpipe crushed slowly in the tiger's vice-like grip. Claws ripped the furry skin from his back. As he felt another set of jaws clamp painfully around his leg, Lars had just enough time to thank Eli for sparing him from his own sinful desires before he vanished into everlasting darkness.

* * *

Henrik and Josie Potter brought the Long Scouts to the place they had found the children. Lars was where they had left him early in the morning. Archer was annoyed that they hadn't bothered to try to bring the body of the boy back or at least cover him. The wild animals of the forest hadn't left much for the Long Scouts to bring back to the parents, and what was left was covered in a thick cloud of black flies. Thank god he had decided against bringing the young man's folks.

"There shouldn't have been any Lutins here," Henrik growled. "Wicker and I scouted this area this morning. I don't see how we could have missed these smelly creatures." Henrik was a white tiger morph but he wasn't exactly the stealthy type, Archer knew. Especially if he hadn't been fully sober, which the Long Scout suspected.

"It's not your fault, Henrik," Josie said. "The boys should not have been this far away from the Keep, playing Predator and Prey of all things."

"I just wish I had found them sooner."

Archer just glared at the civilians with a mild dose of disgust. He was no Follower, but he agreed with their sentiment that idle hands were begging for trouble. Too many folk were allowing the first few years of the curse to be something of a second childhood. Never mind that the curse could actually grant you that. "What exactly happened here? Where's Wicker, now?"

"He went to get Lars' clothes." Josie spoke up quickly with a glance at the ruined, naked body of the impala morph. "He didn't want the boy's parents seeing him like this… naked and…"

Archer held up a paw, the last thing he needed was a crying she-wolf. "Okay, but I'll need to make a report to George, so I'll have to talk to him."

"When I found him, he was holding Lars and trying to lick the boy's wounds clean. But it was too late." The white tiger looked down and bit his lower lip. He spoke to the ground, "I'd never seen him like that."

Archer nodded. Wicker was known as something of a bully, but witnessing death for the first time often softened the hardest hearts. He'd leave the soul-healing to the parents. "What about the other boys?"

"They were just sitting there, in shock. They had defended themselves well, but, they couldn't save Lars."

Archer nodded. There were a dozen Lutin corpses, and one that hadn't been mauled too badly had distinctive hoof marks on its body. With only claws and teeth to defend themselves with and so little real training, Archer was admittedly impressed. He made a mental note to ask to have Custard transferred from the civil guard to the Long Scouts when he was ready; maybe even Carnegie and Elvis, too, if that was what they wanted. There was something about the tiger morph he did not like. He reminded Archer of a young Misha or Rickkter but without the honor or conscience of either.

A little reptilian Long Scout who'd been looking at the dead Keeper's body trotted over to Craig. "He's covered in Lutin blood on what's left of his belly. You can smell it on him, but, Archer…" Archer motioned the scout to spit the rest of it out. "They took his tail."

Archer rolled his cat eyes. Lutin trophy hunters! He did not need that. "Look for that tail," he called out to the other scouts. Josie buried her face in Henrik's chest with a wet gasp. The tiger glared at him as it comforted his wife. Civilians.

The tiger started speaking again, uncomfortable with comforting his wife. "Lars won," Wicker said. He got out of the hunting area before any of them had been able to bring him down. That's when the boy ran full tilt into the Lutins."

Josie looked up, her white canine eyes thick with tears. "Wicker said he scratched up Lars, drew blood. He thinks the scent of blood might have drawn them to Lars. He thinks it's his fault."

It could be. It probably was. Archer only shrugged. He needed to get everyone out of here as quickly as possible.

"They found Lars surrounded by them. He was in some kind of circle they had drawn, battling a knife wielding Lutin child. Their idea of sport, I suppose. Wicker just ripped right into them but Lars was too tired to properly defend himself."

Archer nodded and spit on the ground, a feat he had cultivated over the years to a near art. "As soon as Wicker gets back here with those clothes, I want to move back to the Keep as quickly as possible. If we can't find that tail, we can assume a Lutin escaped with it, and—as much I like killing the damn goblin things—our job right now is to get the body back to the Keep in one piece. Can't do that if we have to fight off scores of Lutins out for revenge."

* * *

Wicked stopped when he came to the rock where they had put their clothes and scooped up Lars' clothes, careful not to get his drying blood on them, just as a regretful friend would be careful about such things.

Ba'al must be very proud of him, he thought. He had not only managed to kill his prey and eat of its flesh, but he had shamed it in almost every way the herbivore could be shamed. There was one more thing he could have done, but it would have diminished him in his eyes of the others, and that would have not done at all. Ba'al understood pragmatism.

Besides, Lars probably would have liked it.

He'd only stopped to wash his paws, arms and muzzle at the nearby stream and then, in a last minute inspiration, took out his prey's tail and forced his eyes wide open. He poked himself in the eyes several times until they felt scratchy and red, and he could feel the tears rolling down his eyes.

Wicker hid the tail under the rock, knowing he'd be back for it. He had to go through the motions now and pretend to be upset and miserable that a stupid gazelle was dead.

But that was okay.

If that was the price to be paid, he could be a good sport about it.

Aubrey Darger is human. Sir Blackthorpe Ravenscairn de Plus Precieux (better known as "Surplus") is a well-dressed bioengineered anthro dog. They are two con-men living in the Postutopian Future, which is rather like a fantasy Steampunk Victorian England. In this story, anyway. "The Dog Said Bow-Wow" (2001) is the first in the "Darger and Surplus" series; others (so far) are the stories "The Little Cat Laughed To See Such Sport" (2002; Paris), "Girls and Boys, Come Out to Play" (2005; Arcadian Greece), "Tawny Petticoats" (2014; New Orleans), and two novels: Dancing With Bears *(Night Shade Books, May 2011; Muscovy), and* Chasing the Phoenix *(Tor Books, August 2015; China). There are also four short-shorts (all 2011); "Song of the Lorelei", "American Cigarettes", "The Brain-Baron", and "The Nature of Mirrors".*

Darger and Surplus' adventures take place in a world that is "set in a not-very-distant future". Hmmm. You can read this and decide for yourselves how "not-very-distant" their future is. Humanity still dominates, but there are numerous very weird robots and bioengineered intelligent animals, all of whom have full civil rights. Greece has been turned over to man-made centaurs, satyrs, fauns, and other creatures of mythology. It's a breathtaking world that furry fans will enjoy.

Swanwick says "The Dog Said Bow-Wow" is his most popular story. It won the Hugo Award, and was nominated for the Nebula, in 2002 for the Best Science Fiction Short Story of 2001. It is in The Best of Michael Swanwick *(Subterranean Press, October 2008) and other books, including Swanwick's collection of the same name (Tachyon Publications, September 2007). "The Little Cat Laughed To See Such Sport", also in the same collection, was a finalist for the Hugo Award for Best Short Story of 2002.*

The Dog Said Bow-Wow

by Michael Swanwick

The dog looked like he had just stepped out of a children's book. There must have been a hundred physical adaptations required to allow him to walk upright. The pelvis, of course, had been entirely reshaped. The feet alone would have needed dozens of changes. He had knees, and knees were tricky.

To say nothing of the neurological enhancements.

But what Darger found himself most fascinated by was the creature's costume. His suit fit him perfectly, with a slit in the back for the tail, and—again—a hundred invisible adaptations that caused it to hang on his body in a way that looked perfectly natural.

"You must have an extraordinary tailor," Darger said.

The dog shifted his cane from one paw to the other, so they could shake, and in the least affected manner imaginable replied, "That is a common observation, sir."

"You're from the States?" It was a safe assumption, given where they stood—on the docks—and that the schooner *Yankee Dreamer* had sailed up the Thames with the morning tide. Darger had seen its bubble sails over the rooftops, like so many rainbows. "Have you found lodgings yet?"

"Indeed I am, and no I have not. If you could recommend a tavern of the cleaner sort?"

"No need for that. I would be only too happy to put you up for a few days in my own rooms." And, lowering his voice, Darger said, "I have a business proposition to put to you."

"Then lead on, sir, and I shall follow you with a right good will."

The dog's name was Sir Blackthorpe Ravenscairn de Plus Precieux, but "Call me Sir Plus," he said with a self-denigrating smile, and "Surplus" he was ever after.

Surplus was, as Darger had at first glance suspected and by conversation confirmed, a bit of a rogue—something more than mischievous and less than a cut-throat. A dog, in fine, after Darger's own heart.

Over drinks in a public house, Darger displayed his box and explained his intentions for it. Surplus warily touched the intricately carved teak housing, and then drew away from it. "You outline an intriguing scheme, Master Darger—"

"Please. Call me Aubrey."

"Aubrey, then. Yet here we have a delicate point. How shall we divide up the… ah, *spoils* of this enterprise? I hesitate to mention this, but many a promising partnership has foundered on precisely such shoals."

Darger unscrewed the salt cellar and poured its contents onto the table. With his dagger, he drew a fine line down the middle of the heap. "I divide—you choose. Or the other way around, if you please. From self-interest, you'll not find a grain's difference between the two."

"Excellent!" cried Surplus and, dropping a pinch of salt in his beer, drank to the bargain.

* * *

It was raining when they left for Buckingham Labyrinth. Darger stared out the carriage window at the drear streets and worn buildings gliding by and sighed. "Poor, weary old London! History is a grinding-wheel that has been applied too many a time to thy face."

"It is also," Surplus reminded him, "to be the making of our fortunes. Raise your eyes to the Labyrinth, sir, with its soaring towers and bright surfaces rising above these shops and flats like a crystal mountain rearing up out of a ramshackle wooden sea, and be comforted."

"That is fine advice," Darger agreed. "But it cannot comfort a lover of cities, nor one of a melancholic turn of mind."

"Pah!" cried Surplus, and said no more until they arrived at their destination.

At the portal into Buckingham, the sergeant-interface strode forward as they stepped down from the carriage. He blinked at the sight of Surplus, but said only, "Papers?"

Surplus presented the man with his passport and the credentials Darger had spent the morning forging, and then added with a negligent wave of his paw, "And this is my autistic."

The sergeant-interface glanced once at Darger, and forgot about him completely. Darger had the gift, priceless to one in his profession, of a face so nondescript that once someone looked away, it disappeared from that person's consciousness forever. "This way, sir. The officer of protocol will want to examine these himself."

A dwarf savant was produced to lead them through the outer circle of the Labyrinth. They passed by ladies in bioluminescent gowns and gentlemen with boots and gloves cut from leathers cloned from their own skin. Both women and men were extravagantly bejeweled—for the ostentatious display of wealth was yet again in fashion—and the halls were lushly clad and pillared in marble, porphyry and jasper. Yet Darger could not help noticing how worn the carpets were, how chipped and soot covered the oil lamps were. His sharp eye espied the remains of an antique electrical system, and traces as well of telephone lines and fiber optic cables from an age when those technologies were yet workable.

These last he viewed with particular pleasure.

The dwarf savant stopped before a heavy black door carved over with gilt griffins, locomotives, and fleurs-de-lis. "This is a door," he said. "The wood is ebony. Its binomial is *Diospyros ebenum*. It was harvested in Serendip. The gilding is of gold. Gold has an atomic weight of 197.2."

He knocked on the door and opened it.

The officer of protocol was a dark-browed man of imposing mass. He did not stand for them. "I am Lord Coherence-Hamilton, and this—" he indicated the slender, clear-eyed woman who stood beside him—"is my sister, Pamela."

Surplus bowed deeply to the Lady, who dimpled and dipped a slight curtsey in return.

The protocol officer quickly scanned the credentials. "Explain these fraudulent papers, sirrah. The Demesne of Western Vermont! Damn me if I have ever heard of such a place."

"Then you have missed much," Surplus said haughtily. "It is true we are a young nation, created only seventy-five years ago during the Partition of New England. But there is much of note to commend our fair land. The glorious beauty of Lake Champlain. The gene-mills of Winooski, that ancient seat of learning the *Universitas Viridis Montis* of Burlington, the Technarchaeological Institute of—" He stopped. "We have much to be proud of, sir, and nothing of which to be ashamed."

The bearlike official glared suspiciously at him, then said, "What brings you to London? Why do you desire an audience with the queen?"

"My mission and destination lie in Russia. However, England being on my itinerary and I a diplomat, I was charged to extend the compliments of my nation to your monarch." Surplus did not quite shrug. "There is no more to it than that. In three days I shall be in France, and you will have forgotten about me completely."

Scornfully, the officer tossed the credentials to the savant, who glanced at and politely returned them to Surplus. The small fellow sat down at a little desk scaled to his own size and swiftly made out a copy. "Your papers will be taken to Whitechapel and examined there. If everything goes well— which I doubt—and there's an opening—not likely—you'll be presented to the queen sometime between a week and ten days hence."

"Ten days! Sir, I am on a very strict schedule!"

"Then you wish to withdraw your petition?"

Surplus hesitated. "I... I shall have to think on't, sir."

Lady Pamela watched coolly as the dwarf savant led them away.

* * *

The room they were shown to had massive framed mirrors and oil paintings dark with age upon the walls, and a generous log fire in the hearth. When their small guide had gone, Darger carefully locked and bolted the door. Then he tossed the box onto the bed, and bounced down alongside it. Lying flat on his back, staring up at the ceiling, he said, "The Lady Pamela is a strikingly beautiful woman. I'll be damned if she's not."

Ignoring him, Surplus locked paws behind his back, and proceeded to pace up and down the room. He was full of nervous energy. At last, he expostulated, "This is a deep game you have gotten me into, Darger! Lord Coherence-Hamilton suspects us of all manner of blackguardry,"

"Well, and what of that?"

"I repeat myself: We have not even begun our play yet, and he suspects us already! I trust neither him nor his genetically remade dwarf."

"You are in no position to be displaying such vulgar prejudice."

"I am not *bigoted* about the creature, Darger, I *fear* him! Once let suspicion of us into that macroencephalic head of his, and he will worry at it until he has found out our every secret."

"Get a grip on yourself, Surplus! Be a man! We are in this too deep already to back out. Questions would be asked, and investigations made."

"I am anything but a man, thank God," Surplus replied. "Still, you are right. In for a penny, in for a pound. For now, I might as well sleep. Get off the bed. You can have the hearth-rug."

"I! The rug!"

"I am groggy of mornings. Were someone to knock, and I to unthinkingly open the door, it would hardly do to have you found sharing a bed with your master."

* * *

The next day, Surplus returned to the Office of Protocol to declare that he was authorized to wait as long as two weeks for an audience with the queen, though not a day more.

"You have received new orders from your government?" Lord Coherence-Hamilton asked suspiciously. "I hardly see how."

"I have searched my conscience, and reflected on certain subtleties of phrasing in my original instructions," Surplus said. "That is all."

He emerged from the office to discover Lady Pamela waiting outside. When she offered to show him the Labyrinth, he agreed happily to her plan. Followed by Darger, they strolled inward, first to witness the changing of the guard in the forecourt vestibule, before the great pillared wall that was the front of Buckingham Palace before it was swallowed up in the expansion of architecture during the mad, glorious years of Utopia. Following which, they proceeded toward the viewer's gallery above the chamber of state.

"I see from your repeated glances that you are interested in my diamonds, 'Sieur Plus Precieux," Lady Pamela said. "Well might you be. They are a family treasure, centuries old and manufactured to order, each stone flawless and perfectly matched. The indentures of a hundred autistics would not buy the like."

Surplus smiled down again at the necklace, draped about her lovely throat and above her perfect breasts. "I assure you, madame, it was not your necklace that held me so enthralled."

She colored delicately, pleased. Lightly, she said, "And that box your man carries with him wherever you go? What is in it?"

"That? A trifle. A gift for the Duke of Muscovy, who is the ultimate object of my journey," Surplus said. "I assure you, it is of no interest whatsoever."

"You were talking to someone last night," Lady Pamela said. "In your room."

"You were listening at my door? I am astonished and flattered."

She blushed. "No, no, my brother… it is his job, you see, surveillance."

"Possibly I was talking in my sleep. I have been told I do that occasionally."

"In accents? My brother said he heard two voices."

Surplus looked away. "In that, he was mistaken."

England's queen was a sight to rival any in that ancient land. She was as large as the lorry of ancient legend, and surrounded by attendants who hurried back and forth, fetching food and advice and carrying away dirty plates and signed legislation. From the gallery, she reminded Darger of a queen bee, but unlike the bee, this queen did not copulate, but remained proudly virgin.

Her name was Gloriana the First, and she was a hundred years old and still growing.

Lord Campbell-Supercollider, a friend of Lady Pamela's met by chance, who had insisted on accompanying them to the gallery, leaned close to Surplus and murmured, "You are impressed, of course, by our queen's magnificence." The warning in his voice was impossible to miss. "Foreigners invariably are."

"I am dazzled," Surplus said.

"Well might you be. For scattered through her majesty's great body are thirty-six brains, connected with thick ropes of ganglia in a hypercube configuration. Her processing capacity is the equal of many of the great computers from Utopian times."

Lady Pamela stifled a yawn. "Darling Rory," she said, touching the Lord Campbell-Supercollider's sleeve. "Duty calls me. Would you be so kind as to show my American friend the way back to the outer circle?"

"Or course, my dear." He and Surplus stood (Darger was, of course, already standing) and paid their compliments. Then, when Lady Pamela was gone and Surplus started to turn toward the exit, "Not that way. Those stairs are for commoners. You and I may leave by the gentlemen's staircase."

The narrow stairs twisted downward beneath clouds of gilt cherubs-and-airships, and debouched into a marble-floored hallway. Surplus and Darger stepped out of the stairway and found their arms abruptly seized by baboons.

There were five baboons all told, with red uniforms and matching choke collars with leashes that gathered in the hand of an ornately mustached officer whose gold piping identified him as a master of apes. The fifth baboon bared his teeth and hissed savagely.

Instantly, the master of apes yanked back on his leash and said, "There, Hercules! There, sirrah! What do you do? What do you say?"

The baboon drew himself up and bowed curtly. "Please come with us," he said with difficulty. The master of apes cleared his throat. Sullenly, the baboon added, "Sir."

"This is outrageous!" Surplus cried. "I am a diplomat, and under international law immune to arrest."

"Ordinarily, sir, this is true," said the master of apes courteously. "However, you have entered the inner circle without her majesty's invitation and are thus subject to stricter standards of security."

"I had no idea these stairs went inward. I was led here by—" Surplus looked about helplessly. Lord Campbell-Supercollider was nowhere to be seen.

So, once again, Surplus and Darger found themselves escorted to the Office of Protocol.

* * *

"The wood is teak. Its binomial is *Tectona grandis*. Teak is native to Burma, Hind, and Siam. The box is carved elaborately but without refinement." The dwarf savant opened it. "Within the casing is an archaic device for electronic intercommunication. The instrument chip is a gallium-arsenide ceramic. The chip weighs six ounces. The device is a product of the Utopian end-times."

"A modem!" The protocol officer's eyes bugged out. "You dared bring a *modem* into the inner circle and almost into the presence of the queen?" His chair stood and walked around the table. Its six insectile legs looked too slender to carry his great, legless mass. Yet it moved nimbly and well.

"It is harmless, sir. Merely something our technarchaeologists unearthed and thought would amuse the Duke of Muscovy, who is well known for his love of all things antiquarian. It is, apparently, of some cultural or historical significance, though without rereading my instructions, I would be hard pressed to tell you what."

Lord Coherence-Hamilton raised his chair so that he loomed over Surplus, looking dangerous and domineering. "*Here* is the historic significance of your modem: The Utopians filled the world with their computer webs and nets, burying cables and nodes so deeply and plentifully that they shall never be entirely rooted out. They then released into that virtual universe demons and mad gods. These intelligences destroyed Utopia and almost destroyed humanity as well. Only the valiant worldwide destruction of all modes of interface saved us from annihilation.

"Oh, you lackwit! Have you no history? These creatures hate us because our ancestors created them. They are still alive, though confined to their electronic netherworld, and want only a modem to extend themselves into the physical realm. Can you wonder, then, that the penalty for possessing such a device is—" he smiled menacingly—"death?"

"No, sir, it is not. Possession of a *working* modem is a mortal crime. This device is harmless. Ask your savant."

"Well?" the big man growled at his dwarf. "Is it functional?"

"No. It—"

"Silence." Lord Coherence-Hamilton turned back to Surplus. "You are a fortunate cur. You will not be charged with any crimes. However, while you are here, I will keep this filthy device locked away and under my control. Is that understood, Sir Bow-Wow?"

Surplus sighed. "Very well," he said. "It is only for a week, after all."

* * *

That night, the Lady Pamela Coherence-Hamilton came by Surplus's room to apologize for the indignity of his arrest, of which, she assured him, she had just now learned. He invited her in. In short order they somehow found themselves kneeling face-to-face on the bed, unbuttoning each other's clothing.

Lady Pamela's breasts had just spilled delightfully from her dress when she drew back, clutching the bodice closed again, and said, "Your man is watching us."

"And what concern is that to us?" Surplus said jovially. "The poor fellow's an autistic. Nothing he sees or hears matters to him. You might as well be embarrassed by the presence of a chair."

"Even were he a wooden carving, I would his eyes were not on me."

"As you wish." Surplus clapped his paws. "Sirrah! Turn around."

Obediently, Darger turned his back. This was his first experience with his friend's astonishing success with women. How many sexual adventuresses, he wondered, might one tumble, if one's form were unique? On reflection, the question answered itself.

Behind him, he heard the Lady Pamela giggle. Then, in a voice low with passion, Surplus said, "No, leave the diamonds on."

With a silent sigh, Darger resigned himself to a long night. Since he was bored and yet could not turn to watch the pair cavorting on the bed without giving himself away, he was perforce required to settle for watching them in the mirror.

They began, of course, by doing it doggy-style.

* * *

The next day, Surplus fell sick. Hearing of his indisposition, Lady Pamela sent one of her autistics with a bowl of broth and then followed, herself, in a surgical mask.

Surplus smiled weakly to see her. "You have no need of that mask," he said. "By my life, I swear that what ails me is not communicable. As you doubtless know, we who have been remade are prone to endocrinological imbalance."

"Is that all?" Lady Pamela spooned some broth into his mouth, then dabbed at a speck of it with a napkin. "Then fix it. You have been very wicked to frighten me over such a trifle."

"Alas," Surplus said sadly, "I am a unique creation, and my table of endocrine balances was lost in an accident at sea. There are copies in Vermont, of course. But by the time even the swiftest schooner can cross the Atlantic twice, I fear me I shall be gone."

"Oh, dearest Surplus!" The Lady caught up his paws in her hands. "Surely there is some measure, however desperate, to be taken?"

"Well…" Surplus turned to the wall in thought. After a very long time, he turned back and said, "I have a confession to make. The modem your brother holds for me? It is functional."

"Sir!" Lady Pamela stood, gathering her skirts, and stepped away from the bed in horror. "Surely not!"

"My darling and delight, you must listen to me." Surplus glanced weakly toward the door, and then lowered his voice. "Come close and I shall whisper."

She obeyed.

"In the waning days of Utopia, during the war between men and their electronic creations, scientists and engineers bent their efforts toward the creation of a modem that could be safely employed by humans. One immune from the attack of demons. One that could, indeed, compel their obedience. Perhaps you have heard of this project."

"There are rumors, but… no such device was ever built."

"Say rather that no such device was built *in time*. It had just barely been perfected when the mobs came rampaging through the laboratories, and the Age of the Machine was over. Some few, however, were hidden away before the last technicians were killed. Centuries later, brave researchers at the Technarchaeological Institute of Shelburne recovered six such devices and mastered the art of their use. One device was destroyed in the process. Two are kept in Burlington. The others were given to trusted couriers and sent to the three most powerful allies of the Demesne—one of which is, of course, Russia."

"This is hard to believe," Lady Pamela said wonderingly. "Can such marvels be?"

"Madame, I employed it two nights ago in this very room! Those voices your brother heard? I was speaking with my principals in Vermont. They gave me permission to extend my stay here to a fortnight."

He gazed imploringly at her. "If you were to bring me the device, I could then employ it to save my life."

Lady Coherence-Hamilton resolutely stood. "Fear nothing, then. I swear by my soul, the modem shall be yours tonight."

* * *

The room was lit by a single lamp which cast wild shadows whenever anyone moved, as if of illicit spirits at a witch's Sabbath.

It was an eerie sight. Darger, motionless, held the modem in his hands. Lady Pamela, who had a sense of occasion, had changed to a low-cut gown of clinging silks, dark-red as human blood. It swirled about her as she hunted through the wainscoting for a jack left unused for centuries. Surplus sat up weakly in bed, eyes half-closed, directing her. It might have been, Darger thought, an allegorical tableau of the human body being directed by its sick animal passions, while the intellect stood by, paralyzed by lack of will.

"There!" Lady Pamela triumphantly straightened, her necklace scattering tiny rainbows in the dim light.

Darger stiffened. He stood perfectly still for the length of three long breaths, then shook and shivered like one undergoing seizure. His eyes rolled back in his head.

In hollow, unworldly tones, he said, "What man calls me up from the vasty deep?" It was a voice totally unlike his own, one harsh and savage and eager for unholy sport. "Who dares risk my wrath?"

"You must convey my words to the autistic's ears," Surplus murmured. "For he is become an integral part of the modem—not merely its operator, but its voice."

"I stand ready," Lady Pamela replied.

"Good girl. Tell it who I am."

"It is Sir Blackthorpe Ravenscairn de Plus Precieux who speaks, and who wishes to talk to..." She paused.

"To his most august and socialist honor, the mayor of Burlington."

"His most august and socialist honor," Lady Pamela began. She turned toward the bed and said quizzically, "The mayor of Burlington?"

"'Tis but an official title, much like your brother's, for he who is in fact the spy-master for the Demesne of Western Vermont," Surplus said weakly. "Now repeat to it: I compel thee on threat of dissolution to carry my message. Use those exact words."

Lady Pamela repeated the words into Darger's ear.

He screamed. It was a wild and unholy sound that sent the Lady skittering away from him in a momentary panic. Then, in mid-cry, he ceased.

"Who is this?" Darger said in an entirely new voice, this one human. "You have the voice of a woman. Is one of my agents in trouble?"

"Speak to him now, as you would to any man: forthrightly, directly, and without evasion." Surplus sank his head back on his pillow and closed his eyes.

So (as it seemed to her) the Lady Coherence-Hamilton explained Surplus's plight to his distant master, and from him received both condolences and the needed information to return Surplus's endocrine levels to a functioning harmony. After proper courtesies, then, she thanked the American spy-master and unjacked the modem. Darger returned to passivity.

The leather-cased endocrine kit lay open on a small table by the bed. At Lady Pamela's direction, Darger began applying the proper patches to various places on Surplus's body. It was not long before Surplus opened his eyes.

"Am I to be well?" he asked and, when the Lady nodded, "Then I fear I must be gone in the morning. Your brother has spies everywhere. If he gets the least whiff of what this device can do, he'll want it for himself."

Smiling, Lady Pamela hoisted the box in her hand. "Indeed, who can blame him? With such a toy, great things could be accomplished."

"So he will assuredly think. I pray you, return it to me."

She did not. "This is more than just a communication device, sir," she said. "Though in that mode it is of incalculable value. You have shown that it can enforce obedience on the creatures that dwell in the forgotten nerves of the ancient world. Ergo, they can be compelled to do our calculations for us."

"Indeed, so our technarchaeologists tell us. You must—"

"We have created monstrosities to perform the duties that were once done by machines. But with this, there would be no necessity to do so. We have allowed ourselves to be ruled by an icosahexadexal-brained freak. Now we have no need for Gloriana the Gross, Gloriana the Fat and Grotesque, Gloriana the Maggot Queen."

"Madame!"

"It is time, I believe, that England had a new queen. A human queen."

"Think of my honor!"

Lady Pamela paused in the doorway. "You are a very pretty fellow indeed. But with this, I can have the monarchy and keep such a harem as will reduce your memory to that of a passing and trivial fancy."

With a rustle of skirts, she spun away.

"Then I am undone!" Surplus cried, and fainted onto the bed.

Quietly, Darger closed the door. Surplus raised himself from the pillows, began removing the patches from his body, and said, "Now what?"

"Now we get some sleep," Darger said. "Tomorrow will be a busy day."

* * *

The master of apes came for them after breakfast, and marched them to their usual destination. By now Darger was beginning to lose track of exactly how many times he had been in the Office of Protocol. They entered to find Lord Coherence-Hamilton in a towering rage, and his sister, calm and knowing, standing in a corner with her arms crossed, watching. Looking at them both now, Darger wondered how he could ever have imagined that the brother outranked his sister.

The modem lay opened on the dwarf-savant's desk. The little fellow leaned over the device, studying it minutely.

Nobody said anything until the master of apes and his baboons had left. Then Lord Coherence-Hamilton roared, "Your modem refuses to work for us!"

"As I told you, sir," Surplus said coolly, "it is inoperative."

"That's a bold-arsed fraud and a goat-buggering lie!" In his wrath, the Lord's chair rose up on its spindly legs so high that his head almost bumped against the ceiling. "I know of your activities—" he nodded toward his sister—"and demand that you show us how this whoreson device works!"

"Never!" Surplus cried stoutly. "I have my honor, sir."

"Your honor, too scrupulously insisted upon, may well lead to your death, sir."

Surplus threw back his head. "Then I die for Vermont!"

At this moment of impasse, Lady Hamilton stepped forward between the two antagonists to restore peace. "I know what might change your mind." With a knowing smile, she raised a hand to her throat and denuded herself of her diamonds. "I saw how you rubbed them against your face the other night. How you licked and fondled them. How ecstatically you took them into your mouth."

She closed his paws about them. "They are yours, sweet 'Sieur Precieux, for a word."

"You would give them up?" Surplus said, as if amazed at the very idea. In fact, the necklace had been his and Darger's target from the moment they'd seen it. The only barrier that now stood between them and the merchants of Amsterdam was the problem of freeing themselves from the Labyrinth before their marks finally realized that the modem was indeed a cheat. And to this end they had the invaluable tool of a thinking man whom all believed to be an autistic, and a plan that would give them almost twenty hours in which to escape.

"Only think, dear Surplus." Lady Pamela stroked his head and then scratched him behind one ear, while he stared down at the precious stones. "Imagine the life of wealth and ease you could lead, the women, the power. It all lies in your hands. All you need do is close them."

Surplus took a deep breath. "Very well," he said. "The secret lies in the condenser, which takes a full day to recharge. Wait but—"

"Here's the problem," the savant said unexpectedly. He poked at the interior of the modem. "There was a wire loose."

He jacked the device into the wall.

"Oh, dear God," Darger said.

A savage look of raw delight filled the dwarf savant's face, and he seemed to swell before them.

"I am free!" he cried in a voice so loud it seemed impossible that it could arise from such a slight source. He shook as if an enormous electrical current were surging through him. The stench of ozone filled the room.

He burst into flames and advanced on the English spy-master and her brother.

While all stood aghast and paralyzed, Darger seized Surplus by the collar and hauled him out into the hallway, slamming the door shut as he did.

* * *

They had not run twenty paces down the hall when the door to the Office of Protocol exploded outward, sending flaming splinters of wood down the hallway.

Satanic laughter boomed behind them.

Glancing over his shoulder, Darger saw the burning dwarf, now blackened to a cinder, emerge from a room engulfed in flames, capering and dancing. The modem, though disconnected, was now tucked under one arm, as if it were exceedingly valuable to him. His eyes were round and white and lidless. Seeing them, he gave chase.

"Aubrey!" Surplus cried. "We are headed the *wrong way!*"

It was true. They were running deeper into the Labyrinth, toward its heart, rather than outward. But it was impossible to turn back now. They plunged through scattering crowds of nobles and servitors, trailing fire and supernatural terror in their wake.

The scampering grotesque set fire to the carpets with every footfall. A wave of flame tracked him down the hall, incinerating tapestries and wallpaper and wood trim. No matter how they dodged, it ran straight toward them. Clearly, in the programmatic literalness of its kind, the demon from the web had determined that having early seen them, it must early kill them as well.

Darger and Surplus raced through dining rooms and salons, along balconies and down servants' passages. To no avail. Dogged by their hyper-natural nemesis, they found themselves running down a passage, straight toward two massive bronze doors, one of which had been left just barely ajar. So fearful were they that they hardly noticed the guards.

"Hold, sirs!"

The mustachioed master of apes stood before the doorway, his baboons straining against their leashes. His eyes widened with recognition. "By gad, it's you!" he cried in astonishment.

"Lemme kill 'em!" one of the baboons cried. "The lousy bastards!" The others growled agreement.

Surplus would have tried to reason with them, but when he started to slow his pace, Darger put a broad hand on his back and shoved. "Dive!" he commanded. So of necessity the dog of rationality had to bow to the man of action. He tobogganed wildly across the polished marble floor between two baboons, straight at the master of apes, and then between his legs.

The man stumbled, dropping the leashes as he did.

The baboons screamed and attacked.

For an instant all five apes were upon Darger, seizing his limbs, snapping at his face and neck. Then the burning dwarf arrived and, finding his target obstructed, seized the nearest baboon. The animal shrieked as its uniform burst into flames.

As one, the other baboons abandoned their original quarry to fight this newcomer who had dared attack one of their own.

In a trice, Darger leaped over the fallen master of apes, and was through the door. He and Surplus threw their shoulders against its metal surface and pushed. He had one brief glimpse of the fight, with the baboons aflame, and their master's body flying through the air. Then the door slammed shut. Internal bars and bolts, operated by smoothly oiled mechanisms, automatically latched themselves.

For the moment, they were safe.

Surplus slumped against the smooth bronze, and wearily asked, "Where did you *get* that modem?"

"From a dealer of antiquities." Darger wiped his brow with his kerchief. "It was transparently worthless. Whoever would dream it could be repaired?"

Outside, the screaming ceased. There was a very brief silence. Then the creature flung itself against one of the metal doors. It rang with the impact.

A delicate girlish voice wearily said, "What is this noise?"

They turned in surprise and found themselves looking up at the enormous corpus of Queen Gloriana. She lay upon her pallet, swaddled in satin and lace, and abandoned by all, save her valiant (though doomed) guardian apes. A pervasive yeasty smell emanated from her flesh. Within the tremendous folds of chins by the dozens and scores was a small human face. Its mouth moved delicately and asked, "What is trying to get in?"

The door rang again. One of its great hinges gave.

Darger bowed. "I fear, madame, it is your death."

"Indeed?" Blue eyes opened wide and, unexpectedly, Gloriana laughed. "If so, that is excellent good news. I have been praying for death an extremely long time."

"Can any of God's creations truly pray for death and mean it?" asked Darger, who had his philosophical side. "I have known unhappiness myself, yet even so life is precious to me."

"Look at me!" Far up to one side of the body, a tiny arm - though truly no tinier than any woman's arm—waved feebly. "I am not God's creation, but Man's. Who would trade ten minutes of their own life for a century of mine? Who, having mine, would not trade it all for death?"

A second hinge popped. The doors began to shiver. Their metal surfaces radiated heat.

"Darger, we must leave!" Surplus cried. "There is a time for learned conversation, but it is not now."

"Your friend is right," Gloriana said. "There is a small archway hidden behind yon tapestry. Go through it. Place your hand on the left wall and run. If you turn whichever way you must to keep from letting go of the wall, it will lead you outside. You are both rogues, I see, and doubtless deserve punishment, yet I can find nothing in my heart for you but friendship."

"Madame..." Darger began, deeply moved.

"Go! My bridegroom enters."

The door began to fall inward. With a final cry of "Farewell!" from Darger and "Come *on!*" from Surplus, they sped away.

By the time they had found their way outside, all of Buckingham Labyrinth was in flames. The demon, however, did not emerge from the flames, encouraging them to believe that when the modem it carried finally melted down, it had been forced to return to that unholy realm from whence it came.

* * *

The sky was red with flames as the sloop set sail for Calais. Leaning against the rail, watching, Surplus shook his head. "What a terrible sight! I cannot help feeling, in part, responsible."

"Come! Come!" Darger said. "This dyspepsia ill becomes you. We are both rich fellows, now. The Lady Pamela's diamonds will maintain us lavishly for years to come. As for London, this is far from the first fire it has had to endure. Nor will it be the last. Life is short, and so, while we live, let us be jolly."

"These are strange words for a melancholiac," Surplus said wonderingly.

"In triumph, my mind turns its face to the sun. Dwell not on the past, dear friend, but on the future that lies glittering before us."

"The necklace is worthless," Surplus said. "Now that I have the leisure to examine it, free of the distracting flesh of Lady Pamela, I see that these are not diamonds, but mere imitations." He made to cast the necklace into the Thames.

Before he could, though, Darger snatched away the stones from him and studied them closely. Then he threw back his head and laughed. "The biters bit! Well, it may be paste, but it looks valuable still. We shall find good use for it in Paris."

"We are going to Paris?"

"We are partners, are we not? Remember that antique wisdom that whenever a door closes, another opens. For every city that burns, another beckons. To France, then, and adventure! After which, Italy, the Vatican Empire, Austro-Hungary, perhaps even Russia! Never forget that we have yet to present your credentials to the Duke of Muscovy."

"Very well," Surplus said. "But when we do, I'll pick out the modem."

MGM's Tom and Jerry. *Famous Studios'* Herman and Katnip. *Terrytoons'* Little Roquefort and Percy. *Hanna-Barbera's* Pixie and Dixie and Mr. Jinks. *("I hate meeses to pieces!") Hanna-Barbera's* Motormouse and Autocat. *Hanna-Barbera's* Punkin' Puss & Mushmouse. *Gracie Films'* Itchy and Scratchy.

But mostly the mega-popular animated Tom and Jerry *series. Steven Millhauser's unnamed cat 'n' mouse pair are a surrealistic deconstruction of the animated-cartoon cat-versus-mouse stereotype, from the 1940s to the present. The cat chasing the mouse—the cat & mouse-silhouette holes in the door—the cat crashing into a wall and folding like an accordion, or into a bottle and becoming the bottle's shape—the cat getting an anvil dropped on him. It's all here! Read this and you don't need to see any of the above.*

Steven Millhauser has written many novels and short stories. "Cat 'n' Mouse", first published in The New Yorker, *may be his most popular. It is the lead story in his collection* Dangerous Laughter: Thirteen Stories *(Knopf, February 2008). Even when reviewers or critics cover one of his more recent works, they often work a mention of "Cat 'n' Mouse" into it.*

(Yes, we know about Trans-Artists Productions' Courageous Cat and Minute Mouse *and Hanna-Barbera's* Snooper and Blabber. *They were teammates and friends, not rivals.)*

Cat 'n' Mouse

by Steven Millhauser

The cat is chasing the mouse through the kitchen: between the blue chair legs, over the tabletop with its red-and-white checkered tablecloth that is already sliding in great waves, past the sugar bowl falling to the left and the cream jug falling to the right, over the blue chair back, down the chair legs, across the waxed and butter-yellow floor. The cat and the mouse lean backward and try to stop on the slippery wax, which shows their flawless reflections. Sparks shoot from their heels, but it's much too late: the big door looms. The mouse crashes through, leaving a mouse-shaped hole. The cat crashes through, replacing the mouse-shaped hole with a larger, cat-shaped hole. In the living room, they race over the back of the couch, across the piano keys (delicate mouse tune, crash of cat chords), along the blue rug. The fleeing mouse snatches a glance over his shoulder, and when he looks forward again he sees the floor lamp coming closer and closer. Impossible to stop—at the last moment, he splits in half and rejoins himself on the other side. Behind him the rushing cat fails to split in half and crashes into the lamp: his head and body push the brass pole into the shape of a trombone. For a moment, the cat hangs sideways there, his stiff legs shaking like the clapper of a bell. Then he pulls free and rushes after the mouse, who turns and darts into a mousehole in the baseboard. The cat crashes into the wall and folds up like an accordion. Slowly, he unfolds, emitting accordion music. He lies on the floor with his chin on his upraised paw, one eyebrow lifted high in disgust, the claws of his other forepaw tapping the floorboards. A small piece of plaster drops on his head. He raises an outraged eye. A framed painting falls heavily on his head, which plunges out of sight between his shoulders. The painting shows a green tree with bright-red apples. The cat's head struggles to rise, then pops up with the sound of a yanked cork, lifting the picture. Apples fall from the tree and land with a thump on the grass. The cat shudders, winces. A final apple falls. Slowly it rolls toward the frame, drops over the edge, and lands on the cat's head. In the cat's eyes, cash registers ring up "No Sale."

The mouse, dressed in a bathrobe and slippers, is sitting in his plump armchair, reading a book. He is tall and slim. His feet rest on a hassock, and a pair of spectacles rest on the end of his long, whiskered nose. Yellow light from a table lamp pours onto the book and dimly illuminates the cozy brown room. On the wall hang a tilted sampler bearing the words "Home Sweet Home," an oval photograph of the mouse's mother with her gray hair in a bun, and a reproduction of Seurat's "Sunday Afternoon" in which all the figures are mice. Near the armchair is a bookcase filled with books, with several titles visible: "Martin Cheddarwit," Gouda's "Faust," "The Memoirs of Anthony Edam," "A History of the Medicheese," the sonnets of Shakespaw. As the mouse reads his book, he reaches without looking toward a dish on the table. The dish is empty: his fingers tap about inside it. The mouse rises and goes over to the cupboard, which is empty except for a tin box with the word "Cheese" on it. He opens the box and turns it upside down. Into his palm drops a single toothpick. He gives it a melancholy look. Shaking his head, he returns to his chair and takes up his book. In a bubble above his head a picture appears: He is seated at a long table covered with a white tablecloth. He is holding a fork upright in one fist and a knife upright in the other. A mouse butler dressed in tails sets before him a piece of cheese the size of a wedding cake.

From the mousehole emerges a red telescope. The lens looks to the left, then to the right. A hand issues from the end of the telescope and beckons the mouse forward. The mouse steps from the mousehole, collapses the telescope, and thrusts it into his bathrobe pocket. In the moonlit room, he tiptoes carefully, lifting his legs very high, over to the base of the armchair. He dives under the chair and peeks out through the fringe. He emerges from beneath the armchair, slinks over to the couch, and dives under. He peeks out through the fringe. He emerges from beneath the couch and approaches the slightly open kitchen door. He stands flat against the doorjamb, facing the living room, his eyes darting left and right. One leg tiptoes delicately around the jamb. His stretched body snaps after it like a rubber band. In the kitchen, he creeps to a moonlit chair, stands pressed against a chair leg, begins to climb. His nose rises over the tabletop: he sees a cream pitcher, a gleaming knife, a looming pepper mill. On a breadboard sits a wedge of cheese. The mouse, hunching his shoulders, tiptoes up to the cheese. From a pocket of his robe he removes a white handkerchief that he ties around his neck. He bends over the cheese, half closing his eyes, as if he were sniffing a flower. With a crashing sound, the cat springs onto the table. As he chases the mouse, the tablecloth bunches in waves, the sugar bowl topples, and waterfalls of sugar spill to the floor. An olive from a fallen cocktail glass rolls across the table, knocking into a cup, a saltshaker, a trivet: the objects light up and cause bells to ring, as in a pinball machine. On the floor, a brigade of ants is gathering the sugar: one ant catches the falling grains in a bucket, which he dumps into the bucket of a second ant, who dumps the sugar into the bucket of a third ant, all the way across the room, until the last ant dumps it into a waiting truck. The cat chases the mouse over the blue chair back, down the chair legs, across the waxed floor. Both lean backward and try to stop as the big door comes closer and closer.

* * *

The mouse is sitting in his armchair with his chin in his hand, looking off into the distance with a melancholy expression. He is thoughtful by temperament, and he is distressed at the necessity of interrupting his meditations for the daily search for food. The search is wearying and absurd in itself, but is made unbearable by the presence of the brutish cat. The mouse's disdain for the cat is precise and abundant: he loathes the soft, heavy paws with their hidden hooks, the glinting teeth, the hot, fish-stinking breath. At the same time, he confesses to himself a secret admiration for the cat's coarse energy and simplicity. It appears that the cat has no other aim in life than to catch the mouse. Although the faculty of astonishment is not highly developed in the mouse, he is constantly astonished by the cat's unremitting enmity. This makes the cat dangerous, despite his stupidity, for the mouse recognizes that he himself has long periods when the cat fades entirely from his mind. Moreover, despite the fundamental simplicity of the cat's nature, it remains true that the cat is cunning: he plots tirelessly against the mouse, and his ludicrous wiles require in the mouse an alert attention that he would prefer not to give. The mouse is aware of the temptation of indifference; he must continually exert himself to be wary. He feels that he is exhausting his nerves and harming his spirit by attending to the cat; at the same time, he realizes that his attention is at best imperfect, and that the cat is thinking uninterruptedly, with boundless energy, of him. If only the mouse could stay in his hole, he would be happy, but he cannot stay in his hole, because of the need to find cheese. It is not a situation calculated to produce the peace of mind conducive to contemplation.

The cat is standing in front of the mousehole with a hammer in one hand and a saw in the other. Beside him rests a pile of yellow boards and

221

a big bag of nails. He begins furiously hammering and sawing, moving across the room in a cloud of dust that conceals him. Suddenly, the dust clears and the cat beholds his work: a long, twisting pathway that begins at the mousehole and passes under the couch, over the back of the armchair, across the piano, through the kitchen door, and onto the kitchen table. On the tablecloth, at the end of the pathway, is a large mousetrap on which sits a lump of cheese. The cat tiptoes over to the refrigerator, vanishes behind it, and slyly thrusts out his head: his eyes dart left and right. There is the sound of a bicycle bell: ring ring. A moment later, the mouse appears, pedaling fiercely. He speeds from the end of the pathway onto the table. As he screeches to a stop, the round wheels stretch out of shape and then become round again. The mouse is wearing riding goggles, a riding cap, and gloves. He leans his bicycle against the sugar bowl, steps over to the mousetrap, and looks at it with interest. He steps onto the mousetrap, sits down on the brass bar, and puts on a white bib. From a pocket of his leather jacket he removes a knife and fork. He eats the cheese swiftly. After his meal, he replaces the knife and fork in his pocket and begins to play on the mousetrap. He swings on a high bar, hangs upside down by his legs, walks the parallel bars, performs gymnastic stunts. Then he climbs onto his bicycle and disappears along the pathway, ringing his bell. The cat emerges from behind the refrigerator and springs onto the table beside the mousetrap. He frowns down at the trap. From the top of his head he plucks a single hair: it comes loose with the sound of a snapping violin string. Slowly, he lowers the hair toward the mousetrap. The hair touches the spring. The mousetrap remains motionless. He presses the spring with a spoon. The mousetrap remains motionless. He bangs the spring with a sledgehammer. The mousetrap remains motionless. He looks at the trap with rage. Cautiously, he reaches out a single toe. The mousetrap springs shut with the sound of a slammed iron door. The cat hops about the table holding his trapped foot as the toe swells to the size of a light bulb, bright red.

The cat enters on the left, disguised as a mouse. He is wearing a blond wig, a nose mask, and a tight black dress slit to the thigh. He has high and very round breasts, a tiny waist, and round, rolling hips. His lips are bright red, and his black lashes are so tightly curled that when he blinks his eyes the lashes roll out and snap back like window shades. He walks slowly and seductively, resting one hand on a hip and one hand on his blond hair. The mouse is standing in the mousehole, leaning against one side with his hands in his pockets. His eyes protrude from their sockets in the shape of telescopes. In the lens of each telescope is a thumping heart. Slowly, as if mesmerized, the mouse sleepwalks into the room. The cat places a needle on a record, and rumba music begins to play. The cat dances with his hands clasped behind his neck, thrusting out each hip, fluttering his long lashes, turning to face the other way: in the tight black dress, his twitching backside is shaped like the ace of spades. The mouse faces the cat and begins to dance. They stride back and forth across the room, wriggling and kicking in step. As they dance, the cat's wig comes loose, revealing one cat ear. The cat dances over to a bearskin rug and lies down on his side. He closes his long-lashed eyes and purses his red, red lips. The mouse steps up to the cat. He reaches into his pocket, removes a cigar, and places it between the big red lips. The cat's eyes open. They look down at the cigar, look up, and look down again. The cat removes the cigar and stares at it. The cigar explodes. When the smoke clears, the cat's face is black. He gives a strained, very white smile. Many small lines appear in his teeth. The teeth crack into little pieces and fall out.

The cat is lying on his back in his basket in the kitchen. His hands are clasped behind his head, his left knee is raised, and his right ankle rests sideways on the raised knee. He is filled with rage at the thought of the mouse, who he knows despises him. He would like to tear the mouse to pieces, to roast him over a fire, to plunge him into a pan of burning butter. He understands that his rage is not the rage of hunger and he wonders whether the mouse himself is responsible for evoking this savagery, which burns in his chest like indigestion. He despises the mouse's physical delicacy, his weak arms as thin as the teeth of combs, his frail, crushable skull, his fondness for books and solitude. At the same time, he is irritably aware that he admires the mouse's elegance, his air of culture and languor, his easy self-assurance. Why is he always reading? In a sense, the mouse intimidates the cat: in his presence, the cat feels clumsy and foolish. He thinks obsessively about the mouse and suspects with rage that the mouse frequently does not think about him at all, there in his brown room. If the mouse was less indifferent, would he burn with such hatred? Might they learn to live peacefully together in the same house? Would he be released from this pain of outrage in his heart?

The mouse is standing at his workbench, curling the eyelashes of a mechanical cat. Her long black hair is as shiny as licorice; her lips look like licked candy. She is wearing a tight red dress, black fishnet stockings, and red high heels. The mouse stands the mechanical cat on her feet, unzips the back of her dress, and winds a big key. He zips up the dress and aims her toward the mousehole. In the living room, the mechanical cat struts slowly back and forth; her pointy breasts stick out like party hats. The cat's head rises over the back of the armchair. In his eyes appear hearts pierced by arrows. He slithers over the chair and slides along the floor like honey. When he reaches the strutting cat, he glides to an upright position and stands mooning at her. His heart is thumping so hard that it pushes out the skin of his chest with each beat. The cat reaches into a pocket and removes a straw boater, which he places on his head at a rakish angle. He fastens at his throat a large polka-dot bow tie. He becomes aware of a ticking sound. He removes from his pocket a round yellow watch, places it against his ear, frowns, and returns it to his pocket. He bends close to the face of the cat and sees in each of her eyes a shiny round black bomb with a burning fuse. The cat turns to the audience and then back to the dangerous eyes. The mechanical cat blows up. When the smoke clears, the cat's skin hangs in tatters about him, revealing his raw pink flesh and a pair of polka-dot boxer shorts.

Outside the mousehole, the cat is winding up a mouse that exactly resembles the real mouse. The mechanical mouse is wearing a bathrobe and slippers, stands with hands in pockets, and has a pair of eyeglasses perched at the end of its nose. The cat lifts open the top of the mouse's head, which is attached in the manner of a hinged lid. He inserts a sizzling red stick of dynamite and closes the lid. He sets the mouse in front of the hole and watches as it vanishes through the arched opening. Inside, the mouse is sitting in his chair, reading a book. He does not raise his eyes to the visitor, who glides over with its hands in its pockets. Still reading, the mouse reaches out and lifts open the head of his double. He removes the sizzling dynamite, thrusts it into a cake, and inserts the cake into the mouse's head. He turns the mechanical mouse around and continues reading as it walks out through the arch. The cat is squatting beside the hole with his eyes shut and his fingers pressed in his ears. He opens his eyes and sees the mouse. His eyebrows rise. He snatches up the mouse, opens its head, and lifts out a thickly frosted cake that says "Happy Birthday." In the center of the cake is a sizzling red stick of dynamite. The cat's hair leaps up. He takes a tremendous breath and blows out the fuse with such force that for a moment the cake is slanted. Now the cat grins, licks his teeth, and opens his jaws. He hears a sound. The cake is ticking loudly: tock tock, tock tock. Puzzled, the cat holds it up to one ear. He listens closely. A terrible knowledge dawns in his eyes.

The cat rides into the living room in a bright-yellow crane. From the boom hangs a shiny black wrecking ball. He drives up to the mousehole and stops. He pushes and pulls a pair of levers, which cause the wrecking ball to be inserted into a gigantic rubber band attached to a gigantic slingshot. The rubber band stretches back and back. Suddenly, it releases the shiny black ball, which smashes into the wall. The entire house collapses, leaving only a tall red chimney standing amid the ruins. On top of the chimney is a stork's nest, in which a stork sits with a fishing pole. He is wearing a blue baseball cap. Below, in the rubble, a stirring is visible. The cat rises unsteadily, leaning on a crutch. His head is covered with a white bandage that conceals an eye; one leg is in a cast and one arm in a sling. With the tip of his crutch, he moves away a pile of rubble and exposes a fragment of baseboard. In the baseboard we see the unharmed mousehole. Inside the mousehole, the mouse sits in his chair, reading a book.

The mouse understands that the clownishly inept cat has the freedom to fail over and over again, during the long course of an inglorious lifetime, while he himself is denied the liberty of a single mistake. It is highly unlikely, of course, that he will ever be guilty of an error, since he is much cleverer than the cat and immediately sees through every one of his risible stratagems. Still, might not the very knowledge of his superiority lead to a relaxation of vigilance that will prove fatal, in the end? After all, he is not invulnerable; he is invulnerable only insofar as he is vigilant. The mouse is bored, deeply bored, by the ease with which he outwits the cat; there are times when he longs for a more worthy enemy, someone more like himself. He understands that his boredom is a dangerous weakness against which he must perpetually be on his guard. Sometimes he thinks, If only I could stop watching over myself, if only I could let myself go! The thought alarms him and causes him to look over his shoulder at the mousehole, across which the shadow of the cat has already fallen.

The cat enters from the left, carrying a sack over one shoulder. He sets the sack down beside the mousehole. He unties a rope from the neck of the sack, plunges both hands in, and carefully lifts out a gray cloud. He places the cloud in the air above the mousehole. Rain begins to fall from the cloud, splashing down in great drops. The cat reaches into the sack and removes some old clothes. He swiftly disguises himself as a peddler and rings the mouse's bell. The mouse appears in the arched doorway, leaning against the side with his arms folded across his stomach and his ankles crossed as he stares out at the rain. The cat removes from the sack an array of mouse-size umbrellas, which he opens in turn: red, yellow, green, blue. The mouse shakes his head. The cat removes from the sack a yellow slicker, a pair of hip boots, a fishing rod and tackle box. The mouse shakes his head. The cat removes a red rubber sea horse, a compressed-air tank, a diving bell, a rowboat, a yacht. The mouse shakes his head, steps into his house, and slams the door. He opens the door, hangs a sign on the knob, and slams the door again. The sign reads "Not Home." The rain falls harder. The cat steps out from under the cloud, which rises above his head and begins to follow him about the room. The storm grows worse: he is pelted with hailstones the size of golf balls. In the cloud appear many golfers, driving golf balls

225

into the room. Forked lightning flashes; thunder roars. The cat rushes around the room trying to escape the cloud and dives under the couch. His tail sticks out. Lightning strikes the tail, which crackles like an electric wire. The couch rises for an instant, exposing the luminous, electrified cat rigid with shock; inside the cat's body, with its rim of spiked fur, his blue-white skeleton is visible. Now snow begins to fall from the cloud, and whistling winds begin to blow. Snow lies in drifts on the rug, rises swiftly up the sides of the armchair, sweeps up to the mantelpiece, where the clock looks down in terror and covers its eyes with its hands. The cat struggles slowly through the blizzard but is soon encased in snow. Icicles hang from his chin. He stands motionless, shaped like a cat struggling forward with bent head. The door of the mousehole opens and the mouse emerges, wearing earmuffs, scarf, and gloves. The sun is shining. He begins shovelling a path. When he comes to the snow-cat, he climbs to the top of his shovel and sticks a carrot in the center of the snowy face. Then he climbs down, steps back, and begins throwing snowballs. The cat's head falls off.

The cat is pacing angrily in the kitchen, his hands behind his back and his eyebrows drawn down in a V. In a bubble above his head a wish appears: He is operating a circular saw that moves slowly, with high whining sounds, along a yellow board. At the end of the board is the mouse, lying on his back, tied down with ropes. The image vanishes and is replaced by another: The cat, wearing an engineer's hat, is driving a great train along a track. The mouse is stretched across the middle of the track, his wrists fastened to one rail and his ankles to the other. Sweat bursts in big drops from the mouse's face as the image vanishes and is replaced by another: The cat is turning a winch that slowly lowers an anvil toward the mouse, who is tied to a little chair. The mouse looks up in terror. Suddenly, the cat lets go of the crank and the anvil rushes down with a whistling sound as the winch spins wildly. At the last moment, the mouse tumbles away. The anvil falls through the bubble onto the cat's head.

The cat understands that the mouse will always outwit him, but this tormenting knowledge serves only to inflame his desire to catch the mouse. He will never give up. His life, in relation to the mouse, is one long failure, a monotonous succession of unspeakable humiliations; his unhappiness is relieved only by moments of delusional hope, during which he believes, despite doubts supported by a lifetime of bitter experience, that at last he will succeed. Although he knows that he will never catch the mouse, who will forever escape into his mousehole a half inch ahead of the reaching claw, he also knows that only if he catches the mouse will his wretched life be justified. He will be transformed. Is it therefore his own life that he seeks, when he lies awake plotting against the mouse? Is it, when all is said and done, himself that he is chasing? The cat frowns and scratches his nose.

The cat stands before the mousehole holding in one hand a piece of white chalk. On the blue wall he draws the outline of a large door. The mousehole is at the bottom of the door. He draws the circle of a doorknob and opens the door. He steps into a black room. At the end of the room stands the mouse with a piece of chalk. The mouse draws a white mousehole on the wall and steps through. The cat kneels down and peers into the mousehole. He stands up and draws another door. He opens the door and steps into another black room. At the end of the room stands the mouse, who draws another mousehole and steps through. The cat draws another door, the mouse draws another mousehole. Faster and faster they draw: door, hole, door, hole, door. At the end of the last room, the mouse draws on the wall a white stick of dynamite. He draws a white match, which he takes in his hand and strikes against the wall. He lights the dynamite and hands it to the cat. The cat looks at the white outline of the dynamite. He offers it to the mouse. The mouse shakes his head. The cat points to himself and raises his eyebrows. The mouse nods. The stick of dynamite explodes.

* * *

The cat enters on the left, wearing a yellow hard hat and pushing a red wheelbarrow. The wheelbarrow is piled high with boards. In front of the mousehole, the cat puts down the handles of the barrow, pulls a hammer and saw from the pile of boards, and thrusts a fistful of black nails between his teeth. He begins sawing and hammering rapidly, moving from one end of the room to the other as a cloud of dust conceals his work. Suddenly, the dust clears and the cat beholds his creation: he has constructed a tall guillotine, connected to the mousehole by a stairway. The blue-black glistening blade hangs between posts high above the opening for the head. Directly below the opening, on the other side, stands a basket. On the rim of the basket the cat places a wedge of cheese. The cat loops a piece of string onto a lever in the side of the guillotine and fastens the other end of the string to the wedge of cheese. Then he tiptoes away with hunched shoulders and vanishes behind a fire shovel. A moment later, the mouse climbs the stairs onto the platform of the guillotine. He stands with his hands in the pockets of his robe and contemplates the blade, the opening for the head, and the piece of cheese. He removes from one pocket a yellow package with a red bow. He leans over the edge of the platform and slips the loop from the lever. He thrusts his head through the head hole, removes the piece of cheese from the rim of the basket, and sets the package in its place. He ties the string to the package, slides his head back through the hole, and fits the loop of the string back over the lever. From his pocket he removes a large pair of scissors, which he lays on the platform. He next removes a length of rope, which he fastens to the lever so that the rope hangs nearly to the floor. On the floor, he stands cross-ankled against the wheel of the barrow, eating his cheese. A moment later, the cat leaps onto the platform. He looks up in surprise at the unfallen blade. He crouches down, peers through the head hole, and sees the yellow package. He frowns. He looks up at the blade. He looks at the yellow package. Gingerly, he reaches a paw through the opening and snatches it back. He frowns at the string. A cunning look comes into his eyes. He notices the pair of scissors, picks them up, and cuts the string. He waits, but nothing happens. Eagerly, he thrusts his head through the opening and reaches for the package. The mouse, eating his cheese with one hand, lazily tugs at the rope with the other. The blade rushes down with the sound of a roaring train; a forlorn whistle blows. The cat tries to pull his head out of the hole. The blade slices off the top half of his head, which drops into the basket and rolls noisily around like a coin. The cat pulls himself out of the hole and stumbles about until he falls over the edge of the platform into the basket. He seizes the top of his head and puts it on like a hat. It is backward. He straightens it with a half turn. In his hand, he sees with surprise the yellow package with the red bow. Frowning, he unties it. Inside is a bright-red stick of dynamite with a sizzling fuse. The cat looks at the dynamite and turns his head to the audience. He blinks once. The dynamite explodes. When the smoke clears, the cat's face is black. In each eye a ship cracks in half and slowly sinks in the water.

* * *

The mouse is sitting in his chair with his feet on the hassock and his open book face down on his lap. A mood of melancholy has invaded him, as if the brown tones of his room had seeped into his brain. He feels stale and out of sorts: he moves within the narrow compass of his mind, utterly devoid of fresh ideas. Is he perhaps too much alone? He thinks of the cat and wonders whether there is some dim and distant possibility of a connection, perhaps a companionship. Is it possible that they might become friends? Perhaps he could teach the cat to appreciate the things of the mind, and learn from the cat to enjoy life's simpler pleasures. Perhaps the cat, too, feels an occasional sting of loneliness. Haven't they much in common, after all? Both are bachelors, indoor sorts, who enjoy the comforts of a cozy domesticity; both are secretive; both take pleasure in plots and schemes. The more the mouse pursues this line of thought, the more it seems to him that the cat is a large, soft mouse. He imagines the cat with mouse ears and gentle mouse paws, wearing a white bib, sitting across from him at the kitchen table, lifting to his mouth a fork at the end of which is a piece of cheese.

* * *

The cat enters from the right with a chalkboard eraser in one hand. He goes over to the mousehole, bends down, and erases it. He stands up and erases the wall, revealing the mouse's home. The mouse is sitting in his chair with his feet on the hassock and his open book face down on his lap. The cat bends over and erases the book. The mouse looks up in irritation. The cat erases the mouse's chair. He erases the hassock. He erases the entire room. He tosses the eraser over his shoulder. Now there is nothing left in the world except the cat and the mouse. The cat snatches him up in a fist. The cat's red tongue slides over glistening teeth sharp as ice picks. Here and there, over a tooth, a bright star expands and contracts. The cat opens his jaws wider, closes his eyes, and hesitates. The death of the mouse is desirable in every way, but will life without him really be pleasurable? Will the mouse's absence satisfy him entirely? Is it conceivable that he may miss the mouse, from time to time? Is it possible that he needs the mouse, in some disturbing way?

As the cat hesitates, the mouse reaches into a pocket of his robe and removes a red handkerchief. With swift circular strokes he wipes out the cat's teeth while the cat's eyes watch in surprise. He wipes out the cat's eyes. He wipes out the cat's whiskers. He wipes out the cat's head. Still held in the cat's fist, he wipes out the entire cat, except for the paw holding him. Then, very carefully, he wipes out the paw. He drops lightly down and slaps his palms together. He looks about. He is alone with his red handkerchief in a blank white world. After a pause, he begins to wipe himself out, moving rapidly from head to toe. Now there is nothing left but the red handkerchief. The handkerchief flutters, grows larger, and suddenly splits in half. The halves become red theatre curtains, which begin to close. Across the closing curtains, words write themselves in black script:

"The End."

Scott Bradfield is a literary professor and critic who has taught at colleges and universities from California to England, and whose reviews have appeared in such journals as The Times Literary Supplement. *He is best-known for his novels (read and enjoy* Animal Planet, *his satiric version of Orwell's* Animal Farm, *available on Kindle now) and short stories that usually lampoon some foible of modern society.*

In P~~ig~~ Paradise, *Hubert (a pig) and Harry (a wolf) work in the same office. Harry has never been anything but friendly—maybe too friendly. The nervous pig can't concentrate on his job with a gregarious, sharp-fanged wolf insisting on being buddy-buddy with him in his face all the time. So Hubie files an interspecies harassment complaint with Employee Relations. Matters quickly escalate out of control from there.*

~~Pig~~ Paradise

by Scott Bradfield

> If it's true, as some German fellow has said,
> that without phosphorus there is no thought,
> it is still more true that there is no
> kindness of heart without
> certain amount of imagination.
>
> - Joseph Conrad, "Amy Foster"

Hubert was breaking into a sweat around his twitchy pink snout and trying to look casual with an icy glass of Évian. His bare bottom and the Naugahyde chair were starting to feel like a potentially embarrassing match.

"Look at me, Hubert. Why won't you *look* at me?"

Harry leaned across the Swedish modern office desk. His paws came together in a blunt arrow aimed directly at Hubert.

"I *am* looking at you, Harry. I mean, I'm looking at you right now."

Harry's red, lupine gaze was cool and unremitting.

"No, you're not, Hubert. You're looking at my paws. You're looking at my sharp teeth. You never look me in the eye, Hubert. Do you think I don't notice?"

Hubert rested the water glass against his monogrammed red cotton weskit. He knew he should meet Harry's gaze, but he couldn't do it. He simply couldn't.

"I'm doing my best," Hubert told the glass. "I just wish, you know. I wish you wouldn't take it so personal."

"Take it personal," Harry said simply. "I shouldn't take it personal."

Hubert shifted in his squeaky seat. The hairs on the back of his neck bristled.

"You've got every right to be, well, not pissed off, Harry. I haven't done anything wrong. But your feelings, I'm sure your feelings *are* hurt, and I'm trying, Harry. I'm trying to understand."

Harry showed Hubert one digit after another of his right forepaw, ticking off each remonstrance. "You don't look at me. If you see me on the bus, you pretend not to. If you see me coming down the corridor, you duck the other way. If I ask for a meeting, you're too busy, you're ill, whatever. Everybody notices, Hubie. And how do you think it makes me feel? To be treated like some sort of, Jesus, some wild animal. Like I'm going to hunt you down and rip out your belly. Is that what you see when you look at me, Hubert? A savage beast that wants you for breakfast?"

Hubert looked out the window at the revolving corporate icon: a house-size aluminum kettle being stirred by a smiling wolf and an equally smiling pig.

Mama O'Brian's All-Veggie Pies
— today's food for today's world —

It was the first surge of pure anger that Hubert had felt in weeks.

"I didn't make me who I am, Harry. And I don't know what good you think you're doing putting so much pressure on me all the time. Like I can't come to work anymore without these guilt trips you're always laying on me about the way I feel, Harry, and I can't *help* the way I feel, but my whole inner being, Harry. According to you and the way you look at me, there's something wrong with how I feel deep inside."

Hubert thumped his red weskit twice with his hard, pale trotter. It gave him courage and a sense of resonance. He looked up.

Here's my eye contact, his expression told Harry. If this is what you want—you got it.

"Don't get upset," Harry said softly. "All I'm trying to say—"

"You're trying to say that I hurt your feelings, I'm not open-minded enough, I don't treat you like, like an equal or something. Like everybody's an equal and I'm supposed to walk down these corridors going Hi, hello, how you doing, equal equal equal, bing bing bing. But life isn't like that, Harry. Everybody's different, and everybody treats each other different, and I don't care what they say in the 'Employee Guidelines.'"

The tension seemed to bend in Harry's direction. Harry leaned back in his swivel chair, breaking into a sweat around his snout and collar.

"There's no need to raise your voice, Hubert. And as far as putting pressure on you, I never meant… This wasn't supposed…"

Hubert regained his breath. Now it was Harry who better keep out of *his* way.

"If you've got problems with my sales figures, Harry, then send me a memo and hey, better yet, copy it to the entire Sales Department and that's corporate, Harry. That's a matter we should set straight. But if you've got *personal* problems with me? Maybe you don't think I'm friendly enough, or respect you enough, or I don't look you in the eye, or whatever. You learn to *live* with that, Harry. Because I won't be harassed, Harry. I won't be harassed by *you* ever again."

* * *

"How'd it go, Mr. Armstrong?"

"I'd rather not talk about it, Stacey. Did my wife call?"

"She did. She and Mrs. Conroy left the kids with a sitter to attend some PTA thingie. She suggested you pick up dinner on the way home."

"How about those orders from the Franciscan winery?"

"On your desk."

"And the corporate earnings?"

"Ditto, Mr. Armstrong."

"Thanks, Stacey. For the next hour or so I don't want to be disturbed."

Stacey nodded curtly and turned back to her flat screen. Hubert watched her for a few seconds—just to make sure she wasn't watching him.

"Oh, and Stacey?"

"Uh-huh." The glowing spreadsheets were reflected by her pink eyes like a scheme of inner mathematics.

"I'll tell you if I need anything. Okay?"

"Okay, Hubie."

As Hubert shoved the door shut behind himself, it felt like letting all the air out of a balloon. He exhaled with a long, expiring whoosh and loosened his damp collar. He hyperventilated ten times and then held it, feeling the subsidence of blood in his brain. The room had gone white around the edges. The intercom on his desk began to buzz.

"Hubert Armstrong."

"How'd it go, old buddy? You marched past in the hall and didn't even look at me."

"Stan, I swear. I can't breathe or something. I still can't believe it. The things I said."

The intercom issued a long, staticky sigh.

"What sort of things, Hubert? What sort of things did you say?"

Hubert felt the small, crowded room yawn open around him. The clumsy metal bookshelves filled with account ledgers and sales catalogs. The company calendar and wall clock. The framed photo of Angela and the kids.

"I think I told him to piss off, get away from me or else, you know."

"Or else what?"

"I'd file a report with Employee Relations. For the one thing, you know, the one thing they could nail him for."

"Interspecies harassment."

Hubert collapsed into his wide-back swivel chair. He closed his eyes and placed his hand on the cold, hissing intercom.

"And the scary thing, Stan? I think I meant it, too."

* * *

"I don't think it's because Harry's a wolf," Angela confessed to Muriel on their way home that night from the fund-raising committee. "I think it's more because he's a guy, and a middle management guy at that. Other guys, especially guys higher up the corporate ladder, make Hubie nervous; they always have. Anyway, Hubie has never been what you'd call a social individual. Not like your Harry."

Muriel lit her long, filtered menthol off the dashboard lighter and peered through her thwipping wipers at the foggy, dim-lit street ahead.

"I know there's nothing you can do, Angela. It just seems such a shame."

"I know, Muriel. I *know*."

Angela hated driving through the border regions, even in a car as large, luxurious and well equipped as Muriel's SUV. Ever since the Cultural Intercession, it was the one part of town which hadn't changed, populated by the same bankrupt strip malls, triple-X-rated bookstores and velour-curtained massage parlors.

"I keep thinking it'll blow over," Angela thought out loud, "and they'll get used to each other. Like you and me, Muriel; or even the kids. You think Hubie'd appreciate the open-minded ones like Harry who were so instrumental, you know. In creating so many new opportunities."

Muriel had yet to shift beyond first gear as they crawled through the close-packed urban streets, rocky with potholes, overturned trash bins and soggy, unraked leaves. Every few seconds, Muriel reactivated the door-lock mechanism. Just to make sure.

"It bothers Harry, that's all. And I can't pretend it doesn't," Muriel said. "You know, the way Hubie acts around us, those nervous little flinches of his. And the way he paces around until he's memorized every possible exit before he'll even sit in the same room as us. That night we had you over for dinner, Jesus. He made me so uncomfortable; even the kids noticed. And by the time we sat down to those veggieburgers I couldn't eat a thing and then Hubie—"

"Please, Muriel. It's not like I don't remember."

"Please let me finish. And then the way Hubie got up and pretended he'd been beeped on his cell phone and took off like that, problem with the sales brochures or something, and knocking over his bowl on the floor he was in such a hurry to leave he didn't even look back he just—"

"*Watch out!*"

In that fractured moment it was as if some belated impulse had caught up with them. Muriel slammed on the brakes.

We've been here before, Angela thought mystically. Muriel and I, floating through space for eternities, finding our way home to this recurring moment, again and again.

There was a terrible, short-lived *thunk* and a brief glimpse of aborted momentum. Then a clutch of brightly adorned rags landed solidly in the street.

The large fat rat sat frozen in the electric white glare of the SUV's high beams, partially turned to regard them, glinty mouth agape.

"Oh Jesus, Angela. I didn't see him. I really didn't."

The rat, clad in a hooded sweatshirt and latex jogging trunks, shook animation into his face and fingers. He got to his feet. He rubbed his furry forehead.

After a stunned moment, he exploded into words.

"What the *fuck* do you think you're doing!"

"Come on, Muriel. Let's get out of here."

The rat acquired a weird stature in the SUV's moonish emanations. He started towards them slowly, swinging his scraggly arms from side to side.

"You drive these boats though our neighborhoods like you *own* the place!"

Muriel looked over both shoulders while groping blindly for the clutch.

"Just back up, Muriel. Back up and get us out of here."

"You hear what I'm telling you? You fucking wolves and pigs think you own the place? Well, not in my book, sisters! Come on! Get outta that fucking car! Talk to me face to face!"

There was a backward lurch and kick from the clutch as the motor stalled and Muriel hit the ignition. The starter was grinding brokenly, like an obstructed blender.

"I really didn't see him," Muriel whispered as the engine finally caught and fired. Then, with two sweeps of the steering wheel, she backed into a driveway and took them swerving down the opposite side of the street. "I mean, why would I, he's acting like—"

"Come back here and show me your driver's license you crazy bitches! You think you can just knock us down in the street and run away from your responsibilities!"

Angela watched the shrouded rat recede in the rearview window until distance and street engulfed him. Every few moments or so, the SUV hit an obstruction, lifted off the ground, and came down again with a smooth, well-engineered glide.

"Don't tell Harry," Muriel said. "He's been so worried about the office. I don't want him to start worrying about me and the kids, too."

But Angela couldn't hear her. All she could think about was what she was going to tell Hubie when she got home.

* * *

"You practically got us *killed!*" she shouted palely, shaking her red weskit at him like a hyperactive toreador. "We should have been watching the road and paying attention. But all we could think about was *you*, Hubert P. Armstrong! You and your petty, childish, and yes, Hubie, your *bigoted*, old-fashioned attitudes about wolves. Maybe you haven't quite noticed yet, Hubie, but this *is* the twenty-first century. Wolves don't exactly run in packs and howl at the moon any more than we root around in our own feces. Animals change over time, Hubie. They adopt, adapt, improve. Otherwise the world wouldn't get any better, we wouldn't learn anything, we wouldn't grow up. Harry's sick over the way you treat him. And Muriel, and me—even *I'm* sick of the way you act. I mean, Muriel is like my only friend left since the Intercession, and I'm *proud* of the way I've opened our home to her and the kids. And I'm telling you, Hubert. If you're not proud of me, too, if you're not going to support me in showing a little animal decency to our new neighbors, then, then…"

Angela was running out of gas, issuing faint, grayish sputters from her thin, pink lips, like a dying outboard. Meanwhile, Hubert sat alone at the dining room table, staring ashamedly into his cardboard container of truffles in black bean sauce.

"I never meant to upset you, Angel," he said softly. "I just can't help the way I feel."

The red weskit fell from her hand to the floor, distinctly, like punctuation.

"Your feelings, Hubert, have nothing, they haven't got anything to do with, I mean—*my* feelings, Hubert, and *Muriel's* feelings…"

Hubert didn't feel capable of replying or moving a muscle. But then, somewhere deep inside himself, words gathered and cohered. Words that didn't have anything to do with him, or Angela, or even Harry.

He replaced the carton of Chinese food upon the stain it had left on his white cotton napkin. Carton and stain—a perfect fit.

"I've thought long and hard about everybody's feelings, Angela. I really have. I went to work with Harry every day on the same bus for months. I watched him and the kids move in next door, attend block parties, and play with our kids in the yard. I never sneered at them or shouted insults, and when I saw those kids down the road throwing rocks at their car that day, remember. You remember what I did?"

"I remember, Hubert." Angela sat down in the crimson stuffed chair. Hubert often thought of it as the sad chair.

"I told them to go home, I'd call their parents, and they *went*, Angel. Look, I know my behavior hasn't been, well, exemplary, but I never meant to be rude, and I still keep wondering. Don't I have any rights in this matter? Don't my feelings count, too? I know I should look Harry in the eye and smile at Muriel and let the kids snap at my heels but I just *can't* do it. It sends me into a panic. I can't even sleep anymore. And I just keep asking myself, maybe I'm wrong. Maybe wolves *have* changed, and maybe I *haven't* changed enough. But this daily corporate and social pressure they're exerting, it's just not fair. I thought freedom meant being free to think the wrong thing from time to time. But the sort of freedom you guys are talking? Well, I'm sorry. That doesn't feel like freedom at all."

* * *

Long after he tucked Angela into bed and kissed her good night, Hubert sat awake watching an old cop-buddy movie from his childhood. Entitled *Fatal Fire*, it featured exploding automobiles, collapsing skyscrapers, and two scowling, innately sentimental action stars who were constantly following one another into scenes of rapid-fire mayhem—a wolf who hated being partner to a pig, and a pig who hated being partner to a wolf. Hubert was surprised to find himself two beats ahead of the more memorable dialogue.

"Bite my pink butt, Furball!"

Or: "You know what I like best about pigs, short stuff? The gravy!"

It was where the Cultural Intercession had begun several years ago, just before the schools were merged and the suburbs desegregated. And to this day, it was where Hubert felt the Cultural Intercession should have ended.

* * *

Just before dawn, Hubert awoke on the sofa in a pale, crinkly moondust of Pringles. He heard the toilet flush upstairs and the soft, distant burbling of *Chick Chat* on Cissy's transistor radio. *Which pup bands are your favorite, Allison from Maidenhead? Which pup stars? Have you entered our Become a Pup Star competition? Submit your photos now.*

Hubert rubbed his puffy cheeks, went to the front window, and pried back the insulated curtains to see the glowing green lawns and dimming streetlights of Paradise Village Estates. A few early risers were already leaning rickety aluminum stepladders against rooftops, or washing their cars with sudsy water. Harry the Wolf, clad in his wife's billowy chiffon robe and a pair of tattered sweat-pants, stood at the foot of his driveway, unsnapping the *Herald* and saying something to Sid Field across the street. Sid, the first pig to be booted upstairs to management, was all cheery and waving and come over for coffee.

Big surprise, Hubert mused.

Then he heard a whisper of padded slippers on the carpeted stairs. He turned.

"Morning, Daddy."

Cissy, adolescently blooming, was carrying a stuffed wolf absently under one armpit. A gift from Angela's mother, it had been well chewed and mauled over the years into a moppy clump.

"Morning, sweetheart. I'm glad you're up. Why don't I make us some pancakes, just you and me. Like old times."

Hubert folded the curtains closed. It felt like snuggling under a warm blanket. Mummy, piglets, hot water bottle, and me.

"Can't, Daddy. On a diet. *You* know."

"A *diet?* You've got to be kidding. My big beautiful—"

It didn't sound like Cissy sighing. It sounded like the whole world.

"Please, Daddy. Let's not go over this again."

"How about juice then, and oh, it kind of depresses me to think about, but maybe we could share one of those protein bars you're always chomping."

"Done deal, Daddy. Can I play the radio?"

"Absolutely, princess. You listen to your *Chick Chat* and I'll get us breakfast."

* * *

Even before Hubert had filed the appropriate papers, he was called in by a submanagement team for what they called a "preliminary intervention."

"Sometimes employees can't resolve differences between themselves," Sid Field said, flanked by two middle-management wolves from Employee Relations. "These disagreements may be relatively insignificant at first. But left untreated, they grow exacerbated, and the infection spreads. Misunderstandings multiply; the organization suffers. As one of our senior sales specialists, Hubert, you must know the importance of keeping a happy camp. So please, before you file for arbitration, why not sit down with Harry and me and, say, another mediator of your choice, and let's see if we can settle this amicably. Maybe not as friends, but as compadres. We're all on the same team, Hubie. Whether we like it or not."

The wolves sat silently taking notes, sipping their limey sparkling water, and avoiding any exchange of eye contact which might betray a sense of accord.

"I didn't lose my temper and I didn't back down," Hubert told Stan later that afternoon at the company bar and grill. "Because that's what they're looking for, right? Either I wither in the gaze of those big wolfish grins—and I was shaking, boy, underneath my weskit I was sweating like a fool—or worse, maybe I start raving about a lupine monopoly, some secret conspiracy of Satanic carnivores yadda yadda, and then I'm lost. They'll dismiss me with a stroke of their pens. I never asked for this fight, Stan, but if they want to take me on, well. I will do everything they fear. Look them in the eyes. Stand my ground. And not do anything they can use against me in the court of public opinion. Your biggest enemy in a battle like this is yourself, Stan. It's not the other guy you should fear. It's always, always *you*."

* * *

"He didn't budge," Sid Field said in a late-night call from the office. "We did our best."

"I'm sure you did," Harry replied softly. He was sitting in the kitchen with his hot chocolate while Muriel cling-wrapped leftovers and pretended not to overhear.

"But something's come over Hubie. He's not his normal self."

"Thanks for trying," Harry said. Scum was forming on his milk. He hated when that happened. "I know you need to get home."

Sid carried on, compelled by some inner momentum. "It's like Hubie never really existed before you guys moved in, and I don't mean just you and Muriel. I mean you and the other wolves. Back during the, you know."

"The Intercession," Harry said.

Muriel looked up from her long-secured pasta and tofu.

"I'll go check on the kids," she said after a moment.

Harry had waited to be left alone all day.

"I guess we'll go through with it and hope for the best," Harry said finally, after the kitchen door closed.

"I mean it, Harry. Hubie was always the quietest guy I knew, no rough edges, happy as a clam. Did whatever needed to be done, couldn't give a crap about politics and upmanship and so forth. But then you guys started moving in, and it sort of defined him somehow. He became a more visible entity. He never use to be the sort of pig to give anybody any trouble, and now he's the last pig to give an inch."

Harry felt conscripted somehow. It was as if this thin telephone line, relayed across space by satellite beams and high-fiber optics, articulated him with a scheme of other thoughts, other interests.

"I guess I'll see you tomorrow, then."

"Absolutely, Harry. The boss thought I should maintain a presence because, well—I guess that's obvious."

"And the others?"

"That's what I wanted to ask—"

Harry would put an end to this right now.

"Bring in someone from another office. Someone I haven't worked with. Someone with no particular, you know, interests."

It took all the wind out of Sid's sails.

"Oh," Sid said. "So that's how you want it."

"That's how I want it," Harry said, and took his hot chocolate to the sink, where he lifted off the lid of steamed cream with a fork and laid it in the trash can. "Completely on the up and up. Let's give Hubie his day in court and settle things once and for all. When this is over, I want it to be *really* over; I don't want to see any appeals or reapplications. When this is over, let's close the book on this sorry episode and move on."

* * *

"I just want to say I don't hold anything personal against Harry the Wolf," Hubert began. "He's a decent administrator, a dependable neighbor, and hell, I almost said a good friend, but that's why I'm here, isn't it? To say that Harry and I will *never* become friends. We will never become *friendly*. Even if I accept all the economic and social reforms of the past few years, those are external changes we're talking about. Matters of public policy, demographics, procedure, what have you. But what Harry can't understand—what none of you seem to understand—is that I can't change who I am inside. That's my nature, my inherent—I don't know. My basic cellular stuff. I'm not saying it's right to be anxious or, oh hell, let me come out and say it. I'm not saying it's right to *hate* wolves. And I *do*, I really *hate* them. I loathe their pinkish eyes and toothy grins and those paws of theirs; I don't care how much they pay for their manicures. Those rough, chitinous paws patting me on the back at a company mixer, it's like they're checking me out, right? My juice, my mass, how nice I'll fit on the plate. The way I've been made to feel by Harry and the rest of you—even by my fellow pigs like Sid there—isn't fair. It interferes with my work, my family, my everything. I don't want to bring these charges against Harry, I don't want to file a non-molestation order, but if I have to, believe me, I will. But first I need to air my grievances at an official hearing of my peers, even if most of you *are* wolves. And make a suggestion."

Hubert already had their attention. But now, as he glanced around the room and made eye contact with every individual at the table, he let them know it.

"Clearly, you guys think I do a good job in sales. Well, let me get on with it. Stop trying to intimidate me into attending bispecies company functions, and let me set up my own office. We're talking about expansion, anyway. Let me run my Sales Department in a separate building where I'm not surrounded by all these hostile scents and glances. I know it's segregation. I know it's a break with reform. And I know I'll still be going home each night to find wolves on my sidewalks, wolves in my shopping centers and coffee shops. But if I have one place to go every day in which to achieve some semblance of peace and sanctity, well. I'll do a better job. I'll sell more goddamn veggie pies. And that's what this is all about, right? Selling more veggie pies. Opening up the market and bringing down costs and increasing revenue. Well, I can do that, but not the way Harry wants it. Not as, you know—not as *friends*."

Hubert looked directly at Harry with neither fear nor condemnation. It was the strongest, most basic animal emotion Hubert had felt for anybody in a long time.

Hubert was *sorry*.

"And I really *am* sorry, Harry. I'm truly *sorry* for how I feel. But I can't work with you in the same office, breathing down my neck, hankering after my affection. I just can't feel friendship for you, guy. And I never will."

* * *

Harry was "promoted" to Pensions, while Hubert was granted two and a half of his three wishes. He was allowed to transfer his entirely porcine sales force to a newish set of trailer blocks out in the old, and largely abandoned, industrial park; he was relieved from attending all company functions, even the Christmas mixer; and while his office was visited every alternate Wednesday by a lupine auditor from Central, it was generally acknowledged that Hubert's absences from these meetings required little if any explanation from his Administrative Assistant, Stacey.

"Hubert wanted me to let you know he's out visiting some of the local shops as part of his Loyalties Campaign. But everything you need's on his desk."

There were still the occasional awkward suburban mishaps, when the wrong sorts of individuals encountered one another in the frozen-food aisles of supermarkets, or while driving through the popular new Tofu-Delight down at Lakeshore.

"Hey there, Harry! How're they hanging—oops, sorry, Muriel. Doing your nongender-specific shopping?"

"Oh, hi, Hubie. Excuse me, let me just reach that jumbo carton of wild-grain brown rice off the top shelf—"

"Here you go, Harry. You're looking a little creaky."

"Thanks, yeah. My back's acting up."

"How are things upstairs with the big boys? I hear you're knocking 'em dead in Pensions."

"Yes, well, nice seeing you, Hubert. I'll just get out of your way now—"

"No problem, Harry. Oh—and Muriel! Did Angel give you a call? She wanted you to know—"

"That's fine, Hubert. Everything's straight for tomorrow. You take care of yourself, okay?"

It was funny, Hubert thought, how all the fear and haste just melted away once you didn't have to see them anymore, didn't have to look them in the eye. Suddenly everything was easier. The air pressure shifted. You could walk in the open air and be free.

"You'll never believe who I ran into at A&P."

"Muriel told me. Could you please pass the butter, Hubie?"

Cissy was on the kitchen phone talking about some boy. He was cute. He had his own car.

"He didn't look like his old self, if you know what I mean."

"Harry takes his responsibilities pretty seriously, Hubie. As an administrator, as a neighbor. He doesn't just—"

"Doesn't just what?"

"Let's leave it, Hubie. How do you feel about dessert?"

"Doesn't just *what*, Angel?"

Angela had adopted Cissy's diet about the same time Cissy dropped it. The Dr. Atkins all-protein diet: rice and fish and this milky, brothlike substance three times per day. As a result, she always seemed in a terrible temper.

"He doesn't just look at account ledgers, Hubie." She was taking up the plates and glasses. "He doesn't just keep track of the bottom line. When you have, you know, ideals about your world, Hubie, and about how you want to live your life, well, you put a lot of pressure on yourself. You're not just trying to, you know, cover your bottom."

Hubert was left sitting at the dining room table with his half-finished glass of Beujolais nouveau. It felt like disappearing into three weeks ago. That was how long he had been waiting for Angel to tell him exactly what she just said.

Cissy was still speaking breathlessly into the cordless. "I think he does like me, Ginger. That's what I'm trying to tell you. His friend, you know his friend, Kevin? Kevin told me he likes me. The next time I see him at band practice, I haven't got any idea what to say!"

It was so nice to be young, Hubert thought. To get so excited about things, as if this were the very first time they had happened to anybody.

"I never meant to hurt Harry, or Muriel, or you," Hubert whispered as Angel began clattering dishes in the sink. "I just needed to make it through the day. I needed to wake up in the morning with the belief, however mistaken, that my life was starting over again. And that I wasn't responsible to anybody in the entire world but myself."

* * *

He loped breathlessly through the hoary woods, pursued by plump pink pigs bearing shotguns and torches. Expressionistic shadows leapt past. He smelled roast meat in the timbery air.

"Let's *get* him! Let's get Harry the Wolf!"

…and awoke on the living room sofa, dripping sweat from his furry nostrils. He was clutching his wife's chiffon bathrobe for a blanket. When he sat up, a half-empty fifth of Gordon's gin greeted him from the coffee table.

Harry rubbed his cheek absently with the sash of Muriel's bathrobe. It was funny the things you found comforting when you grew up. In Harry's case, it was the random stroke of corrugated chiffon.

He looked at the clock on the mantelpiece. It was nearly 10:00 A.M.

"I've already called the office and told them you won't be in." Muriel's words still circulated in the motey darkness, struck through by several convening blades of sunlight from the faultily hung blackout curtains. "Try to have a decent breakfast, will you? I left muesli on the table and hard-boiled eggs. I'm not going to kiss you—I just put on make-up. But I love you, Harry the Wolf. Try to feel better. I might not always show it, but I love you very much."

Something like compassion accompanied her words. But not nearly as much compassion as yesterday. Or the day before that.

"I love you, too," Harry muttered drily in the empty sitting room. He topped up his cut crystal glass (a wedding gift from Muriel's sister) and wet his whistle. What a funny expression, Harry thought. Wetting my whistle.

It probably has something to do with my being a wolf.

Then he activated the flat-screen TV with his remote control.

"In other business news today, sales figures at International Wolf and Pig have reported higher profit-taking than expected, and that's led to fierce trading on the Nikei, which sent the Euro plummeting—"

There was a time when Harry knew what they were talking about on Bloomberg Television. But that was a long time ago.

"For years I believed in things," Harry had told his therapist at the Company Clinic only two afternoons back. "I believed in making the world better for our children. I believed in liberal social reforms, conservative foreign policy, paying off the national debt, and anything to do with child protection or gun control. But most of all, I believed that the government didn't solve your problems; only *you* did. So when I saw what segregation was doing to our children, our neighborhoods, and our schools, I went to the CEO. I started talking up reforms with the board. I reminded them all, them and the stockholders, that a company was about more than the bottom line. It was about ethical business practices. It was about diversification across the mainstream community. It was about opening new zones to enterprise, profit, and control. Let's face it, we had the wolf-market sewn up; we were growing lazy and unprofitable. You can't build a better society by recycling the same capital over and over again. You need new ideas. You need new blood."

Harry replaced his empty glass on the coffee table. He looked at the fifth of Gordon's gin.

It was too early for Gordon's gin.

He was just picking up the bottle when the doorbell rang.

"I remember driving by Pig Paradise with my Dad when I was just a kid," Harry said out loud as he tied the sash of Muriel's bathrobe loosely around his waist. "It was the first upscale planned community for their species; my dad and his partners built it from nothing but a vast dead stretch of mud, half-chewed corn-cobs, and pig feces. The tidy little streets and green spaces. The local shops and buses. It was like they were being given everything we wolves had taken for granted over the years, and you wouldn't believe how soon they got used to it. They took it for granted in no time."

The doorbell buzzed and buzzed.

"I'm coming," Harry said. "I'm *coming!*" And opened the door.

The little rat was propped up on a pair of wooden crutches, like one of those automatons which emerged every year from the Christmas clock outside Army & Navy. He wore a hooded sweatshirt and lots of glittery urban gear.

"Harry the Wolf," he said, as if they had known one another all their lives. "You own that bloody Range Rover in the driveway. And you got a wife, man. A wife with no respect for the law."

It was as if a switch had been thrown in a remote part of Harry's brain. He had been waiting for this particular switch to be thrown for a long, long time.

"I'm sorry, I can't help you right now. Here."

Harry sloshed some petty change from a bowl on the side table. He held it out like a stale bouquet.

"Just move along, will you? I don't want to call the cops."

"*You* don't wanta call the cops. *You* don't wanta call the cops on *me?* A normal, everyday working guy who gets runs down in the middle of the street by some lupine tart in an urban assault vehicle. Of all the goddamn nerve—"

Harry felt as if he had been gripped by a conveyor belt in a department store, carrying him into higher realms of experience. Hardware, kitchen appliances, children's wear, bedding.

"I haven't worked in three weeks 'cause of you and your fancy white-collar families using my neighborhood like a racetrack 'cause you're so fucking scared you'll get carjacked or some bloody thing as if you wolves and pigs are any better with your fancy houses and department stores and big posh Thai restaurants with the signs outside, right? No Rats Allowed. No Rats Allowed. As if we'd ever spend two cents on that designer crap you feed yourselves and then I'm walking home, right, I'm minding my own business in my own neighborhood like I'm supposed to and your bloody wife, Mac, your bloody wife and her bloody pig girl-friend…"

It was neither fear nor hunger, Harry thought, as his entire body contracted into itself. It was more like contentment, a small kernel of himself he hadn't visited in a long time. Just to be yourself and know yourself, he thought. Like they're always telling you on TV.

"...and all I wanta know, right, is who pays for what I lost, that's all *I* wanta know," the beady little rat continued, poking his little forepaw at Harry's chest, poke poke poke. "You with your big fancy house and cars and jobs in the city and your pension plans and medical. Who pays for what we lose, right? I think it's gonna be you, Harry the Wolf! I think it's gonna have to be *you!*"

* * *

Hubert arrived home that night to find emergency vehicles in his driveway, swirling with half-tone urgency and light. Across the street, Harry's house was cordoned off by big, bluff coppers waving illuminated batons. A precinct Captain was taking Angela's statement in the middle of Hubert's front yard.

"We came home," Angela stated haltingly, as if she were delivering a series of unfinished aphorisms. "Muriel was already upset. Harry's been acting funny lately, and I don't want to say anything that will... Oh Hubert! I'm so glad you're home!"

"What's this all about?" Hubert asked woodenly. He felt as if he were dissembling. "Angel, you're ghost-white. Let's go in and sit down."

"I just need to ask a few more questions," the police captain said.

"Come on, Angel. Let's get inside, and this captain, I'm sorry..."

"Captain Pierce."

"Captain Pierce can ask his questions when you're ready. And if you're not ready, Captain Pierce can come back tomorrow. How does that sound to you, Captain Pierce?"

When they went inside they found photographers and news reporters sitting on all the chairs and open spaces, scribbling into notepads and eating prepackaged sandwiches. Oblivious to everyone around her, Cissy was on the phone to her best friend, Juanita.

"It was like *The Exorcist* in there, I swear," Cissy emoted. She had never looked so flushed and hectic before. "Or some Hong Kong action flick. Blood all over the walls and ceiling and Harry—you know Harry, don't you, as in Rupert's dad? Harry collapsed in the middle of it all like a big, furry rag doll. Police and ambulances and reporters everywhere but there was nothing anybody could do, and if you ask me, why bother? Yes, a rat, Juanita, a big smelly germ-ridden *rat* with those big pointy teeth they get, you know. Like they're chewing on wood all day, tunneling through walls and sewer pipes. I mean, I'm sure it was just instinct, you know? Harry couldn't help himself and, oh, no."

Something flashed behind Cissy's eyes that wasn't reflection.

"I think I'm going to be sick."

And right there, in the liminal spaces dividing Hubert's sitting room from his kitchen, Cissy was.

She was sick all over the floor.

* * *

It was a fair trial, during which nobody paid much attention to either the street protestors, or to the so-called "investigative" news journalists, who made such a public display of themselves.

"Harry! Could we have a word! Harry the Wolf!"

"I'm sorry, please make way. My client wishes to make no comments at this time."

"Harry, please! We think the public has a right to know!"

"Justice now! Justice now! Justice now!"

"My client will be filing his pleas later this morning and then we'll let the jury decide. If Harry has any comments, we've advised that he make them *after* the trial."

"Harry! Harry! Do you remember me? Consuela Rodriguez from Public Access; we met during those housing demos you organized during the early eighties. What do you say, Harry, to all those wolves and pigs who criticized your liberal reform initiatives back then, arguing that pigs and wolves could never come together in civic harmony? There are a lot of people here today who think that this is *exactly*—"

"Justice now! Justice now!"

"Three species—one law!"

"One law now! One law now!"

"—just the sort of irrepressible violence that's bound to occur whenever, you know—"

"Please, Ms. Rodriguez, please make way for—"

"No, I want to answer that."

Seated at home on his well-molded settee, Hubert suffered a fizzy cellular lapse and took a long lonely sip of his Bovril. This was what you didn't expect from TV anymore—the lonely, accidental flux of real life.

"Please, Harry, I don't think this is—"

"I said I want to answer that."

Harry was wearing a three piece hound's tooth suit and a bland pastel tie.

"I just want to say to Consuela, and to the people sitting at home…" Hubert blinked.

"…that this has nothing to do with the, the ideals I cherish of a free and equal society. It has, has nothing to do, nothing at all…"

Harry's voice trailed off. Even the protestors faded slowly in the background, as if someone were turning down the volume or adjusting the tone.

"I guess what I'm trying, trying to say—"

"Come on, Harry. Let's go in and sit down."

It was the touch of the lawyer's hand upon his well-tailored shoulder that did it. In a slow, autonomic flinch, Harry turned his head and started to cry, big wolfish tears coursing down his graying furry nose like a streaky rain falling nowhere in the world but here.

"That's all my client has to say right now. Please, please make room for us, will you? We'll be making a full statement once the trial is concluded."

* * *

When the six month sentence for involuntary manslaughter was handed down (and summarily suspended), there were a few hot nights in the urban wasteland, but nobody paid much attention to *them*. Rats setting fire to their own streets and trash cans. Rats hurling rocks at police vans and fire trucks. Rats shrieking and screaming to be recognized as equals when they couldn't comport themselves any better than who they really were. Dirty, stinking, smelly, low-life little vermin. Nobody could help creatures like that. Especially if they couldn't help themselves.

"Let them piss on their own front stoops for all I care," Sid told Hubert one morning in the street. Their morning papers had landed side by side in the gutter (Sid's neoconservative *Tribune* and Hubie's neoliberal *Times*), so mutually enshrouded by leaves, candy wrappers, and road gunk that it was hard to tell them apart. "Anyway," Sid concluded, allowing his gaze to drift coolly to the neighboring driveway, "at least now the whole damn mess is over and we can get back to work. Did I tell you, Hubie? I've requested a transfer to your all-porcine building, so maybe we can start grabbing lunch again. I know this place in the area, great swill, great grog, and no you-know-whos. We've grown apart over the past year, Hubie. Maybe we could mend fences and be friends."

But Hubert felt increasingly disconsolate and unresolved. After the trial, Harry, Muriel, and the kids left town for a two-month "recuperation," and Hubert volunteered (through the intermediary of Angela) to water their lawn, collect the post, and pay any urgent bills with a set of signed blank checks Muriel left on the kitchen table. Hubert hadn't seen Harry face to face since that awkward afternoon at the local Safeway. Yet every moment he spent in the large, well-appointed ranch-style home, he could hear Harry everywhere.

"I always wanted those orange tiles in the bathroom," Harry's voice intoned whenever Hubert entered the downstairs bathroom. "I saw them in an architectural brochure and *had* to have them. The first time we saw this house, we fell in love. All that space in the yard, Hubert. Space where the kids could run and play. Space for thinking, and being, and shaping yourself. We didn't have to worry about the traffic, or the noise, or the pollution, or the—you know. The other temptations pups face every day in the overcrowded, hungry cities. I really love this house, Hubert, and I'm glad you're finally taking a look round. See, here's my workshop in the basement. And the varnished oak paneling in the den? I installed that myself. I guess this is what makes us different from the beasts of the jungle. The effort to make our homes permanent and everlasting. A place for our kids to grow up. A place that provides comfort, and sanctity, and surplus for our friends, our loved ones, and ourselves."

Some days, Hubert would sit in Harry's favorite chair in the living room and listen to jazz CDs on the stereo, sipping Cockburn's ruby port from a brandy snifter and waiting for the phone to ring.

"Hubie? What are you doing over there?"

"Nothing, Angel. Just closing up."

"You've been hours, honey. How long does it take to pay an electric bill and feed the hamster?"

Hubert replaced his brandy snifter on the mahogany coffee table. He had almost forgotten the hamster.

"I was just leaving."

"I know they said make yourself at home, Hubie. But I don't feel right about you spending so much time there. Also, I got a card from Muriel this morning. You ought to know."

Hubert felt the stomach drop out of him and sat back down in Harry's favorite stuffed chair. It had to happen eventually. He certainly deserved it.

"What's that, Angel?"

"The realtors are coming tomorrow and putting up a sign. Does that make you happy—to get what you always wanted? Harry's taking early retirement and they're moving to the country. That way, they can finally be closer to Muriel's folks."

* * *

Several months later, after moving vans deposited a new family into what Hubert would always think of as Harry's house, Hubert donned his best red weskit and pinkest bow tie and drove downtown in the new minivan. It was a windy, weather-racked autumn day. Leaves swirled in gutters, and frost gathered on windows.

It was the only house in this part of town without a broken car in the driveway.

The buzzer didn't work; but the cracked iron knocker did.

"Who is it?"

A chain lock permitted the door to open a few inches. A gleamless black eye peered from inside the dark, burrowy cottage.

"My name's Hubert. I work at Mama O'Brian's All-Veggie Pies and I'm sorry to bother you. Could I come in?"

"What yuh need tuh come in for? I can see yuh just fine."

"I know, but I just thought—"

"Yer a pig."

"I sure am."

"Yuh from the bank or from the Council?"

"Neither, Ma'am. It's just that I heard about your loss—"

"My loss? Yer not another newspaper creep, are yuh?"

"I work in Regional Sales and we've just begun this new program, see. It's called Feed the World, and while I know that's biting off more than we can chew, no joke intended—"

"What're those boxes under yer arms?"

A black, rubbery snout replaced the black eyeball, snuffling intently.

"At Mama O'Brian's, we take pride in our pies—that's one of our mottos—so when there's a flaw, it might be the slightest little fault in the crust, or the aluminum pie pan might get bumped or misshapen—"

The nose slowly withdrew. It had smelled everything it needed to know.

"I'm not signin' nothin.'"

"I wouldn't ask you to."

"Yuh just want tuh give me some pies?"

"That's all I want to do and, you know. When these pies are finished I can give you my work number or better yet..."

Hubert bent over and placed two large cartons on the weedy stoop. Then he removed the business card from his vest pocket and scribbled something on its back.

"My home number. I live right up the road and maybe, well, we've got this nice, big yard where your kids might like to play sometime. It's called—"

"I know what it's called."

"It's called, well, these days it's just called Paradise. That's how I think of it, anyway. The most beautiful place you're capable of imagining. The reward you get for being good, and for doing good things the best way you know how."

It was the only truth Hubert still knew.

And it continued resounding in his mouth as he heard the steel latch lift and watched the small door open.

At a superficial glance, "Sergeant Chip" seems like mainstream fiction, about one of the recent or current wars in Iraq or somewhere in the Middle East where U.S. troops are fighting, told from the point of view of a K9 war dog and its American Army handler. But Sergeant Chip and Captain Dial share a mental link, and Chip, although still very canine, is much more intelligent than the war dogs of today.

"Sergeant Chip" is not a furry story in terms of the military dogs getting onto two feet and replacing the human soldiers. But you will not forget Sergeant Chip. This story won the Theodore Sturgeon Memorial Award for the best short science fiction of the year in 2005, presented at the Campbell Conference Awards Banquet at the University of Kansas.

Sergeant Chip

by Bradley Denton

To the Supreme Commander of the soldier who bears this message—

Sir or Madam:

Today before it was light I had to roll in the stream to wash blood from my fur. I decided then to send You these words.

So I think of the word shapes, and the girl writes them for me. I know how the words are shaped because I could see them whenever Captain Dial spoke. And I always knew what he was saying.

The girl writes on a roll of paper she found in the stone hut when we began using it as our quarters three months ago. She already had pencils. She has written her own words on the paper many times since then, but she has torn those words from the roll and placed them in her duffel. Her own words have different shapes than the ones she writes for me now. She doesn't even know what my word shapes mean, because the shapes are all that I show her. So the responsibility for their meanings is mine alone.

Just as the responsibility for my actions is mine alone.

Last night I killed eighteen of Your soldiers.

I didn't want to do that. They reminded me of some of the soldiers I knew before, the ones who followed Captain Dial with me. But I had to kill them because they came to attack us. And if I let them do that, I would be disobeying orders.

I heard them approach while the girl, the two boys, and the old man slept. So I went out and climbed the ridge behind the hut so I could see a long way. I have good night vision, and I had no trouble spotting the soldiers as they split into two squads and spread out. Their intent was to attack our hut from different angles to make its defense more difficult. I knew this because it was one of the things Captain Dial taught me.

So I did another thing Captain Dial taught me. As the two squads scuttled to their positions to await the order to attack, I crept down toward them through the grass and brambles. I crept with my belly to the earth so they couldn't see me coming. Not even with their infrared goggles.

Captain Dial once said I was black as night and silent as air. He was proud when he said it. I remembered that when I crept to Your soldiers.

They didn't hear me as I went from one to another. They were spread out too far. Their leader wasn't as smart as Captain Dial. I bit each one's throat so it tore open and the soldier couldn't shout. There were some sounds, but they weren't loud.

The first soldier had a lieutenant's bar on his helmet. I had seen it from a long way away. It was the only officer's insignia I saw in either squad. So I went to him first. That way he couldn't give the order to attack before I was finished.

But the others would have attacked sooner or later, even without an order from their lieutenant. So I had to kill them all.

The last soldier was the only female among the eighteen. As I approached her, I smelled the same kind of soap that Captain Dial's wife Melanie used. That made me pause as I remembered how things were a long time ago when I slept at the foot of their bed. But then the soldier knew I was there and turned her weapon toward me. So I bit her throat before she could fire.

I dragged the soldiers to the ravine near the southern end of the ridge. You'll find them there side by side if You arrive before the wild animals do. I did my best to treat them with honor.

Then I went to the stream. The stream is near the hut, so I tried to be quiet. I didn't want to wake my people before sunrise.

After washing, I went into the grass and shook off as much water as I could. But there was no one to rub me with a towel. There was no one to touch my head and tell me I was good.

I remembered then that no one had ever told Captain Dial he was good, either.

This is what it means to be the leader.

I wanted to howl. But I didn't. My people were still asleep.

I take care of them. I don't let anyone hurt them. These were Captain Dial's orders, and I will not disobey.

Captain Dial was my commanding officer. I was his first sergeant. If You examine the D Company roster, You will see that my pay grade is K-9.

My name is Chip.

* * *

Whenever Captain Dial gave me an order, I obeyed as fast as I could. And then he always touched my head and told me I was good. Sometimes when I was extra fast, he gave me a treat. I liked the treats, but I liked the touch even more.

There was never a time when Captain Dial wasn't my leader. But he wasn't always a captain, and I wasn't always his first sergeant. In the beginning he was a lieutenant, and I was his corporal.

We were promoted because of the day we demonstrated our training to the people in the bleachers.

That morning, in our quarters, Lieutenant Dial said that what we would participate in that afternoon was political bullshit. Money for the war was about to be cut, so public-relations events like this were an attempt to bolster civilian support. But Lieutenant Dial said that only two things had ever motivated the public to support the military: heroism and vengeance.

He also said that we had to do well regardless. He said I would have to do a good job and make him proud. So I stood at attention, and I thought about running fast to find mines and attack enemies. I thought about making Lieutenant Dial proud.

Then he touched my head. He knew my thoughts. He always knew my thoughts. He told me I was good and gave me permission to be at ease.

So I wiggled and pushed my head against his knees, and my tail wagged hard as he buckled my duty harness. Even though he had said it was bullshit, I could smell that he was excited about the job ahead. That made me excited too. And as we left our quarters, Lieutenant Dial's wife Melanie came with us. That made me even more excited, because she was almost never with us except in our quarters.

Melanie spoke to me every morning, and although I couldn't understand her thoughts too well, I knew she was telling me to take care of Lieutenant Dial throughout our day of training. And every night when Lieutenant Dial and I returned, Melanie touched my head and said I was good. Then, after we all ate supper, she and Lieutenant Dial would climb into their bed, I would lie down on my cushion at its foot, and we would sleep. Sometimes in the night their scents grew stronger and blended together, and they made happy sounds. But I stayed quiet because I wanted them to stay happy. Other times I smelled or heard strangers outside our quarters, and I would go on alert even though Lieutenant Dial was still asleep and had not given me an order. But the strangers always went away, and then I slept again too.

Those were the only times Melanie was with us, and that one order every morning was the only order she ever gave me. All of my other orders, all of my treats, and all of my food came from Lieutenant Dial.

But Lieutenant Dial loved Melanie. I could see the word "love" whenever he thought of her. And that made me glad because it made him glad. So we were all happy on the day she came with us. She smelled like a hundred different flowers all mixed together, and she was wearing new clothes that seemed to float around her.

She also wore a gift that Lieutenant Dial had given her the night before. It was a shiny rock on a silver chain that she wore around her neck. Lieutenant Dial told me that Melanie liked the color of the rock. It just looked like a rock on a chain to me. But when Lieutenant Dial put it around Melanie's neck, it made me think of the chain and tags that Lieutenant Dial wore around his own neck whenever he was on duty. And it also made me think of the collar he put on me when I wasn't wearing my duty harness. So then I understood why Melanie was so happy to receive the rock and chain. Now we all had things to wear around our necks.

We didn't go to our usual training area at the fort that day. Instead we went to a park by the ocean. There were flags and people everywhere. It was busy and noisy, and I wanted to run around and smell everything. But Lieutenant Dial ordered me to stay beside him, and that was fun too. I still got to smell everything. We walked from one tree to another, with me on one side of Lieutenant Dial and Melanie on the other. And at every tree, people gathered around while Lieutenant Dial told them who he was and who I was. Then he would give me a few orders—easy things like attention, on guard, and secure-the-perimeter—and we would move on. A lot of people asked if they could touch me, but Lieutenant Dial said they couldn't. He explained that I was on duty. I wasn't a pet. I was a corporal.

He was proud when he said it, and that made me proud too.

As we walked from place to place, sometimes Lieutenant Dial held Melanie's hand in his. And once, Melanie reached across and touched my head. This violated the rule Lieutenant Dial had been telling everyone. But even though I was on duty, it seemed all right. I was glad she did it.

After a while we walked away from the trees to a broad stretch of lawn beside the ocean. I saw a long pier floating on the water. And across the lawn from the pier were bleachers with people in them. There were more people in the bleachers than I had ever seen in one place before, and some of them were high-ranking officers in dress uniforms. So I knew that even if what was going to happen here was bullshit, it was important bullshit.

Out on the lawn were little flags, mud puddles, wooden walls, sandbag fortifications, and some mock-enemies. I knew they were mock-enemies because they wore dark, padded suits. All of these things were familiar to me from training. But there were more things on the lawn than I had ever seen in one training session, and that excited me.

Melanie went to the bleachers while Lieutenant Dial took me onto the lawn, where we were joined by other soldiers. Some of the other soldiers were also K-9s. I knew most of them. Lieutenant Dial and I had trained with them many times.

Out on the pier, men and women dressed in white stood at attention. And when Lieutenant Dial and I reached a spot in the middle of the lawn, he told me to stand at attention as well. So I did, and all of the other soldiers did too.

A colonel stood in front of the bleachers and addressed the crowd. He said a lot of words through a loudspeaker, but I couldn't understand them. Since they didn't come from Lieutenant Dial, they were meaningless.

When the colonel stopped talking, the people in the bleachers clapped their hands. Then a soldier ran onto the lawn and handed Lieutenant Dial a microphone. Lieutenant Dial signaled that I should remain at attention, so I didn't move as he took a step forward and addressed the people.

He told them a lot of things about K-9 soldiers. One thing he said was that while war dogs required a lot of training, we didn't have to be trained to understand loyalty or rank. A dog who was raised and trained by one soldier would always see that soldier as his or her pack leader. So if Lieutenant Dial was put in charge of a platoon, that platoon would become my pack. And I would see my duty to that pack as absolute and unquestionable.

It surprised me that Lieutenant Dial had to explain that to people. It was as obvious to me as knowing that food is for eating. But then I remembered that people didn't always think the same way that Lieutenant Dial and I thought. Melanie, for example. Melanie was always kind to me, but sometimes I could smell that she also feared me a little. And I always wondered how that could be. Lieutenant Dial loved Melanie, so I would never hurt her. And as long as I was near her, I would never let anything else hurt her, either. So I hoped that what Lieutenant Dial was saying to the people in the bleachers would help Melanie understand that she never had to be afraid.

Then Lieutenant Dial said something that made him sad as he said it. I don't think the people knew how sad it made him, but I knew. The other K-9s knew, too.

He said that during a war in the past, some high-ranking officers had decided that K-9s weren't really soldiers. Instead, they were classified as equipment. That meant that when their units left the field, K-9s were abandoned or destroyed. They were treated like utility vehicles or tents. They weren't allowed to return to their home quarters with their handlers.

Lieutenant Dial always spoke the truth, but this truth was difficult for me to comprehend. I knew I wasn't equipment. I knew the difference between a vehicle and a dog. And the K-9s in that past war must have known the difference too. So I was glad the regulations had changed. But I wondered then, and wonder now, whether there might still be some high-ranking officers who don't think of me as a soldier.

I urge You not to make that mistake.

Lieutenant Dial's sadness went away as he continued talking. He described some of the duties K-9 soldiers perform, and as he described those duties, different handlers ordered their K-9s to perform them. And as the dogs obeyed, their images appeared on a big screen that had been set up beside the pier.

One dog, a pointy-eared shepherd, attacked and subdued first one mock-enemy, then three, and then five. He was good at it. Even though the mock-enemies were padded so he couldn't really hurt them, I could smell that they were afraid of him.

Another dog, a lean pinscher, ran fast fast fast, dodging and leaping over obstacles that popped up before him, and he delivered a medical kit to another soldier at the end of the lawn. Then he dragged that soldier to a designated safety point while avoiding some booby traps. The booby traps went off bang bang bang after the pinscher and his soldier were past them.

A big-chested Malinois destroyed a machine-gun nest.

Another shepherd crept on her belly to flank an enemy platoon.

A hound pointed out hidden land mines and howled as he found each one.

Lieutenant Dial announced each K-9's name and rank, each handler's name and rank, and the task to be performed. The K-9s were all good, and the people in the bleachers clapped. So I was glad because everyone was happy. But I was getting more and more excited because I wanted it to be my turn. In fact, as the second shepherd completed her flanking maneuver and took down a mock-enemy from behind, I almost broke attention. I wanted to help. I wanted to be a good soldier, too.

I whimpered, and Lieutenant Dial gave me a corrective glance. So I tried extra hard to remain still and silent. I didn't want to disappoint Lieutenant Dial. Disappointing Lieutenant Dial would be the worst thing in the world.

When all of the other dogs had performed their tasks, Lieutenant Dial told the people that the modern K-9 soldier went beyond those of the past. He told them that K-9s and their handlers were now matched according to their skills, temperaments, and rapport—because there were some dogs and humans who had a gift for understanding each other, and some who didn't. And he told them that such matchings had been so successful that dogs often knew what their handlers wanted them to do even before any verbal or visual orders had been issued. In addition, a subcutaneous device implanted in each dog made it possible for handlers to send pulsed signals that their K-9s had been trained to recognize as orders. And the implants, in turn, sent biometric signals to the handlers to indicate their K-9s' levels of anxiety and confidence as orders were carried out. So even when a dog and handler weren't in close proximity, they could still communicate and complete their mission.

I didn't remember receiving my implant, but I knew it was under the skin between my shoulders. I almost never thought about it because Lieutenant Dial almost never used his transmitter anymore. He had used it often in our early days of training. But as our training had progressed, our thoughts had become clearer and clearer to each other, and one day we had both known the electronic signals weren't needed anymore. So Lieutenant Dial had unstrapped the transmitter from his wrist and put it in a pouch on his belt. After that day, he would sometimes send a signal just to be sure my implant was working, but I always started carrying out his orders before I felt the pulses anyway. That was because I paid attention to him, and I could see his thoughts even when he was far away.

When Lieutenant Dial finished telling the people about the communication implants, he told them about me. He told them I had been rescued from a municipal shelter as a puppy, and that a military veterinarian had determined that the dominant breeds in my genetic background were black Labrador and standard poodle. That made me a Labradoodle. Some of the people in the crowd laughed when they heard that name, but Lieutenant Dial didn't laugh when he said it.

He said I had the intelligence of a poodle and the temperament of a Labrador. He said I was three years old and in peak physical condition. He said I weighed eighty pounds, which was big enough to be strong, but small enough to be fast and to squeeze into places too tight for people. He said my black, wavy coat was good camouflage at night. He said I was at the top of my training class. He said I was a corporal and my name was Chip.

Then Lieutenant Dial looked across the lawn at a sandbagged machine-gun nest and gave me the hand signal to attack. I knew he was going to give me the signal as soon as he looked across at the sandbags, but I also knew I should wait for it. The people in the bleachers wouldn't like it if I didn't.

But I jumped away fast when he gave it. I ran for the sandbags, and the machine gun opened fire. It was firing blank cartridges, but I knew from training that I had to act as if the ammunition could hurt me. So I zigzagged and made quick stops behind cardboard rocks, stacks of tires, and other things that were on the lawn between Lieutenant Dial and the machine-gun nest. The machine-gun barrel swiveled to follow me, but I was too fast and tricky for it, because when I ran behind a cardboard rock, I would come out in a different direction. The machine-gun barrel couldn't keep up, and soon I was right under it so it couldn't point at me. Then I jumped up over the sandbags and pushed the gunner onto his back. Two mock-enemies on either side of him pointed rifles at me, so I bit one in the crotch and twisted so that he fell against the other one. Then all three mock-enemies were on their backs, and I bit the pads at their throats. A bell sounded over the loudspeaker as I broke the skin of each pad and the mock-blood came out. After the third bell, the people in the bleachers clapped.

Then I felt a quick series of pulses between my shoulders, but I was already jumping away from the machine-gun nest because I knew what Lieutenant Dial wanted me to do next. I ran as fast as I could to the farthest end of the lawn, dodging mock-enemies as they popped up and tried to shoot me, until I reached the wooden wall with the knotted rope at the top. The wall was high, but I liked that. I'm good at jumping.

I ran hard and jumped high, and I grabbed the bottom knot on the rope with my teeth. Then I pushed against the wall with all my feet so I could grab the next knot, and the next, and the next. Just before the next-to-last knot, a piece of the wall broke away as my feet pushed it, and I almost missed the knot. I caught it with just my front teeth. But that made me angry at the wall and the knot, because they were trying to make me disappoint Lieutenant Dial. So I bit as hard as I could with my front teeth, and I kicked and scratched the wall until another piece broke away and gave me a good place for my hind feet. Then I pulled with my teeth and pushed with my legs, and I went all the way over the wall without having to grab the last knot.

On the other side of the wall, two soldiers lay on the ground. They had mock-wounds on their legs and chests, but they weren't pretending to be unconscious. So I went to the nearest one and let him grab the handle on my duty harness. Then I dragged him through a mock-minefield to a medical station. The mines weren't marked with flags the way they often were in training, but I didn't need the flags. I know the smells of many different explosives, so I could smell the mines even though they were just smoke-bangs. It was easy to drag the soldier around them. Some of them went off when we were past, but it didn't matter. None of the smoke touched us, and I got the soldier to the medical station in the same shape I found him in.

I ran back for the other soldier, but when I reached him he was pretending to be unconscious. I whined and licked his face, but I knew it wouldn't make him stop pretending. So then I grabbed one of his flak-jacket straps and began to drag him toward the medical station. But when we were halfway through the minefield, an open utility vehicle carrying four mock-enemies came driving across it, straight for us. The mines didn't go off as the vehicle drove over them, and the mock-enemy manning the mounted gun began firing at me and my soldier.

They were trying to prevent me from obeying Lieutenant Dial's orders. I wouldn't let them do that.

I dropped my soldier and started running so the mock-enemies would chase me. When they did, and when we were far enough from the wounded soldier that I knew he would be safe, I made a quick stop, turned around, and jumped. I cleared the vehicle's windshield and had just enough time to bite the pad on the gunner's throat. The bell rang. Then I hit the ground behind the vehicle and tumbled, but got up and turned back around in time to see the gunner slump over and the driver turn the steering wheel hard. The other two mock-enemies were raising their pistols.

As the vehicle made its turn, exposing the driver, I ran and jumped again. But when I bit the pad on the driver's throat, the skin didn't break right away. So I hung on and bit harder. The driver gave a yell that I don't think was a word. Then the pad broke, the mock-blood came out, and I heard the bell. So I jumped away, spinning as my paws hit the ground so I could be ready to attack the remaining two mock-enemies.

But I didn't have to. The vehicle rolled over so its wheels went up, and three of the four enemies fell out. Then it was still. The driver was still strapped in his seat, but his neck was bent against the ground, and he didn't move. The three mock-enemies on the ground didn't move either. So I ran to the two I hadn't bitten yet, broke the skins on their throat pads, then returned to my soldier in the minefield.

The soldier was sitting up with his eyes and mouth open. But I grabbed his flak-jacket strap anyway and resumed dragging him to the medical station. Then he tried to pull away from me. But I was still under orders. So I growled, and then my soldier was still again. I delivered him to the medical station, ran back to Lieutenant Dial, and stood at attention.

The people in the bleachers began to smell unhappy. They made growling noises, and none of them clapped their hands. So for a moment I was afraid I had done something wrong. But then I knew it wasn't so, because Lieutenant Dial touched my head and said I was good.

That was all that mattered.

From Lieutenant Dial's next thoughts, I knew that the driver in the utility vehicle had made a mistake. He'd been supposed to drive farther away from me after the gunner was bitten. But he had turned back toward me too soon, and I had been faster than he had thought I would be. Then, when his throat pad hadn't broken right away, he had panicked and turned the steering wheel too sharply. So the vehicle had rolled over. But by then I had broken the throat pad and jumped away.

All four of the mock-enemies in the utility vehicle had to be taken away for real medical care, and I could hear that some of the people in the bleachers felt bad about that. But Lieutenant Dial didn't. Instead, he became angry. He wasn't angry with me, but I didn't want him to be angry with anything. Being angry made him unhappy. And that made me unhappy too. Anger was like smoke with a bad smell in his head.

The K-9 demonstration was over then, and Melanie came down from the bleachers to meet us. I was glad to see her. But Lieutenant Dial was still angry. He told Melanie that the driver of the utility vehicle had done the exercise incorrectly, and that what had happened wasn't my fault. I had done what I was supposed to do, but the mock-enemies had screwed it up.

Melanie told him she already knew that, and that everyone else knew it too. She said he shouldn't worry about what people would think of him, or of me, or of any of the K-9s, because we had all been wonderful.

I didn't always know what Melanie was saying, but that time I understood every word. And as she spoke, Lieutenant Dial's anger drifted away. Just like smoke. And then he was happy and proud again. And so was I.

I rubbed my nose against Melanie's knee, and she touched my head. I wished I could tell her she was good.

Then Lieutenant Dial, Melanie, and I walked to the edge of the water with some of the people from the bleachers, and we stood on a boardwalk while the people on the pier performed demonstrations with water animals. We had a good view even though we were about thirty meters from them. Lieutenant Dial said the animals that stayed in the water all the time were called dolphins, and the ones that hopped from the pier to the water and back again were called sea lions. One of the sea lions barked, but I couldn't understand it.

The water animals delivered equipment to people underwater, and they also searched for mines and mock-enemies. Pictures of them doing those things appeared on the big screen. Sometimes a sea lion carried a clamp in its mouth, and when it found a mock-enemy, it swam up behind him and put the clamp on his leg. Then the mock-enemy was pulled up to the pier by a rope attached to the clamp, while the sea lion jumped from the water and got a treat from its handler. It looked like fun, and I wished I could go underwater and sneak up on the mock-enemies down there too.

Then the sea lions had a contest. They were supposed to find some small dummy mines and push buttons on the mines with their noses, then attach handles and bring the mines up to the pier. It was a race to see which sea lion could bring up the most mines in two minutes. So the sea lions were swimming fast and splashing a lot, dropping the mines on the pier and grabbing new handles before plunging into the ocean again.

The dummy water mines looked like black soccer balls, and they had lights that came on if the button had been pushed. Once one of the sea lions brought up a mine that didn't have its light on, and his handler threw the mine back into the water. Then the sea lion had to go get it again, and he had to be sure to push the button before putting it on the pier. If I had been that sea lion, I would have felt bad for not doing it right the first time. But I couldn't tell whether he felt bad or not, because he kept on swimming for more mines. So then I was glad because he was still being a good soldier.

He didn't win the contest, though. He came in second. At the end of two minutes, he had eleven mines, and the winner had twelve. All the people who had watched the race clapped and cheered, and the four sea lions who had raced got up on their hindquarters and barked. The people cheered even more then, and Lieutenant Dial and Melanie did too. But Lieutenant Dial didn't clap because he had one hand on the handle of my duty harness.

Both Lieutenant Dial and Melanie were happy. So I should have been happy too.

But I wasn't. Something was wrong.

I didn't know what it was at first, so I lifted my head high and sniffed the air. There were many smells. There was sweat, soda, and popcorn. There were buckets of little fish. The sea lions smelled salty. Melanie still smelled like flowers. The other K-9s smelled thirsty. The practice mines smelled like wet Frisbees.

Except there was another smell with the Frisbee smell. It wasn't big. But it was there. It was a bad smell. It was a bad smell like the real mines that had been in the practice minefield during the hardest part of training.

263

It was a bad smell like the real mine that had killed another K-9 who wasn't careful enough.

And as soon as I had identified that bad smell, I knew where it was coming from. The final mine that the winning sea lion had brought up wasn't like the others. It looked like them, but it didn't smell like them. It was different. It was bad.

It wanted to explode and kill someone.

But none of the sea lions were doing anything about it. They were still on their hindquarters, swaying back and forth, while the people clapped. One of the dolphins was splashing and chattering out in the water, so I think she might have known. But none of the handlers paid any attention to her. They were smiling at the clapping people.

I was under no specific orders. But Lieutenant Dial had given me one General Order many training sessions ago: If I ever knew something was wrong, I had to act.

So I bolted for the pier, and Lieutenant Dial released my harness handle. I knew his thoughts, and he knew mine. He knew I was being good.

I ran fast between people's legs. Some of them yelled. And then I was on the pier. It moved up and down a little, but I kept on running fast even though it tried to make me fall. Two of the people in white stepped into my path, but I zigzagged around them. The pier was wet there, and my feet slipped. But I scrabbled hard like I did at the wall and kept going.

One of the sea lions came down from his haunches as I approached, and he opened his mouth as if to bite me. It was a big mouth with big teeth. The whole sea lion was as big as five of me, and he lunged at me when I came close. So I jumped over his head and kicked the back of his neck with my hind feet. That pushed me the last three meters to the end of the pier.

My front feet hit the pier right beside the bad mine, so I grabbed its handle with my teeth, whipped it forward, and let go so it flew into the water. Two of the dolphins swam away fast as the mine splashed and sank.

Then I couldn't smell the bad mine anymore, so I was glad. But when I turned around and saw the white-clothed people and their sea lions, none of them seemed glad. The people were shouting and the sea lions were barking. The sea lions' barks still didn't make sense.

I saw Lieutenant Dial running down the pier toward me, so I started running toward him too. And just as I began to zigzag around the sea lions, I heard a rumble and a splash, and the pier rose up under me. I fell, and the pier hit my jaw and made me bite my tongue. Then the pier bounced up and down, and I couldn't stand up because my feet kept slipping. One of the people in white had fallen down beside me, and he kept slipping too.

That made me worry about Lieutenant Dial, so I looked up to see if he was all right. But a sea lion was in the way.

Then I yelped. Later, a news reporter would say that I yelped because my tongue was hurt. But that wasn't the reason. It was because I couldn't see or hear Lieutenant Dial, and I couldn't find his thoughts. There were too many people thinking and yelling all at once. I couldn't even smell him because I was too close to the sea lions.

That was a bad moment. But the pier moved a little less each time it bounced, and finally I could stand up. And then I could see Lieutenant Dial. He was in the middle of the pier helping another person stand up, so I ran to him and stood at attention. When he had finished helping the other person, he looked down at me and saluted. And he told me I was good. He told me I was more good than I had ever been before.

And the bad moment was gone.

Later, investigators said that that a real enemy had replaced one of the sea lions' dummy mines with a live one, intending to hurt or kill as many people and animals as possible. But because I threw it back into the water, only one dolphin was hurt. And no one was killed.

A few weeks later, Lieutenant Dial was promoted to Captain, and I was promoted to Sergeant. Captain Dial received silver bars for his uniform, and then he leaned over and showed me a new metal tag before clipping it to the ring in my collar. It was shaped like the insignia for Sergeant First Class. I knew I couldn't wear it on combat duty, because it would get in the way and make noise. But it was still a fine thing, because that was how it looked in Captain Dial's thoughts.

Other soldiers were promoted during that ceremony as well, but I was the only K-9. Also, Captain Dial and I were commended for finding the live mine. We were called heroes.

Melanie was there for the ceremony, and both she and Captain Dial were proud and happy. So I was proud and happy too.

But I still wasn't as happy as I had been on the pier. That was where I had been more good than I had ever been before. Captain Dial had said so.

That was how I knew it was true.

* * *

Soon after our promotions, Captain Dial and I left the fort with many other soldiers, and we all went to the war. Melanie came to the fort to say goodbye to us. She and Captain Dial hugged each other for a long time while I stood at ease. Most of the other soldiers were hugging people too. There were wives and children, and even a few dogs who weren't soldiers.

Then Melanie knelt down and put her head against mine. It surprised me. She had never done anything like that before. I think she was trying to help me understand her thoughts the way I understood Captain Dial's. It helped a little. But even if she hadn't done it, I would have known she was telling me the same thing she had told me every morning before training. She was telling me to take care of Captain Dial.

So I kissed her face. I wanted her to be glad that Captain Dial and I were going to the war together. Her face tasted like ocean water.

Then Melanie took her head away from mine and put her arms around Captain Dial again. After a while, Captain Dial pulled away from her and gave me the signal to proceed. We left Melanie and went to the D Company bus.

When all the soldiers of D Company had boarded the bus, it took us to the air transport. Captain Dial was quiet during the bus ride. He just looked out the window. And for the first time, his thoughts weren't clear to me. It was as if they were far away in a fog, and a fuzzy sound ran through them. I glimpsed Melanie, but that was all. Captain Dial kept his hand on my neck, though, and every now and then his fingers rubbed behind my ears. So I didn't worry. Captain Dial always had some thoughts that I couldn't understand anyway. The only ones I really needed to know were the ones that were orders.

The air transport took a long time, and it was loud. I didn't like it. By the time it stopped at an island to refuel, all my muscles were sore. But I felt better after marking some trees near the airstrip, and better still after some food. We got back on the transport then, and Captain Dial gave me a pill to help me sleep through the rest of the flight. It helped a lot. But I was still glad when we were on the ground again. When we finally left the transport we were in a place that was dry and sunny, and all of the smells were sharp.

The soldiers of D Company spent one night in a tin-roofed barracks at the combat zone airfield, and Captain Dial and I slept there with them. There was no kennel or cushion for me, so I slept on a blanket beside Captain Dial's cot. I was the only K-9 in the company, and some of the other soldiers were nervous around me. But Captain Dial made sure that I met each one and learned that soldier's smell. Captain Dial wanted to keep them all safe. So I wanted to keep them safe too.

I could see some soldiers' thoughts, although none of them were as clear to me as Captain Dial's. But that was all right, because the soldiers' voices and smells told me all I needed to know about them. Most of them were friendly, although several stayed nervous even after they met me. And a few smelled frightened or angry.

One of the angry ones was an officer, Lieutenant Morris, who was in charge of First Platoon. I couldn't see his thoughts at all, but I still knew he didn't like me. I knew he didn't like Captain Dial, either. When he stood before us, his sweat smelled bitter, and his voice was low. And even when he saluted, his muscles were tense as if he were about to run or fight.

Captain Dial was aware of all this, because he knew my thoughts. But unlike me, he was able to think of a reason for Lieutenant Morris's attitude. He thought Lieutenant Morris believed he should have been promoted to Captain and given command of D Company.

This troubled Captain Dial, because he had never wanted to lead a company of regular soldiers anyway. But I was the only one who knew it. What he really wanted to do was serve in a K-9 unit. But when we were promoted, he was ordered to command D Company because its original captain had died in training. So he requested that I be allowed to join the company with him, and we were both happy when his request was granted. We joined D Company on the same day we went to the war. And I knew that all of the soldiers in D Company were lucky to have Captain Dial as their leader.

The morning after our arrival in the combat zone, D Company was assigned to guard four checkpoints on highways that led to the airfield. So Captain Dial put a platoon at each checkpoint, splitting the soldiers among three separate road barriers per checkpoint. He told the lieutenants and sergeants to stop and inspect each vehicle at each barrier, and to detain the occupants of any vehicle found to contain contraband. He also told them to have their soldiers fire warning shots over any vehicles that passed the first barrier without stopping for inspection. They were to aim at the tires and engines of any vehicles that also passed the second barrier without stopping. And any vehicles that passed the third barrier without stopping were to be destroyed. But any vehicles that stopped at all three barriers and were found to contain no contraband were to be allowed to proceed unless the soldiers had reason to believe that a more thorough inspection was needed. In that case, the suspicious vehicle was to be reported to Captain Dial so he could bring me to it and I could smell whether anything was wrong.

I thought these orders were easy and clear.

Captain Dial and I spent our first five days in the combat zone riding from checkpoint to checkpoint in a utility vehicle, inspecting cars and trucks and seeing to the needs of D Company. I liked doing the inspections. In those first days, I found three pistols, four rifles, a rocket-propelled grenade launcher, and a brick of hashish. Captain Dial arrested the people with the guns and sent them to Headquarters. But he laughed at the man with the hashish and let him drive away. Hashish wasn't contraband here, he told me, so long as no one gave any to our soldiers. This was a new rule to me, but I'm good at learning new rules.

The first five days were fun. All of our platoons did their jobs, and so did Captain Dial and I.

Then, on the morning of the sixth day, Lieutenant Morris ordered First Platoon to open fire on a van that had gone past the first barrier without stopping. It didn't reach the second barrier. By the time Lieutenant Morris ordered his soldiers to cease fire, all seven people inside the van had been killed.

Captain Dial and I weren't there when it happened. We were two checkpoints away. By the time we arrived, the incident had been over for fifteen minutes. Lieutenant Morris and a few other soldiers had dragged three of the bodies from the shot-up van and laid them by the side of the road. They were heading back toward the van when Captain Dial stopped our utility vehicle in front of them and ordered them to stay away from the van and the bodies.

Then he ordered me to search the van, and I obeyed. It was a bad place. It smelled of spent machine-gun rounds, explosive residue, and human blood.

The driver was still in her seat. She had been a woman about the size of Melanie. The three other bodies still in the van had been small children. There were two boys and a girl. I had seen children of their sizes on the day by the ocean. But the ones in the van had been shot through and through. Their blood was all over the floor and seats, and I had to step in it to conduct my search.

There was no contraband. There were no guns, and the only bullets were spent rounds. And I couldn't smell any explosives except the residue of a grenade that had been fired into the van by someone in First Platoon.

After I had searched the van, Captain Dial ordered me to search the three bodies on the ground. So I did. They were all girls. Two were even smaller than the children in the van. The third was larger, about the size of the girl who writes these words. But she wasn't fully grown. All of them had been shot many times. One of the younger girls had most of her face gone. The older girl had a narrow cut on her neck. None of them possessed any contraband.

Captain Dial was angrier than he had ever been before. The smoke in his head was thick and turbulent. And there were sounds. I could hear Melanie crying. I could hear a hundred Melanies crying.

Then Captain Dial began shouting at Lieutenant Morris. I had never heard him shout like that before, and it made me cringe even though he wasn't shouting at me. All the soldiers of First Platoon cringed, too, especially when Captain Dial said he would bring Lieutenant Morris up on charges for disobeying orders.

But Lieutenant Morris's bitter smell was acrid and strong now, and he stood with his head thrust forward and his arms straight down at his sides. He didn't salute. It was as if he was challenging Captain Dial. It was as if he thought he had done a good thing, and that Captain Dial's orders had been wrong.

That made me angry, because Captain Dial always gave good orders. So I took a step toward Lieutenant Morris and growled.

Lieutenant Morris reached for his sidearm, but Captain Dial slapped his hand away from it. Then Lieutenant Morris made a fist and started to swing it at Captain Dial's face. I was on him before his fist was halfway there, and I put him on his back on the highway.

I stood with my front paws on Lieutenant Morris's chest and my teeth touching his throat, and Captain Dial ordered him to remain still. This time, Lieutenant Morris obeyed. I could feel the pulse in his neck and the shallow motion of his chest as he breathed, but those were the only movements he made until Captain Dial ordered me to stand down. Then I took my paws from Lieutenant Morris's chest and backed away.

But now I smelled something wrong in a pocket of Lieutenant Morris's fatigues. It smelled like the girl with the cut on her neck. It smelled like her blood.

I pointed at Lieutenant Morris's pocket and barked. So Captain Dial knelt down, opened the pocket, and brought out a slender chain with a shiny rock on it. It wasn't just like the one he had given Melanie, but it didn't look much different. Except that this one had blood on its chain.

The clasp on the chain was closed, but the chain had been broken in another place. The rock slid down against the clasp when Captain Dial pulled the chain from Lieutenant Morris's pocket, and it dangled there as he held it up. It caught the sun so that it seemed to have a light inside it.

Captain Dial remained on one knee, looking at the necklace, for a long time. Lieutenant Morris started to speak, but I growled and he shut up. I was doing him a favor, because one of Captain Dial's thoughts was clear. He was thinking of using his sidearm to shoot Lieutenant Morris in the head. He was thinking that if Lieutenant Morris said even one word, that was what he would do.

What happened instead was that Captain Dial stood up and told a First Platoon sergeant to call for military police. Then he returned to our utility vehicle, leaving Lieutenant Morris on his back on the highway. I went with Captain Dial, and we waited in our vehicle until the military police came. When they did, Captain Dial gave the rock and chain to one of them.

I didn't understand everything that happened after that. But Lieutenant Morris was back with D Company just two days after he ordered First Platoon to attack the van. And Captain Dial was unhappy because he didn't think there would ever be a court-martial. For one thing, none of the soldiers of First Platoon were sure about what had happened. Some of them even thought that the van had been loaded with explosives, and they continued to think so even after Captain Dial told them I hadn't smelled any. Also, Lieutenant Morris said that he had found the girl's necklace on the ground. And there were no soldiers who would say that he hadn't. Except me. I hadn't smelled any dirt or asphalt on it. All I had smelled was skin and blood from the girl's neck plus sweat from Lieutenant Morris's hand. But the only officer who could hear my testimony was Captain Dial. And unless there was a court-martial, he had already done all he could do.

Besides, the military police said they lost the necklace.

Captain Dial was sad from then on. I don't think anyone else in the company knew that. But I did.

I wanted to make Captain Dial happy again, so I tried even harder to be good. And he told me I was. He told me I was the best sergeant he had ever seen.

But he was still sad. So I was sad too.

* * *

Two weeks later, D Company was assigned to a combat mission. A few hours before dawn on a Friday morning, thirty enemy guerrillas had attacked our supply depot using mortars and small arms—and although they had been repelled, four of our soldiers had been killed. So the guerrillas had to be followed and destroyed, and D Company was chosen to do it. Captain Dial thought it was strange that an entire company was being sent after only thirty enemies, but he followed the order without hesitation.

D Company was in pursuit of the guerrillas within an hour of the attack. The guerrillas had a big head start, but they were on foot, and D Company had armored personnel carriers, utility vehicles, and me. So we were able to move fast over both roads and fields, and every few minutes Captain Dial had me run ahead and correct the direction of our pursuit. The guerrillas were staying in one group, so their trail was easy to smell.

We had almost caught up to them as they reached the hills fifteen kilometers west of our airfield. We were so close that Captain Dial could see them through his night-vision field glasses. They were making their way up a narrow, ascending valley, and they were still in one group.

This troubled Captain Dial. It seemed to him that once the guerrillas had reached the hills, they should have scattered to make our pursuit more difficult. But they were staying together. So Captain Dial used his radio to consult with Headquarters, and Headquarters said a refugee camp of about three hundred souls lay a short distance up the valley, a few hundred meters beyond a natural curve. The guerrillas probably intended to stay together long enough to reach that camp—and then they would disperse and blend in with the civilians. This would force Captain Dial to either let them escape, or arrest the entire camp.

So we had to stop the guerrillas before they reached the refugee camp. Captain Dial increased our speed, then dropped off two squads from Fourth Platoon with ten mortars as soon as we were in range. His plan was for those squads to fire the mortars just beyond the guerrillas, forcing them to turn away from the refugee camp . . . and perhaps also to run back into our pursuit.

As the rest of D Company started up the valley, the mortar squads put a dozen rounds where Captain Dial had ordered. But instead of reversing direction, the guerrillas began to ascend a hill on the south side of the valley. They remained in one group, though, and we gained on them. When we were close enough that we might be hit by stray mortar rounds, Captain Dial radioed the squads and told them to hold fire. But they were to stay put to intercept any enemies that might be flushed back toward them.

We rushed toward the base of the hill the guerrillas were climbing. They were moving much more slowly now, and in the light of dawn it was clear that we would overtake them before they reached the crest of the hill. I became excited as I thought of knocking them down and holding them, one by one, until my fellow soldiers could take them prisoner. And as the utility vehicle that carried me, Captain Dial, and Staff Sergeant Owens began to climb the hill, I readied myself to leap out and attack.

Our vehicle was in the lead, so most of the company was still on the valley floor as we started up the hill. It was at that moment that rocket-propelled grenades and mortar shells began raining down around us from the opposite hillside to the north. And then the guerrillas we were chasing took up positions and began to fire down on us with small arms.

Captain Dial radioed orders to our platoon leaders to take cover and return fire. Then he had Staff Sergeant Owens turn our utility vehicle broadside to the enemy fire, and the three of us exited on the downhill side. We crawled downhill as fast as we could until we reached one of D Company's APCs, and we took cover behind it with soldiers from First and Second Platoons. The soldiers were jumping up and leaning out to fire quick bursts from their rifles, and Captain Dial shouted for them to keep it up as he got on the radio again to call Headquarters for air support. Our helicopters and drones were always out on missions, but two or three could be diverted if soldiers were in trouble. And we were in trouble.

But now Captain Dial couldn't raise Headquarters on the radio. He tried every possible frequency, and there was nothing but silence.

Lieutenant Morris crawled to us and told Captain Dial that we were all going to be killed, and that it was Captain Dial's fault. I wanted to bite Lieutenant Morris's throat then. But Captain Dial ignored him, so I tried to ignore him too. He wasn't a good soldier. He didn't belong in D Company.

There was a loud explosion up the hill, and a soldier told Captain Dial that our abandoned utility vehicle had been hit by a rocket from the other side of the valley. They were zeroing in on us. So Captain Dial said we couldn't stay behind the armored personnel carrier, because it would be targeted next. He ordered First and Second Platoons to retreat to the valley floor, and then he got on the radio and told the mortar squads from Fourth Platoon to fire on the northern hillside. Finally he called to Third Platoon and the remaining two squads of Fourth Platoon, who were all still at the base of the hill, and told them to abandon their APCs and move up the valley on foot, doubletime. All platoons were to return fire as best they could. No one was to retreat back toward the plain.

As Captain Dial and I moved downhill with First and Second Platoons, Lieutenant Morris shouted that Captain Dial's orders were insane. The soldiers in APCs should stay in them, he said. Without armor, he said, they would be picked off in the valley like cattle in a chute.

But Captain Dial knew that the armor was what the enemy would try to destroy first, unless it was moving fast. And it couldn't move fast in the terrain we were in. So getting the soldiers away from it was the only thing to do. And sure enough, before we reached the bottom of the hill, the APC we had been using for cover was hit by a rocket and destroyed.

Our mortars began hitting the northern hill as Captain Dial and I reached the base of the southern hill, and Captain Dial stood his ground there while urging the soldiers of First and Second Platoons to run past our abandoned APCs and continue up the valley. And even now, Lieutenant Morris kept telling him he was wrong, and that D Company ought to be heading back to the plain in full retreat.

But I knew Captain Dial's thoughts, and I knew he was right. Headquarters had been tricked into having D Company follow the guerrillas into an ambush—but Captain Dial wouldn't let the guerrillas trick him any further. He knew that once the ambush began, the enemy would expect D Company to retreat toward the plain. So there would be another trap waiting at the mouth of the valley. The enemy would close us in, then fire down upon us until we were annihilated.

So Captain Dial would confound their expectations. D Company would continue up the valley, on foot, until we could reach an elevated position. With our mortar squads out on the plain providing harassing fire, we could be well up the valley before the guerrillas could leave their hillsides. And then we would transform the enemy's ambush into an attack of our own.

But we would have to take up our battle position before reaching the refugee camp. So we would doubletime around the curve to get out of sight of the enemy, then run up the hill on the backside of the curve. The guerrillas would have no clear shot from their current positions—and if they followed us, we would be able to pour fire down on them as they rounded the curve. So even without air support, we could prevail.

Captain Dial's plan was good, and as D Company rushed up the valley, it began to work. Two more of our abandoned vehicles were hit and began to burn, but despite the constant fire from the enemy, we had not yet lost a single soldier. Our mortar squads were hitting the hillsides as ordered, and the guerrillas' weapons fire became erratic. Captain Dial paused every few meters to shout orders and encouragement to his running soldiers, and once he sent me back to nip at the heels of a few stragglers. But the stragglers weren't stragglers for long, and I was able to rejoin Captain Dial in less than a minute. Then, bringing up the rear, he and I rounded the curve and began running up the slope to take our positions with the rest of our soldiers. They were already following Captain Dial's orders, taking cover behind rocks and in gullies. And they were readying their weapons.

Some of the guerrillas had chased after us, and a few of them came around the curve before Captain Dial and I were far enough up the slope to take our positions. But we hit the dirt so our soldiers could fire on them, and only two of these enemies survived long enough to come within twenty meters of me and Captain Dial. So I turned, charged, and bit their throats. Then I returned to Captain Dial, and we joined several of our soldiers behind a jumble of rocks and dirt.

More guerrillas came around the curve, and D Company shot them. Then some came up the slope in a truck, and one of our soldiers destroyed it with a rocket-propelled grenade. We were winning the battle despite being ambushed.

Then strange things happened.

They didn't seem strange at first. At first, I heard the buzz of airborne drones. Captain Dial couldn't hear them yet, but he knew that I could, and he was glad. It seemed that Headquarters had heard his request after all.

But almost as soon as I heard the drones, I also heard distant explosions, and our mortar squads stopped firing. So Captain Dial radioed them for a status report. But there was no reply. Then he tried again to contact Headquarters, but there was still no reply there either.

The buzz became loud, and two drones appeared around the curve of the valley, flying low. They were narrow-winged and sleek, and almost invisible against the sky. They didn't have any insignia on their wings.

Then they fired rockets at us. They fired rockets at D Company. And at least twenty soldiers died as the rockets exploded. Dirt and rocks pelted me and Captain Dial where we crouched. My ears hurt.

The drones rose up over the opposite hill, then turned back toward us. Captain Dial shouted into his radio, trying one frequency after another, doing his best to raise Headquarters, to raise the remote drone pilots, to raise anyone who should have been listening. He shouted to his lieutenants to try their own radios too. And they did. But no one received a reply.

The drones came swooping toward us, and it became clear that their first attack hadn't been a mistake. Captain Dial's thoughts were tangled as he realized this. The enemy had no such weapons. So he couldn't understand why the drones were attacking us. Their cameras should have seen who we were, and their pilots should have known that D Company wasn't the enemy.

But even in his confusion, Captain Dial was a good leader. He ordered Sergeant Owens to fire a flare to identify us, but he didn't wait to see whether the cameras had seen it and understood its meaning. Instead, he shouted for D Company's surviving lieutenants and sergeants to get their soldiers up and moving again. If the drones were returning to attack our position again, he was going to put us somewhere else.

The soldiers of D Company were already running down the slope when the drones launched their second wave of rockets, so most of them made it to the valley floor. But eight more were killed. Captain Dial and I were bringing up the rear again, and the rocket that killed the eight exploded in front of us just as another exploded behind us. Captain Dial dove to the ground, putting his arms around me and pushing me down. Then he covered me with his body as more rockets exploded on the slope above us.

I didn't like it. Captain Dial wasn't supposed to shield me from harm. I was supposed to do that for him. So I tried to reverse our positions, but Captain Dial ordered me to stay put. Of course I had to obey. But I didn't understand. Captain Dial was more important to D Company than I was.

The rockets stopped exploding, and the drones passed over us again. They were so close that the dirt under my jaw hummed. Then Captain Dial was on his feet again, shouting orders as the drones flew behind the hilltop. The surviving soldiers of D Company were to run like hell up the valley and to take whatever cover they could find—rocks, trees, ditches, anything—if the drones made another pass. But the soldiers were to avoid entering the refugee camp, wherever it was, at all costs. If they came upon it while still on the run, they were to find a way around it.

Captain Dial was smart. But even Captain Dial could only make his choices based on what he knew. And he didn't know that the refugees weren't gathered in a single camp, as Headquarters had said. He didn't know that they were scattered in small clusters throughout the rest of the valley.

And he didn't know that the drones would return so soon, or that they would swoop up and down the valley firing their Gatling guns at anything that moved. The valley was full of sunlight now, so the pilots should have been able to see our soldiers' uniforms. There was nothing to block the view of the cameras. But the drones kept firing on us.

I wished I could jump high enough to tear them out of the sky.

As D Company's lieutenants and sergeants began shouting and radioing Captain Dial, telling him that they were losing more soldiers and that every scrap of cover was occupied by noncombatants, Captain Dial made a decision he didn't want to make. He tried one more time to contact Headquarters—and when that failed, he ordered D Company to return fire. Then he took a rifle from a fallen corporal and fired the first shots at the lead drone as it swooped toward us again.

I couldn't fire a weapon, so I did the only thing I could do to help. I ran in a zigzag pattern toward the drones in an attempt to draw their fire and give the rest of D Company a better chance to make their shots count. And I could hear Captain Dial shouting that I was good.

That made me glad.

The lead drone turned toward me, and in that instant the soldiers of D Company were able to hit it broadside with small-arms fire and at least one RPG. The drone began spewing smoke, and then it turned and almost collided with the second drone. The second drone pulled up and vanished behind a hill just as the first one began to spiral downward.

I returned to Captain Dial, who ordered me and the soldiers who were closest to follow him. We ran up a hillside and dove into a gully that cut across it. There were six of us: Captain Dial, Lieutenant Morris, Sergeant Owens, two specialists, and me. And in the gully we found five civilians: An old man, a woman, an adolescent girl, and two young boys. They scrambled away from us as we tumbled into the gully, and they seemed about to climb out until Captain Dial spoke to them in their language. I think he told them they would be safer if they stayed put.

He had no sooner gotten the words out than the ground shook with the biggest explosion yet. I smelled burning fuel, and I knew the drone had crashed. Captain Dial shouted for everyone to hit the dirt, but I was the only one in the gully who heard him. There was a roaring noise and more explosions. The drone's remaining weapons were detonating.

One of the boys tried to climb out of the gully. The woman jumped up to stop him, and something from the exploding drone hit her in the face. She fell back into the gully. So Captain Dial tried to get to the panicked boy to pull him down. But Lieutenant Morris clutched Captain Dial's leg and stopped him.

Captain Dial made a gesture, and I followed the order. I leaped over him and Lieutenant Morris, and I grabbed the boy's ankle and pulled him down. My teeth broke his skin, but it couldn't be helped. When the boy fell to the dirt beside the woman, I pressed my chest against his to hold him there.

The girl started to move as if to protect the boy from me, but then she looked at my eyes. And for that moment, she knew my thoughts. So she crawled to the woman instead and wiped blood from her face.

The woman wasn't breathing, and I knew she was dead. The girl knew it too, but she tried to make the woman breathe again anyway.

There were a few more explosions from the fallen drone, and then the only noise from it was a muted roar as it burned. So I listened for the other drone, and I heard it flying farther and farther away.

Captain Dial told me I could let the boy up, so I did. He tried to run away again, but this time the girl stopped him. He was crying, and so was the girl. So was the other boy. The girl looked at me again, and I knew then that the dead woman was their mother and the old man was their grandfather. The old man was sitting against the wall of the gully with his knees pulled up to his face and his eyes closed tight.

I looked at Captain Dial then and saw that he was hurt. His left sleeve was turning dark at the shoulder, just below the edge of his flak jacket. But I could hardly smell his blood among all the other bloody smells. I went to him and whined, and he touched my head and told me he was all right. I wanted to go find a medic for him, but he ordered me to stay.

Then he used his radio to ask the rest of D Company for a status report, but he couldn't hear the replies because Lieutenant Morris began shouting. I couldn't understand all of the words, but I understood that Lieutenant Morris blamed Captain Dial for what had happened. He accused Captain

Dial of treason for shooting down one of our own aircraft. And he said that the civilians weren't refugees at all, but guerrillas like those we had been pursuing. He said that was why the drones had attacked. And he said it was Captain Dial's fault that D Company had been in the line of fire when that happened.

Nothing Lieutenant Morris was shouting made any sense. But nothing that had happened to us had made any sense either. I knew that much from Captain Dial's thoughts. He didn't understand why things had happened the way they had happened. He slumped with his back against the wall of the gully, and he wondered whether Melanie would still love him after this.

Lieutenant Morris turned to Sergeant Owens and the two specialists, and he announced that Captain Dial was incapacitated. So he was now ranking officer, he said, and he ordered them to turn their weapons toward the old man, the girl, and the boys. If any of them moved, he said, the soldiers were to shoot them all.

Sergeant Owens and the specialists did as they were told. Then Lieutenant Morris reached for the radio in Captain Dial's right hand, but I jumped in his way and snarled at him. So Lieutenant Morris unholstered his sidearm and pointed it at me.

But before he could fire, Captain Dial spoke. He ordered Lieutenant Morris to lower his weapon, and after some hesitation, Lieutenant Morris obeyed. Then Captain Dial ordered Sergeant Owens and the specialists to lower their weapons as well, and they obeyed too.

Captain Dial was strong again. His shoulder was bleeding, but his thoughts were clear. He stood up, pushing himself off the gully wall with his right forearm, and peered over the rim at the burning drone. He spoke into his radio and told his soldiers to stay put if they were in a safe place, and to keep trying to find one if they weren't. He would assess the situation and issue new orders within the next few minutes.

But we didn't have a few minutes. I could hear the second drone returning.

I barked to let Captain Dial know it was coming. So then he shouted into his radio and ordered all of his soldiers to remain still and refrain from returning fire unless directly fired upon. Then he ordered those of us in the gully to hit the dirt. The girl and the two boys didn't understand at first, but the old man put his hands on their shoulders and made them lie down close to their dead mother.

Then Captain Dial lowered himself to a sitting position with his back against the gully wall. He couldn't lie down flat with his wounded shoulder. I lay down next to him and put my chin on his knee, and we waited while the drone flew back and forth. Its Gatling gun chattered three or four times, and I hoped it was shooting enemy guerrillas and not D Company soldiers or civilians.

One of the little boys began to cry, but the girl and the old man whispered to him, and then he was quiet again. I was glad they could calm him like that. They were being good leaders. Like Captain Dial.

But a good leader needs good soldiers.

On the drone's fourth pass, Lieutenant Morris stood and fired his weapon into the air. I was on him fast, my front paws hitting his back and pushing him down, but it was too late. Even as I pinned Lieutenant Morris to the bottom of the gully, I could hear the drone turning and the barrels of its Gatling guns beginning to spin.

Lieutenant Morris shouted into the dirt that we had to show ourselves to the drone so it would know who we were and so it could help us kill the rest of the enemy. He worked a hand free from under his chest and pointed at the family with the dead mother.

I wanted to bite Lieutenant Morris and bite him hard. And I smelled something in one of his pockets that made me feel that way even more. It smelled like the dead girl at the highway checkpoint.

But I didn't bite him, because I knew Captain Dial wouldn't like it. Captain Dial was busy with his radio, telling the rest of D Company that they were not to give away their positions by firing on the drone if it attacked those of us in the gully—not unless there was a clear shot for an RPG. Otherwise, we were on our own. But D Company would survive.

I heard the drone dip low. It was flying on a path directly in line with our gully. It would be able to pour bullets and rockets on us with ease.

Captain Dial was on his feet. It was as if he had been yanked up on a rope from the sky. His left sleeve was so wet that it dripped.

He shouted two orders. First, Sergeant Owens and the two specialists were to get out of the gully at the south rim and run through the smoke of the downed aircraft until they could find other cover in the valley. Second, I was to take the civilians over the north rim and head up into the hills until I could find another gully, a cave, or some other sheltered position. I was to keep them safe.

Sergeant Owens and the specialists clambered over the south rim, rolled, and ran into the smoke. I jumped off Lieutenant Morris and started toward the civilians. But after a few steps, I stopped. The drone's Gatling guns had begun to fire.

I looked back and saw Captain Dial pull Lieutenant Morris to his feet. Captain Dial could only use his right arm, so he had dropped his radio. Lieutenant Morris seemed dazed, and Captain Dial had to hold him up and drag him.

Captain Dial shouted for me to obey my order. I was not to wait for him and Lieutenant Morris. They would catch up, he said.

But I knew Captain Dial's thoughts. I knew he didn't think that he and Lieutenant Morris would make it.

So for the first time ever, I decided to disobey a direct order. I would obey my General Order instead. That was what I had done on the day beside the ocean, and Captain Dial had told me I was good. He had told me I was more good than I had ever been before. So I would do that again.

I ran back to Captain Dial, and he yelled at me. He said I had to obey his order immediately.

But instead I grabbed one of Lieutenant Morris's flak-jacket straps, and I pulled him away from Captain Dial and began dragging him up the gully wall. He was heavy, but I'm strong.

Captain Dial knew then that he should take charge of the civilians. Dragging soldiers to safety was one of my jobs, and keeping civilians safe was one of his. But first, he jumped to me and hooked Lieutenant Morris's arm through my harness loop. Then he pulled the strap to tighten the loop. Now I could let go of the flak-jacket strap and drag Lieutenant Morris a lot faster.

Captain Dial touched my head and told me to go.

I went up the gully wall and over the top with Lieutenant Morris while Captain Dial ran to the civilians and told them that they must go with him. One of the boys cried because he wanted to stay with his mother, but the old man and the girl listened to Captain Dial and wouldn't let the boy stay. They all climbed up from the gully.

Captain Dial's foot slipped on the way up and he almost fell, but the girl grabbed his arm to steady him. It was his wounded arm, but she couldn't reach the other one. I saw a flash like a grenade exploding in Captain Dial's thoughts. But Captain Dial didn't cry out even though it hurt a lot. He was a good soldier. The girl was, too. She didn't hesitate to help Captain Dial. She didn't flinch from his blood.

When we were all out of the gully, we ran north through the smoke. Captain Dial and the civilians were a few meters west of me and Lieutenant Morris, and they were moving up the slope a little faster. Every few steps, Captain Dial would look back and call encouragement to me. And I would pull harder and could feel Lieutenant Morris's boots bouncing on the ground behind us.

I didn't look back, but I heard the buzz of the drone as it flew low over the gully we had just left. I could smell its exhaust. Its Gatling guns chattered, and the slugs made dull thumps in the dirt.

And then, as we ran higher and came up out of the smoke, I heard the drone swoop out over the valley, turn, and head right for us. It was attacking us from behind, and there was no place for us to take cover when its guns started firing again. I looked ahead and saw a shadow on the ground that looked like another gully, but it was too far away. Lieutenant Morris and I wouldn't reach it before the drone strafed us.

I looked over at Captain Dial. Although he was wounded, he was now carrying one of the boys. The girl was carrying the other one. The old man was breathing hard and stumbling. So they were losing speed, and Lieutenant Morris and I had almost caught up to them. They wouldn't reach the next gully either. The drone would be able to hit all of us with the same burst of gunfire, or with just one rocket.

Captain Dial looked over at me as I looked at him, and we each knew the other's thoughts. There was only one thing to do. And when his thoughts said now, I followed his order.

He and the civilians cut left, where there was still a little smoke, and I cut right, where the air was clear. We ran away from each other as fast as we could. I could hear Captain Dial's breath getting farther and farther away behind me. I could hear it even over the noise from Lieutenant Morris's boots.

I would have dropped Lieutenant Morris if I could, because he would have been safer lying still. But I couldn't. The loop on my harness was pulled tight around his arm, and there was no time for me to turn my head to yank it loose.

The drone came after me and Lieutenant Morris. I was sorry for what that meant for Lieutenant Morris, but glad because it gave Captain Dial a better chance to get himself and the civilians to cover. And I was glad because it gave me a chance to be good.

I ran hard, and I zigzagged as much as I could while dragging Lieutenant Morris. The engine buzz became a roar, and the Gatling gun chattered loud and long. And it almost missed us. But the last slugs in the burst came ripping through the dirt right behind us, and Lieutenant Morris jerked as they reached him. I was slapped down at my hindquarters, and I fell. Lieutenant Morris and I rolled a little way down the hill, and the drone flew over us so low that I could see the rivets in its belly. It rose up over the ridge, hung there for a moment, and then started toward us again.

But this time it bloomed fire from its tail, and it twisted sideways and dove into the hillside above us. There was a loud noise and more fire when it hit, and smoke like there had been from the first one.

I tried to get up, but Lieutenant Morris was lying on my hind legs. And my back hurt, close to my tail. But I couldn't see or hear Captain

Dial, and I had to find him. So I twisted my head around far enough to tug on my harness loop until Lieutenant Morris's arm slipped out. I couldn't hear Lieutenant Morris's breath or heartbeat, and I could smell that he had blood coming out of his legs, back, chest, and neck. He was dead, and there was no place I could drag him where he would be all right again.

When his arm came free, I was able to scramble with my front legs and pull myself out from under him. And then I was able to stand up all the way even though my back hurt. I looked for Captain Dial and the civilians, but I couldn't see them. There was a lot more smoke now, and it made my eyes itch. It also made it hard to smell anything else. But I heard the girl say something, faint and soft, so I left Lieutenant Morris and followed her voice.

I found her with the other civilians and Captain Dial. Captain Dial was lying on the ground, and the girl was kneeling beside him with her hand on his head. The old man was standing nearby holding the little boys' hands. The boys were scared. They were looking at the body of a D Company soldier lying nearby. It was torn in two.

Captain Dial smiled when I came up to him and licked his face. I had to step over an RPG launcher to reach him, and when I touched him I knew what he had done. He had found the RPG launcher with the dead soldier, and he had used it to bring down the second drone. But it had recoiled against his wounded shoulder, and now the wound was bleeding even more.

He saw my thoughts and knew what had happened to Lieutenant Morris. But he said I had done everything right. He said he was proud of me. He said I was good.

And just as he said that, I heard a buzzing noise far off in the south. It was heading toward us fast. More drones were coming.

Captain Dial couldn't hear them. But he knew I did. And he said that they might not be coming to attack us, because their pilots might have realized that the first two had been firing on allies and civilians. But we couldn't count on it. So I was to take the four civilians away and find shelter for them. I was to do so immediately.

I didn't understand at first, because the picture I saw in Captain Dial's thoughts was a picture only of me and the civilians. He wasn't in it. He wasn't walking with us, and I wasn't dragging him with my harness.

And then he made me understand. He was too dizzy to walk, and I couldn't drag him without making his wound worse.

I wanted to follow his orders, but first I wanted to go back down the hill and find a D Company medic to take care of him. But Captain Dial said there was no time for that. Not if I was going to take the civilians to safety before the new drones arrived. And I knew he was right, because the girl could hear the drones now too. She still had her hand on Captain Dial's head, but she was looking at the sky.

I whined. I didn't want to go off with the civilians and leave Captain Dial all alone, even for a little while.

Captain Dial reached up with his right hand to touch my head. He told me it was all right to leave him for now, because I could come back as soon as I had taken the civilians to a safe place. It could be a cave or a deep ravine. It just had to be somewhere they couldn't be hurt. Once I had made sure of that, I could return. And if a medic hadn't come to help Captain Dial yet, I could go find one for him then.

But for now, I had to go. I had to keep the civilians safe.

Captain Dial took his hand from my head and spoke to the girl, and he took his pulse transmitter from the pouch on his belt and gave it to her. I knew he was telling her to go with me, and that the transmitter would help us communicate. She shook her head at first, but I could understand her thoughts well enough to know that it wasn't because she was afraid of me. It was because she didn't want to leave Captain Dial alone any more than I did.

I knew then that I liked her. But we were under orders now, and we had to follow them. So I took the girl's hand in my mouth, and I gave a tug to pull her away from Captain Dial. She didn't want to go, but she didn't fight me. She knew what we had to do. She strapped the transmitter to her wrist and stood up. She was good, too.

We left Captain Dial and went to the old man and the boys. I released the girl's hand as she told them they were all going with me. She put the old man's hand on the handle of my harness, and then he held the hand of one of the boys. The girl held the hand of the other one. We all started up the hill again, pushing through the smoke. My hind legs hurt, but I was still strong. I helped the old man go fast. The girl kept pace beside me as I sniffed and listened to find the best path for us.

I could still see Captain Dial's thoughts for a long way up the hill. At first he was thinking of me and what I was doing, and he was proud. That made me glad.

Then he thought the two words he had thought about on the day we performed our demonstration by the ocean. He thought the words "heroism" and "vengeance."

And then he worried about the other soldiers in D Company. So that made me worry, too. But I couldn't go back to check on them yet. I had orders to follow.

Finally, as the civilians and I came out of the smoke onto a sloping field of rocks, I saw one last strong thought from Captain Dial. It was of Melanie. It was of Melanie with him in their bed, sleeping. And I was on my cushion at their feet.

It was a happy thought, and it made me happy too.

Then Captain Dial's thoughts became fuzzy as the civilians and I went higher, and soon they were gone. I paused near the crest of the hill and looked back down the slope, but I couldn't see the place where Captain Dial lay because of the rocks and smoke. And I thought for a moment that maybe the civilians were safe now, and that I could leave them and go back to where I could know Captain Dial's thoughts again.

But the sound of the approaching drones was loud now, and as I watched, one of them came flying up out of the smoke below us. So I led the civilians behind a big rock. We all crouched down, and I heard the drone turn away and fly back down the hillside again.

Then I heard Gatling guns firing, and I remembered my orders. So I got up from my crouch, and the girl and I took the old man and the boys over the top of the hill and down the other side.

I didn't like not being able to see Captain Dial's thoughts. But now I could see the girl's thoughts almost as well as I had seen his, and she had some good ideas about where we might find a safe place to hide. So we started off in the direction she thought was best.

We had to alter our path many times because of things I smelled or heard. And once we had to make a long detour because the girl remembered there were land mines ahead. I couldn't smell them yet, but she warned me by sending pulses to my implant. And then I saw her thoughts, and I knew they were true. So we found another way.

I became tired and thirsty, and my hind legs hurt. The girl and her family became tired and thirsty too. But we could hear gunfire and explosions behind us, so the girl and I wouldn't let the others stop. Not until we found someplace safe.

Not until we had done what Captain Dial had ordered us to do.

* * *

We went up and down through the hills all that day. At dusk we found a guerrilla camp that had been bombed many weeks before. But there were still some matches, a knife, and three plastic jugs of water. So we were able to get a drink. The water tasted like plastic, but we drank a lot of it. There was only one jug left when we were finished. The girl tied it to my harness, and we set out again. The girl carried the matches and the knife.

After nightfall, the girl couldn't see where we were or where we were going. Clouds covered the sky, so she couldn't find any stars to help her. That meant our path was up to me. So I followed my nose and my ears, and I took us farther and farther away from cities, camps, and roads. I took us away from anything that smelled or sounded like people with weapons. We had to go a long way.

At last, when the eastern sky had begun to brighten, we found a shelf of rock in the side of a hill. Under the shelf was a cave that was narrow but deep. It was well hidden by brush. I went in first and found some bone fragments and a ring of stones for a fire, but I could smell that they were old. No one had used the cave in a long time.

So I brought the people inside, and they slept on the bare rock. I didn't sleep right away because I had to lick the cuts on my hind legs. Then I dozed. But I kept my ears and nose alert. The only sounds were of the wind blowing through the rocks and brush. The only smells were of rabbits, birds, and other small animals nearby. There were no guerrillas, soldiers, or other people anywhere near us.

When I had rested for a few hours, I went out into the morning sunlight and killed three rabbits. I had to chase them, and that made my legs hurt again. But I still caught them with no trouble. I tore one apart and ate most of him, and then I took the other two back to the cave. The girl was awake, and she knew what to do. She woke up the boys and had them gather brush and sticks while she used the knife from the guerrilla camp to skin the rabbits. The old man made a spit from the sticks, and they cooked the rabbits over a fire the girl started inside the old ring of stones. It filled the cave with smoke, but the people didn't care. They were hungry.

While they ate, I scouted the area around the cave in widening circles. I sniffed, smelled, and listened. I marked a broad perimeter to warn off animal intruders. Then I did it all over again. And then I was sure my people were safe.

I had followed and completed Captain Dial's order. So I went to the girl and pushed my nose into her hand to be sure she knew my thoughts. I made sure she knew that she and her family should stay close to the cave. They could kill more rabbits to eat, and they still had the jug of water from the guerrilla camp. When that ran out, they could catch rain and dew.

The girl understood.

So I started back to the battlefield where I had left Captain Dial. I was able to go faster now because I didn't have people with me, and because my legs felt better. I could also choose a path that took me closer to dangerous smells. And I found a pond where I could get a drink. But that was the only time I stopped. I wanted to get back to Captain Dial as soon as I could.

There was still some light in the sky when I came over the hilltop and looked down the rocky slope at the battlefield. The two fallen drones had stopped burning, and there was no more smoke. A number of people were walking around down near the gully where Captain Dial and I had found the civilians, and the wind brought me their smells along with the smells of many dead D Company soldiers and refugees. The walking people didn't smell like soldiers or refugees. But they didn't smell like the enemy, either. They didn't make much noise, but occasionally one of them would fire a single shot. It sounded as if they were firing into the ground.

I didn't care who they were, or why they were shooting at the ground. Because now I smelled something else, too.

When I reached Captain Dial, I lay down beside him with my chin on his chest. There was nothing else I could do. I didn't nudge him with my nose or lick his face. I didn't try to wake him up. I'm not stupid. That was one of the things Captain Dial liked best about me. He liked that I was smart.

I closed my eyes. I didn't have an order for what to do next, so I would do nothing. I was tired, and there were no D Company soldiers left for me to help. I would stay there with my chin on Captain Dial.

I closed my eyes and fell asleep. And I dreamed. I dreamed about the day I found the live mine on the pier and about how proud Captain Dial was. I dreamed about running fast in training so I could complete my orders and get back to Captain Dial before the buzzer sounded. I dreamed about lying curled up on my cushion on the floor while Captain Dial and Melanie made soft noises above me.

Then I woke up and opened my eyes. Three of the people below were coming up the slope. They were solid shadows in the dusk. And their smell was sharper now. They smelled like men who used shampoo and soap and who wore clean clothes. They smelled like the men in the crowd the day I found the mine. They smelled like civilians from home.

And as they came toward me and Captain Dial, I heard something behind me. Something higher up the slope, moving down through the rocks. It wasn't loud, so I knew the men coming up the slope couldn't hear it. I couldn't identify it by scent because the wind was blowing the wrong way, but I could hear that it was small and alone. So I didn't think it would hurt anyone. Besides, none of the men coming up the slope was my commanding officer. I wasn't required to alert them.

The three men approached within a few meters of me and Captain Dial, and now I saw that they were dressed in dark clothes that weren't uniforms. But they carried pistols in holsters. One of them pointed a camera at me and Captain Dial. I couldn't see the men's thoughts, but they

285

spoke in the same language as D Company, so I understood some of what they said. One of them said something was great, and the others agreed.

I didn't know what they thought was great, but I knew there was nothing there that was.

One of them stepped closer and leaned down as if about to touch Captain Dial. So I raised my head and snarled at him, and he moved back. Then I put my head down again, but I stayed ready. I didn't know who they were, but they weren't part of D Company. They weren't even soldiers. I wouldn't let them touch Captain Dial.

The one with the camera kept aiming it at me and Captain Dial. But the other two put their hands on their pistols and conferred. And I understood enough to know they were talking about shooting me. So I did what Captain Dial had taught me to do. I planned how to attack them so they couldn't get off a shot. If either of their pistols began to rise from its holster, I would execute the plan. And I would decide what to do about the one with the camera based on how he reacted.

But another thing that Captain Dial had taught me was that a battlefield situation can change quickly.

The thing coming down the slope sent some pebbles skittering through the brush. And the three men heard it. They backed away from me and Captain Dial, and the one with the camera let it drop to dangle on a cord around his neck. They all three began taking their pistols from their holsters. But now they were looking past me toward whatever had made the pebbles skitter.

I kept my eyes on the three men. But I sniffed the air, and even though the wind was still going the wrong way, I caught a faint scent that told me who was on the slope behind me. It was the girl I had taken to safety on Captain Dial's order. She was still and quiet now, probably crouched behind a rock. But even so, she wasn't safe anymore.

All three men were raising their pistols. They were farther away from me than when I had made my plan of attack. But they weren't looking at me now. The light of day was almost gone. And I am black as night. I am silent as air.

The third one got off a shot as I hit his chest, but the bullet went into the sky. The other two were already on the ground, their throats torn out, their weapons in the dirt. The third one tried to fight me off once he was down, but that didn't last long.

When he was still, I looked back up the slope, beyond Captain Dial, and saw the girl standing beside a clump of brush. She was almost invisible because the sun was gone now. But I saw her shape against the brush. And the wind had shifted so I could smell her better. She smelled scared.

I was angry that she had returned to the battlefield. I had done my duty and made her safe, and she had spoiled it. I didn't understand why she had done that.

Then she came down the hill past Captain Dial, past me, and past the three men on the ground. She didn't walk fast, but she walked steady and strong even though she was scared. She said something soft to me as she went by, and I saw a flash of her thoughts. Then I understood. She was going down to the gully, to her mother. She wanted to wrap the body and take it somewhere to bury it. She had returned by herself to do this, leaving her brothers in the care of the old man.

I looked past her and knew I couldn't let her do as she planned. There were more people down there. They were like the three men I had just killed. The girl wouldn't be safe among them. Already, I could see and hear several of them starting toward her. She couldn't see them yet. But she would encounter them before she could reach the gully.

So I ran down to the girl and got in front of her. But she just walked around me. Then I took her hand in my mouth, but she just pulled it away and kept going. She wouldn't stay in contact with me long enough to see my thoughts. She was determined to reach her mother.

I couldn't knock her down or bite her to make her come with me. But I couldn't let her keep going. I had to make her pay attention to me long enough so she would understand what we had to do. So I turned and ran fast across the hillside, away from both the girl and Captain Dial. I ran to the body of Lieutenant Morris, and I tore open one of his pockets. Some ammo clips fell out, but that wasn't what I wanted. I wanted what I had smelled when I'd pushed Lieutenant Morris down in the gully.

And I found it curled up in the corner of the pocket. It was the necklace from the dead girl at the checkpoint. There was still enough blood on it that I had been able to smell it. The necklace had been taken from Lieutenant Morris for the investigation, but he had stolen it back. Now I took it from him again.

I ran back to the girl with it, got in front of her, and pushed my nose against her hand so she would feel the necklace hanging from my mouth.

She stopped walking. Her palm was against my nose. Her fingers brushed the silver chain. The transmitter on her wrist hummed. And then, as someone shouted below us, I thought hard and showed her what had happened to the girl who had worn the necklace. So she saw that girl lying on the side of the road with her sisters. She saw me find the necklace in Lieutenant Morris's pocket. She saw how angry Captain Dial had been at what Lieutenant Morris had done.

The shouting below us grew louder. I could hear six voices now, and weapons being readied. More of the armed-men-who-weren't-soldiers were coming toward us.

But I didn't turn away from the girl. I kept my nose in her palm because I had to be sure she understood. I had to be sure she understood that Captain Dial was my commanding officer, and that I hated to leave him there on the hillside again. But I would. And she would have to leave her mother there, too. We both had to follow Captain Dial's last order. And if the men coming up the hillside reached us, we would fail. I wouldn't be good. And she would be like the other girl. The one who had worn the necklace.

The girl was smart. I saw in her thoughts that her mother wouldn't want her to die like that other girl. But when she understood what I was telling her, she began to cry. She hadn't cried before this. But she cried now, taking the necklace from my mouth and clutching it in her fist. She wanted to fight the men coming up the hill. She thought they were responsible for her mother's death. She thought they had made the drones attack.

I didn't know why she thought that. But I understood why she would want to fight whoever had made the drones fire on D Company. I wanted to fight those people too. But even if those people were the men who were coming up the hill, we couldn't fight them now. I had already killed three of them, but I had caught those three by surprise. There were more than three coming now, and they had their weapons ready to fire.

So we had to go back up over the hill. And while the girl stood there with the necklace clenched in her fist, I took her other hand in my mouth. And then I started up the hill, pulling her with me.

At first, she came with me without knowing what she was doing. She was still crying and thinking of what she wanted to do to the people who had sent the drones. So the men coming up the hill gained on us, and a shot was fired. I heard the bang and then heard the slug hiss through the air. It hit the dirt several meters ahead of us.

Then the girl's thoughts came back to where we were and what we needed to do. So she began to run, and I was able to release her hand. We ran together back up the hill, through the rocks and brush, up toward the night sky.

We paused for a few seconds when we reached Captain Dial again. He lay still in the twilight. He made no sound. He had no thoughts. He didn't even smell like Captain Dial anymore. So it was all right for the girl to take his sidearm and empty his pockets. And this time, it was easier to leave. This time, I knew I wouldn't need to return.

In training, Captain Dial had told me that when a soldier was gone, he was gone forever. But he had also told Melanie that they would be together forever. So it was always a hard word for me to understand. But whenever I didn't understand something, it was because it was something only someone as smart as Captain Dial could understand. And in those cases, I would just have to believe whatever Captain Dial said. Because Captain Dial always spoke the truth.

So that was what I did as I left his body there on the hillside for the last time. I remembered what Captain Dial had said, and I was glad that even though he was gone, he and Melanie would still be together.

I wished I could be with them, too. But I didn't know how to get to wherever they were.

The girl and I went up over the top of the hill, and soon I couldn't smell or hear the men behind us anymore. Then the twilight was gone, and the girl held my harness so I could lead her through the darkness. She knew my thoughts most of the time now, so I promised her I would do a good job. And she promised me the same thing.

We had our orders. So we would follow them.

Forever.

* * *

I took the girl back to the cave where the old man and the boys were waiting, and we stayed there several weeks until I smelled men with weapons approaching. Then we left, and I led the way deeper into the hills, taking us as far from danger as I could. The weather grew colder, but my fur grew thicker, and we found winter clothing in an abandoned village. The old man also found sewing tools, and he made blankets from the skins of the rabbits I caught. The girl stretched some skins between two long pieces of wood, and that was where we kept our growing collection of supplies. The people and I took turns dragging it as we traveled.

We traveled this way for many days, until we came upon the stone hut near the stream.

It's been a good place. We found more things that my people could use here. But the people who had stayed in the hut before us had been gone for a long time when we arrived. I couldn't even smell them on the things they had left. So I believed my company would be safe here for the winter.

Food was easy to obtain. All I had to do was go up and down the stream until I found rabbits. Once I killed a small deer, and the girl said its skin should be my bed. So now I sleep on it even though I like the bare ground just as well. I have thick fur. But it makes my people happy to see me lie down on the deer's skin, and that makes me glad.

In recent weeks the bushes and trees have grown leaves, and the grass that was dry and thin is now thick and juicy. The girl and the old man have been making plans to plant seeds they found in the abandoned village. We've all been looking forward to warmer days.

Then, last night, eighteen of Your soldiers came to kill us. You must have told them we were the enemy. So they didn't know I was trained by Captain Dial. They didn't know that even when I sleep, my ears and nose are awake.

I took the girl to their bodies this morning, and it made her sad. But she understood that I had to follow orders. She understands a lot. She and I often help each other figure out things that are puzzling.

I didn't understand how Your soldiers could have found us, or why You would want them to, because we've traveled far from anything that should matter to You. Besides, we're not Your enemies. And even if we were, we wouldn't be important enough for You to bother with. Or so I thought.

Then the girl remembered the implant under the skin between my shoulders, and the transmitter that Captain Dial had given her. We had used these things to help us understand each other in our first weeks together, but then—just as Captain Dial and I had found—they had become unnecessary. So the girl had placed the transmitter in her duffel, and we hadn't thought of it or of my implant since. But now the girl said that machines in the sky could probably hear signals from them at any time, and that the machines could then tell You where I was. So that was how Your soldiers found us.

The girl also says she knows why You want to attack us.

She found a radio receiver in the abandoned village, and now she listens to its voices for a few minutes each evening. I can't understand the voices, but the girl has told me some of the things they've said. They've said that all Your soldiers were about to be sent home because the money for the war was almost gone. But then D Company was ambushed and destroyed by enemy guerrillas, and the bad publicity from what Lieutenant Morris had done at the checkpoint was obliterated by the heroism of his company's sacrifice. So Your public support surged, and more money was provided so Your soldiers could avenge the ambush by destroying the enemy.

This is what the radio voices say. They don't say anything about the drones. But if the drones hadn't come, D Company would not only have beaten the guerrillas, but would have suffered almost no casualties. Captain Dial would have seen to it.

But the drones did come. They came from our own airfield. They came from You.

Then the men-who-weren't-soldiers came too, and the girl thinks she knows why they fired shots at the ground. She thinks they killed any soldier or refugee who was still alive. And we believe those men were sent by You as well.

The girl says that our knowledge of this is why You want to attack us. We're the only survivors of that battle. So as long as we still live, You fear that we may reveal the truth of what happened to D Company and the refugees. And the girl says that then all of Your public support and money will go away again.

I have tried to think of what Captain Dial might do if these things had been revealed to him. But he was much smarter than me. And I can't see his thoughts anymore.

But I still know the final order he gave me: To keep my people safe.

So I've thought of things I can do to obey.

The first thing I thought of was to have the girl write this message. Again, she doesn't know what she writes. Only that I require her to write it. And what I'm asking her to write now is a promise that You have nothing to fear from me if You leave us alone. If You allow me to keep my people safe, we will never tell the radio voices what Your drones and men-who-weren't-soldiers did to D Company. The second thing made the girl cry again. Before beginning this message, I told her to use her knife to cut between my shoulders and find the communication implant. She cried because she didn't want to hurt me, and then she cried more because the device was smaller than we had imagined, and it was hard to find. She had to make the cut longer and deeper. But she finally found the tiny glass bean and gave it to the boys, who took turns hitting it and the transmitter with a hammer until both were dust. Then the old man cleaned my wound and sewed it shut. I growled once because the needle hurt, and he stepped back. But then I licked his hand, and he finished the job. Afterward, I was proud of all of them for following orders so well.

The third thing makes us unhappy. But it's necessary. We must leave the stone hut. We must leave this good place with its water and rabbits. Your soldiers found us here, so You know where we are.

But since I no longer have the communication implant, You won't know where we'll go next.

Finally, there is a fourth thing I'll do.

If the above measures fail, and if You send more soldiers or men-who-aren't-soldiers to find us, I will kill them all. I'll always know they're coming, so they'll never be able to attack us before I attack them first.

You may even send some of my fellow K-9s, because they could find us more quickly than people could. But Captain Dial said that the K-9s in my training class were the best war dogs there had ever been, and I was ranked first in that class. So there are no K-9s that I can't find and defeat before they can find and defeat me.

And if You attack us with drones instead of people or dogs, we're now equipped to fight them. Some of the soldiers I killed last night were carrying RPGs, and others carried guns with armor-piercing rounds. We have taken these weapons.

But if You bomb us from high in the sky so we can't fight, there may be nothing I can do to stop You. Then You will have made me fail to carry out my orders.

In that event, I'll do whatever I must to survive. And then I will find You. I don't know Your name or Your rank, but I will find You anyway. I will hunt and kill every officer in every company and every battalion until I reach You. I will read their thoughts as they die and will use that knowledge to hunt You. I will climb walls and dig tunnels. I will swim and run. I will stow away in trucks, ships, and aircraft that will bring me closer to You. I will find something You have touched so I know Your scent. And then I will find You in Your bed or at Your table or wherever You may be.

And I will bite Your throat so it tears out.

So I hope You heed this message. It will be left with one of Your dead soldiers, so I know it will reach their unit's commanding officer. And then it will reach that officer's commanding officer, and then that officer's commanding officer, and so on until it reaches the officer who gave the orders that resulted in the current situation. Until it reaches You.

My company has its equipment and is ready to move out. The two boys are my specialists. The old man is my medic and quartermaster.

As for the girl—

She now wears the metal tag I received when I was promoted to sergeant. She found it in Captain Dial's pocket as we left the battlefield, and today she put it on the chain of her necklace beside the shiny rock. Sergeant is the toughest enlisted job. But she can do it.

I myself am no longer a sergeant. I didn't realize that until this morning. But after I showed the girl what I had done in the night, she touched my head. And I heard her thoughts. I heard what she called me.

She called me Captain.

Then she took the silver bars that she found with the sergeant's tag, and she pinned them to my duty harness.

I am the ranking survivor of D Company, and my final order from Captain Dial was a commission. I know this because what he told me to do was what a good officer does.

A good officer takes care of his soldiers.

But if You attack us again, You will not be a good officer. You will not be taking care of Your soldiers. And if You make me fail in my duty to take care of mine, You will not be an officer of any kind for much longer.

Captain Dial told me what I am, and he always spoke the truth. So now I tell You:

I am black as night. I am silent as air.

My sergeant touches my head, and I tell her she's good.

This message is complete.

Respectfully,
Chip, K-9
Captain and Commanding Officer
D Company

Peter S. Beagle said in his introduction to this story in his collection The Line Between *(Tachyon Publications, August 2006): "The first draft of 'Gordon, The Self-Made Cat' was written more than forty years ago, when I was living on nine wild acres in the hills north of Santa Cruz, California, with my young family. [...] I made up the valiant Gordon to amuse the children, sent his story off to an animation company that had requested ideas for a feature film, shrugged at their almost immediate rejection, then buried the piece in my battered filing cabinet [...] I'm currently working on expanding it, adding new characters and more adventures, for eventual book publication. I've always loved* Charlotte's Web *and* Stuart Little; *the longer version of* Gordon *will be my own small nod in that very challenging direction."*

It's now 2015, and there is no sign of "the longer version of Gordon". *But this short story is so delightful by itself that a longer version does not seem necessary. It is good to know, though, that Gordon was never intended to fade away.*

Gordon, the Self-Made Cat

by Peter S. Beagle

Once upon a time to a family of house mice there was born a son named Gordon. He looked very much like his father and mother and all his brothers and sisters, who were gray and had bright, twitchy, black eyes, but what went on inside Gordon was very different from what went on inside the rest of his family. He was forever asking why everything had to be the way it was, and never satisfied with the answer. Why did mice eat cheese? Why did they live in the dark and only go out when it was dark? Where did mice come from, anyway? *What were people?* Why did people smell so funny? Suppose mice were big and people were tiny? Suppose mice could fly? Most mice don't ask many questions, but Gordon never stopped.

One evening, when Gordon was only a few weeks old, his next-to-eldest sister was sent out to see if anything interesting had been left open in the pantry. She never returned. Gordon's father shrugged sadly and spread his front paws, and said, "The cat."

"What's a cat?" Gordon asked.

His mother and father looked at one another and sighed. "They have to know sometime," his father said. "Better he learns it at home than on the streets."

His mother sniffled a little and said, "But he's so young," and his father answered, "Cats don't care." So they told Gordon about cats right then, expecting him to start crying and saying that there weren't any such things. It's a hard idea to get used to. But Gordon only asked, "Why do cats eat mice?"

"I guess we taste very good," his father said.

Gordon said, "But cats don't have to eat mice. They get plenty of other food that probably tastes as good. Why should anybody eat anybody if he doesn't have to?"

"Gordon," said his father. "Listen to me. There are two kinds of creatures in the world. There are animals that hunt, and animals that are hunted. We mice just happen to be the kind of animal that gets hunted, and it doesn't really matter if the cat *is* hungry or not. It's the way life is. It's really a great honor to be the hunted, if you just look at it the right way."

"Phooey on that," said Gordon. "Where do I go to learn to be a cat?"

They thought he was joking, but as soon as Gordon was old enough to go places by himself, he packed a clean shirt and some peanut butter, and started off for cat school. "I love you very much," he said to his parents before he left, "but this business of being hunted for the rest of my life just because I happened to be born a mouse is not for me." And off he went, all by himself.

All cats go to school, you know, whether you ever see them going or not. Dogs don't, but cats always have and always will. There are a great many cat schools, so Gordon found one easily enough, and he walked bravely up the front steps and knocked at the door. He said that he wanted to speak to the Principal.

He almost expected to be eaten right there, but the cats—students and teachers alike—were so astonished that they let him pass through, and one of the teachers took him to the Principal's office. Gordon could feel the cats looking at him, and hear the sounds their noses made as they smelled how good he was, but he held on tight to the suitcase with his shirt and the peanut butter, and he never looked back.

The Principal was a fat old tiger cat who chewed on his tail all the time he was talking to Gordon. "You must be out of your mind," he said when Gordon told him he wanted to be a cat. "I'd smack you up this minute, but it's bad luck to eat crazies. Get out of here! The day mice go to cat school…"

"Why not?" said Gordon. "Is it in writing? Where does it say that I can't go to school here if I want?"

Well, of course there's nothing in the rules of cat schools that says mice can't enroll. Nobody ever thought of putting it in.

The Principal folded his paws and said, "Gordon, look at it this way—"

"You look at it *my* way," said Gordon. "I want to be a cat, and I bet I'd make a better one than the dopey-looking animals I've seen in this school. Most of them look as if they wouldn't even make good mice! So let's make a deal. You let me come to school here and study for one term, and if at the end of that time I'm not doing better than any cat in the school—if even one cat has better grades than I have—then you can eat me and that'll be the end of it. Is that fair?"

No cat can resist a challenge like that. But before agreeing, the Principal insisted on one small change: at the end of the term, if Gordon didn't have the very best marks in the school, then the privilege of eating him would go to the cat that did.

"Ought to encourage some of those louts to work harder," the Principal said to himself, as Gordon left his office. "He's crazy, but he's right—most of them wouldn't even make good mice. I almost hope he does it."

So Gordon went to cat school. Every day he sat at his special little desk, surrounded by a hundred kittens and half-grown cats who would have liked nothing better than to leap on him and play games with him for a while before they gobbled him. He learned how to wash himself, and what to do to keep his claws sharp, and how to watch everything in the room while pretending to be asleep. There was a class on Dealing With Dogs, and another on Getting Down From Trees, which is much harder than climbing up, and also a particularly scholarly seminar on the various meanings of "Bad Kitty!" Gordon's personal favorite was the Visions class, which had to do with the enchanting things all cats can see that no one else ever does—the great, gliding ancestors, and faraway castles, and mysterious forests full of monsters to chase. The Professor of Visions told his colleagues that he had never had such a brilliant student. "It would be a crime to eat such a mouse!" he proclaimed everywhere. "An absolute, shameful, yummy crime."

The class in Mouse-Hunting was a bit awkward at first, because usually the teacher asks one of the students to be the mouse, and in Gordon's case the Principal felt that would be too risky. But Gordon insisted on being chased like everyone else, and not only was he never caught (well, *almost* never; there was one blue Persian who could turn on a dime), but when he took his own turn at chasing, he proved to be a natural expert. In fact his instant mastery of the Flying Pounce caused his teacher and the entire class to sit up and applaud. Gordon took three bows and an encore.

There was also a class where the cats learned the necessities of getting along with people: how to lie in laps, how to keep from scratching furniture even when you feel you have to, what to do when children pick you up, and how to ask for food or affection in such a sweet manner that people call other people to look at you. These classes always made Gordon a little sad. He didn't suppose that he would ever be a real "people" cat, for who would want to hold a mouse on his lap, or scratch it behind the ears while it purred? Still, he paid strict attention in People Class, as he did in all the others, for all the cats knew that whoever did best in school that term would be the one who ate him, and they worked harder than they ever had in their lives. The Principal said that they were becoming the best students in the school's history, and he talked openly about making this a regular thing, one mouse to a term

When all the marks were in, and all the grades added up, two students led the rankings: Gordon and the blue Persian. Their scores weren't even a whisker's thickness apart. In the really important classes, like Running And Pouncing, Climbing, Stalking, and Waiting For The Prey To Forget You're Still There; and in matters of feline manners such as Washing, Tail Etiquette, The Elegant Yawn, Sleeping In Undignified Positions, and Making Sure You Get Enough Food Without Looking Greedy (101 *and* 102)—in all of these Gordon and the blue Persian were first, and the rest nowhere. Besides that, both could meow in five different dialects: Persian, Abyssinian, Siamese, Burmese (which almost no cat who isn't Burmese ever learns), and basic tiger.

But there can only be one Top Cat to a term; no ties allowed. In order to decide the matter once and for all between them, the Principal announced that Gordon and the blue Persian would have to face one another in a competitive mouse roundup.

The Persian and Gordon got along quite well, all things considered, so they shook paws—carefully—and the Persian purred, "No hard feelings."

"None at all," Gordon answered. "If anyone here got to eat me, I'd much rather it was you."

"Very sporting of you," the Persian said. "I hope so too."

"But it won't happen," Gordon said.

The blue Persian never had a chance. Once he and Gordon were set on their marks in a populous mouse neighborhood, Gordon ambushed and outsmarted and cornered all but a handful of the very quickest mice, and did it in a style so smooth, so effortlessly elegant—so *catlike*—that the Persian finally threw up his paws and surrendered. In front of the entire faculty and student body of the cat school, he announced, "I yield to Gordon. He's a better cat than I am, and I'm not ashamed to admit it. If all mice were like him, we cats would be vegetarians." (Persians are *very* dramatic.)

The cheering was so wild and thunderous that no one objected in the least when Gordon freed all the mice he had captured. Cats can appreciate a grand gesture, and everyone had already had lunch.

Gordon had won his bet, and, like the blue Persian, the Principal was cat enough to accept it graciously. He scheduled a celebration, which the whole school attended, and at the end of the party he announced that Gordon was now to be considered as much a cat as any student in the school, if not more so. He gave Gordon a little card to show that he was a cat in good standing, and all the students cheered, and Gordon made another speech that began, "Fellow cats…" As he spoke, he wished very much that his parents could be there to see what he had accomplished, and just how different things could be if you just asked questions and weren't afraid of new ideas.

Being acknowledged the best cat in the school didn't make Gordon let up in his studies. Instead, he worked even harder, and did so well that he graduated with the special degree of *felis maximus*, which is Latin for *some cat!* He stayed on at the school to teach a seminar in Evasive Maneuvers, which proved very popular, and a course in the Standing Jump (for a bird that comes flying over when you weren't looking).

The story of his new life spread everywhere among all mice, and grew very quickly into a myth more terrifying than any cat could have been. They whispered of "Gordon the Terrible," "Gordon, the Self-Made Cat," and, simply, "The Unspeakable," and told midnight tales of a gigantic mouse who lashed his tail and sprang at them with his razor claws out and his savage yellow eyes blazing; a mouse without pity who hunted them out in their deepest hiding places, walking without a sound. They believed unquestioningly that he ate mice like gingersnaps, and laughingly handed over to his cat friends those he was too full to devour. There was even a dreadful legend that Gordon had eaten his own family, and that he frequently took kittens from the school on field trips in order to teach them personally the secret mouse ways that no mere cat could ever have known.

These stories made Gordon deeply unhappy when he heard them, because he believed with absolute conviction that what he had achieved was for the good of all mice everywhere. Whether he trapped a lone mouse or cornered a dozen trembling in an attic or behind a refrigerator, he would say the same thing to them: "Look at me. *Look at me!* I am a mouse like you—nothing more, nothing less—and yet I walk with cats every day, and I am not eaten! I am respected, I am admired, I am even powerful among cats—and every one of you could be like me! Do not believe that we mice are born only to be hunted, humiliated, tormented, and finally gobbled up. It is not true! Instead of huddling in the shadows, in constant lifelong terror, pitiful little balls of fur, we too can be sleek, fierce hunters, fearing nothing and no one. Run now and spread the word! You must spread the word!"

Saying that, he would step back and let the mice scatter, hoping each time that they would finally understand what he was trying to show them. But it simply never happened. The mice always scurried away, convinced that they had escaped only by great good fortune, and myths and legends of the terrible Self-Made Cat were all that spread among them, growing ever more horrifying, ever more chilling. It didn't matter that not one mouse had ever actually seen Gordon doing any of the frightful things he was supposed to have done. That's the way it is with legends.

Now it happened that Gordon was walking down the street one day, on his way to a faculty meeting, padding along like a leopard, twitching his tail like a lion, and making the eager little noises in his throat that a tiger makes when he smells food. Quite suddenly an enormous shadow fell across his path, so big that he looked up to see if he were going through a tunnel. What he saw was a dog. What he actually saw was a leg, for this dog was huge, too big for even a full-grown cat to have understood his real size without looking twice. The dog rumbled, "Oh, goody! I love mice. Lots of phosphorus in mice. Yummy."

Gordon crouched, tail lashing, and lifted the fur along his spine. "Watch it, dog," he said warningly. "Don't mess with me, I'm telling you."

"Oh, how cute," the dog said. "He's playing he's a cat. I'm a cat too. Meow."

"I *am* a cat!" Gordon arched his back until it ached, hissing and spitting and growling in his throat, all more or less at the same time. "I *am*! You want to see my card? Look, right here."

"A crazy," the dog said wonderingly. "They say its bad luck to eat a crazy. Good thing I'm not superstitious."

Having given the proper First Warning, exactly as he'd been taught, Gordon moved quickly to the Second—the lightning-swift slash of the right paw across the nose. Gordon had to leap straight up to reach the dog's big wet nose, but even with that handicap, he executed the Second Warning in superb style.

Instead of yelping and retreating in a properly humbled state, however, the dog only sneezed.

This, Gordon thought, is the difference between theory and practice.

But there was a reason that Gordon's seminar in Evasive Maneuvers was always so well attended. With astonishing daring, he went directly from the Second Warning right into the Fourth Avoidance, which involves a double feint—head looking *this* way, tail jerking *that* way—followed by a quick, threatening charge directly at the attacker, and *then* a leap to the side, which, done correctly, leaves one perfectly poised either for escape or the Flying Pounce, depending on the situation.

But the big dog had no idea that a classic Evasive Maneuver had just been performed upon him, leaving him looking like an idiot. He was used to looking like an idiot. He gave a delighted bounce, wuffed, "*Tag*—you're it!" and went straight for Gordon, who responded by going up a tree with the polished grace that always left his students too breathless to cheer. He found a comfortable branch and rested there, thinking ruefully that a real cat wouldn't have been so proud of being a cat as to waste time arguing about it.

The dog sat down too, grinning. "Be a bird now," he called to Gordon. "Let's see you be a bird and fly away."

Normally, Gordon could easily have stayed up in the tree longer than the dog felt like waiting below, but he was tired and rather thirsty, not to mention annoyed at the thought of being late for the faculty meeting. Something had to be done. But what?

He was bravely considering an original plan of leaping straight down at the dog, when three young mice happened along. They had been out shopping for their mother.

They were really very young, and as they had never seen Gordon the Terrible—though they had heard about him since they were blind babies—they didn't know who it was in the tree. All they saw was a fellow mouse in danger, and, being at the age when they didn't know any better than to do things like that, they carefully put down their packages and began luring the dog away from the tree. First one mouse would rush in at him and make the dog chase him a little way, and then another would come scampering from somewhere else, so that the dog would leave off chasing the first mouse and go after him.

The dog, who was actually quite good-natured, and not very hungry, had a fine time running after them all. He followed them farther and farther away from the tree, and had probably forgotten all about Gordon by the time the Unspeakable was able to spring down from the tree and vanish into the bushes.

Gordon would have waited to thank the three mice, but they had disappeared, along with the dog. Anxious not to miss his meeting, he dashed back to the school, slowing down before he got there to catch his breath and smooth his whiskers. "It could happen to anyone," he told himself. "There's nothing to be ashamed of." Yet there was something fundamentally troubling to Gordon about having run away. Feeling uncertain for the first time since he had marched up the front steps, he washed himself all over and stalked on into the school, outwardly calm and proud, the best cat anyone there would ever see, Gordon the Terrible, the Unspeakable—yes, the Self-Made Cat.

But another cat—the Assistant Professor of Tailchasing, in fact—had seen the whole incident, and had already interrupted the faculty meeting with the shocking tale.

The Principal tried to brush the news aside. "When it's time to climb a tree, you climb a tree," he said. "Any cat knows that." (He had become quite fond of Gordon, in his way.)

It wasn't enough. The Assistant Professor of Tailchasing (a chocolate-point Siamese who dreamed of one day heading the school himself) led the opposition. As the Assistant Professor saw it, Gordon was plainly a fraud, a pretender, a cat in card only, so friendly with his fellow mice that they had rushed to help him when he was in danger. In light of that, who could say what Gordon's *real* plans might be? Why had he come to the school in the first place? What if more like him followed? What if the mice were plotting to attack the cat school, all cat schools?

This thought rattled everyone at the table. With a mouse like Gordon in their midst, a mouse who knew far more about being a cat than the cats themselves, was any feline safe?

Just that quickly, fear replaced reason. Within minutes everyone but the Principal forgot how much they had liked and admired Gordon. Admitting him to the school had been a catastrophic mistake, one that must be set right without a moment's delay!

The Principal groaned and covered his eyes and sent for Gordon. He was almost crying as he took Gordon's cat card away.

Gordon protested like mad, of course. He spoke of Will and Choice, and Freedom, and the transforming power of Questioning Assumptions. But the Principal said sadly, "We just can't trust you, Gordon. Go away now, before I eat you myself. I always wondered what you'd taste like." Then he put his head down on his desk and really did begin to cry.

So Gordon packed his clean shirt and his leftover peanut butter and left the cat school. All the cats formed a double line to let him pass, their faces turned away, and nobody said a word. The Assistant Professor of Tailchasing was poised to pounce at the very last, but the Principal stepped on his tail.

Nobody ever heard of Gordon again. There were stories that he'd gone right on being a cat, even without his card; and there were other tales that said he had been driven out of the country by the mice themselves. But only the Principal knew for sure, because only the Principal had heard the words that Gordon was muttering to himself as he walked away from the cat school with his head held high.

"Woof," Gordon was murmuring thoughtfully. "Woof. Bow-wow. Shouldn't be too hard."

The talking animal fable is one of the oldest forms of literature. Aesop used it to preach morals. Today, Renee Carter Hall and others use it just for entertainment.

Just for entertainment? Red and Buddy, the two hound dogs, and the nameless raccoon can talk with each other, but not with humans. There are many fables, and modern novels (the "Mrs. Murphy" mysteries by Rita Mae Brown, and the "Midnight Louie" mysteries by Carole Nelson Douglas, for example), in which all the animals can speak with each other but not with humans. Are humans really that different from "animals"?

In any case, the talking animal fable is alive and well after more than 2,500 years. Enjoy.

The Wishing Tree

by Renee Carter Hall

He was the oldest raccoon in the backwoods, and he not only knew every trick, he'd invented half of them himself. He'd seen the leaves change so many times that he'd lost all count of how many years he'd lived, but though his gray-brown fur had gone silvery white in places, he was still as spry and limber a coon as any hound had ever chased. He had no name, not even one he called himself, but when anyone in the woods talked about him, everyone understood who they meant.

He was curled up in a cozy hollow that day, dozing as afternoon settled into dusk, when he heard the hounds baying.

He recognized their voices. One of the hounds was young and green. The other one—wasn't. And he hadn't lived so many years without learning to respect at least a few of his enemies.

So he hauled himself out of the tree and set about his usual course, adding in bits as the opportunity arose: a few leaps from one branch to another, a quick splash in the stream, a doubling-back here and a figure eight there.

And it was almost enough.

But he hadn't been counting on that rotten branch to give way, sending him tumbling nose over tail in a most undignified manner, down to the ground just as the hounds found his trail.

They were close. He could smell their hot breath—what *did* that hunter feed them, anyway?—and he had just enough time to bolt up the nearest tree, which happened to be a tall oak newly-dressed in its autumn bronze. An instant later, the hounds burst through the underbrush, raced to the base of the tree, and bawled.

The raccoon closed his eyes briefly. Treed. By the blessed Lady Moon, he hadn't been treed since these dogs' sires were suckling pups. It was clear enough there'd be no doubling back this time. This was going to take some fast thinking and some faster talking. Fortunately, he was a master at both.

He cleared his throat. "Good evening, gentlemen."

The hounds looked at each other. The younger one, Buddy, was a bluetick barely more than a pup, all wiggle and wag, eager to get even a pat on the head for a job well done. The older hound, Red, was a battle-worn redbone. His coat was snarled with burrs and etched with ragged scars, and a spark of hellfire blazed in each eye. His teeth—the raccoon noted—were yellow, but they were still sharp.

"Is he talking to us?" Buddy asked Red.

Red snarled. "Of course he's talking to us—who else is here?" He called up the tree's thick trunk. "And good evening to you too, mister. I hope you've enjoyed it, because I haven't seen food all day, and I'm figuring on getting the tender parts as soon as you hit the ground."

Buddy yelped laughter. "That's a good one."

"Well," the raccoon replied calmly, "if you can't see farther than your belly, I suppose that's your loss. Still, I'd have thought a... a *sophisticated* canine like yourself would know the legend if anyone did."

The hounds exchanged another glance. "What legend?" Red asked.

The raccoon feigned surprise. "Then you don't know about this tree?"

Red looked the trunk up and down. "What about it?"

"It's the Wishing Tree. I thought everyone in these woods knew about the Wishing Tree."

"What's a wishing tree?" Buddy piped up.

"Shut up, you," Red snapped. He looked back up at the raccoon. "What's a wishing tree?"

"A magic tree that gets you whatever you want most," the raccoon explained. "Of course, you have to climb it and get an acorn from up here to wish on, and I don't think those nails of yours are up to it."

Buddy was already scrabbling at the bark with his front paws, trying to grab hold. "Stop it," Red said with a growl. "Everyone knows dogs can't climb trees."

"Yes, that's true," the raccoon said. "Of course... I could make your wishes for you."

Buddy's tail wagged so hard it stirred up dead leaves in the underbrush. "Really?"

"Don't see why not. There are plenty of acorns up here. I can reach two right—from—here. Now," the raccoon said, "after we make your wishes, you have to close your eyes, turn around seven times, and run home. And you can't open your eyes until you get there, or your wish won't come true."

Buddy looked at Red. "But how're we gonna get home if we can't see?"

Red rolled his eyes. "Use your nose, stupid. Are you a hunting dog or not?"

The raccoon heard rustling, and the shifting breeze carried the oily scent of human. "Better make those wishes quick. How about the little one first?"

"Well..." Buddy lowered his head in a canine blush. "It's sorta..."

"Out with it," Red snapped, "or we won't have time for mine! The master's coming!"

"Well, there's a... a lady down the road. She's..."

"Pretty?" the raccoon prompted.

"Oh, yes. But we're always tied up, so..."

Red rolled his eyes again. "You wouldn't know a bitch's backside from a woodchuck hole."

"Say no more," the raccoon said, clutching the acorn and closing his eyes. "Okay. Now what about you?"

"Steak," Red said dreamily, licking his lips. "Had it once when I was a pup. Back when the master was different." He sighed. "Long time ago."

"All you think about is food," Buddy said.

"Yeah, well, someday you'll learn what's *really* important in life. And it's not a little show dog with more scent than sense."

The raccoon held the second acorn, closed his eyes, and opened them again. "Done!" he said, and as soon as the hounds' eyes closed, he hauled himself down the tree and as far away as he could get while still being in the woods.

A minute later, the hunter arrived—and nearly got barreled down by his two hounds, their eyes still shut tight, galloping full-speed all the way home.

* * *

Red stretched and settled, trying to find a position that would accommodate his swollen belly. It had been a good night.

He chuckled to himself, remembering. It had started just after sundown, when they'd woken up from a long nap. Buddy had started up his lovesick howling again—*he* called it singing—and then broke off in surprise when he found he didn't have a rope around his neck anymore. It lay in the dirt like a dead snake. Wasn't chewed through, and wasn't cut. And when Red turned his head to look closer, he realized his was gone too.

But before he'd been able to investigate, the master had come out, yelling for Buddy to shut up if he knew what was good for him. Buddy was young, but he had enough sense to take his chance, and when the master saw his prize bluetick coonhound take off down the hill and down the road, he went chasing after.

And he left the cabin door open.

Red had enough sense to take his chance, too. That open door was all the invitation he needed, and inside, his nose led him right to the dinner his master had left behind: a gorgeous raw steak, deep pink and marbled, waiting to be slapped into the cast-iron skillet. He grabbed it, turned to run, and then paused.

He remembered this cabin. He remembered curling up by that woodstove in the corner, feeling the fire's warmth washing over him like his mother's tongue, back from when he was too little to know anything except touch. He remembered getting tidbits of master's dinner, remembered pats on the head and scratches behind the ears.

He glanced back at the kitchen table. One of the bottles was there, too, right next to the skillet. His hackles went up, and he growled around the dripping meat.

The bottles had started everything. Once they showed up, the bad times started and never stopped. Not being able to wake the master. Being shut inside all day, all night, and then hit when he did what he had to do on the floor. Pain that made him want to bite, and worse pain if he did. Once, his master's own rifle aimed at him. And then the halfhearted doghouse, and the rope tied tight.

But there was no rope around his neck now.

He held the steak firmly in his teeth—those lovely salt-sweet juices pooling on his tongue—and decided.

On his way out, he paused at the master's chair. Once it had smelled good, as the master did, but now it smelled only of the bottles. As the master did.

His bladder was conveniently full. He lifted his leg to the worn upholstery and, when finished, trotted off into the night. Nothing in his life had ever tasted so good as a fine steak eaten in the shelter of a hollow log, and nothing had ever felt so good as falling asleep afterward with the night woods singing around him.

* * *

Nudge.

"Hey."

Nudge.

"*Hey.*"

Red woke, looking bleary-eyed at the log overhead and the woods beyond. Buddy was standing next to him. What were they... Then he felt the faint breeze against the ring on his neck where the rope had chafed the fur away, and he remembered.

He yawned until he squeaked, then looked at Buddy. "How'd you get here?"

"Tracked you. I'm a hunting dog, aren't I?"

"I guess so." Red stretched. "Did you find her?"

"Oh, yes." Buddy rolled onto his back and sighed blissfully. "It was wonderful."

"Hmph."

"So what do we do now?" Buddy asked.

"I'm not going back."

"We could find a new master."

Red laid his head on his paws. "Done with masters."

"Come on. A little one. The little ones are fun. I had one when I was a pup."

"You're *still* a pup," Red grumbled, but his ears came up a little, considering it. "And how are we supposed to find one?"

Buddy thought a moment, scratched an itch behind his left ear, chased his tail, then sat down and thought some more. "We could wish for one!" he declared finally.

"*Wish* for..." Red trailed off. After all, the taste of steak still lingered in his mouth, and Buddy reeked of that show dog down the road. "Well... Couldn't hurt, I guess."

* * *

The raccoon watched the two hounds approach from his perch on the oak tree. They weren't baying, and his curiosity won out enough that he came out and let them see him. "On the hunt again, boys?"

"Nope," Buddy said, tail wagging. "We want to make another wish."

The raccoon blinked. *Well, now you've started something...* "Another wish?"

"Just one," Buddy continued. "For both of us."

The raccoon shrugged and plucked an acorn. "All right. What is it?"

"We want a new master. A little one."

"And no bottles, ever," Red added.

"Okay, why not." The raccoon closed his eyes. "There you go. Enjoy."

"And..." Red started.

The raccoon peered down at him. "You said *one* wish."

The old hound looked embarrassed. "And one for you. Whatever you want. You know, to thank you, for the other ones."

What were they putting in dog food these days? "Why not," he repeated. He grabbed another acorn and closed his eyes—*and no hunters anymore, ever.*

The hounds turned around seven times and ran. The raccoon chuckled, turned around seven times just to see what it felt like, got dizzy, and nearly fell off the branch. His front paws still ached a little from untying those ropes, but if it made for two less hounds in the woods, it was worth it.

And then, just because he was curious and had nothing better to do, he followed the hounds. Their trail was easy to follow, what with all the trampled underbrush and broken branches, and it led down to the road.

He stopped in a tree at the edge of the woods—and winced when he heard the screech of brakes. The hounds, their eyes still closed, had run right into the path of a navy-blue minivan. Buddy, he saw, had been knocked off his feet, but he still looked to be breathing well enough. Red stood over him and growled when the driver got out.

"Dad!" A boy leapt out of the back.

"Stay back," the man warned. "They might bite if they're hurt." He edged closer.

Red sized him up. He smelled good, as the old master had long ago. A bit of woodsmoke, clean human skin with a little sweat, and the scent of others mingled with his. The scent of family.

And no bottles, either, not a hint. It was good. Red looked up, searching the man's eyes, and wagged his tail once, then twice.

"Hey, buddy," the man said softly. "Easy now, that's a good boy. Just want a look at your friend here..."

The old hound backed up and sat. Buddy whined as the man came close, then relaxed.

From the tree, the raccoon watched as the man took out a cell phone and made a call. The boy brought a blanket from the car, and they carried the little hound carefully inside. Red hesitated just an instant, then jumped in, and the minivan drove away.

Well, that's two less hounds for sure, the raccoon thought. Still... it *was* a little odd. He'd made that Wishing Tree up in the time it took a leaf to fall... but what were the chances...?

He turned to head back into the woods—and stopped. There was something new on this tree. He looked down at the trunk. A yellow sign, bright and fresh, was nailed there. He couldn't read it, but he knew what it meant, and there was one on nearly every tree that bordered the road, as far as he could see: POSTED. NO HUNTING.

No hunters anymore.

Well.

The raccoon hurried back to the oak, clambered up, and clutched an acorn tightly in both paws.

"Crawdads without pinchers," he whispered, and closed his eyes.

About the Authors

<u>Peter S. Beagle</u>

Peter S. Beagle (1939-current) was raised in the Bronx, where he grew up surrounded by the arts and education: both his parents were teachers, three of his uncles were world-renowned gallery painters, and his immigrant grandfather was a respected writer, in Hebrew, of Jewish fiction and folktales. As a child Peter used to sit by himself in the stairwell of apartment building he lived in, staring at the mailboxes across the way and making up stories to entertain himself. Today, thanks to classics like *The Last Unicorn* (The Viking Press, March 1968), *A Fine and Private Place* (The Viking Press, May 1960), and *"Two Hearts"* (*The Magazine of Fantasy and Science Fiction*, October-November 2005), he is a living icon of fantasy fiction.

In addition to eight novels and over one hundred pieces of short fiction, Peter has written many teleplays and screenplays (including the animated versions of *The Lord of the Rings* and *The Last Unicorn*); six nonfiction books (among them the classic travel memoir *I See By My Outfit*); the libretto for one opera; and more than seventy published poems and songs. He currently makes his home in Oakland, California.

<u>John Gregory Betancourt</u>

John Gregory Betancourt (1963-current) has largely retired from writing to focus on running his publishing company, Wildside Press (http://www.wildsidepress.com/).

He still manages to produce at least one short story each year, though, usually for *Alfred Hitchcock's Mystery Magazine* (where his Black Orchid Award-winning Peter "Pit Bull" Geller crime series appears).

<u>Scott Bradfield</u>

Just facts, Ma'am: Born in California, Scott Bradfield (1955-current) is former Professor of English at University of Connecticut, and has lived primarily in London for the past thirty years. His novels and short story collections include: *Animal Planet* (Picador USA, October 1995), *The History of Luminous Motion* (Knopf, August 1989), *The People Who*

Watched Her Pass By (Two Dollar Radio, April 2010), and *Hot Animal Love: Tales of Modern Romance* (Carroll & Graf, July 2005).

His stories, essays and reviews have appeared in *The New York Times Book Review, The Vintage Book of Contemporary Short Stories*, ed. by Tobias Wolff (Vintage, September 1994), and numerous year's best anthologies.

L. Sprague de Camp

L(yon) Sprague de Camp (1907-2000) was a popular and prolific science-fiction author throughout most of the 20th century. He specialized in humorous s-f & fantasy, such as "Nothing in the Rules" (1939) about a small-town swimming contest in which a mermaid is entered. (She gets drunk on the chlorine in the pool.) Many of his novels and stories featured anthropomorphized aliens and animals; notably the four "Johnny Black" stories (1938-1940) about an experimentally intelligent black bear, one of the first appearances in s-f of an "uplifted" animal. He and Fritz Leiber coined the phrase "sword & sorcery", and he edited the first s&s anthology in 1963.

De Camp's 1939 "The Blue Giraffe" is one of the earliest s-f tales to show the mutation of animals by a means other than vivisection. It's dated in several respects, not least in its prediction of a 1976 setting that has South Africa still a British Dominion. But it's still good fun.

Bradley Denton

Bradley Denton (1958-current)'s first professional story appeared in *The Magazine of Fantasy and Science Fiction* in March 1984. Since then, he's published dozens more stories and five novels, including *Wrack and Roll* (Headline Book Publishing, August 1987), *Blackburn* (St. Martin's Press, February 1993), *Lunatics* (St. Martin's Press, June 1996), *Laughin' Boy* (Subterranean Press, July 2005), and the 1992 John W. Campbell Memorial Award-winning *Buddy Holly is Alive and Well on Ganymede* (Morrow, September 1991). Brad's two-volume story collection *A Conflagration Artist* and *The Calvin Coolidge Home for Dead Comedians* (Wildside Press, November 1993) won the World Fantasy Award in 1995 . . . and his novella "Sergeant Chip" was honored with the Theodore Sturgeon Memorial Award in 2005.

"Sergeant Chip" is dedicated to the many dogs throughout Brad's life who served as models for the title character—especially Misty, Buff, Watson, Linus, Lucy, and an early-childhood German Shepherd-mix companion who was also named Chip. Born and raised in Kansas, Brad now lives in Central Texas with his wife Barbara and their current canine family members, Tater and Sugar.

Philip K. Dick

Philip K. Dick (1928-1982) was well-known as an award-winning novelist (notably for his Hugo-winning *The Man in the High Castle*) within the science-fiction field, but he did not become well-known to the public until the release of several big-budget s-f movies based upon his works, just after his death: *Blade Runner* (1982), *Total Recall* (1990), *Screamers* (1995), *Minority Report* (2002), *Paycheck* (2003), *A Scanner Darkly* (2006), and *The Adjustment Bureau* (2011). As a result of his posthumous fame, most of his novels that were unsalable during his lifetime have been published, many to critical acclaim. His s-f fans were surprised to learn that he had written several novels outside the s-f field.

Dick's short fiction tends to remain overlooked today, but not entirely so. His short story "The King of the Elves" (*Beyond Fantasy Fiction*, September 1953) is being developed by Walt Disney Animation Studios for release as a big-budget animated feature, tentatively for release in November 2019.

Phil Geusz

Phil Geusz (1961-current) is the author of more than twenty-five novels and novellas, many of them furry, as well as numerous columns and articles in various furry venues. He began writing in a serious way in 1997, and soon after became active in the furry fandom.

Today Phil is retired from his "day job", but still writing as eagerly as ever. He prides himself in writing furry (as well as in some cases non-furry) tales in many genres, including action-adventure, literary fiction, fantasy, horror, and even political fiction.

Renee Carter Hall

Renee Carter Hall (1977-current) works as a medical transcriptionist by day and as a writer, poet, and artist all the time. Her short fiction has appeared in a variety of publications, including the magazines *Strange Horizons*, *Daily Science Fiction*, and *STRAEON Quarterly*, and the book *Hero's Best Friend; An Anthology of Animal Companions*, ed. by Scott M. Sandridge (Seventh Star Press, February 2014).

She lives in West Virginia with her husband, their cat, and a ridiculous number of creative works-in-progress. Readers can find her online at www. reneecarterhall.com and on Twitter as @RCarterHall.

Chris Hoekstra

Chris Hoekstra (1980-current) was born and lives in Canada. The majority of people are, by definition, normal. What fun is there in doing what everyone else is doing when there's so much else out there? That sentiment has influenced many of Chris' interests in life. Such was his mindset when he stumbled upon the furry community during the twilight years of the 1990's. Furry takes the world and reinterprets it with odd and stranger players, making it all the more interesting.

Writing has always been a part of Chris' life, usually occurring in bursts throughout the years. The Internet and the Transformation Story Archive community were the first place that talent was not only widely shared but embraced by others. The collaborative environment found there fostered friendships that have endured to this day. Furries are a group that celebrates the other and each other. We drive our own content and are beholden to no larger outside influence. Each member has the opportunity to contribute to the whole. And that is something remarkable and virtually wholly unique amongst fandoms. "Daylight Fading" will be his first published story.

Bill Kieffer

Bill "Greyflank" Kieffer (1963-current) is a greymuzzle, in his 50's. His motto is "Blurring the Line Between Gifted and Twisted Every Day!" He's written for comic books, APAs, porn, short stories, articles, interviews, and computer help files. He studied under Denny O'Neil in the early 90's. He wrote a treatment for a Vertigo version of *The Amazing Zoo Crew* and his lovely wife said, "I don't think there's a market for sexually active funny animals. You should research that a little before pitching it..." Things went a little crazy after that for a few years.

Metamor Keep is a shared universe. I like to think I brought a unique perspective to my vision of life in the Keep. For my other fan fiction, see https://www.fanfiction.net/~greyflank.

Clifton B. Kruse

Clifton B. Kruse (1905-2000) was an active s-f short-story writer during the 1930s, but his last science-fiction story was published in 1943. He was later a Midwestern minister, the Reverend Clifton B. Kruse, Sr.

He is often confused with his son, Clifton B. Kruse Jr. (1934-2008), a well-known lawyer and author who specialized in estate planning, and did not always use the Jr.

Sharyn McCrumb

Sharyn McCrumb (1948-current) is an award-winning Southern writer, best known for her Appalachian "Ballad" novels, including the *New York Times* best sellers *The Ballad of Tom Dooley* (Thomas Dunne Books, September 2011), *The Ballad of Frankie Silver* (Dutton, May 1998), and Ghost Riders (Dutton, July 2003), which won the Wilma Dykeman Award for Literature from the East Tennessee Historical Society and the national *Audie Award* for Best Recorded Book. Her Revolutionary War novel, *King's Mountain* (St. Martin's Press, September 2013), tells the story of the Overmountain Men in the American Revolution. Her next novel, *Prayers the Devil Answers*, will be published next year by Atria, a division of Simon & Schuster.

Sharyn McCrumb, named a Virginia Woman of History by the Library of Virginia, was awarded the Mary Hobson Prize for Arts & Letters in 2014. In addition to presenting programs at universities, libraries, and other organizations throughout the U. S., Sharyn McCrumb has taught a writers workshop in Paris, and served as writer-in-residence at King University in Tennessee, and at the Chautauqua Institute in western New York.

Steven Millhauser

Steven Millhauser (1943-current) is the author of thirteen books of fiction, including the recently published *Voices in the Night* (Knopf, April 2015), a collection of stories. His short fiction has appeared in the magazines *Harper's*, *The New Yorker*, *McSweeney's*, and *Tin House*.

"Eisenheim the Illusionist" was adapted for the film *The Illusionist* (2006), and "The Sisterhood of Night" was adapted for the recently released *Sisterhood of Night* (2015).

Michael H. Payne

Michael H. Payne (1965-current)'s stories have appeared in venues ranging from *Asimov's Science Fiction* magazine to the annual *Marion Zimmer Bradley's Sword and Sorceress* anthologies, edited by Elisabeth Waters, to *The Ursa Major Awards Anthology*, ed. by Fred Patten (FurPlanet Productions, June 2012). His novels have been published by Tor Books, Sofawolf Press, and his own "Hey, Your Nose is on Fire" Industries imprint. Other "Ottersgate" stories include the novels *The Blood Jaguar* (Tor Books, December 1998; reprinted by Sofawolf Press, June 2012) and *Rat's Reputation* (Sofawolf Press, forthcoming), as well as the e-book collection *A Curial Quartet* (October 2011) containing four stories about the Twelve Curials.

His webcomics *Daily Grind* and *Terebinth* appear a combined six times a week at pandora.xepher.net, he's a pre-reader for *Equestria Daily*, and his *My Little Pony* fanfiction can be found at Fimfiction.net under the names AugieDog and Baal Bunny.

Saki

Hector Hugh Munro (1870-1916) was born in Burma, where his father was an officer in the British Army. He and his siblings were sent back to England to be raised. After reaching adulthood, Munro returned to the British military in Burma, but soon contracted malaria and was invalided out. He returned to England, where he became a noted author and playwright, usually using the pseudonym "Saki". He specialized in satirizing the boring and frivolous upper-class Edwardian society, just before it disappeared. One of his novels, *When William Came; A Story of London Under the Hohenzollerns* (1913), a pointing-with-alarm at Britain's unpreparedness for the coming war with the German Empire, is borderline science-fiction.

Although he was too old for World War I, he volunteered for the Army and was killed at the front by a German sniper. His reported last words, "Put that bloody cigarette out!", are credited for the World War I superstition about "three men on a match: bad luck".

Will Stanton

Will Stanton (1918-1996) was not primarily a s-f author. He was on the staff of *Readers Digest*, and his usually humorous short stories appeared in such magazines as *Atlantic Monthly, Esquire, Good Housekeeping, Look, McCall's, The New Yorker, Redbook, The Saturday Evening Post,* and *Woman's Day* for over fifty years. His "How to Tell a Democrat From a Republican" in *Ladies' Home Journal* was read into the *Congressional Record*.

"Barney" was an uncharacteristic venture into the s-f magazine field. It's humorous, but with a bite.

Michael Swanwick

Michael Swanwick (1950-current) has received the Nebula, Theodore Sturgeon, World Fantasy and Hugo Awards, and has the pleasant distinction of having been nominated for and lost more of these same awards than any other human being. He has written nine novels, a hundred and fifty short stories, and countless works of flash fiction. His latest novel, *Chasing the Phoenix*, in which post-Utopian con men Darger and Surplus accidentally conquer China, will be published by Tor Books on August 11, 2015.

At the Worldcon in London, this past August, it was announced that Swanwick will be guest of honor at MidAmeriCon II, the 2016 Worldcon in Kansas City.

He lives in Philadelphia with his wife, Marianne Porter.

Steven Utley

Steven Utley (1948-2013) started as a member of the Turkey City Writer's Workshop, a group of s-f authors in Austin, Texas, in the early 1970s. He often co-wrote with Howard Waldrop, another Turkey City Writer. His & Waldrop's "Black as the Pit, from Pole to Pole" (*New Dimensions #7*, ed. by Robert Silverberg, April 1977) is often mentioned as a precursor of and influence on steampunk s-f. His short stories were published in just about every print s-f magazine and several electronic ones; and were often included in "best of the year" s-f anthologies.

His last s-f story was published just after his death from cancer. He also wrote poetry and comic book stories.

Edd Vick

Edd Vick (1958-current) is a graduate of the 2002 Clarion SF Writing Workshop. His stories have appeared in magazines including *Asimov's Science Fiction, Jim Baen's Universe,* and *Analog,* and anthologies including *First Contact Cafe,* ed. by Phyllis Irene Radford (Sky Warrior Book Publishing, February 2015), *New Writings in the Fantastic,* ed. by John Grant (Pendragon Press, September 2007), and *Northwest Passages: A Cascadian Anthology,* ed. by Cris DiMarco (Fandom Press, September 2005). His story "Moon Does Run" from *Electric Velocipede* was chosen for inclusion in *Year's Best SF 12,* ed. by David G. Hartwell & Kathryn Cramer (Harper Voyager, May 2007).

By day a bookseller, he lives in Seattle with s-f novelist Amy Thomson and their adopted daughter Katie (also five chickens, a cat, and a dog).

Howard Waldrop

Howard Waldrop was born in Mississippi in 1946, which makes him almost a geezer. He has spent most of his life in Texas, where he is a frequent attendee of Austin's annual ArmadilloCon. His writing career started in 1969, and he's filled more magazines and anthologies than most people have filled dreams. He's been nominated for lots of awards (which he refers to as "tickets to Palookaville").

He's still finishing *The Moone World,* announced as coming tentatively in Summer 2008, and *The Search for Tom Purdue,* which he has been writing since 2003. (A novella version was published in 2005.)

James White

James White (1928-1999) was an almost-lifelong resident of Belfast, Northern Ireland. He became active in s-f fandom in 1941, co-published (with Walt Willis) two of the best-known fanzines in the 1940s and '50s, *Slant* and *Hyphen*, and was encouraged to become a professional author. He did not, but four of his "hobbyist" works were finalists for the Hugo and Nebula Awards, and he was often a guest-of-honor at international s-f conventions.

His best-known works were his Sector General stories, about life on a huge interstellar hospital space station that cared for patients of many spacegoing species. Many s-f scholars have noted strong similarities between his works and episodes of the later TV series *Star Trek: Deep Space Nine* and *Babylon 5*. He was commonly credited with defining serious medical s-f. After his death, the James White Award was started for the best s-f story of the year by a non-professional author.

About the Artists

<u>Mark Brill</u>
Mark Brill, or Werepuppy, is an illustrator who is most well known for his comics *Rocketship Rodents* and *Fur and Fury*, his work on card illustrations for Magic: The Gathering, and *The Mark of Aeacus* comic series.

<u>Dark Natasha</u>
Dark Natasha is an artist with a truly international following. Working mostly with mixed media, she is most recognized for painting animal and bird life with anthropomorphic overtones. At first glance a wolf portrait is simply that but look closer there is a feather braided into the mane and an amulet hangs around its neck.

About the Editor

<u>Fred Patten</u>
Fred Patten (1940-current) joined the Los Angeles Science Fantasy Society in 1960 while in college, and has been an active s-f & fantasy fan ever since. He began writing for and publishing fanzines in 1961 (see http://www.zinewiki.com/Salamander), and has written over a thousand reviews of anthropomorphic literature since 1962, irregularly for s-f fanzines in the 1960s, 1970s, and 1980s; for *Yarf!* from 1990 to 2003, for *Claw & Quill* in 2004-2005, for *Anthro* from 2005 to 2008, for *Renard's Menagerie* in 2008, and for *Flayrah* since 2011. He has written two books and edited six anthologies of furry fiction. He founded the Ursa Major Awards and has been on its administrative Anthropomorphic Literature and Arts Association since 2001. He is a member of the Furry Writers' Guild and the Furry Hall of Fame. He co-founded Japanese anime fandom in 1977, and was awarded the Comic-Con's Inkpot Award in 1980 for helping to introduce anime to America. He writes a weekly column on animation, *Funny Animals and More*, for Jerry Beck's Cartoon Research website.

A stroke in 2005 has left him partly paralyzed and bedridden, from which he carries on his fanac via a MacBook Pro laptop.